I0764659

Written In Blood: Vampire Tales

Start Publishing PD LLC
Copyright © 2024 by Start Publishing PD LLC

All rights reserved, including the right to reproduce this book or portions thereof in any form whatsoever.

Start Publishing PD is a registered trademark of Start Publishing PD LLC
Manufactured in the United States of America

Cover art: Shutterstock/Taisiya Kozorez

Cover design: Jennifer Do

10 9 8 7 6 5 4 3 2 1

ISBN 979-8-8809-2503-2

Written In Blood: Vampire Tales

Contents

THE VAMPYRE
by John William Polidori

EXTRACT OF A LETTER FROM GENEVA.

"I breathe freely in the neighbourhood of this lake; the ground upon which I tread has been subdued from the earliest ages; the principal objects which immediately strike my eye, bring to my recollection scenes, in which man acted the hero and was the chief object of interest. Not to look back to earlier times of battles and sieges, here is the bust of Rousseau—here is a house with an inscription denoting that the Genevan philosopher first drew breath under its roof. A little out of the town is Ferney, the residence of Voltaire; where that wonderful, though certainly in many respects contemptible, character, received, like the hermits of old, the visits of pilgrims, not only from his own nation, but from the farthest boundaries of Europe. Here too is Bonnet's abode, and, a few steps beyond, the house of that astonishing woman Madame de Stael: perhaps the first of her sex, who has really proved its often claimed equality with, the nobler man. We have before had women who have written interesting-novels and poems, in which their tact at observing drawing-room characters has availed them; but never since the days of Heloise have those faculties which are peculiar to man, been developed as the possible inheritance of woman. Though even here, as in the case of Heloise, our sex have not been backward in alledging the existence of an Abeilard in the person of M. Schlegel as the inspirer of her works. But to proceed: upon the same side of the lake, Gibbon, Bonnivard, Bradshaw, and others mark, as it were, the stages for our progress; whilst upon the other side there is one house, built by Diodati, the friend of Milton, which has contained within its walls, for several months, that poet whom we have so often read together, and who—if human passions remain the same, and human feelings, like chords, on being swept by nature's impulses shall vibrate as before—will be placed by posterity in the first rank of our English Poets. You must have heard, or the Third Canto of Childe Harold will have informed you, that Lord Byron resided many months in this neighbourhood. I went with some friends a few days ago, after having seen Ferney, to view this mansion. I trod the floors with the same feelings of awe and respect as we did, together, those of Shakespeare's dwelling at Stratford. I sat down in a chair of the saloon, and satisfied myself that I was resting on what he had made his constant seat. I found a servant there who had lived with him; she, however, gave me but little information. She pointed out his bed-chamber upon the same level as the saloon and dining-room, and informed me that he retired to rest at three, got up at two, and employed himself a long time over his toilette; that he never went to sleep without a pair of pistols and a dagger by his side, and that he never eat animal food. He apparently spent some part of every day upon the lake in an English boat. There is a balcony from the saloon which looks upon the lake and the mountain Jura; and I imagine, that it must have been hence, he contemplated the storm so magnificently described in the Third Canto; for you have from here a most extensive view of all the points he has therein depicted. I can fancy him like the scathed pine, whilst all around was sunk to repose, still waking to observe, what gave but a weak image of the storms which had desolated his own breast.

The sky is changed!—and such a change; Oh, night!
And storm and darkness, ye are wond'rous strong,
Yet lovely in your strength, as is the light
Of a dark eye in woman! Far along
From peak to peak, the rattling crags among,
Leaps the lire thunder! Not from one lone cloud,
But every mountain now hath found a tongue,
And Jura answers thro' her misty shroud,
Back to the joyous Alps who call to her aloud!

And this is in the night:—Most glorious night!
Thou wer't not sent for slumber! let me be
A sharer in thy far and fierce delight,—
A portion of the tempest and of me!
How the lit lake shines a phosphoric sea,
And the big rain comet dancing to the earth!
And now again 'tis black,—and now the glee
Of the loud hills shakes with its mountain mirth,
As if they did rejoice o'er a young; earthquake's birth,

Now where the swift Rhine cleaves his way between
Heights which appear, as lovers who have parted

In haste, whose mining depths so intervene,
That they can meet no more, tho' broken hearted;
Tho' in their souls which thus each other thwarted,
Love was the very root of the fond rage
Which blighted their life's bloom, and then departed—
Itself expired, but leaving; them an age
Of years all winter—war within themselves to wage.

I went down to the little port, if I may use the expression, wherein his vessel used to lay, and conversed with the cottager, who had the care of it. You may smile, but I have my pleasure in thus helping my personification of the individual I admire, by attaining to the knowledge of those circumstances which were daily around him. I have made numerous enquiries in the town concerning him, but can learn nothing. He only went into society there once, when M. Pictet took him to the house of a lady to spend the evening. They say he is a very singular man, and seem to think him very uncivil. Amongst other things they relate, that having invited M. Pictet and Bonstetten to dinner, he went on the lake to Chillon, leaving a gentleman who travelled with him to receive them and make his apologies. Another evening, being invited to the house of Lady D—— H——, he promised to attend, but upon approaching the windows of her ladyship's villa, and perceiving the room to be full of company, he set down his friend, desiring him to plead his excuse, and immediately returned home. This will serve as a contradiction to the report which you tell me is current in England, of his having been avoided by his countrymen on the continent. The case happens to be directly the reverse, as he has been generally sought by them, though on most occasions, apparently without success. It is said, indeed, that upon paying his first visit at Coppet, following the servant who had announced his name, he was surprised to meet a lady carried out fainting; but before he had been seated many minutes, the same lady, who had been so affected at the sound of his name, returned and conversed with him a considerable time—such is female curiosity and affectation! He visited Coppet frequently, and of course associated there with several of his countrymen, who evinced no reluctance to meet him whom his enemies alone would represent as an outcast.

Though I have been so unsuccessful in this town, I have been more fortunate in my enquiries elsewhere. There is a society three or four miles from Geneva, the centre of which is the Countess of Breuss, a Russian lady, well acquainted with the agrémens de la Société, and who has collected them round herself at her mansion. It was chiefly here, I find, that the gentleman who travelled with Lord Byron, as physician, sought for society. He used almost every day to cross the lake by himself, in one of their flat-bottomed boats, and return after passing the evening with his friends, about eleven or twelve at night, often whilst the storms were raging in the circling summits of the mountains around. As he became intimate, from long acquaintance, with several of the families in this neighbourhood, I have gathered from their accounts some excellent traits of his lordship's character, which I will relate to you at some future opportunity. I must, however, free him from one imputation attached to him—of having in his house two sisters as the partakers of his revels. This is, like many other charges which have been brought against his lordship, entirely destitute of truth. His only companion was the physician I have already mentioned. The report originated from the following circumstance: Mr. Percy Bysshe Shelly, a gentleman well known for extravagance of doctrine, and for his daring, in their profession, even to sign himself with the title of ATHeos in the Album at Chamouny, having taken a house below, in which he resided with Miss M. W. Godwin and Miss Clermont, (the daughters of the celebrated Mr. Godwin) they were frequently visitors at Diodati, and were often seen upon the lake with his Lordship, which gave rise to the report, the truth of which is here positively denied.

Among other things which the lady, from whom I procured these anecdotes, related to me, she mentioned the outline of a ghost story by Lord Byron. It appears that one evening Lord B., Mr. P. B. Shelly, the two ladies and the gentleman before alluded to, after having perused a German work, which was entitled Phantasmagoriana, began relating ghost stories; when his lordship having recited the beginning of Christabel, then unpublished, the whole took so strong a hold of Mr. Shelly's mind, that he suddenly started up and ran out of the room. The physician and Lord Byron followed, and discovered him leaning against a mantle-piece, with cold drops of perspiration trickling down his face. After having given him something to refresh him, upon enquiring into the cause of his alarm, they found that his wild imagination having pictured to him the bosom of one of the ladies with eyes (which was reported of a lady in the neighbourhood where he lived) he was obliged to leave the room in order to destroy the impression. It was afterwards proposed, in the course of conversation, that each of the company present should write a tale depending upon some supernatural agency, which was undertaken by Lord B., the physician, and Miss M. W. Godwin. My friend, the lady above referred to, had in her possession the outline of each of these stories; I obtained them as a great favour, and herewith Forward them to you, as I was assured you would feel as much curiosity as myself, to peruse the ebauches of so great a genius, and those immediately under his influence."

INTRODUCTION

THE superstition upon which this tale is founded is very general in the East. Among the Arabians it appears to be common: it did not, however, extend itself to the Greeks until after the establishment of Christianity; and it has only assumed its present form since the division of the Latin and Greek churches; at which time, the idea becoming prevalent, that a Latin body could not corrupt if buried in their territory, it gradually increased, and formed the subject of many wonderful stories, still extant, of the dead rising from their graves, and feeding upon the blood of the young and beautiful. In the West it spread, with some slight variation, all over Hungary, Poland, Austria, and Lorraine, where the belief existed, that vampyres nightly imbibed a certain portion of the blood of their victims, who became emaciated, lost their strength, and speedily died of consumptions; whilst these human blood-suckers fattened—and their veins became distended to such a state of repletion, as to cause the blood to flow from all the passages of their bodies, and even from the very pores of their skins.

In the London Journal, of March, 1732, is a curious, and, of course, credible account of a particular case of vampyrism, which is stated to have occurred at Madreyga, in Hungary. It appears, that upon an examination of the commander-in-chief and magistrates of the place, they positively and unanimously affirmed, that, about five years before, a certain Heyduke, named Arnold Paul, had been heard to say, that, at Cassovia, on the frontiers of the Turkish Servia, he had been tormented by a vampyre, but had found a way to rid himself of the evil, by eating some of the earth out of the vampyre's grave, and rubbing himself with his blood. This precaution, however, did not prevent him from becoming a vampyre himself; for, about twenty or thirty days after his death and burial, many persons complained of having been tormented by him, and a deposition was made, that four persons had been deprived of life by his attacks. To prevent further mischief, the inhabitants having consulted their Hadagni, took up the body, and found it (as is supposed to be usual in cases of vampyrism) fresh, and entirely free from corruption, and emitting at the mouth, nose, and ears, pure and florid blood. Proof having been thus obtained, they resorted to the accustomed remedy. A stake was driven entirely through the heart and body of Arnold Paul, at which he is reported to have cried out as dreadfully as if he had been alive. This done, they cut off his head, burned his body, and threw the ashes into his grave. The same measures were adopted with the corses of those persons who had previously died from vampyrism, lest they should, in their turn, become agents upon others who survived them.

This monstrous rodomontade is here related, because it seems better adapted to illustrate the subject of the present observations than any other instance which could be adduced. In many parts of Greece it is considered as a sort of punishment after death, for some heinous crime committed whilst in existence, that the deceased is not only doomed to vampyrise, but compelled to confine his infernal visitations solely to those beings he loved most while upon earth—those to whom he was bound by ties of kindred and affection.—A supposition alluded to in the "Giaour."

But first on earth, as Vampyre sent,
Thy corse shall from its tomb be rent;
Then ghastly haunt the native place,
And suck the blood of all thy race;
There from thy daughter, sister, wife,
At midnight drain the stream of life;
Yet loathe the banquet which perforce
Must feed thy livid living corse,
Thy victims, ere they yet expire,
Shall know the demon for their sire;
As cursing thee, thou cursing them,
Thy flowers are withered on the stem.
But one that for thy crime must fall,
The youngest, best beloved of all,
Shall bless thee with a father's name—
That word shall wrap thy heart in flame!
Yet thou must end thy task and mark
Her cheek's last tinge—her eye's last spark,
And the last glassy glance must view
Which freezes o'er its lifeless blue;
Then with unhallowed hand shall tear
The tresses of her yellow hair,
Of which, in life a lock when shorn
Affection's fondest pledge was worn—
But now is borne away by thee
Memorial of thine agony!

Yet with thine own best blood shall drip;
Thy gnashing tooth, and haggard lip;
Then stalking to thy sullen grave,
Go—and with Gouls and Afrits rave,
Till these in horror shrink away
From spectre more accursed than they.

Mr. Southey has also introduced in his wild but beautiful poem of "Thalaba," the vampyre corse of the Arabian maid Oneiza, who is represented as having returned from the grave for the purpose of tormenting him she best loved whilst in existence. But this cannot be supposed to have resulted from the sinfulness of her life, she being pourtrayed throughout the whole of the tale as a complete type of purity and innocence. The veracious Tournefort gives a long account in his travels of several astonishing cases of vampyrism, to which he pretends to have been an eyewitness; and Calmet, in his great work upon this subject, besides a variety of anecdotes, and traditionary narratives illustrative of its effects, has put forth some learned dissertations, tending to prove it to be a classical, as well as barbarian error.

Many curious and interesting notices on this singularly horrible superstition might be added; though the present may suffice for the limits of a note, necessarily devoted to explanation, and which may now be concluded by merely remarking, that though the term Vampyre is the one in most general acceptation, there are several others synonimous with it, made use of in various parts of the world: as Vroucolocha, Vardoulacha, Goul, Broucoloka, &c.

THE VAMPYRE

IT happened that in the midst of the dissipations attendant upon a London winter, there appeared at the various parties of the leaders of the ton a nobleman, more remarkable for his singularities, than his rank. He gazed upon the mirth around him, as if he could not participate therein. Apparently, the light laughter of the fair only attracted his attention, that he might by a look quell it, and throw fear into those breasts where thoughtlessness reigned. Those who felt this sensation of awe, could not explain whence it arose: some attributed it to the dead grey eye, which, fixing upon the object's face, did not seem to penetrate, and at one glance to pierce through to the inward workings of the heart; but fell upon the cheek with a leaden ray that weighed upon the skin it could not pass. His peculiarities caused him to be invited to every house; all wished to see him, and those who had been accustomed to violent excitement, and now felt the weight of ennui, were pleased at having something in their presence capable of engaging their attention. In spite of the deadly hue of his face, which never gained a warmer tint, either from the blush of modesty, or from the strong emotion of passion, though its form and outline were beautiful, many of the female hunters after notoriety attempted to win his attentions, and gain, at least, some marks of what they might term affection: Lady Mercer, who had been the mockery of every monster shewn in drawing-rooms since her marriage, threw herself in his way, and did all but put on the dress of a mountebank, to attract his notice:—though in vain:—when she stood before him, though his eyes were apparently fixed upon her's, still it seemed as if they were unperceived;—even her unappalled impudence was baffled, and she left the field. But though the common adultress could not influence even the guidance of his eyes, it was not that the female sex was indifferent to him: yet such was the apparent caution with which he spoke to the virtuous wife and innocent daughter, that few knew he ever addressed himself to females. He had, however, the reputation of a winning tongue; and whether it was that it even overcame the dread of his singular character, or that they were moved by his apparent hatred of vice, he was as often among those females who form the boast of their sex from their domestic virtues, as among those who sully it by their vices.

About the same time, there came to London a young gentleman of the name of Aubrey: he was an orphan left with an only sister in the possession of great wealth, by parents who died while he was yet in childhood. Left also to himself by guardians, who thought it their duty merely to take care of his fortune, while they relinquished the more important charge of his mind to the care of mercenary subalterns, he cultivated more his imagination than his judgment. He had, hence, that high romantic feeling of honour and candour, which daily ruins so many milliners' apprentices. He believed all to sympathise with virtue, and thought that vice was thrown in by Providence merely for the picturesque effect of the scene, as we see in romances: he thought that the misery of a cottage merely consisted in the vesting of clothes, which were as warm, but which were better adapted to the painter's eye by their irregular folds and various coloured patches. He thought, in fine, that the dreams of poets were the realities of life. He was handsome, frank, and rich: for these reasons, upon his entering into the gay circles, many mothers surrounded him, striving which should describe with least truth their languishing or romping favourites: the daughters at the same time, by their brightening countenances when he approached, and by their sparkling eyes, when he opened his lips, soon led him into false notions of his talents and his merit. Attached as he was to the romance of his solitary hours, he was startled at finding, that, except in the tallow and wax candles that flickered, not from the presence of a ghost, but from want of snuffing, there was no foundation in real life for any of that congeries of pleasing pictures and descriptions contained in those volumes, from which he had formed his study. Finding, however, some compensation in his gratified vanity, he was about to relinquish his dreams, when the extraordinary being we have above described, crossed him in his career.

He watched him; and the very impossibility of forming an idea of the character of a man entirely absorbed in himself, who gave few other signs of his observation of external objects, than the tacit assent to their existence, implied by the avoidance of their contact: allowing his imagination to picture every thing that flattered its propensity to extravagant ideas, he soon formed this object into the hero of a romance, and determined to observe the offspring of his fancy, rather than the person before him. He became acquainted with him, paid him attentions, and so far advanced upon his notice, that his presence was always recognised. He gradually learnt that Lord Ruthven's affairs were embarrassed, and soon found, from the notes of preparation in —— Street, that he was about to travel. Desirous of gaining some information respecting this singular character, who, till now, had only whetted his curiosity, he hinted to his guardians, that it was time for him to perform the tour, which for many generations has been thought necessary to enable the young to take some rapid steps in the career of vice towards putting themselves upon an equality with the aged, and not allowing them to appear as if fallen from the skies, whenever scandalous intrigues are mentioned as the subjects of pleasantry or of praise, according to the degree of skill shewn in carrying them on. They consented: and Aubrey immediately mentioning his intentions to Lord Ruthven, was surprised to receive from him a proposal to join him. Flattered by such a mark of esteem from him, who, apparently, had nothing in common with other men, he gladly accepted it, and in a few days they had passed the circling waters.

Hitherto, Aubrey had had no opportunity of studying Lord Ruthven's character, and now he found, that, though many more of his actions were exposed to his view, the results offered different conclusions from the apparent motives to his conduct. His companion was profuse in his liberality;—the idle, the vagabond, and the beggar, received from his hand more than enough to relieve their immediate wants. But Aubrey could not avoid remarking, that it was not upon the virtuous, reduced to indigence by the misfortunes attendant even upon virtue, that he bestowed his alms;—these were sent from the door with hardly suppressed sneers; but when the profligate came to ask something, not to relieve his wants, but to allow him to wallow in his lust, or to sink him still deeper in his iniquity, he was sent away with rich charity. This was, however, attributed by him to the greater importunity of the vicious, which generally prevails over the retiring bashfulness of the virtuous indigent. There was one circumstance about the charity of his Lordship, which was still more impressed upon his mind: all those upon whom it was bestowed, inevitably found that there was a curse upon it, for they were all either led to the scaffold, or sunk to the lowest and the most abject misery. At Brussels and other towns through which they passed, Aubrey was surprized at the apparent eagerness with which his companion sought for the centres of all fashionable vice; there he entered into all the spirit of the faro table: he betted, and always gambled with success, except where the known sharper was his antagonist, and then he lost even more than he gained; but it was always with the same unchanging face, with which he generally watched the society around: it was not, however, so when he encountered the rash youthful novice, or the luckless father of a numerous family; then his very wish seemed fortune's law—this apparent abstractedness of mind was laid aside, and his eyes sparkled with more fire than that of the cat whilst dallying with the half-dead mouse. In every town, he left the formerly affluent youth, torn from the circle he adorned, cursing, in the solitude of a dungeon, the fate that had drawn him within the reach of this fiend; whilst many a father sat frantic, amidst the speaking looks of mute hungry children, without a single farthing of his late immense wealth, wherewith to buy even sufficient to satisfy their present craving. Yet he took no money from the gambling table; but immediately lost, to the ruiner of many, the last gilder he had just snatched from the convulsive grasp of the innocent: this might but be the result of a certain degree of knowledge, which was not, however, capable of combating the cunning of the more experienced. Aubrey often wished to represent this to his friend, and beg him to resign that charity and pleasure which proved the ruin of all, and did not tend to his own profit;—but he delayed it—for each day he hoped his friend would give him some opportunity of speaking frankly and openly to him; however, this never occurred. Lord Ruthven in his carriage, and amidst the various wild and rich scenes of nature, was always the same: his eye spoke less than his lip; and though Aubrey was near the object of his curiosity, he obtained no greater gratification from it than the constant excitement of vainly wishing to break that mystery, which to his exalted imagination began to assume the appearance of something supernatural.

They soon arrived at Rome, and Aubrey for a time lost sight of his companion; he left him in daily attendance upon the morning circle of an Italian countess, whilst he went in search of the memorials of another almost deserted city. Whilst he was thus engaged, letters arrived from England, which he opened with eager impatience; the first was from his sister, breathing nothing but affection; the others were from his guardians, the latter astonished him; if it had before entered into his imagination that there was an evil power resident in his companion, these seemed to give him sufficient reason for the belief. His guardians insisted upon his immediately leaving his friend, and urged, that his character was dreadfully vicious, for that the possession of irresistible powers of seduction, rendered his licentious habits more dangerous to society. It had been discovered, that his contempt for the adultress had not originated in hatred of her character; but that he had required, to enhance his gratification, that his victim, the partner of his guilt, should be hurled from the pinnacle of unsullied virtue, down to the lowest abyss of infamy and degradation: in fine, that all those females whom he had sought, apparently on account of their virtue, had, since his departure, thrown even the mask aside, and had not scrupled to expose the whole deformity of their vices to the public gaze.

Aubrey determined upon leaving one, whose character had not yet shown a single bright point on which to rest the eye. He resolved to invent some plausible pretext for abandoning him altogether, purposing, in the mean while, to watch him more closely, and to let no slight circumstances pass by unnoticed. He entered into the same circle, and soon perceived, that his Lordship was endeavouring to work upon the inexperience of the daughter of the lady whose house he chiefly frequented. In Italy, it is seldom that an unmarried female is met with in society; he was therefore obliged to carry on his plans in secret; but Aubrey's eye followed him in all his windings, and soon discovered that an assignation had been appointed, which would most likely end in the ruin of an innocent, though thoughtless girl. Losing no time, he entered the apartment of Lord Ruthven, and abruptly asked him his intentions with respect to the lady, informing him at the same time that he was aware of his being about to meet her that very night. Lord Ruthven answered, that his intentions were such as he supposed all would have upon such an occasion; and upon being pressed whether he intended to marry her, merely laughed. Aubrey retired; and, immediately writing a note, to say, that from that moment he must decline accompanying his Lordship in the remainder of their proposed tour, he ordered his servant to seek other apartments, and calling upon the mother of the lady, informed her of all he knew, not only with regard to her daughter, but also concerning the character of his Lordship. The assignation was prevented. Lord Ruthven next day merely sent his servant to notify his complete assent to a separation; but did not hint any suspicion of his plans having been foiled by Aubrey's interposition.

Having left Rome, Aubrey directed his steps towards Greece, and crossing the Peninsula, soon found himself at Athens. He then fixed his residence in the house of a Greek; and soon occupied himself in tracing the faded records of ancient glory upon monuments that apparently, ashamed of chronicling the deeds of freemen only before slaves, had hidden themselves beneath the sheltering soil or many coloured lichen. Under the same roof as himself, existed a being, so beautiful and delicate, that she might have formed the model for a painter, wishing; to pourtray on canvass the promised hope of the faithful in Mahomet's paradise, save that her eyes spoke too much mind for any one to think she could belong to those who had no souls. As she danced upon the plain, or tripped along the mountain's side, one would have thought the gazelle a poor type of her beauties; for who would have exchanged her eye, apparently the eye of animated nature, for that sleepy luxurious look of the animal suited but to the taste of an epicure. The light step of Ianthe often accompanied Aubrey in his search after antiquities, and often would the unconscious girl, engaged in the pursuit of a Kashmere butterfly, show the whole beauty of her form, floating as it were upon the wind, to the eager gaze of him, who forgot the letters he had just decyphered upon an almost effaced tablet, in the contemplation of her sylph-like figure. Often would her tresses falling, as she flitted around, exhibit in the sun's ray such delicately brilliant and swiftly fading hues, its might well excuse the forgetfulness of the antiquary, who let escape from his mind the very object he had before thought of vital importance to the proper interpretation of a passage in Pausanias. But why attempt to describe charms which all feel, but none can appreciate?—It was innocence, youth, and beauty, unaffected by crowded drawing-rooms and stifling balls. Whilst he drew those remains of which he wished to preserve a memorial for his future hours, she would stand by, and watch the magic effects of his pencil, in tracing the scenes of her native place; she would then describe to him the circling dance upon the open plain, would paint, to him in all the glowing colours of youthful memory, the marriage pomp she remembered viewing in her infancy; and then, turning to subjects that had evidently made a greater impression upon her mind, would tell him all the supernatural tales of her nurse. Her earnestness and apparent belief of what she narrated, excited the interest even of Aubrey; and often as she told him the tale of the living vampyre, who had passed years amidst his friends, and dearest ties, forced every year, by feeding upon the life of a lovely female to prolong his existence for the ensuing months, his blood would run cold, whilst he attempted to laugh her out of such idle and horrible fantasies; but Ianthe cited to him the names of old men, who had at last detected one living among themselves, after several of their near relatives and children had been found marked with the stamp of the fiend's appetite; and when she found him so incredulous, she begged of him to believe her, for it had been, remarked, that those who had dared to question their existence, always had some proof given, which obliged them, with grief and heartbreaking, to confess it was true. She detailed to him the traditional appearance of these monsters, and his horror was increased, by hearing a pretty accurate description of Lord Ruthven; he, however, still persisted in persuading her, that there could be no truth in her fears, though at the same time he wondered at the many coincidences which had all tended to excite a belief in the supernatural power of Lord Ruthven.

Aubrey began to attach himself more and more to Ianthe; her innocence, so contrasted with all the affected virtues of the women among whom he had sought for his vision of romance, won his heart; and while he ridiculed the idea of a young man of English habits, marrying an uneducated Greek girl, still he found himself more and more attached to the almost fairy form before him. He would tear himself at times from her, and, forming a plan for some antiquarian research, he would depart, determined not to return until his object was attained; but he always found it impossible to fix his attention upon the ruins around him, whilst in his mind he retained an image that seemed alone the rightful possessor of his thoughts. Ianthe was unconscious of his love, and was ever the same frank infantile being he had first known. She always seemed to part from him with reluctance; but it was because she had no longer any one with whom she could visit her favourite haunts, whilst her guardian was occupied in sketching or uncovering some fragment which had yet escaped the destructive hand of time. She had appealed to her parents on the subject of Vampyres, and they both, with several present, affirmed their existence, pale with horror at the very name. Soon after, Aubrey determined to proceed upon one of his excursions, which was to detain him for a few hours; when they heard the name of the place, they all at once begged of him not to return at night, as he must necessarily pass through a wood, where no Greek would ever remain, after the day had closed, upon any consideration. They described it as the resort of the vampyres in their nocturnal orgies, and denounced the most heavy evils as impending upon him who dared to cross their path. Aubrey made light of their representations, and tried to laugh them out of the idea; but when he saw them shudder at his daring thus to mock a superior, infernal power, the very name of which apparently made their blood freeze, he was silent.

Next morning Aubrey set off upon his excursion unattended; he was surprised to observe the melancholy face of his host, and was concerned to find that his words, mocking the belief of those horrible fiends, had inspired them with such terror. When he was about to depart, Ianthe came to the side of his horse, and earnestly begged of him to return, ere night allowed the power of these beings to be put in action;—he promised. He was, however, so occupied in his research, that he did not perceive that day-light would soon end, and that in the horizon there was one of those specks which, in the warmer climates, so rapidly gather into a tremendous mass, and pour all their rage upon the devoted country.—He at last, however, mounted his horse, determined to make up by speed for his delay: but it was too late. Twilight, in these southern climates, is almost unknown; immediately the sun sets, night begins: and ere he had advanced far, the power of the storm was above—its echoing thunders had scarcely an interval of rest—its thick heavy rain forced its way through the canopying foliage, whilst the blue forked lightning seemed to fall and radiate at his very feet. Suddenly his horse took fright, and he was carried with dreadful rapidity through the entangled forest. The animal at last, through fatigue, stopped, and he found, by the glare of lightning, that he was in the neighbourhood of a hovel that hardly lifted itself up from the masses of dead leaves and brushwood which surrounded it. Dismounting, he approached, hoping to find some one to guide him to the town, or at least trusting to obtain shelter from the pelting of the storm. As he approached, the thunders, for a moment silent, allowed him to hear the dreadful shrieks of a woman mingling with the stifled, exultant mockery of a laugh, continued in one almost unbroken sound;—he was startled: but, roused by the thunder which again rolled over his head, he, with a sudden effort, forced open the door of the hut. He found himself in utter darkness: the sound, however, guided him. He was apparently unperceived; for, though he called, still the sounds continued, and no notice was taken of him. He found himself in contact with some one, whom he immediately seized; when a voice cried, "Again baffled!" to which a loud laugh succeeded; and he felt himself grappled by one whose strength seemed superhuman: determined to sell his life as dearly as he could, he struggled; but it was in vain: he was lifted from his feet and hurled with enormous force against the ground:—his enemy threw himself upon him, and kneeling upon his breast, had placed his hands upon his throat—when the glare of many torches penetrating through the hole that gave light in the day, disturbed him;—he instantly rose, and, leaving his prey, rushed through the door, and in a moment the crashing of the branches, as he broke through the wood, was no longer heard. The storm was now still; and Aubrey, incapable of moving, was soon heard by those without. They entered; the light of their torches fell upon the mud walls, and the thatch loaded on every individual straw with heavy flakes of soot. At the desire of Aubrey they searched for her who had attracted him by her cries; he was again left in darkness; but what was his horror, when the light of the torches once more burst upon him, to perceive the airy form of his fair conductress brought in a lifeless corse. He shut his eyes, hoping that it was but a vision arising from his disturbed imagination; but he again saw the same form, when he unclosed them, stretched by his side. There was no colour upon her cheek, not even upon her lip; yet there was a stillness about her face that seemed almost as attaching as the life that once dwelt there:—upon her neck and breast was blood, and upon her throat were the marks of teeth having opened the vein:—to this the men pointed, crying, simultaneously struck with horror, "A Vampyre! a Vampyre!" A litter was quickly formed, and Aubrey was laid by the side of her who had lately been to him the object of so many bright and fairy visions, now fallen with the flower of life that had died within her. He knew not what his thoughts were—his mind was benumbed and seemed to shun reflection, and take refuge in vacancy—he held almost unconsciously in his hand a naked dagger of a particular construction, which had been found in the hut. They were soon met by different parties who had been engaged in the search of her whom a mother had missed. Their lamentable cries, as they approached the city, forewarned the parents of some dreadful catastrophe.—To describe their grief would be impossible; but when they ascertained the cause of their child's death, they looked at Aubrey, and pointed to the corse. They were inconsolable; both died broken-hearted.

Aubrey being put to bed was seized with a most violent fever, and was often delirious; in these intervals he would call upon Lord Ruthven and upon Ianthe—by some unaccountable combination he seemed to beg of his former companion to spare the being he loved. At other times he would imprecate maledictions upon his head, and curse him as her destroyer. Lord Ruthven, chanced at this time to arrive at Athens, and, from whatever motive, upon hearing of the state of Aubrey, immediately placed himself in the same house, and became his constant attendant. When the latter recovered from his delirium, he was horrified and startled at the sight of him whose image he had now combined with that of a Vampyre; but Lord Ruthven, by his kind words, implying almost repentance for the fault that had caused their separation, and still more by the attention, anxiety, and care which he showed, soon reconciled him to his presence. His lordship seemed quite changed; he no longer appeared that apathetic being who had so astonished Aubrey; but as soon as his convalescence began to be rapid, he again gradually retired into the same state of mind, and Aubrey perceived no difference from the former man, except that at times he was surprised to meet his gaze fixed intently upon him, with a smile of malicious exultation playing upon his lips: he knew not why, but this smile haunted him. During the last stage of the invalid's recovery, Lord Ruthven was apparently engaged in watching the tideless waves raised by the cooling breeze, or in marking the progress of those orbs, circling, like our world, the moveless sun;—indeed, he appeared to wish to avoid the eyes of all.

Aubrey's mind, by this shock, was much weakened, and that elasticity of spirit which had once so distinguished him now seemed to have fled for ever. He was now as much a lover of solitude and silence as Lord Ruthven; but much as he wished for solitude, his mind could not find it in the neighbourhood of Athens; if he sought it amidst the ruins he had formerly frequented, Ianthe's form stood by his side—if he sought it in the woods, her light step would appear wandering amidst the underwood, in quest of the modest violet; then suddenly turning round, would show, to his wild imagination, her pale face and wounded throat, with a meek smile upon her lips. He determined to fly scenes, every feature of which created such bitter associations in his mind. He proposed to Lord Ruthven, to whom he held himself bound by the tender care he had taken of him during his illness, that they should visit those parts of Greece neither had yet seen. They travelled in every direction, and sought every spot to which a recollection could be attached: but though they thus hastened from place to place, yet they seemed not to heed what they gazed upon. They heard much of robbers, but they gradually began to slight these reports, which they imagined were only the invention of individuals, whose interest it was to excite the generosity of those whom they defended from pretended dangers. In consequence of thus neglecting the advice of the inhabitants, on one occasion they travelled with only a few guards, more to serve as guides than as a defence. Upon entering, however, a narrow defile, at the bottom of which was the bed of a torrent, with large masses of rock brought down from the neighbouring precipices, they had reason to repent their negligence; for scarcely were the whole of the party engaged in the narrow pass, when they were startled by the whistling of bullets close to their heads, and by the echoed report of several guns. In an instant their guards had left them, and, placing themselves behind rocks, had begun to fire in the direction whence the report came. Lord Ruthven and Aubrey, imitating their example, retired for a moment behind the sheltering turn of the defile: but ashamed of being thus detained by a foe, who with insulting shouts bade them advance, and being exposed to unresisting slaughter, if any of the robbers should climb above and take them in the rear, they determined at once to rush forward in search of the enemy. Hardly had they lost the shelter of the rock, when Lord Ruthven received a shot in the shoulder, which brought him to the ground. Aubrey hastened to his assistance; and, no longer heeding the contest or his own peril, was soon surprised by seeing the robbers' faces around him—his guards having, upon Lord Ruthven's being wounded, immediately thrown up their arms and surrendered.

By promises of great reward, Aubrey soon induced them to convey his wounded friend to a neighbouring cabin; and having agreed upon a ransom, he was no more disturbed by their presence—they being content merely to guard the entrance till their comrade should return with the promised sum, for which he had an order. Lord Ruthven's strength rapidly decreased; in two days mortification ensued, and death seemed advancing with hasty steps. His conduct and appearance had not changed; he seemed as unconscious of pain as he had been of the objects about him: but towards the close of the last evening, his mind became apparently uneasy, and his eye often fixed upon Aubrey, who was induced to offer his assistance with more than usual earnestness—"Assist me! you may save me—you may do more than that—I mean not my life, I heed the death of my existence as little as that of the passing day; but you may save my honour, your friend's honour."—"How? tell me how? I would do any thing," replied Aubrey.—"I need but little—my life ebbs apace—I cannot explain the whole—but if you would conceal all you know of me, my honour were free from stain in the world's mouth—and if my death were unknown for some time in England—I—I—but life."—"It shall not be known."—"Swear!" cried the dying man, raising himself with exultant violence, "Swear by all your soul reveres, by all your nature fears, swear that, for a year and a day you will not impart your knowledge of my crimes or death to any living being in any way, whatever may happen, or whatever you may see. "—His eyes seemed bursting from their sockets: "I swear!" said Aubrey; he sunk laughing upon his pillow, and breathed no more.

Aubrey retired to rest, but did not sleep; the many circumstances attending his acquaintance with this man rose upon his mind, and he knew not why; when he remembered his oath a cold shivering came over him, as if from the presentiment of something horrible awaiting him. Rising early in the morning, he was about to enter the hovel in which he had left the corpse, when a robber met him, and informed him that it was no longer there, having been conveyed by himself and comrades, upon his retiring, to the pinnacle of a neighbouring mount, according to a promise they had given his lordship, that it should be exposed to the first cold ray of the moon that rose after his death. Aubrey astonished, and taking several of the men, determined to go and bury it upon the spot where it lay. But, when he had mounted to the summit he found no trace of either the corpse or the clothes, though the robbers swore they pointed out the identical rock: on which they had laid the body. For a time his mind was bewildered in conjectures, but he at last returned, convinced that they had buried the corpse for the sake of the clothes.

Weary of a country in which he had met with such terrible misfortunes, and in which all apparently conspired to heighten that superstitious melancholy that had seized upon his mind, he resolved to leave it, and soon arrived at Smyrna. While waiting for a vessel to convey him to Otranto, or to Naples, he occupied himself in arranging those effects he had with him belonging to Lord Ruthven. Amongst other things there was a case containing several weapons of offence, more or less adapted to ensure the death of the victim. There were several daggers and ataghans. Whilst turning them over, and examining their curious forms, what was his surprise at finding a sheath apparently ornamented in the same style as the dagger discovered in the fatal hut—he shuddered—hastening to gain further proof, he found the weapon, and his horror may be imagined when he discovered that it fitted, though peculiarly shaped, the sheath he held in his hand. His eyes seemed to need no further certainty—they seemed gazing to be bound to the dagger; yet still he wished to disbelieve; but the particular form, the same varying tints upon the haft and sheath were alike in splendour on both, and left no room for doubt; there were also drops of blood on each.

He left Smyrna, and on his way home, at Rome, his first inquiries were concerning the lady he had attempted to snatch from Lord Ruthven's seductive arts. Her parents were in distress, their fortune ruined, and she had not been heard of since the departure of his lordship. Aubrey's mind became almost broken under so many repeated horrors; he was afraid that this lady had fallen a victim to the destroyer of Ianthe. He became morose and silent; and his only occupation consisted in urging the speed of the postilions, as if he were going to save the life of some one he held dear. He arrived at Calais; a breeze, which seemed obedient to his will, soon wafted him to the English shores; and he hastened to the mansion of his fathers, and there, for a moment, appeared to lose, in the embraces and caresses of his sister, all memory of the past. If she before, by her infantine caresses, had gained his affection, now that the woman began to appear, she was still more attaching as a companion.

Miss Aubrey had not that winning grace which gains the gaze and applause of the drawing-room assemblies. There was none of that light brilliancy which only exists in the heated atmosphere of a crowded apartment. Her blue eye was never lit up by the levity of the mind beneath. There was a melancholy charm about it which did not seem to arise from misfortune, but from some feeling within, that appeared to indicate a soul conscious of a brighter realm. Her step was not that light footing, which strays where'er a butterfly or a colour may attract—it was sedate and pensive. When alone, her face was never brightened by the smile of joy; but when her brother breathed to her his affection, and would in her presence forget those griefs she knew destroyed his rest, who would have exchanged her smile for that of the voluptuary? It seemed as if those eyes,—that face were then playing in the light of their own native sphere. She was yet only eighteen, and had not been presented to the world, it having been thought by her guardians more fit that her presentation should be delayed until her brother's return from the continent, when he might be her protector. It was now, therefore, resolved that the next drawing-room, which was fast approaching, should be the epoch of her entry into the "busy scene." Aubrey would rather have remained in the mansion of his fathers, and fed upon the melancholy which overpowered him. He could not feel interest about the frivolities of fashionable strangers, when his mind had been so torn by the events he had witnessed; but he determined to sacrifice his own comfort to the protection of his sister. They soon arrived in town, and prepared for the next day, which had been announced as a drawing-room.

The crowd was excessive—a drawing-room had not been held for a long time, and all who were anxious to bask in the smile of royalty, hastened thither. Aubrey was there with his sister. While he was standing in a corner by himself, heedless of all around him, engaged in the remembrance that the first time he had seen Lord Ruthven was in that very place—he felt himself suddenly seized by the arm, and a voice he recognized too well, sounded in his ear—"Remember your oath." He had hardly courage to turn, fearful of seeing a spectre that would blast him, when he perceived, at a little distance, the same figure which had attracted his notice on this spot upon his first entry into society. He gazed till his limbs almost refusing to bear their weight, he was obliged to take the arm of a friend, and forcing a passage through the crowd, he threw himself into his carriage, and was driven home. He paced the room with hurried steps, and fixed his hands upon his head, as if he were afraid his thoughts were bursting from his brain. Lord Ruthven again before him—circumstances started up in dreadful array—the dagger—his oath.—He roused himself, he could not believe it possible—the dead rise again!—He thought his imagination had conjured up the image, his mind was resting upon. It was impossible that it could be real—he determined, therefore, to go again into society; for though he attempted to ask concerning Lord Ruthven, the name hung upon his lips, and he could not succeed in gaining information. He went a few nights after with his sister to the assembly of a near relation. Leaving her under the protection of a matron, he retired into a recess, and there gave himself up to his own devouring thoughts. Perceiving, at last, that many were leaving, he roused himself, and entering another room, found his sister surrounded by several, apparently in earnest conversation; he attempted to pass and get near her, when one, whom he requested to move, turned round, and revealed to him those features he most abhorred. He sprang forward, seized his sister's arm, and, with hurried step, forced her towards the street: at the door he found himself impeded by the crowd of servants who were waiting for their lords; and while he was engaged in passing them, he again heard that voice whisper close to him—"Remember your oath!"—He did not dare to turn, but, hurrying his sister, soon reached home.

Aubrey became almost distracted. If before his mind had been absorbed by one subject, how much more completely was it engrossed, now that the certainty of the monster's living again pressed upon his thoughts. His sister's attentions were now unheeded, and it was in vain that she intreated him to explain to her what had caused his abrupt conduct. He only uttered a few words, and those terrified her. The more he thought, the more he was bewildered. His oath startled him;—was he then to allow this monster to roam, bearing ruin upon his breath, amidst all he held dear, and not avert its progress? His very sister might have been touched by him. But even if he were to break his oath, and disclose his suspicions, who would believe him? He thought of employing his own hand to free the world from such a wretch; but death, he remembered, had been already mocked. For days he remained in this state; shut up in his room, he saw no one, and eat only when his sister came, who, with eyes streaming with tears, besought him, for her sake, to support nature. At last, no longer capable of bearing stillness and solitude, he left his house, roamed from street to street, anxious to fly that image which haunted him. His dress became neglected, and he wandered, as often exposed to the noon-day sun as to the midnight damps. He was no longer to be recognized; at first he returned with the evening to the house; but at last he laid him down to rest wherever fatigue overtook him. His sister, anxious for his safety, employed people to follow him; but they were soon distanced by him who fled from a pursuer swifter than any—from thought. His conduct, however, suddenly changed. Struck with the idea that he left by his absence the whole of his friends, with a fiend amongst them, of whose presence they were unconscious, he determined to enter again into society, and watch him closely, anxious to forewarn, in spite of his oath, all whom Lord Ruthven approached with intimacy. But when he entered into a room, his haggard and suspicious looks were so striking, his inward shudderings so visible, that his sister was at last obliged to beg of him to abstain from seeking, for her sake, a society which affected him so strongly. When, however, remonstrance proved unavailing, the guardians thought proper to interpose, and, fearing that his mind was becoming alienated, they thought it high time to resume again that trust which had been before imposed upon them by Aubrey's parents.

Desirous of saving him from the injuries and sufferings he had daily encountered in his wanderings, and of preventing him from exposing to the general eye those marks of what they considered folly, they engaged a physician to reside in the house, and take constant care of him. He hardly appeared to notice it, so completely was his mind absorbed by one terrible subject. His incoherence became at last so great, that he was confined to his chamber. There he would often lie for days, incapable of being roused. He had become emaciated, his eyes had attained a glassy lustre;—the only sign of affection and recollection remaining displayed itself upon the entry of his sister; then he would sometimes start, and, seizing her hands, with looks that severely afflicted her, he would desire her not to touch him. "Oh, do not touch him—if your love for me is aught, do not go near him!" When, however, she inquired to whom he referred, his only answer was, "True! true!" and again he sank into a state, whence not even she could rouse him. This lasted many months: gradually, however, as the year was passing, his incoherences became less frequent, and his mind threw off a portion of its gloom, whilst his guardians observed, that several times in the day he would count upon his fingers a definite number, and then smile.

The time had nearly elapsed, when, upon the last day of the year, one of his guardians entering his room, began to converse with his physician upon the melancholy circumstance of Aubrey's being in so awful a situation, when his sister was going next day to be married. Instantly Aubrey's attention was attracted; he asked anxiously to whom. Glad of this mark of returning intellect, of which they feared he had been deprived, they mentioned the name of the

Earl of Marsden. Thinking this was a young Earl whom he had met with in society, Aubrey seemed pleased, and astonished them still more by his expressing his intention to be present at the nuptials, and desiring to see his sister. They answered not, but in a few minutes his sister was with him. He was apparently again capable of being affected by the influence of her lovely smile; for he pressed her to his breast, and kissed her cheek, wet with tears, flowing at the thought of her brother's being once more alive to the feelings of affection. He began to speak with all his wonted warmth, and to congratulate her upon her marriage with a person so distinguished for rank and every accomplishment; when he suddenly perceived a locket upon her breast; opening it, what was his surprise at beholding the features of the monster who had so long influenced his life. He seized the portrait in a paroxysm of rage, and trampled it under foot. Upon her asking him why he thus destroyed the resemblance of her future husband, he looked as if he did not understand her—then seizing her hands, and gazing on her with a frantic expression of countenance, he bade her swear that she would never wed this monster, for he—— But he could not advance—it seemed as if that voice again bade him remember his oath—he turned suddenly round, thinking Lord Ruthven was near him but saw no one. In the meantime the guardians and physician, who had heard the whole, and thought this was but a return of his disorder, entered, and forcing him from Miss Aubrey, desired her to leave him. He fell upon his knees to them, he implored, he begged of them to delay but for one day. They, attributing this to the insanity they imagined had taken possession of his mind, endeavoured to pacify him, and retired.

Lord Ruthven had called the morning after the drawing-room, and had been refused with every one else. When he heard of Aubrey's ill health, he readily understood himself to be the cause of it; but when he learned that he was deemed insane, his exultation and pleasure could hardly be concealed from those among whom he had gained this information. He hastened to the house of his former companion, and, by constant attendance, and the pretence of great affection for the brother and interest in his fate, he gradually won the ear of Miss Aubrey. Who could resist his power? His tongue had dangers and toils to recount—could speak of himself as of an individual having no sympathy with any being on the crowded earth, save with her to whom he addressed himself;—could tell how, since he knew her, his existence, had begun to seem worthy of preservation, if it were merely that he might listen to her soothing accents;—in fine, he knew so well how to use the serpent's art, or such was the will of fate, that he gained her affections. The title of the elder branch falling at length to him, he obtained an important embassy, which served as an excuse for hastening the marriage, (in spite of her brother's deranged state,) which was to take place the very day before his departure for the continent.

Aubrey, when he was left by the physician and his guardians, attempted to bribe the servants, but in vain. He asked for pen and paper; it was given him; he wrote a letter to his sister, conjuring her, as she valued her own happiness, her own honour, and the honour of those now in the grave, who once held her in their arms as their hope and the hope of their house, to delay but for a few hours that marriage, on which he denounced the most heavy curses. The servants promised they would deliver it; but giving it to the physician, he thought it better not to harass any more the mind of Miss Aubrey by, what he considered, the ravings of a maniac. Night passed on without rest to the busy inmates of the house; and Aubrey heard, with a horror that may more easily be conceived than described, the notes of busy preparation. Morning came, and the sound of carriages broke upon his ear. Aubrey grew almost frantic. The curiosity of the servants at last overcame their vigilance, they gradually stole away, leaving him in the custody of an helpless old woman. He seized the opportunity, with one bound was out of the room, and in a moment found himself in the apartment where all were nearly assembled. Lord Ruthven was the first to perceive him: he immediately approached, and, taking his arm by force, hurried him from the room, speechless with rage. When on the staircase, Lord Ruthven whispered in his ear—"Remember your oath, and know, if not my bride to day, your sister is dishonoured. Women are frail!" So saying, he pushed him towards his attendants, who, roused by the old woman, had come in search of him. Aubrey could no longer support himself; his rage not finding vent, had broken a blood-vessel, and he was conveyed to bed. This was not mentioned to his sister, who was not present when he entered, as the physician was afraid of agitating her. The marriage was solemnized, and the bride and bridegroom left London.

Aubrey's weakness increased; the effusion of blood produced symptoms of the near approach of death. He desired his sister's guardians might be called, and when the midnight hour had struck, he related composedly what the reader has perused—he died immediately after.

The guardians hastened to protect Miss Aubrey; but when they arrived, it was too late. Lord Ruthven had disappeared, and Aubrey's sister had glutted the thirst of a VAMPYRE!

EXTRACT OF A LETTER, CONTAINING AN ACCOUNT OF LORD BYRON'S RESIDENCE IN THE ISLAND OF MITYLENE.

ACCOUNT OF LORD BYRON'S RESIDENCE, &c.

"The world was all before him, where to choose his place of rest, and Providence his guide."

IN Sailing through the Grecian Archipelago, on board one of his Majesty's vessels, in the year 1812, we put into the harbour of Mitylene, in the island of that name. The beauty of this place, and the certain supply of cattle and vegetables always to be had there, induce many British vessels to visit it—both men of war and merchantmen; and though it lies rather out of the track for ships bound to Smyrna, its bounties amply repay for the deviation of a voyage. We landed; as usual, at the bottom of the bay, and whilst the men were employed in watering, and the purser bargaining for cattle with the natives, the clergyman and myself took a ramble to the cave called Homer's School, and other places, where we had been before. On the brow of Mount Ida (a small monticule so named) we met with and engaged a young Greek as our guide, who told us he had come from Scio with an English lord, who left the island four days previous to our arrival in his felucca. "He engaged me as a pilot," said the Greek, "and would have taken me with him; but I did not choose to quit Mitylene, where I am likely to get married. He was an odd, but a very good man. The cottage over the hill, facing the river, belongs to him, and he has left an old man in charge of it: he gave Dominick, the wine-trader, six hundred zechines for it, (about L250 English currency,) and has resided there about fourteen months, though not constantly; for he sails in his felucca very often to the different islands."

This account excited our curiosity very much, and we lost no time in hastening to the house where our countryman had resided. We were kindly received by an old man, who conducted us over the mansion. It consisted of four apartments on the ground-floor—an entrance hall, a drawing-room, a sitting parlour, and a bed-room, with a spacious closet annexed. They were all simply decorated: plain green-stained walls, marble tables on either side, a large myrtle in the centre, and a small fountain beneath, which could be made to play through the branches by moving a spring fixed in the side of a small bronze Venus in a leaning posture; a large couch or sofa completed the furniture. In the hall stood half a dozen English cane chairs, and an empty book-case: there were no mirrors, nor a single painting. The bedchamber had merely a large mattress spread on the floor, with two stuffed cotton quilts and a pillow—the common bed throughout Greece. In the sitting-room we observed a marble recess, formerly, the old man told us, filled with books and papers, which were then in a large seaman's chest in the closet: it was open, but we did not think ourselves justified in examining the contents. On the tablet of the recess lay Voltaire's, Shakspeare's, Boileau's, and Rousseau's works complete; Volney's Ruins of Empires; Zimmerman, in the German language; Klopstock's Messiah; Kotzebue's novels; Schiller's play of the Robbers; Milton's Paradise Lost, an Italian edition, printed at Parma in 1810; several small pamphlets from the Greek press at Constantinople, much torn, but no English book of any description. Most of these books were filled with marginal notes, written with a pencil, in Italian and Latin. The Messiah was literally scribbled all over, and marked with slips of paper, on which also were remarks.

The old man said: "The lord had been reading these books the evening before he sailed, and forgot to place them with the others; but," said he, "there they must lie until his return; for he is so particular, that were I to move one thing without orders, he would frown upon me for a week together; he is otherways very good. I once did him a service; and I have the produce of this farm for the trouble of taking care of it, except twenty zechines which I pay to an aged Armenian who resides in a small cottage in the wood, and whom the lord brought here from Adrianople; I don't know for what reason."

The appearance of the house externally was pleasing. The portico in front was fifty paces long and fourteen broad, and the fluted marble pillars with black plinths and fret-work cornices, (as it is now customary in Grecian architecture,) were considerably higher than the roof. The roof, surrounded by a light stone balustrade, was covered by a fine Turkey carpet, beneath an awning of strong coarse linen. Most of the house-tops are thus furnished, as upon them the Greeks pass their evenings in smoking, drinking light wines, such as "lachryma christi," eating fruit, and enjoying the evening breeze.

On the left hand as we entered the house, a small streamlet glided away, grapes, oranges and limes were clustering together on its borders, and under the shade of two large myrtle bushes, a marble seat with an ornamental wooden back was placed, on which we were told, the lord passed many of his evenings and nights till twelve o'clock, reading, writing, and talking to himself. "I suppose," said the old man, "praying" for he was very devout, "and always attended our church twice a week, besides Sundays."

The view from this seat was what may be termed "a bird's-eye view." A line of rich vineyards led the eye to Mount Calcla, covered with olive and myrtle trees in bloom, and on the summit of which an ancient Greek temple appeared in majestic decay. A small stream issuing from the ruins descended in broken cascades, until it was lost in the woods near the mountain's base. The sea smooth as glass, and an horizon unshadowed by a single cloud, terminates the view in front; and a little on the left, through a vista of lofty chesnut and palm-trees, several small islands were distinctly observed, studding the light blue wave with spots of emerald green. I seldom enjoyed a view more than I did this; but our enquiries were fruitless as to the name of the person who had resided in this romantic solitude: none knew his name but Dominick, his banker, who had gone to Candia. "The Armenian," said our conductor, "could tell, but I am sure he will not,"—"And cannot you tell, old friend?" said I—"If I can," said he, "I dare not." We had not time to visit the Armenian, but on our return to the town we learnt several particulars of the isolated lord. He had portioned eight young girls when he was last upon the island, and even danced with them at the nuptial feast. He gave a cow to one man, horses to others, and cotton and silk to the girls who live by weaving these articles. He also bought a new boat for a fisherman who had lost his own in a gale, and he often gave Greek Testaments to the poor children. In short, he appeared to us, from all we collected, to have been a very eccentric and benevolent character. One circumstance we learnt, which our old friend at the cottage thought proper not to disclose. He had a most beautiful daughter, with whom the lord was often seen walking on the sea-shore, and he had bought her a piano-forte, and taught her himself the use of it.

Such was the information with which we departed from the peaceful isle of Mitylene; our imaginations all on the rack, guessing who this rambler in Greece could be. He had money it was evident: he had philanthropy of disposition, and all those eccentricities which mark peculiar genius. Arrived at Palermo, all our doubts were dispelled. Falling in company with Mr. FOSTER, the architect, a pupil of WYATT'S, who had been travelling in Egypt and Greece, "The individual," said he, "about whom you are so anxious, is Lord Byron; I met him in my travels on the island of Tenedos, and I also visited him at Mitylene." We had never then heard of his lordship's fame, as we had been some years from home; but "Childe Harolde" being put into our hands we recognized the recluse of Calcla in every page. Deeply did we regret not having been more curious in our researches at the cottage, but we consoled ourselves with the idea of returning to Mitylene on some future day; but to me that day will never return. I make this statement, believing it not quite uninteresting, and in justice to his lordship's good name, which has been grossly slandered. He has been described as of an unfeeling disposition, averse to associating with human nature, or contributing in any way to sooth its sorrows, or add to its pleasures. The fact is directly the reverse, as may be plainly gathered from these little anecdotes. All the finer feelings of the heart, so elegantly depicted in his lordship's poems, seem to have their seat in his bosom. Tenderness, sympathy, and charity appear to guide all his actions: and his courting the repose of solitude is an additional reason for marking him as a being on whose heart Religion hath set her seal, and over whose head Benevolence hath thrown her mantle. No man can read the preceding pleasing "traits" without feeling proud of him as a countryman. With respect to his loves or pleasures, I do not assume a right to give an opinion. Reports are ever to be received with caution, particularly when directed against man's moral integrity; and he who dares justify himself before that awful tribunal where all must appear, alone may censure the errors of a fellow-mortal. Lord Byron's character is worthy of his genius. To do good in secret, and shun the world's applause, is the surest testimony of a virtuous heart and self-approving conscience.

Fragment of a Novel

by Lord Byron

"June 17, 1816.

"In the year 17—, having for some time determined on a journey through countries not hitherto much frequented by travellers, I set out, accompanied by a friend, whom I shall designate by the name of Augustus Darvell. He was a few years my elder, and a man of considerable fortune and ancient family, advantages which an extensive capacity prevented him alike from undervaluing and overrating. Some peculiar circumstances in his private history had rendered him to me an object of attention, of interest, and even of regard, which neither the reserve of his manners, nor occasional indication of an inquietude at times approaching to alienation of mind, could extinguish.

"I was yet young in life, which I had begun early; but my intimacy with him was of a recent date: we had been educated at the same schools and university; but his progress through these had preceded mine, and he had been deeply initiated into what is called the world, while I was yet in my novitiate. While thus engaged, I heard much both of his past and present life; and, although in these accounts there were many and irreconcilable contradictions, I could still gather from the whole that he was a being of no common order, and one who, whatever pains he might take to avoid remark, would still be remarkable. I had cultivated his acquaintance subsequently, and endeavoured to obtain his friendship, but this last appeared to be unattainable: whatever affections he might have possessed seemed now, some to have been extinguished, and others to be concentred: that his feelings were acute, I had sufficient opportunities of observing; for, although he could control, he could not altogether disguise them; still he had a power of giving to one passion the appearance of another, in such a manner that it was difficult to define the nature of what was working within him; and the expressions of his features would vary so rapidly, though slightly, that it was useless to trace them to their sources. It was evident that he was a prey to some cureless disquiet; but whether it arose from ambition, love, remorse, grief, from one or all of these, or merely from a morbid temperament akin to disease, I could not discover: there were circumstances alleged which might have justified the application to each of these causes; but, as I have before said, these were so contradictory and contradicted, that none could be fixed upon with accuracy. Where there is mystery, it is generally supposed that there must also be evil: I know not how this may be, but in him there certainly was the one, though I could not ascertain the extent of the other — and felt loth, as far as regarded himself, to believe in its existence. My advances were received with sufficient coldness: but I was young, and not easily discouraged, and at length succeeded in obtaining, to a certain degree, that common-place intercourse and moderate confidence of common and every-day concerns, created and cemented by similarity of pursuit and frequency of meeting, which is called intimacy, or friendship, according to the ideas of him who uses those words to express them.

"Darvell had already travelled extensively; and to him I had applied for information with regard to the conduct of my intended journey. It was my secret wish that he might be prevailed on to accompany me; it was also a probable hope, founded upon the shadowy restlessness which I observed in him, and to which the animation which he appeared to feel on such subjects, and his apparent indifference to all by which he was more immediately surrounded, gave fresh strength. This wish I first hinted, and then expressed: his answer, though I had partly expected it, gave me all the pleasure of surprise — he consented; and, after the requisite arrangement, we commenced our voyages. After journeying through various countries of the south of Europe, our attention was turned towards the East, according to our original destination; and it was in my progress through these regions that the incident occurred upon which will turn what I may have to relate.

"The constitution of Darvell, which must from his appearance have been in early life more than usually robust, had been for some time gradually giving away, without the intervention of any apparent disease: he had neither cough nor hectic, yet he became daily more enfeebled; his habits were temperate, and he neither declined nor complained of fatigue; yet he was evidently wasting away: he became more and more silent and sleepless, and at length so seriously altered, that my alarm grew proportionate to what I conceived to be his danger.

"We had determined, on our arrival at Smyrna, on an excursion to the ruins of Ephesus and Sardis, from which I endeavoured to dissuade him in his present state of indisposition — but in vain: there appeared to be an oppression on his mind, and a solemnity in his manner, which ill corresponded with his eagerness to proceed on what I regarded as a mere party of pleasure little suited to a valetudinarian; but I opposed him no longer — and in a few days we set off together, accompanied only by a serrugee and a single janizary.

"We had passed halfway towards the remains of Ephesus, leaving behind us the more fertile environs of Smyrna, and were entering upon that wild and tenantless tract through the marshes and defiles which lead to the few huts yet lingering over the broken columns of Diana — the roofless walls of expelled Christianity, and the still more recent but complete desolation of abandoned mosques — when the sudden and rapid illness of my companion obliged us to halt at a Turkish cemetery, the turbaned tombstones of which were the sole indication that human life had ever been a sojourner in this wilderness. The only caravansera we had seen was left some hours behind us, not a vestige of a town or even cottage was within sight or hope, and this 'city of the dead' appeared to be the sole refuge of my unfortunate friend, who seemed on the verge of becoming the last of its inhabitants.

"In this situation, I looked round for a place where he might most conveniently repose: contrary to the usual aspect of Mahometan burial-grounds, the cypresses were in this few in number, and these thinly scattered over its extent; the tombstones were mostly fallen, and worn with age: upon one of the most considerable of these, and beneath one of the most spreading trees, Darvell supported himself, in a half-reclining posture, with great difficulty. He asked for water. I had some doubts of our being able to find any, and prepared to go in search of it with hesitating despondency: but he desired me to remain; and turning to Suleiman, our janizary, who stood by us smoking with great tranquility, he said, 'Suleiman, verbana su,' (i.e. 'bring some water,') and went on describing the spot where it was to be found with great minuteness, at a small well for camels, a few hundred yards to the right: the janizary obeyed. I said to Darvell, 'How did you know this?' He replied, 'From our situation; you must perceive that this place was once inhabited, and could not have been so without springs: I have also been here before.'

" 'You have been here before! How came you never to mention this to me? and what could you be doing in a place where no one would remain a moment longer than they could help it?'

"To this question I received no answer. In the mean time Suleiman returned with the water, leaving the serrugee and the horses at the fountain. The quenching of his thirst had the appearance of reviving him for a moment; and I conceived hopes of his being able to proceed, or at least to return, and I urged the attempt. He was silent — and appeared to be collecting his spirits for an effort to speak. He began —

" 'This is the end of my journey, and of my life; I came here to die; but I have a request to make, a command — for such my last words must be. — You will observe it?'

" 'Most certainly; but I have better hopes.'

" 'I have no hopes, nor wishes, but this — conceal my death from every human being.'

" 'I hope there will be no occasion; that you will recover, and —'

" 'Peace! it must be so; promise this.'

" 'I do.'

" 'Swear it, by all that —' He here dictated an oath of great solemnity.

" 'There is no occasion for this. I will observe your request; and to doubt me is—'

" 'It cannot be helped, you must swear.'

"I took the oath, it appeared to relieve him. He removed a seal ring from his finger, on which were some Arabic characters, and presented it to me. He proceeded —

" 'On the ninth day of the month, at noon precisely (what month you please, but this must be the day), you must fling this ring into the salt springs which run into the Bay of Eleusis; the day after, at the same hour, you must repair to the ruins of the temple of Ceres, and wait one hour.'

" 'Why?'

" 'You will see.'

" 'The ninth day of the month, you say?'

" 'The ninth.'

"As I observed that the present was the ninth day of the month, his countenance changed, and he paused. As he sat, evidently becoming more feeble, a stork, with a snake in her beak, perched upon a tombstone near us; and, without devouring her prey, appeared to be steadfastly regarding us. I know not what impelled me to drive it away, but the attempt was useless; she made a few circles in the air, and returned exactly to the same spot. Darvell pointed to it, and smiled — he spoke — I know not whether to himself or to me — but the words were only, 'Tis well!'

" 'What is well? What do you mean?'

" 'No matter; you must bury me here this evening, and exactly where that bird is now perched. You know the rest of my injunctions.'

"He then proceeded to give me several directions as to the manner in which his death might be best concealed. After these were finished, he exclaimed, 'You perceive that bird?'

" 'Certainly.'

" 'And the serpent writhing in her beak?'

" 'Doubtless: there is nothing uncommon in it; it is her natural prey. But it is odd that she does not devour it.'

"He smiled in a ghastly manner, and said faintly. 'It is not yet time!' As he spoke, the stork flew away. My eyes followed it for a moment — it could hardly be longer than ten might be counted. I felt Darvell's weight, as it were, increase upon my shoulder, and, turning to look upon his face, perceived that he was dead!

"I was shocked with the sudden certainty which could not be mistaken — his countenance in a few minutes became nearly black. I should have attributed so rapid a change to poison, had I not been aware that he had no opportunity of receiving it unperceived. The day was declining, the body was rapidly altering, and nothing remained but to fulfil his request. With the aid of Suleiman's ataghan and my own sabre, we scooped a shallow grave upon the spot which Darvell had indicated: the earth easily gave way, having already received some Mahometan tenant. We dug as deeply as the time permitted us, and throwing the dry earth upon all that remained of the singular being so lately departed, we cut a few sods of greener turf from the less withered soil around us, and laid them upon his sepulchre.

"Between astonishment and grief, I was tearless."

For the Blood is the Life

by F. Marion Crawford

We had dined at sunset on the broad roof of the old tower, because it was cooler there during the great heat of summer. Besides, the little kitchen was built at one corner of the great square platform, which made it more convenient than if the dishes had to be carried down the steep stone steps broken in places and everywhere worn with age. The tower was one of those built all down the west coast of Calabria by the Emperor Charles V early in the sixteenth century, to keep off the Barbary pirates, when the unbelievers were allied with Francis I against the Emperor and the Church. They have gone to ruin, a few still stand intact, and mine is one of the largest. How it came into my possession ten years ago, and why I spend a part of each year in it, are matters which do not concern this tale. The tower stands in one of the loneliest spots in Southern Italy, at the extremity of a curving, rocky promontory, which forms a small but safe natural harbour at the southern extremity of the Gulf of Policastro, and just north of Cape Scalea, the birthplace of Judas Iscariot, according to the old local legend. The tower stands alone on this hooked spur of the rock, and there is not a house to be seen within three miles of it. When I go there I take a couple of sailors, one of whom is a fair cook, and when I am away it is in charge of a gnome-like little being who was once a miner and who attached himself to me long ago.

My friend, who sometimes visits me in my summer solitude, is an artist by profession, a Scandinavian by birth, and a cosmopolitan by force of circumstances. We had dined at sunset; the sunset glow had reddened and faded again, and the evening purple steeped the vast chain of the mountains that embrace the deep gulf to eastward and rear themselves higher and higher towards the south. It was hot, and we sat at the landward corner of the platform, waiting for the night breeze to come down from the lower hills. The colour sank out of the air, there was a little interval of deep-grey twilight, and a lamp sent a yellow streak from the open door of the kitchen, where the men were getting their supper.

Then the moon rose suddenly above the crest of the promontory, flooding the platform and lighting up every little spur of rock and knoll of grass below us, down to the edge of the motionless water. My friend lighted his pipe and sat looking at a spot on the hillside. I knew that he was looking at it, and for a long time past I had wondered whether he would ever see anything there that would fix his attention. I knew that spot well. It was clear that he was interested at last, though it was a long time before he spoke. Like most painters, he trusts to his own eyesight, as a lion trusts his strength and a stag his speed, and he is always disturbed when he cannot reconcile what he sees with what he believes that he ought to see.

"It's strange," he said. "Do you see that little mound just on this side of the boulder?"

"Yes," I said, and I guessed what was coming.

"It looks like a grave," observed Holger.

"Very true. It does look like a grave."

"Yes," continued my friend, his eyes still fixed on the spot. "But the strange thing is that I see the body lying on the top of it. Of course," continued Holger, turning his head on one side as artists do, "it must be an effect of light. In the first place, it is not a grave at all. Secondly, if it were, the body would be inside and not outside. Therefor, it's an effect of the moonlight. Don't you see it?"

"Perfectly; I always see it on moonlight nights."

"It doesn't seem it interest you much," said Holger.

"On the contrary, it does interest me, though I am used to it. You're not so far wrong, either. The mound is really a grave."

"Nonsense!" cried Holger incredulously. "I suppose you'll tell me that what I see lying on it is really a corpse!"

"No," I answered, "it's not. I know, because I have taken the trouble to go down and see."

"Then what is it?" asked Holger.

"It's nothing."

"You mean that it's an effect of light, I suppose?"

"Perhaps it is. But the inexplicable part of the matter is that it makes no difference whether the moon is rising or setting, or waxing or waning. If there's any moonlight at all, from east or west or overhead, so long as it shines on the grave you can see the outline of the body on top."

Holger stirred up his pipe with the point of his knife, and then used his finger for a stopper. When the tobacco burned well, he rose from his chair.

"If you don't mind," he said, "I'll go down and take a look at it."

He left me, crossed the roof, and disappeared down the dark steps. I did not move, but sat looking down until he came out of the tower below. I heard him humming an old Danish song as he crossed the open space in the bright moonlight, going straight to the mysterious mound. When he was ten paces from it, Holger stopped short, made two steps forward, and then three or four backward, and then stopped again. I know what that meant. He had reached the spot where the Thing ceased to be visible — where, as he would have said, the effect of light changed.

Then he went on till he reached the mound and stood upon it. I could see the Thing still, but it was no longer lying down; it was on its knees now, winding its white arms round Holger's body and looking up into his face. A cool breeze stirred my hair at that moment, as the night wind began to come down from the hills, but it felt like a breath from another world.

The Thing seemed to be trying to climb to its feet helping itself up by Holger's body while he stood upright, quite unconcious of it and apparently looking toward the tower, which is very picturesque when the moonlight falls upon it on that side.

"Come along!" I shouted. "Don't stay there all night!"

It seemed to me that he moved reluctantly as he stepped from the mound, or else with difficulty. That was it. The Thing's arms were still round his waist, but its feet could not leave the grave. As he came slowly forward it was drawn and lengthened like a wreath of mist, thin and white, till I saw distinctly that Holger shook himself, as a man does who feels a chill. At the same instant a little wail of pain came to me on the breeze — it might have been the cry of the small owl that lives amongst the rocks — and the misty presence floated swiftly back from Holger's advancing figure and lay once more at its length upon the mound.

Again I felt the cool breeze in my hair, and this time an icy thrill of dread ran down my spine. I remembered very well that I had once gone down there alone in the moonlight; that presently, being near, I had seen nothing; that, like Holger, I had gone and had stood upon the mound; and I remembered how when I came back, sure that there was nothing there, I had felt the sudden conviction that there was something after all if I would only look back, a temptation I had resisted as unworthy of a man of sense, until, to get rid of it, I had shaken myself just as Holger did.

And now I knew that those white, misty arms had been round me, too; I knew it in a flash, and I shuddered as I remembered that I had heard the night owl then, too. But it had not been the night owl. It was the cry of the Thing.

I refilled my pipe and poured out a cup of strong southern wine; in less than a minute Holger was seated beside me again.

"Of course there's nothing there," he said, "but it's creepy, all the same. Do you know, when I was coming back I was so sure that there was something behind me that I wanted to turn around and look? It was an effort not to."

He laughed a little, knocked the ashes out of his pipe, and poured himself out some wine. For a while neither of us spoke, and the moon rose higher and we both looked at the Thing that lay on the mound.

"You might make a story about that," said Holger after a long time.

"There is one," I answered. "If you're not sleepy, I'll tell it to you."

"Go ahead," said Holger, who likes stories.

Old Aderio was dying up there in the village beyond the hill. You remember him, I have no doubt. They say that he made his money by selling sham jewelry in South America, and escaped with his gains when he was found out.. Like all those fellows, if they bring anything back with them, he at once set to work to enlarge his house, and as there are no masons here, he sent all the way to Paola for two workmen. They were a rough-looking pair of scoundrels—a Neapolitan who had lost one eye and a Sicilian with an old scar half an inch deep across his left cheek. I often saw them, for on Sundays they used to come down here and fish off the rocks. When Alario caught the fever that killed him the masons were still at work. As he had agreed that part of their pay should be their board and lodging, he made them sleep in the house. His wife was dead, and he had an only son called Angelo, who was a much better sort than himself. Angelo was to marry the daughter of the richest man in the village, and, strange to say, though the marriage was arranged by their parents, the young people were said to be in love with eachother.

For that matter, the whole village was in love with Angelo, and among the rest a wild, good-looking creature called Cristina, who was more like a gipsy than any girl I ever saw about here. She had very red lips and very black eyes, she was built like a greyhound, and had the tongue of the devil. But Angelo did not care a straw for her. He was rather a simpleminded fellow, quite different from his old scoundrel of a father, and under what I should call normal circumstances I really believe that he would never have looked at any girl except the nice plump little creature, with a fat dowry, whom his father meant him to marry. But things turned up which were neither normal nor natural.

On the other hand, a very handsome young shepherd from the hills above Maratea was in love with Cristina, who seems to have been quite indifferent to him. Cristina had no regular means of subsistence, but she was a good girl and willing to do any work or go on errands to any distance for the sake of a loaf of bread or a mess of beans, and permission to sleep under cover. She was especially glad when she could get something to do about the house of Angelo's father. There is no doctor in the village, and when the neighbours saw that old Alario was dying they sent Cristina to Scalea to fetch one. That was late in the afternoon, and if they had waited so long it was because the dying miser refused to allow any such extravagance while he was able to speak. But while Cristina was gone matters grew rapidly worse, the priest was brough tothe bedside, and when he had done what he could he gave it as his opinion to the bystanders that the old man was dead, and left the house.

You know these people. They have a physical horror of death. Until the priest spoke, the room had been full of people. The words were hardly out of his mouth before it was empty. It was night now. They hurried down the dark steps and out into the street.

Angelo, as I have said, was away, Cristina had not come back—the simple woman-servant who had nursed the sick man fled with the rest, and the body was left alone in the flickering light of the earthen oil lamp.

Five minutes later two men looked in cautiously and crept forward toward the bed. They were the one-eyed Neapolitan mason and his Sicilian companion. They knew what they wanted. In a moment they had dragged from under the bed a small but heavy iron-bound box, and long before anyone thought of coming back to the dead man they had left the house and the village under cover of darkness. It was easy enough, for Alario's house is the last toward the gorge which leads down here, and the thieves merely went out by the back door, got over the stone wall, and had nothing to risk after that except that possibility of meeting some belated countryman, which was very small indeed, since few of the people use that path. They had a mattock and shovel, and they made their way without accident.

I am telling you this story as it must have happened, for, of course, there were no witnesses to this part of it. The men brought the box down by the gorge, intending to bury it on the beach in the wet sand, where it would have been much safer. But the paper would ahve rotted if they had been obliged to leave it there long,so they dug their hole down there, close to that boulder. Yes, just where the mound is now.

Cristina did not find the doctor in Scalea, for he had been sent for from a place up the valley, half-way to San Domenico. If she had found him we would have come on his mule by the upper road, which is smoother but much longer. But Cristina took the short cut by the rocks, which passes about fifty feet above the mound, and goes round that corner. The men were digging when she passed, and she heard them at work. It would not hav been like her to go by without finding out what the noise was, for she was never afraid of anything in her life, and, besides, the fishermen sometimes come ashore here at night to get a stone for an anchor or to gather sticks to make a little fire. The night was dark and Cristina probably came close to the two men before she could see what they were doing. She knew them, of course, and they knew her, and understood instantly that they were in her power. There was only one thing to be done for their safety, and they did it. They knocked her on the head, they dug the hole deep, and they buried her quickly with the iron-bound chest. They must have understood that their only chance of escaping suspicion lay in getting back to the village before their absence was noticed, for they returned immediately, and were found half and hour later gossiping quietly with the man who was making Alario's coffin. He was a crony of theirs, and had been working at the repairs in the old man's house. So far as I have been able to make out, the only persons who were supposed to know where Alario kept his treasure were Angelo and the one woman-servant I have mentioned. Angelo was away; it was the woman who discovered the theft.

It was easy enough to understand why no one else knew where the money was. The old man kept his door locked and the key in his pocket when he was out, and did not let the woman enter to clean the place unless he was there himself. The whole village knew that he had money somewhere, however, and the masons had probably discovered the whereabouts of the chest by climbing in at the window in his absence. If the old man had not been delirious until he lost conciousness he would have been in frightful agony of mind for his riches. The faithful woman-servant forgot their existence only for a few moments when she fled with the rest, overcome by the horror of death. Twenty minutes had not passed before she returned with the two hideous old hags who are always called in to prepare the dead for burial. Even then she had not at first the courage to go near the bed with them, but she made a pretence of dropping something, went down on her knees as if to find it, and looked under the bedstead. The walls of the room were newly whitewashed down to the floor and she saw at a glance that the chest was gone. It had been there in the afternoon, it had therefore been stolen in the short interval since she had left the room.

There are no carabineers stationed in the village; there is not so much as a municipal watchman, for there is no municipality. There never was such a place, I believe. Scalea is supposed to look after it in some mysterious way, and it takes a couple of hours to get anybody from there. As the old woman had lived in the village all her life, it did not even occur to her to apply to any civil authority for help. She simply set up a howl and ran through the village in the dark, screaming out that her dead master's house had been robbed. Many of the people looked out, but at first no one seemed inclined to help her. Most of them, judging her by themselves, whispered to each other that she had probably stolen the money herself. The first man to move was the father of the girl whom Angelo was to marry; having collected his household, all of whom felt a personal interest in the wealth which was to have come into the family, he declared it to be his opinion that the chest had been stolen by the two journeymen masons who lodged in the house. He headed a search for them, which naturally began in Alario's house and ended in the carpenter's workshop, where the thieves were found discussing a measure of wine with the carpenter over the half-finished coffin, by the light of one earthen lamp filled with oil and tallow. The search-party at once accused the delinquents of the crime, and threatened to lock them up in the cellar till the carabineers could be fetched from Scalea. The two men looked at each other for one moment, and then without the slightest hesitation they put out the single light, seized the unfinished coffin between them, and using it as a sort of battering ram, dashed upon their assailants in the dark. In a few moments they were beyond pursuit.

That is the end of the first part of the story. The tresure had disappeared, and as no trace of it could be found the people supposed that the thieves had succeeded in carrying it off. The old man was buried, and when Angelo came back at last he had to borrow money to pay for the miserable funeral, and had some difficulty in doing so. He hardly needed to be told that in losing his inheritance he had lost his bride. In this part of the world marriages are made on strictly business principles, and if the promised cash is not forthcoming on the appointed day, the bride or the bridegroom whose parents have failed to produce it may as well take themselves off, for there will be no wedding. Poor Angelo knew that well enough. His father had been possessed of hardly any land, and now that the hard cash which he had brought from South America was gone, there was nothing left but debts for the building materials that were to have been used for enlarging and improving the old house. Angelo was beggared, and the nice plump little creature who was to have been his, turned up her nose at him in the most approved fashion. As for Cristina, it was several days before she was missed, for no one remembered that she had been sent to Scalea for the doctor, who had never come. She often disappeared in the same way for days together, when she could find a little work here and there at the distant farms among the hills. But when she did not come back at all, people began to wonder, and at last made up their minds that she had connived with the masons and had escaped with them.

I paused and emptied my glass.

"That sort of thing could not happen anywhere else," observed Holger, filling his everlasting pipe again. "It is wonderful what a natural charm there is about murder and sudden death in a romantic country like this. Deeds that would be simply brutal and disgusting anywhere else become dramatic and mysterious because this is Italy, and we are living in a genuine tower of Charles V built against Barbary pirates."

"There's something in that," I admitted. Holger is the most romantic man in the world inside of himself, but he always thinks it necessary to explain why he feels anything.

"I suppose the found the poor girl's body with the box," he said presently.

"As it seems to interest you," I answered, "I'll tell you the rest of the story."

The mood had risen by this time; the outline of the Thing on the mound was clearer to our eyes than before.

The village very soon settled down to its small dull life. No one missed old Alario, who had been away so much on his voyages to South America that he had never been a familiar figure in his native place. Angelo lived in the half-finished house, and because he had no money to pay the old woman-servant, she would not stay with him, but once in a long time she would come and wash a shirt for him for old acquaintance' sake. Besides the house, he had inherited a small patch of ground at some distance from the village; he tried to cultivate it, but he had no heart in the work, for he knew he could neer pay the taxes on it and on the house, which would certainly be confiscated by the Government, or seized for the debt of the building material, which the man who had supplied it refused to take back.

Angelo was very unhappy. So long as his father had been alive and rich, every girl in the village had been in love with him; but that was all changed now. It had been pleasant to be admired and courted, and invited to drink wine by fathers who had girls to marry. It was hard to be stared at coldly, and sometimes laughed at because he had been robbed of his inheritance. He cooked his miserable meals for himself, and from being sad became melancholy and morose.

At twilight, when the day's work was done, instead of hanging about in the open space before the church with young fellows of his own age, he took to wandering in lonely places on the outskirts of the village till it was quite dark. Then he slunk home and went to bed to save the expense of a light. But in those lonely twilight hours he began to have strange waking dreams. He was not always alone, for often when he sat on the stump of a tree, where the narrow path turns down the gorge, he was sure that a woman came up noiselessly over the rough stones, as if her feet were bare; and she stood under a clump of chestnut trees only half a dozen yards down the path, and beckoned to him without speaking. Though she was in the shadow he knew that her lips were red, and that when they parted a little and smiled at him she showed two small sharp teeth. He knew this at first rather than saw it, and he knew that it was Cristina, and that she was dead. Yet he was not afraid; he only wondered whether it was a dream, for he thought that if he had been awake he should have been frightened.

Besides, the dead woman had red lips, and that could only happen in a dream. Whenever he went near the gorget after sunset she was already there waiting for him, or else she very soon appeared, and he began to be sure of her blood-red mouth, but now each feature grew distinct, and the pale face looked at him with deep and hungry eyes.

It was the eyes that grew dim. Little by little he came to know that someday the dream would not end when he turned away to go home, but would lead him down the gorge out of which the vision rose. She was nearer now when she beckoned to him. Her cheeks were not livid like those of the dead, but pale with starvation, with the furious and unappeased physical hunger of her eyes that devoured him. They feasted on his soul and cast a spell over him, and at last they were close to his own and held him. He could not tell whether her breath was as hot as fire, or as cold as ice; he could not tell whether her red lips burned his or froze them, or whether her five fingers on his wrists seared scorching scars or bit his flesh like frost; he could not tell whether he was awake or asleep, whether she was alive or dead, but he knew that she loved him, she alone of all creatures, earthly or unearthly, and her spell had power over him.

When the moon rose high that night the shadow of that Thing was not alone down there upon the mound.

Angelo awoke in the cool dawn, drenched with dew and chilled through flesh, and blood, and bone. He opened his eyes to the faint grey light, and saw the stars were still shining overhead. He was very weak, and his heart was beating so slowly that he was almost like a man fainting. Slowly he turned his head on the mound, as on a pillow, but the other face was not there. Fear seized him suddenly, a fear unspeakable and unknown; he sprang to his feet and fled up the gorge, and he never looked behind him until he reached the door of the house on the outskirts of the village. Drearily he went to his work that day, and wearily the hours dragged themselves after the sun, till at last it touched the sea and sank, and the great sharp hills above Maratea turned purple against the dove-coloured eastern sky.

Angelo shouldered his heavy hoe and left the field. He felt less tired now than in the morning when he had begun to work, but he promised himself that he would go home without lingering by the gorge, and eat the best supper he could get himself, and sleep all night in his bed like a Christian man. Not again would he be tempted down the narrow way by a shadow with red lips and icy breath; not again would he dream that dream of terror and delight. He was near the village now; it was half an hour since the sun had set, and the cracked church bell sent little discordant echoes across the rocks and ravines to tell all good people that the day was done. Angelo stood still a moment where the path forked, where it led toward the village on the left, and down to the gorge on the right, where a clump of chestnut trees overhung the narrow way. He stood still a minute, lifting his battered hat from his head and gazing at the fast-fading sea westward, and his lips moved as he silently repeated the familiar evening prayer. His lips moved, but the words that followed them in his brain lost their meaning and turned into others, and ended in a name that he spoke aloud — Cristina! With the name, the tension of his will relaxed suddenly, reality went out and the dream took him again, and bore him on swiftly and surely like a man walking in his sleep, down, down, by the steep path in the gathering darkness. And as she glided beside him, Cristina whispered strange, sweet things in his ear, which somehow, if he had been awake, he knew that he could not quite have understood; but now they were the most wonderful words he had ever heard in his life. And she kissed him also, but not upon his mouth. He felt her sharp kisses upon his white throat, and he knew that her lips were red. So the wild dream sped on through twilight and darkness and moonrise, and all the glory of the summer's night. But in the chilly dawn he lay as one half dead upon the mound down there, recalling and not recalling, drained of his blood, yet strangely longing to give those red lips more. Then came the fear, the awful nameless panic, the mortal horror that guards the confines of the world we see not, neither know of as we know of other things, but which we feel when its icy chill freezes our bones and stirs our hair with the touch of a ghostly hand. Once more Angelo sprang from the mound and fled up the gorge in the breaking day, but his step was less sure this time, and he panted for breath as he ran; and when he came to the bright spring of water that rises half way up the hillside, he dropped upon his knees and hands and plunged his whole face in and drank as he had never drunk before — for it was the thirst of the wounded man who has lain bleeding all night upon the battle-field.

She had him fast now, and he could not escape her, but would come to her every evening at dusk until she had drained him of his last drop of blood. It was in vain that when the day was done he tried to take another turning and to go home by a path that did not lead near the gorge. It was in vain that he made promises to himself each morning at dawn when he climbed the lonely way up from the shore to the village. It was all in vain, for when the sun sank burning into the sea, and the coolness of the evening stole out as from a hiding-place to delight the weary world, his feet turned toward the old way, and she was waiting for him in the shadow under the chestnut trees; and then all happened as before, and she fell to kissing his white throat even as she flitted lightly down the way, winding one arm about him. And as his blood failed, she grew more hungry and more thirsty every day, and every day when he awoke in the early dawn it was harder to rouse himself to the effort of climbing the steep path to the village; and when he went to his work his feet dragged painfully, and there was hardly strength in his arms to wield the heavy hoe. He scarcely spoke to anyone now, but the people said he was "consuming himself" for love of the girl he was to have married when he lost his inheritance; and they laughed heartily at the thought, for this is not a very romantic country. At this time Antonio, the man who stays here to look after the tower, returned from a visit to his people, who live near Salerno. He had been away all the time since before Alario's death and knew nothing of what had happened. He has told me that he came back late in the afternoon and shut himself up in the tower to eat and sleep, for he was very tired. It was past midnight when he awoke, and when he looked out toward the mound, and he saw something, and he did not sleep again that night. When he went out again in the morning it was broad daylight, and there was nothing to be seen on the mound but loose stones and driven sand. Yet he did not go very near it; he went straight up the path to the village and directly to the house of the old priest.

"I have seen an evil thing this night," he said; "I have seen how the dead drink the blood of the living. And the blood is the life."

"Tell me what you have seen," said the priest in reply.

Antonio told him everything he had seen.

"You must bring your book and your holy water to-night," he added. "I will be here before sunset to go down with you, and if it pleases your reverence to sup with me while we wait, I will make ready."

"I will come," the priest answered, "for I have read in old books of these strange beings which are neither quick nor dead, and which lie ever fresh in their graves, stealing out in the dusk to taste life and blood."

Antonio cannot read, but he was glad to see that the priest understood the business; for, of course, the books must have been instructed him as to the best means of quieting the half-living Thing for ever.

So Antonio went away to his work, which consists largely in sitting on the shady side of the tower, when he is not perched upon a rock with a fishing-line catching nothing. But on that day he went twice to look at the mound in the bright sunlight, and he searched round and round it for some hole through which the being might get in and out; but he found none. When the sun began to sink and the air was cooler in the shadows, he went up to fetch the old priest, carrying a little wicker basket with him; and in this they placed a bottle of holy water, and the basin, and sprinkler, and the stole which the priest would need; and they came down and waited in the door of the tower till it should be dark. But while the light still lingered very grey and faint, they saw something moving, just there, two figures, a man's that walked, and a woman's that flitted beside him, and while her head lay on his shoulder she kissed his throat. The priest has told me that, too, and that his teeth chattered and he grasped Antonio's arm. The vision passed and disappeared into the shadow. Then Antonio got the leathern flask of strong liquor, which he kept for great occasions, and poured such a draught as made the old man feel almost young again; and gave the priest his stole to put on and the holy water to carry, and they went out together toward the spot where the work was to be done. Antonio says that in spite of the rum his own knees shook together, and the priest stumbled over his Latin. For when they were yet a few yards from the mound the flickering light of the lantern fell upon Angelo's white face, unconscious as if in sleep, and on his upturned throat, over which a very thin red line of blood trickled down into his collar; and the flickering light of the lantern played upon another face that looked up from the feast, upon two deep, dead eyes that saw in spite of death — upon parted lips, redder than life itself — upon two gleaming teeth on which glistened a rosy drop. Then the priest, good old man, shut his eyes tight and showered holy water before him, and his cracked voice rose almost to a scream; and then Antonio, who is no coward after all, raised his pick n one hand and the lantern in the other, as he sprang forward, not knowing what the end should be; and then he swears that he heard a woman's cry, and the Thing was gone, and Angelo lay alone on the mound unconscious, with the red line on his throat and the beads of deathly sweat on his cold forehead. They lifted him, half-dead as he was, and laid him on the ground close by; then Antonio went to work, and the priest helped him, thought he was old and could not do much; and they dug deep, and at last Antonio, standing in the grave, stooped down with his lantern to see what he might see.

His hair used to be dark brown, with grizzled streaks about the temples; in less than a month from that day he was as grey as a badger. He was a miner when he was young, and most of these fellows have seen ugly sights now and then, when accidents have happened, but he had never seen what he saw that night — that Thing which is neither alive nor dead, that Thing that will abide neither above ground nor in the grave. Antonio had brought something with him which the priest had not noticed — a sharp stake shaped from a piece of tough old driftwood. He had it with him now, and he had his heavy pick, and he had taken the lantern down into the grave. I don't think any power on earth could make him speak of what happened then, and the old priest was too frightened to look in. He says he heard Antonio breathing like a wild beast, and moving as if he were fighting with something almost as strong as himself; and he heard an evil sound also, with blows, as of something violently driven through flesh and bone; and then, the most awful sound of all — a woman's shriek, the unearthly scream of a woman neither dead nor alive, but buried deep for many days. And he, the poor old priest, could only rock himself as he knelt there in the sand, crying aloud his prayers and exorcisms to drown these dreadful sounds. Then suddenly a small iron-bound chest was thrown up and rolled over against the old man's knee, and in a moment more Antonio was beside him, his face as white as tallow in the flickering light of the lantern, shoveling the sand and pebbles into the grave with furious haste, and looking over the edge till the pit was half full; and the priest said that there was much fresh blood on Antonio's hands and on his clothes.

I had come to the end of my story. Holger finished his wine and leaned back in his chair.

"So Angelo got his own again," he said. "Did he marry the prim and plump young person to whom he had been betrothed?"

"No; he had been badly frightened. He went to South America, and has not been heard of since."

"And that poor thing's body is there still, I suppose," said Holger. "Is it quite dead yet, I wonder?"

I wonder, too. But whether it be dead or alive, I should hardly care to see it, even in broad daylight. Antonio is as grey as a badger, and he has never been quite the same man since that night.

The Room in the Tower
by E. F. Benson

It is probable that everybody who is at all a constant dreamer has had at least one experience of an event or a sequence of circumstances which have come to his mind in sleep being subsequently realized in the material world. But, in my opinion, so far from this being a strange thing, it would be far odder if this fulfilment did not occasionally happen, since our dreams are, as a rule, concerned with people whom we know and places with which we are familiar, such as might very naturally occur in the awake and daylit world. True, these dreams are often broken into by some absurd and fantastic incident, which puts them out of court in regard to their subsequent fulfilment, but on the mere calculation of chances, it does not appear in the least unlikely that a dream imagined by anyone who dreams constantly should occasionally come true. Not long ago, for instance, I experienced such a fulfilment of a dream which seems to me in no way remarkable and to have no kind of psychical significance. The manner of it was as follows.

A certain friend of mine, living abroad, is amiable enough to write to me about once in a fortnight. Thus, when fourteen days or thereabouts have elapsed since I last heard from him, my mind, probably, either consciously or subconsciously, is expectant of a letter from him. One night last week I dreamed that as I was going upstairs to dress for dinner I heard, as I often heard, the sound of the postman's knock on my front door, and diverted my direction downstairs instead. There, among other correspondence, was a letter from him. Thereafter the fantastic entered, for on opening it I found inside the ace of diamonds, and scribbled across it in his well-known handwriting, "I am sending you this for safe custody, as you know it is running an unreasonable risk to keep aces in Italy." The next evening I was just preparing to go upstairs to dress when I heard the postman's knock, and did precisely as I had done in my dream. There, among other letters, was one from my friend. Only it did not contain the ace of diamonds. Had it done so, I should have attached more weight to the matter, which, as it stands, seems to me a perfectly ordinary coincidence. No doubt I consciously or subconsciously expected a letter from him, and this suggested to me my dream. Similarly, the fact that my friend had not written to me for a fortnight suggested to him that he should do so. But occasionally it is not so easy to find such an explanation, and for the following story I can find no explanation at all. It came out of the dark, and into the dark it has gone again.

All my life I have been a habitual dreamer: the nights are few, that is to say, when I do not find on awaking in the morning that some mental experience has been mine, and sometimes, all night long, apparently, a series of the most dazzling adventures befall me. Almost without exception these adventures are pleasant, though often merely trivial. It is of an exception that I am going to speak.

It was when I was about sixteen that a certain dream first came to me, and this is how it befell. It opened with my being set down at the door of a big red-brick house, where, I understood, I was going to stay. The servant who opened the door told me that tea was being served in the garden, and led me through a low dark-panelled hall, with a large open fireplace, on to a cheerful green lawn set round with flower beds. There were grouped about the tea-table a small party of people, but they were all strangers to me except one, who was a schoolfellow called Jack Stone, clearly the son of the house, and he introduced me to his mother and father and a couple of sisters. I was, I remember, somewhat astonished to find myself here, for the boy in question was scarcely known to me, and I rather disliked what I knew of him; moreover, he had left school nearly a year before. The afternoon was very hot, and an intolerable oppression reigned. On the far side of the lawn ran a red-brick wall, with an iron gate in its center, outside which stood a walnut tree. We sat in the shadow of the house opposite a row of long windows, inside which I could see a table with cloth laid, glimmering with glass and silver. This garden front of the house was very long, and at one end of it stood a tower of three stories, which looked to me much older than the rest of the building.

Before long, Mrs. Stone, who, like the rest of the party, had sat in absolute silence, said to me, "Jack will show you your room: I have given you the room in the tower."

Quite inexplicably my heart sank at her words. I felt as if I had known that I should have the room in the tower, and that it contained something dreadful and significant. Jack instantly got up, and I understood that I had to follow him. In silence we passed through the hall, and mounted a great oak staircase with many corners, and arrived at a small landing with two doors set in it. He pushed one of these open for me to enter, and without coming in himself, closed it after me. Then I knew that my conjecture had been right: there was something awful in the room, and with the terror of nightmare growing swiftly and enveloping me, I awoke in a spasm of terror.

Now that dream or variations on it occurred to me intermittently for fifteen years. Most often it came in exactly this form, the arrival, the tea laid out on the lawn, the deadly silence succeeded by that one deadly sentence, the mounting with Jack Stone up to the room in the tower where horror dwelt, and it always came to a close in the nightmare of terror at that which was in the room, though I never saw what it was. At other times I experienced variations on this same theme. Occasionally, for instance, we would be sitting at dinner in the dining-room, into the windows of which I had looked on the first night when the dream of this house visited me, but wherever we were, there was the same silence, the same sense of dreadful oppression and foreboding. And the silence I knew would always be broken by Mrs. Stone saying to me, "Jack will show you your room: I have given you the room in the tower." Upon which (this was invariable) I had to follow him up the oak staircase with many corners, and enter the place that I dreaded more and more each time that I visited it in sleep. Or, again, I would find myself playing cards still in silence in a drawing-room lit with immense chandeliers, that gave a blinding illumination. What the game was I have no idea; what I remember, with a sense of miserable anticipation, was that soon Mrs. Stone would get up and say to me, "Jack will show you your room: I have given you the room in the tower." This drawing-room where we played cards was next to the dining-room, and, as I have said, was always brilliantly illuminated, whereas the rest of the house was full of dusk and shadows. And yet, how often, in spite of those bouquets of lights, have I not pored over the cards that were dealt me, scarcely able for some reason to see them. Their designs, too, were strange: there were no red suits, but all were black, and among them there were certain cards which were black all over. I hated and dreaded those.

As this dream continued to recur, I got to know the greater part of the house. There was a smoking-room beyond the drawing-room, at the end of a passage with a green baize door. It was always very dark there, and as often as I went there I passed somebody whom I could not see in the doorway coming out. Curious developments, too, took place in the characters that peopled the dream as might happen to living persons. Mrs. Stone, for instance, who, when I first saw her, had been black-haired, became gray, and instead of rising briskly, as she had done at first when she said, "Jack will show you your room: I have given you the room in the tower," got up very feebly, as if the strength was leaving her limbs. Jack also grew up, and became a rather ill-looking young man, with a brown moustache, while one of the sisters ceased to appear, and I understood she was married.

Then it so happened that I was not visited by this dream for six months or more, and I began to hope, in such inexplicable dread did I hold it, that it had passed away for good. But one night after this interval I again found myself being shown out onto the lawn for tea, and Mrs. Stone was not there, while the others were all dressed in black. At once I guessed the reason, and my heart leaped at the thought that perhaps this time I should not have to sleep in the room in the tower, and though we usually all sat in silence, on this occasion the sense of relief made me talk and laugh as I had never yet done. But even then matters were not altogether comfortable, for no one else spoke, but they all looked secretly at each other. And soon the foolish stream of my talk ran dry, and gradually an apprehension worse than anything I had previously known gained on me as the light slowly faded.

Suddenly a voice which I knew well broke the stillness, the voice of Mrs. Stone, saying, "Jack will show you your room: I have given you the room in the tower." It seemed to come from near the gate in the red-brick wall that bounded the lawn, and looking up, I saw that the grass outside was sown thick with gravestones. A curious greyish light shone from them, and I could read the lettering on the grave nearest me, and it was, "In evil memory of Julia Stone." And as usual Jack got up, and again I followed him through the hall and up the staircase with many corners. On this occasion it was darker than usual, and when I passed into the room in the tower I could only just see the furniture, the position of which was already familiar to me. Also there was a dreadful odor of decay in the room, and I woke screaming.

The dream, with such variations and developments as I have mentioned, went on

at intervals for fifteen years. Sometimes I would dream it two or three nights in succession; once, as I have said, there was an intermission of six months, but taking a reasonable average, I should say that I dreamed it quite as often as once in a month. It had, as is plain, something of nightmare about it, since it always ended in the same appalling terror, which so far from getting less, seemed to me to gather fresh fear every time that I experienced it. There was, too, a strange and dreadful consistency about it. The characters in it, as I have mentioned, got regularly older, death and marriage visited this silent family, and I never in the dream, after Mrs. Stone had died, set eyes on her again. But it was always her voice that told me that the room in the tower was prepared for me, and whether we had tea out on the lawn, or the scene was laid in one of the rooms overlooking it, I could always see her gravestone standing just outside the iron gate. It was the same, too, with the married daughter; usually she was not present, but once or twice she returned again, in company with a man, whom I took to be her husband. He, too, like the rest of them, was always silent. But, owing to the constant repetition of the dream, I had

ceased to attach, in my waking hours, any significance to it. I never met Jack Stone again during all those years, nor did I ever see a house that resembled this dark house of my dream. And then something happened.

I had been in London in this year, up till the end of the July, and during the first week in August went down to stay with a friend in a house he had taken for the summer months, in the Ashdown Forest district of Sussex. I left London early, for John Clinton was to meet me at Forest Row Station, and we were going to spend the day golfing, and go to his house in the evening. He had his motor with him, and we set off, about five of the afternoon, after a thoroughly delightful day, for the drive, the distance being some ten miles. As it was still so early we did not have tea at the club house, but waited till we should get home. As we drove, the weather, which up till then had been, though hot, deliciously fresh, seemed to me to alter in quality, and become very stagnant and oppressive, and I felt that indefinable sense of ominous apprehension that I am accustomed to before thunder. John, however, did not share my views, attributing my loss of lightness to the fact that I had lost both my matches. Events proved, however, that I was right, though I do not think that the thunderstorm that broke that night was the sole cause of my depression.

Our way lay through deep high-banked lanes, and before we had gone very far I fell asleep, and was only awakened by the stopping of the motor. And with a sudden thrill, partly of fear but chiefly of curiosity, I found myself standing in the doorway of my house of dream. We went, I half wondering whether or not I was dreaming still, through a low oak-panelled hall, and out onto the lawn, where tea was laid in the shadow of the house. It was set in flower beds, a red-brick wall, with a gate in it, bounded one side, and out beyond that was a space of rough grass with a walnut tree. The facade of the house was very long, and at one end stood a three-storied tower, markedly older than the rest.

Here for the moment all resemblance to the repeated dream ceased. There was no

silent and somehow terrible family, but a large assembly of exceedingly cheerful persons, all of whom were known to me. And in spite of the horror with which the dream itself had always filled me, I felt nothing of it now that the scene of it was thus reproduced before me. But I felt intensest curiosity as to what was going to happen.

Tea pursued its cheerful course, and before long Mrs. Clinton got up. And at that moment I think I knew what she was going to say. She spoke to me, and what she said was:

"Jack will show you your room: I have given you the room in the tower."

At that, for half a second, the horror of the dream took hold of me again. But it quickly passed, and again I felt nothing more than the most intense curiosity. It was not very long before it was amply satisfied.

John turned to me.

"Right up at the top of the house," he said, "but I think you'll be comfortable. We're absolutely full up. Would you like to go and see it now? By Jove, I believe that you are right, and that we are going to have a thunderstorm. How dark it has become."

I got up and followed him. We passed through the hall, and up the perfectly familiar staircase. Then he opened the door, and I went in. And at that moment sheer unreasoning terror again possessed me. I did not know what I feared: I simply feared. Then like a sudden recollection, when one remembers a name which has long escaped the memory, I knew what I feared. I feared Mrs. Stone, whose grave with the sinister inscription, "In evil memory," I had so often seen in my dream, just beyond the lawn which lay below my window. And then once more the fear passed so completely that I wondered what there was to fear, and I found myself, sober and quiet and sane, in the room in the tower, the name of which I had so often heard in my dream, and the scene of which was so familiar.

I looked around it with a certain sense of proprietorship, and found that nothing had been changed from the dreaming nights in which I knew it so well. Just to the left of the door was the bed, lengthways along the wall, with the head of it in the angle. In a line with it was the fireplace and a small bookcase; opposite the door the outer wall was pierced by two lattice-paned windows, between which stood the dressing-table, while ranged along the fourth wall was the washing-stand and a big cupboard. My luggage had already been unpacked, for the furniture of dressing and undressing lay orderly on the wash-stand and toilet-table, while my dinner clothes were spread out on the coverlet of the bed. And then, with a sudden start of unexplained dismay, I saw that there were two rather conspicuous objects which I had not seen before in my dreams: one a life-sized oil painting of Mrs. Stone, the other a black-and-white sketch of Jack Stone, representing him as he had appeared to me only a week before in the last of the series of these repeated dreams, a rather secret and evil-looking man of about thirty. His picture hung between the windows, looking straight across the room to the other portrait, which hung at the side of the bed. At that I looked next, and as I looked I felt once more the horror of nightmare seize me.

It represented Mrs. Stone as I had seen her last in my dreams: old and withered and white-haired. But in spite of the evident feebleness of body, a dreadful exuberance and vitality shone through the envelope of flesh, an exuberance wholly malign, a vitality that foamed and frothed with unimaginable evil. Evil beamed from the narrow, leering eyes, it laughed in the demon-like mouth. The whole face was instinct with some secret and appalling mirth; the hands, clasped together on the knee, seemed shaking with suppressed and nameless glee. Then I saw also that it was signed in the left-hand bottom corner, and wondering who the artist could be, I looked more closely, and read the inscription, "Julia Stone by Julia Stone."

There came a tap at the door, and John Clinton entered.

"Got everything you want?" he asked.

"Rather more than I want," said I, pointing to the picture.

He laughed.

"Hard-featured old lady," he said. "By herself, too, I remember. Anyhow she can't have flattered herself much."

"But don't you see?" said I. "It's scarcely a human face at all. It's the face of some witch, of some devil."

He looked at it more closely.

"Yes; it isn't very pleasant," he said. "Scarcely a bedside manner, eh? Yes; I can imagine getting the nightmare if I went to sleep with that close by my bed. I'll have it taken down if you like."

"I really wish you would," I said. He rang the bell, and with the help of a servant we detached the picture and carried it out onto the landing, and put it with its face to the wall.

"By Jove, the old lady is a weight," said John, mopping his forehead. "I wonder if she had something on her mind."

The extraordinary weight of the picture had struck me too. I was about to reply, when I caught sight of my own hand. There was blood on it, in considerable quantities, covering the whole palm.

"I've cut myself somehow," said I.

John gave a little startled exclamation.

"Why, I have too," he said.

Simultaneously the footman took out his handkerchief and wiped his hand with it. I saw that there was blood also on his handkerchief.

John and I went back into the tower room and washed the blood off; but neither on his hand nor on mine was there the slightest trace of a scratch or cut. It seemed to me that, having ascertained this, we both, by a sort of tacit consent, did not allude to it again. Something in my case had dimly occurred to me that I did not wish to think about. It was but a conjecture, but I fancied that I knew the same thing had occurred to him.

The heat and oppression of the air, for the storm we had expected was still undischarged, increased very much after dinner, and for some time most of the party, among whom were John Clinton and myself, sat outside on the path bounding the lawn, where we had had tea. The night was absolutely dark, and no twinkle of star or moon ray could penetrate the pall of cloud that overset the sky. By degrees our assembly thinned, the women went up to bed, men dispersed to the smoking or billiard room, and by eleven o'clock my host and I were the only two left. All the evening I thought that he had something on his mind, and as soon as we were alone he spoke.

"The man who helped us with the picture had blood on his hand, too, did you notice?" he said.

"I asked him just now if he had cut himself, and he said he supposed he had, but that he could find no mark of it. Now where did that blood come from?"

By dint of telling myself that I was not going to think about it, I had succeeded in not doing so, and I did not want, especially just at bedtime, to be reminded of it.

"I don't know," said I, "and I don't really care so long as the picture of Mrs. Stone is not by my bed."

He got up.

"But it's odd," he said. "Ha! Now you'll see another odd thing."

A dog of his, an Irish terrier by breed, had come out of the house as we talked. The door behind us into the hall was open, and a bright oblong of light shone across the lawn to the iron gate which led on to the rough grass outside, where the walnut tree stood. I saw that the dog had all his hackles up, bristling with rage and fright; his lips were curled back from his teeth, as if he was ready to spring at something, and he was growling to himself. He took not the slightest notice of his master or me, but stiffly and tensely walked across the grass to the iron gate. There he stood for a moment, looking through the bars and still growling. Then of a sudden his courage seemed to desert him: he gave one long howl, and scuttled back to the house with a curious crouching sort of movement.

"He does that half-a-dozen times a day." said John. "He sees something which he both hates and fears."

I walked to the gate and looked over it. Something was moving on the grass outside, and soon a sound which I could not instantly identify came to my ears. Then I remembered what it was: it was the purring of a cat. I lit a match, and saw the purrer, a big blue Persian, walking round and round in a little circle just outside the gate, stepping high and ecstatically, with tail carried aloft like a banner. Its eyes were bright and shining, and every now and then it put its head down and sniffed at the grass.

I laughed.

"The end of that mystery, I am afraid." I said. "Here's a large cat having Walpurgis night all alone."

"Yes, that's Darius," said John. "He spends half the day and all night there. But that's not the end of the dog mystery, for Toby and he are the best of friends, but the beginning of the cat mystery. What's the cat doing there? And why is Darius pleased, while Toby is terror-stricken?"

At that moment I remembered the rather horrible detail of my dreams when I saw through the gate, just where the cat was now, the white tombstone with the sinister inscription. But before I could answer the rain began, as suddenly and heavily as if a tap had been turned on, and simultaneously the big cat squeezed through the bars of the gate, and came leaping across the lawn to the house for shelter. Then it sat in the doorway, looking out eagerly into the dark. It spat and struck at John with its paw, as he pushed it in, in order to close the door.

Somehow, with the portrait of Julia Stone in the passage outside, the room in the tower had absolutely no alarm for me, and as I went to bed, feeling very sleepy and heavy, I had nothing more than interest for the curious incident about our bleeding hands, and the conduct of the cat and dog. The last thing I looked at before I put out my light was the square empty space by my bed where the portrait had been. Here the paper was of its original full tint of dark red: over the rest of the walls it had faded. Then I blew out my candle and instantly fell asleep.

My awaking was equally instantaneous, and I sat bolt upright in bed under the impression that some bright light had been flashed in my face, though it was now absolutely pitch dark. I knew exactly where I was, in the room which I had dreaded in dreams, but no horror that I ever felt when asleep approached the fear that now invaded and froze my brain. Immediately after a peal of thunder crackled just above the house, but the probability that it was only a flash of lightning which awoke me gave no reassurance to my galloping heart. Something I knew was in the room with me, and instinctively I put out my right hand, which was nearest the wall, to keep it away. And my hand touched the edge of a picture-frame hanging close to me.

I sprang out of bed, upsetting the small table that stood by it, and I heard my watch, candle, and matches clatter onto the floor. But for the moment there was no need of light, for a blinding flash leaped out of the clouds, and showed me that by my bed again hung the picture of Mrs. Stone. And instantly the room went into blackness again. But in that flash I saw another thing also, namely a figure that leaned over the end of my bed, watching me. It was dressed in some close-clinging white garment, spotted and stained with mold, and the face was that of the portrait.

Overhead the thunder cracked and roared, and when it ceased and the deathly stillness succeeded, I heard the rustle of movement coming nearer me, and, more horrible yet, perceived an odor of corruption and decay. And then a hand was laid on the side of my neck, and close beside my ear I heard quick-taken, eager breathing. Yet I knew that this thing, though it could be perceived by touch, by smell, by eye and by ear, was still not of this earth, but something that had passed out of the body and had power to make itself manifest. Then a voice, already familiar to me, spoke.

"I knew you would come to the room in the tower," it said. "I have been long waiting for you. At last you have come. Tonight I shall feast; before long we will feast together."

And the quick breathing came closer to me; I could feel it on my neck.

At that the terror, which I think had paralyzed me for the moment, gave way to the wild instinct of self-preservation. I hit wildly with both arms, kicking out at the same moment, and heard a little animal-squeal, and something soft dropped with a thud beside me. I took a couple of steps forward, nearly tripping up over whatever it was that lay there, and by the merest good-luck found the handle of the door. In another second I ran out on the landing, and had banged the door behind me. Almost at the same moment I heard a door open somewhere below, and John Clinton, candle in hand, came running upstairs.

"What is it?" he said. "I sleep just below you, and heard a noise as if—Good heavens, there's blood on your shoulder."

I stood there, so he told me afterwards, swaying from side to side, white as a sheet, with the mark on my shoulder as if a hand covered with blood had been laid there.

"It's in there," I said, pointing. "She, you know. The portrait is in there, too, hanging up on the place we took it from."

At that he laughed.

"My dear fellow, this is mere nightmare," he said.

He pushed by me, and opened the door, I standing there simply inert with terror, unable to stop him, unable to move.

"Phew! What an awful smell," he said.

Then there was silence; he had passed out of my sight behind the open door. Next moment he came out again, as white as myself, and instantly shut it.

"Yes, the portrait's there," he said, "and on the floor is a thing—a thing spotted with earth, like what they bury people in. Come away, quick, come away."

How I got downstairs I hardly know. An awful shuddering and nausea of the spirit rather than of the flesh had seized me, and more than once he had to place my feet upon the steps, while every now and then he cast glances of terror and apprehension up the stairs. But in time we came to his dressing-room on the floor below, and there I told him what I have here described.

The sequel can be made short; indeed, some of my readers have perhaps already guessed what it was, if they remember that inexplicable affair of the churchyard at West Fawley, some eight years ago, where an attempt was made three times to bury the body of a certain woman who had committed suicide. On each occasion the coffin was found in the course of a few days again protruding from the ground. After the third attempt, in order that the thing should not be talked about, the body was buried elsewhere in unconsecrated ground. Where it was buried was just outside the iron gate of the garden belonging to the house where this woman had lived. She had committed suicide in a room at the top of the tower in that house. Her name was Julia Stone.

Subsequently the body was again secretly dug up, and the coffin was found to be full of blood.

Aylmer Vance and the Vampire

by Alice and Claude Askew

Aylmer Vance had rooms in Dover Street, Piccadilly, and now that I had decided to follow in his footsteps and to accept him as my instructor in matters psychic, I found it convenient to lodge in the same house. Aylmer and I quickly became close friends, and he showed me how to develop that faculty of clairvoyance which I had possessed without being aware of it. And I may say at once that this particular faculty of mine proved of service on several important occasions.

At the same time I made myself useful to Vance in other ways, not the least of which was that of acting as recorder of his many strange adventures. For himself, he never cared much about publicity, and it was some time before I could persuade him, in the interests of science, to allow me to give any detailed account of his experiences to the world.

The incidents which I will now narrate occurred very soon after we had taken up our residence together, and while I was still, so to speak, a novice.

It was about ten o'clock in the morning that a visitor was announced. He sent up a card which bore upon it the name of Paul Davenant.

The name was familiar to me, and I wondered if this could be the same Mr Davenant who was so well known for his polo playing and for his success as an amateur rider, especially over the hurdles? He was a young man of wealth and position, and I recollected that he had married, about a year ago, a girl who was reckoned the greatest beauty of the season. All the illustrated papers had given their portraits at the time, and I remember thinking what a remarkably handsome couple they made.

Mr Davenant was ushered in, and at first I was uncertain as to whether this could be the individual whom I had in mind, so wan and pale and ill did he appear. A finely-built, upstanding man at the time of his marriage, he had now acquired a languid droop of the shoulders and a shuffling gait, while his face, especially about the lips, was bloodless to an alarming degree.

And yet it was the same man, for behind all this I could recognize the shadow of the good looks that had once distinguished Paul Davenant.

He took the chair which Aylmer offered him—after the usual preliminary civilities had been exchanged—and then glanced doubtfully in my direction. 'I wish to consult you privately, Mr Vance,' he said. 'The matter is of considerable importance to myself, and, if I may say so, of a somewhat delicate nature.'

Of course I rose immediately to withdraw from the room, but Vance laid his hand upon my arm.

'If the matter is connected with research in my particular line, Mr Davenant,' he said, 'if there is any investigation you wish me to take up on your behalf, I shall be glad if you will include Mr Dexter in your confidence. Mr Dexter assists me in my work. But, of course—.'

'Oh, no,' interrupted the other, 'if that is the case, pray let Mr Dexter remain. I think,' he added, glancing at me with a friendly smile, 'that you are an Oxford man, are you not, Mr Dexter? It was before my time, but I have heard of your name in connection with the river. You rowed at Henley, unless I am very much mistaken.'

I admitted the fact, with a pleasurable sensation of pride. I was very keen upon rowing in those days, and a man's prowess at school and college always remain dear to his heart. After this we quickly became on friendly terms, and Paul Davenant proceeded to take Aylmer and myself into his confidence.

He began by calling attention to his personal appearance. 'You would hardly recognize me for the same man I was a year ago,' he said. 'I've been losing flesh steadily for the last six months. I came up from Scotland about a week ago, to consult a London doctor. I've seen two—in fact, they've held a sort of consultation over me—but the result, I may say, is far from satisfactory. They don't seem to know what is really the matter with me.'

'Anaemia—heart,' suggested Vance. He was scrutinizing his visitor keenly, and yet without any particular appearance of doing so. 'I believe it not infrequently happens that you athletes overdo yourselves—put too much strain upon the heart —'

'My heart is quite sound,' responded Davenant. 'Physically it is in perfect condition. The trouble seems to be that it hasn't enough blood to pump into my veins. The doctors wanted to know if I had met with an accident involving a great loss of blood—but I haven't. I've had no accident at all, and as for anaemia, well, I don't seem to show the ordinary symptoms of it. The inexplicable thing is that I've lost blood without knowing it, and apparently this has been going on for some time, for I have been getting steadily worse. It was almost imperceptible at first—not a sudden collapse, you understand, but a gradual failure of health.'

'I wonder,' remarked Vance slowly, 'what induced you to consult me? For you know, of course, the direction in which I pursue my investigations. May I ask if you have reason to consider that your state of health is due to some cause which we may describe as super-physical?'

A slight colour came to Davenant's white cheeks.

'There are curious circumstances,' he said in a low and earnest tone of voice. 'I've been turning them over in my mind, trying to see light through them. I daresay it's all the sheerest folly—and I must tell you that I'm not in the least a superstitious sort of man. I don't mean to say that I'm absolutely incredulous, but I've never given thought to such things—I've led too active a life. But, as I have said, there are curious circumstances about my case, and that is why I decided upon consulting you.'

'Will you tell me everything without reserve?' said Vance. I could see that he was interested.

He was sitting up in his chair, his feet supported on a stool, his elbows on his knees, his chin in his hands—a favourite attitude of his. 'Have you,' he suggested, slowly, 'any mark upon your body, anything that you might associate, however remotely, with your present weakness and ill-health?'

'It's a curious thing that you should ask me that question,' returned Davenant, 'because I have got a curious mark, a sort of scar, that I can't account for. But I showed it to the doctors, and they assured me that it could have nothing whatever to do with my condition. In any case, if it had, it was something altogether outside their experience. I think they imagined it to be nothing more than a birthmark, a sort of mole, for they asked me if I'd had it all my life. But that I can swear I haven't. I only noticed it for the first time about six months ago, when my health began to fail. But you can see for yourself.'

He loosened his collar and bared his throat. Vance rose and made a careful scrutiny of the suspicious mark. It was situated a very little to the left of the central line, just above the clavicle, and, as Vance pointed out, directly over the big vessels of the throat. My friend called to me so that I might examine it, too. Whatever the opinion of the doctors may have been, Aylmer was obviously deeply interested. And yet there was very little to show. The skin was quite intact, and there was no sign of inflammation. There were two red marks, about an inch apart, each of which was inclined to be crescent in shape. They were more visible than they might otherwise have been owing to the peculiar whiteness of Davenant's skin.

'It can't be anything of importance,' said Davenant, with a slightly uneasy laugh. 'I'm inclined to think the marks are dying away.'

'Have you ever noticed them more inflamed than they are at present?' inquired Vance. 'If so, was it at any special time?'

Davenant reflected. 'Yes,' he replied slowly, 'there have been times, usually, I think perhaps invariably, when I wake up in the morning, that I've noticed them larger and more angry looking. And I've felt a slight sensation of pain—a tingling—oh, very slight, and I've never worried about it. Only now you suggest it to my mind, I believe that those same mornings I have felt particularly tired and done up—a sensation of lassitude absolutely unusual to me. And once, Mr Vance, I remember quite distinctly that there was a stain of blood close to the mark. I didn't think anything of it at the time, and just wiped it away.'

'I see.' Aylmer Vance resumed his seat and invited his visitor to do the same. 'And now,' he resumed, 'you said, Mr Davenant, that there are certain peculiar circumstances you wish to acquaint me with. Will you do so?'

And so Davenant readjusted his collar and proceeded to tell his story. I will tell it as far as I can, without any reference to the occasional interruptions of Vance and myself.

Paul Davenant, as I have said, was a man of wealth and position, and so, in every sense of the word, he was a suitable husband for Miss Jessica MacThane, the young lady who eventually became his wife. Before coming to the incidents attending his loss of health, he had a great deal to recount about Miss MacThane and her family history.

She was of Scottish descent, and although she had certain characteristic features of her race, she was not really Scotch in appearance. Hers was the beauty of the far South rather than that of the Highlands from which she had her origin. Names are not always suited to their owners, and Miss MacThane's was peculiarly inappropriate. She had, in fact, been christened Jessica in a sort of pathetic effort to counteract her obvious departure from normal type. There was a reason for this which we were soon to learn.

Miss MacThane was especially remarkable for her wonderful red hair, hair such as one hardly ever sees outside of Italy—not the Celtic red—and it was so long that it reached to her feet, and it had an extraordinary gloss upon it so that it seemed almost to have individual life of its own.

Then she had just the complexion that one would expect with such hair, the purest ivory white, and not in the least marred by freckles, as is so often the case with red-haired girls. Her beauty was derived from an ancestress who had been brought to Scotland from some foreign shore—no one knew exactly whence.

Davenant fell in love with her almost at once and he had every reason to believe, in spite of her many admirers, that his love was returned. At this time he knew very little about her personal history. He was aware only that she was very wealthy in her own right, an orphan, and the last representative of a race that had once been famous in the annals of history—or rather infamous, for the MacThanes had distinguished themselves more by cruelty and lust of blood than by deeds of chivalry. A clan of turbulent robbers in the past, they had helped to add many a blood-stained page to the history of their country.

Jessica had lived with her father, who owned a house in London, until his death when she was about fifteen years of age. Her mother had died in Scotland when Jessica was still a tiny child. Mr MacThane had been so affected by his wife's death that, with his little daughter, he had abandoned his Scotch estate altogether—or so it was believed—leaving it to the management of a bailiff—though, indeed, there was but little work for the bailiff to do, since there were practically no tenants left. Blackwick Castle had borne for many years a most unenviable reputation.

After the death of her father, Miss MacThane had gone to live with a certain Mrs Meredith, who was a connection of her mother's—on her father's side she had not a single relation left.

Jessica was absolutely the last of a clan once so extensive that intermarriage had been a tradition of the family, but for which the last two hundred years had been gradually dwindling to extinction.

Mrs Meredith took Jessica into Society—which would never have been her privilege had Mr MacThane lived, for he was a moody, self-absorbed man, and prematurely old—one who seemed worn down by the weight of a great grief.

Well, I have said that Paul Davenant quickly fell in love with Jessica, and it was not long before he proposed for her hand. To his great surprise, for he had good reason to believe that she cared for him, he met with a refusal; nor would she give any explanation, though she burst into a flood of pitiful tears.

Bewildered and bitterly disappointed, he consulted Mrs Meredith, with whom he happened to be on friendly terms, and from her he learnt that Jessica had already had several proposals, all from quite desirable men, but that one after another had been rejected.

Paul consoled himself with the reflection that perhaps Jessica did not love them, whereas he was quite sure that she cared for himself. Under these circumstances he determined to try again.

He did so, and with better result. Jessica admitted her love, but at the same time she repeated that she would not marry him. Love and marriage were not for her. Then, to his utter amazement, she declared that she had been born under a curse—a curse which, sooner or later was bound to show itself in her, and which, moreover, must react cruelly, perhaps fatally, upon anyone with whom she linked her life. How could she allow a man she loved to take such a risk? Above all, since the evil was hereditary, there was one point upon which she had quite made up her mind: no child should ever call her mother—she must be the last of her race indeed.

Of course, Davenant was amazed and inclined to think that Jessica had got some absurd idea into her head which a little reasoning on his part would dispel. There was only one other possible explanation. Was it lunacy she was afraid of? But Jessica shook her head, She did not know of any lunacy in her family. The ill was deeper, more subtle than that. And then she told him all that she knew.

The curse—she made us of that word for want of a better—was attached to the ancient race from which she had her origin. Her father had suffered from it, and his father and grandfather before him. All three had taken to themselves young wives who had died mysteriously, of some wasting disease, within a few years. Had they observed the ancient family tradition of intermarriage this might possibly not have happened, but in their case, since the family was so near extinction, this had not been possible.

For the curse—or whatever it was—did not kill those who bore the name of MacThane. It only rendered them a danger to others. It was as if they absorbed from the blood-soaked walls of their fatal castle a deadly taint which reacted terribly upon those with whom they were brought into contact, especially their nearest and dearest.

'Do you know what my father said we have it in us to become?' said Jessica with a shudder.

'He used the word vampires. Paul, think of it—vampires—preying upon the life blood of others.'And then, when Davenant was inclined to laugh, she checked him. 'No,' she cried out, 'it is not impossible. Think. We are a decadent race. From the earliest times our history has been marked by bloodshed and cruelty. The walls of Blackwick Castle are impregnated with evil—every stone could tell its tale, of violence, pain, lust, and murder. What can one expect of those who have spent their lifetime between its walls?'

'But you have not done so,' exclaimed Paul. 'You have been spared that, Jessica. You were taken away after your mother died, and you have no recollection of Blackwick Castle, none at all. And you need never set foot in it again.'

'I'm afraid the evil is in my blood,' she replied sadly, 'although I am unconscious of it now.

And as for not returning to Blackwick—I'm not sure I can help myself. At least, that is what my father warned me of. He said there is something there, some compelling force, that will call me to it in spite of myself. But, oh, I don't know—I don't know, and that is what makes it so difficult. If I could only believe that all this is nothing but an idle superstition, I might be happy again, for I have it in me to enjoy life, and I'm young, very young, but my father told me these things when he was on his death-bed.' She added the last words in a low, awe-stricken tone.

Paul pressed her to tell him all that she knew, and eventually she revealed another fragment of family history which seemed to have some bearing upon the case. It dealt with her own astonishing likeness to that ancestress of a couple of hundred years ago, whose existence seemed to have presaged the gradual downfall of the clan of the MacThanes.

A certain Robert MacThane, departing from the traditions of his family, which demanded that he should not marry outside his clan, brought home a wife from foreign shores, a woman of wonderful beauty, who was possessed of glowing masses of red hair and a complexion of ivory whiteness—such as had more or less distinguished since then every female of the race born in the direct line.

It was not long before this woman came to be regarded in the neighbourhood as a witch. Queer stories were circulated abroad as to her doings, and the reputation of Blackwick Castle became worse than ever before.

And then one day she disappeared. Robert MacThane had been absent upon some business for twenty-four hours, and it was upon his return that he found her gone. The neighbourhood was searched, but without avail, and then Robert, who was a violent man and who had adored his foreign wife, called together certain of his tenants whom he suspected, rightly or wrongly, of foul play, and had them murdered in cold blood. Murder was easy in those days, yet such an outcry was raised that Robert had to take to flight, leaving his two children in the care of their nurse, and for a long while Blackwick Castle was without a master.

But its evil reputation persisted. It was said that Zaida, the witch, though dead, still made her presence felt. Many children of the tenantry and young people of the neighbourhood sickened and died—possibly of quite natural causes; but this did not prevent a mantle of terror settling upon the countryside, for it was said that Zaida had been seen—a pale woman clad in white—flitting about the cottages at night, and where she passed sickness and death were sure to supervene.

And from that time the fortune of the family gradually declined. Heir succeeded heir, but no sooner was he installed at Blackwick Castle than his nature, whatever it may previously have been, seemed to undergo a change. It was as if he absorbed into himself all the weight of evil that had stained his family name—as if he did, indeed, become a vampire, bringing blight upon any not directly connected with his own house. And so, by degrees, Blackwick was deserted of its tenantry. The land around it was left uncultivated—the farms stood empty. This had persisted to the present day, for the superstitious peasantry still told their tales of the mysterious white woman who hovered about the neighbourhood, and whose appearance betokened death—and possibly worse than death.

And yet it seemed that the last representatives of the MacThanes could not desert their ancestral home. Riches they had, sufficient to live happily upon elsewhere, but, drawn by some power they could not contend against, they had preferred to spend their lives in the solitude of the now half-ruined castle, shunned by their neighbours, feared and execrated by the few tenants that still clung to their soil.

So it had been with Jessica's grandfather and great-grandfather. Each of them had married a young wife, and in each case their love story had been all too brief. The vampire spirit was still abroad, expressing itself—or so it seemed—through the living representatives of bygone generations of evil, and young blood had been demanded as the sacrifice.

And to them had succeeded Jessica's father. He had not profited by their example, but had followed directly in their footsteps. And the same fate had befallen the wife whom he passionately adored. She had died of pernicious anaemia—so the doctors said—but he had regarded himself as her murderer.

But, unlike his predecessors, he had torn himself away from Blackwick—and this for the sake of his child. Unknown to her, however, he had returned year after year, for there were times when the passionate longing for the gloomy, mysterious halls and corridors of the old castle, for the wild stretches of moorland, and the dark pinewoods, would come upon him too strongly to be resisted. And so he knew that for his daughter, as for himself, there was no escape, and he warned her, when the relief of death was at last granted to him, of what her fate must be.

This was the tale that Jessica told the man who wished to make her his wife, and he made light of it, as such a man would, regarding it all as foolish superstition, the delusion of a mind overwrought. And at last—perhaps it was not very difficult, for she loved him with all her heart and soul—he succeeded in inducing Jessica to think as he did, to banish morbid ideas, as he called them from her brain, and to consent to marry him at an early date.

'I'll take any risk you like,' he declared. 'I'll even go and live at Blackwick if you should desire it. To think of you, my lovely Jessica, a vampire! Why, I never heard such nonsense in my life.'

'Father said I'm very like Zaida, the witch,' she protested, but he silenced her with a kiss.

And so they were married and spent their honeymoon abroad, and in the autumn Paul accepted an invitation to a house party in Scotland for the grouse shooting, a sport to which he was absolutely devoted, and Jessica agreed with him that there was no reason why he should forgo his pleasure.

Perhaps it was an unwise thing to do, to venture to Scotland, but by this time the young couple, more deeply in love with each other than ever, had got quite over their fears. Jessica was redolent with health and spirits, and more than once she declared that if they should be anywhere in the neighbourhood of Blackwick she would like to see the old castle out of curiosity, and just to show how absolutely she had got over the foolish terrors that used to assail her.

This seemed to Paul to be quite a wise plan, and so one day, since they were actually staying at no great distance, they motored over to Blackwick, and finding the bailiff, got him to show them over the castle.

It was a great castellated pile, grey with age, and in places falling into ruin. It stood on a steep hillside, with the rock of which it seemed to form part, and on one side of it there was a precipitous drop to a mountain stream a hundred feet below. The robber MacThanes of the old days could not have desired a better stronghold.

At the back, climbing up the mountainside were dark pinewoods, from which, here and there, rugged crags protruded, and these were fantastically shaped, some like gigantic and misshapen human forms, which stood up as if they mounted guard over the castle and the narrow gorge, by which alone it could be approached.

This gorge was always full of weird, uncanny sounds. It might have been a storehouse for the wind, which, even on calm days, rushed up and down as if seeking an escape, and it moaned among the pines and whistled in the crags and shouted derisive laughter as it was tossed from side to side of the rocky heights. It was like the plaint of lost souls—that is the expression Davenant made use of—the plaint of lost souls.

The road, little more than a track now, passed through this gorge, and then, after skirting a small but deep lake, which hardly knew the light of the sun so shut in was it by overhanging trees, climbed the hill to the castle.

And the castle! Davenant used but a few words to describe it, yet somehow I could see the gloomy edifice in my mind's eye, and something of the lurking horror that it contained communicated itself to my brain. Perhaps my clairvoyant sense assisted me, for when he spoke of them I seemed already acquainted with the great stone halls, the long corridors, gloomy and cold even on the brightest and warmest of days, the dark, oak-panelled rooms, and the broad central staircase up which one of the early MacThanes had once led a dozen men on horseback in pursuit of a stag which had taken refuge within the precincts of the castle. There was the keep, too, its walls so thick that the ravages of time had made no impression upon them, and beneath the keep were dungeons which could tell terrible tales of ancient wrong and lingering pain.

Well, Mr and Mrs Davenant visited as much as the bailiff could show them of this ill-omened edifice, and Paul, for his part, thought pleasantly of his own Derbyshire home, the fine Georgian mansion, replete with every modern comfort, where he proposed to settle with his wife. And so he received something of a shock when, as they drove away, she slipped her hand into his and whispered:

'Paul, you promised, didn't you, that you would refuse me nothing?'

She had been strangely silent till she spoke those words. Paul, slightly apprehensive, assured her that she only had to ask—but the speech did not come from his heart, for he guessed vaguely what she desired.

She wanted to go and live at the castle—oh, only for a little while, for she was sure she would soon tire of it. But the bailiff had told her that there were papers, documents, which she ought to examine, since the property was now hers—and, besides, she was interested in this home of her ancestors, and wanted to explore it more thoroughly. Oh, no, she wasn't in the least influenced by the old superstition—that wasn't the attraction—she had quite got over those silly ideas. Paul had cured her, and since he himself was so convinced that they were without foundation he ought not to mind granting her her whim.

This was a plausible argument, not easy to controvert. In the end Paul yielded, though it was not without a struggle. He suggested amendments. Let him at least have the place done up for her—that would take time; or let them postpone their visit till next year—in the summer—not move in just as the winter was upon them.

But Jessica did not want to delay longer than she could help, and she hated the idea of redecoration. Why, it would spoil the illusion of the old place, and, besides, it would be a waste of money since she only wished to remain there for a week or two. The Derbyshire house was not quite ready yet; they must allow time for the paper to dry on the walls.

And so, a week later, when their stay with their friends was concluded, they went to Blackwick, the bailiff having engaged a few raw servants and generally made things as comfortable for them as possible. Paul was worried and apprehensive, but he could not admit this to his wife after having so loudly proclaimed his theories on the subject of superstition.

They had been married three months at this time—nine had passed since then, and they had never left Blackwick for more than a few hours—till now Paul had come to London—alone.

'Over and over again,' he declared, 'my wife has begged me to go. With tears in her eyes, almost upon her knees, she has entreated me to leave her, but I have steadily refused unless she will accompany me. But that is the trouble, Mr Vance, she cannot; there is something, some mysterious horror, that holds her there as surely as if she were bound with fetters. It holds her more strongly even than it held her father—we found out that he used to spend six months at least of every year at Blackwick—months when he pretended that he was travelling abroad. You see the spell—or whatever the accursed thing may be—never really relaxed its grip of him.'

'Did you never attempt to take your wife away?' asked Vance.

'Yes, several times; but it was hopeless. She would become so ill as soon as we were beyond the limit of the estate that I invariably had to take her back. Once we got as far as Dorekirk—that is the nearest town, you know—and I thought I should be successful if only I could get through the night. But she escaped me; she climbed out of a window—she meant to go back on foot, at night, all those long miles. Then I have had doctors down; but it is I who wanted the doctors, not she. They have ordered me away, but I have refused to obey them till now.'

'Is your wife changed at all—physically?' interrupted Vance.

Davenant reflected. 'Changed,' he said, 'yes, but so subtly that I hardly know how to describe it. She is more beautiful than ever—and yet it isn't the same beauty, if you can understand me. I have spoken of her white complexion, well, one is more than ever conscious of it now, because her lips have become so red—they are almost like a splash of blood upon her face. And the upper one has a peculiar curve that I don't think it had before, and when she laughs she doesn't smile—

'Do you know what I mean? Then her hair—it has lost its wonderful gloss. Of course, I know she is fretting about me; but that is so peculiar, too, for at times, as I have told you, she will implore me to go and leave her, and then perhaps only a few minutes later, she will wreathe her arms round my neck and say she cannot live without me. And I feel that there is a struggle going on within her, that she is only yielding slowly to the horrible influence—whatever it is—that she is herself when she begs me to go, but when she entreats me to stay—and it is then that her fascination is most intense—oh, I can't help remembering what she told me before we were married, and that word'—he lowered his voice-'the word "vampire"—'

He passed his hand over his brow that was wet with perspiration. 'But that's absurd, ridiculous,' he muttered; 'these fantastic beliefs have been exploded years ago. We live in the twentieth century.'

A pause ensued, then Vance said quietly, 'Mr Davenant, since you have taken me into your confidence, since you have found doctors of no avail, will you let me try to help you? I think I may be of some use—if it is not already too late. Should you agree, Mr Dexter and I will accompany you, as you have suggested, to Blackwick Castle as early as possible—by tonight's mail North. Under ordinary circumstances I should tell you as you value your life, not to return —'. Davenant shook his head. 'That is advice which I should never take,' he declared. 'I had already decided, under any circumstances, to travel North tonight. I am glad that you both will accompany me.'

And so it was decided. We settled to meet at the station, and presently Paul Davenant took his departure. Any other details that remained to be told he would put us in possession of during the course of the journey.

'A curious and most interesting case,' remarked Vance when we were alone. 'What do you make of it, Dexter?'

'I suppose,' I replied cautiously, 'that there is such a thing as vampirism even in these days of advanced civilization? I can understand the evil influence that a very old person may have upon a young one if they happen to be in constant intercourse—the worn-out tissue sapping healthy vitality for their own support. And there are certain people—I could think of several myself—who seem to depress one and undermine one's energies, quite unconsciously, of course, but one feels somehow that vitality has passed from oneself to them. And in this case, when the force is centuries old, expressing itself, in some mysterious way, through Davenant's wife, is it not feasible to believe that he may be physically affected by it, even though the whole thing is sheerly mental?'

'You think, then,' demanded Vance, 'that it is sheerly mental? Tell me, if that is so, how do you account for the marks on Davenant's throat?'

This was a question to which I found no reply, and though I pressed him for his views, Vance would not commit himself further just then.

Of our long journey to Scotland I need say nothing. We did not reach Blackwick Castle till late in the afternoon of the following day. The place was just as I had conceived it—as I have already described it. And a sense of gloom settled upon me as our car jolted us over the rough road that led through the Gorge of the Winds—a gloom that deepened when we penetrated into the vast cold hall of the castle.

Mrs Davenant, who had been informed by telegram of our arrival, received us cordially. She knew nothing of our actual mission, regarding us merely as friends of her husband's. She was most solicitous on his behalf, but there was something strained about her tone, and it made me feel vaguely uneasy. The impression that I got was that the woman was impelled to everything that she said or did by some force outside herself—but, of course, this was a conclusion that the circumstances I was aware of might easily have conduced to. In every other aspect she was charming, and she had an extraordinary fascination of appearance and manner that made me readily understand the force of a remark made by Davenant during our journey.

'I want to live for Jessica's sake. Get her away from Blackwick, Vance, and I feel that all will be well. I'd go through hell to have her restored to me—as she was.'

And now that I had seen Mrs Davenant I realized what he meant by those last words. Her fascination was stronger than ever, but it was not a natural fascination—not that of a normal woman, such as she had been. It was the fascination of a Circe, of a witch, of an enchantress—and as such was irresistible.

We had a strong proof of the evil within her soon after our arrival. It was a test that Vance had quietly prepared. Davenant had mentioned that no flowers grew at Blackwick, and Vance declared that we must take some with us as a present for the lady of the house. He purchased a bouquet of pure white roses at the little town where we left the train, for the motorcar has been sent to meet us. Soon after our arrival he presented these to Mrs Davenant. She took them it seemed to me nervously, and hardly had her hand touched them before they fell to pieces, in a shower of crumpled petals, to the floor.

'We must act at once,' said Vance to me when we were descending to dinner that night. 'There must be no delay.'

'What are you afraid of?' I whispered.

'Davenant has been absent a week,' he replied grimly. 'He is stronger than when he went away, but not strong enough to survive the loss of more blood. He must be protected. There is danger tonight.'

'You mean from his wife?' I shuddered at the ghastliness of the suggestion.

'That is what time will show.' Vance turned to me and added a few words with intense earnestness. 'Mrs Davenant, Dexter, is at present hovering between two conditions. The evil thing has not yet completely mastered her—you remember what Davenant said, how she would beg him to go away and the next moment entreat him to stay? She has made a struggle, but she is gradually succumbing, and this last week, spent here alone, has strengthened the evil. And that is what I have got to fight, Dexter—it is to be a contest of will, a contest that will go on silently till one or the other obtains the mastery. If you watch, you may see. Should a change show itself in Mrs Davenant you will know that I have won.'

Thus I knew the direction in which my friend proposed to act. It was to be a war of his will against the mysterious power that had laid its curse upon the house of MacThane. Mrs Davenant must be released from the fatal charm that held her.

And I, knowing what was going on, was able to watch and understand. I realized that the silent contest had begun even while we ate dinner. Mrs Davenant ate practically nothing and seemed ill at ease; she fidgeted in her chair, talked a great deal, and laughed—it was the laugh without a smile, as Davenant had described it. And as soon as she was able to she withdrew.

Later, as we sat in the drawing-room, I could feel the clash of wills. The air in the room felt electric and heavy, charged with tremendous but invisible forces. And outside, round the castle, the wind whistled and shrieked and moaned—it was as if all the dead and gone MacThanes, a grim army, had collected to fight the battle of their race.

And all this while we four in the drawing-room were sitting and talking the ordinary commonplaces of after—dinner conversation! That was the extraordinary part of it—Paul Davenant suspected nothing, and I, who knew, had to play my part. But I hardly took my eyes from Jessica's face. When would the change come, or was it, indeed, too late!

At last Davenant rose and remarked that he was tired and would go to bed. There was no need for Jessica to hurry. We would sleep that night in his dressing-room and did not want to be disturbed.

And it was at that moment, as his lips met hers in a goodnight kiss, as she wreathed her enchantress arms about him, careless of our presence, her eyes gleaming hungrily, that the change came.

It came with a fierce and threatening shriek of wind, and a rattling of the casement, as if the horde of ghosts without was about to break in upon us. A long, quivering sigh escaped from Jessica's lips, her arms fell from her husband's shoulders, and she drew back, swaying a little from side to side.

'Paul,' she cried, and somehow the whole timbre of her voice was changed, 'what a wretch I've been to bring you back to Blackwick, ill as you are! But we'll go away, dear; yes, I'll go, too. Oh, will you take me away—take me away tomorrow?' She spoke with an intense earnestness—unconscious all the time of what had been happening to her. Long shudders were convulsing her frame. 'I don't know why I've wanted to stay here,' she kept repeating. 'I hate the place, really—it's evil—evil.'

Having heard these words I exulted, for surely Vance's success was assured. But I was to learn that the danger was not yet past.

Husband and wife separated, each going to their own room. I noticed the grateful, if mystified glance that Davenant threw at Vance, vaguely aware, as he must have been, that my friend was somehow responsible for what had happened. It was settled that plans for departure were to be discussed on the morrow.

'I have succeeded,' Vance said hurriedly, when we were alone, 'but the change may be a transitory. I must keep watch tonight. Go you to bed, Dexter, there is nothing that you can do.'

I obeyed—though I would sooner have kept watch, too—watch against a danger of which I had no understanding. I went to my room, a gloomy and sparsely furnished apartment, but I knew that it was quite impossible for me to think of sleeping. And so, dressed as I was, I went and sat by the open window, for now the wind that had raged round the castle had died down to a low moaning in the pinetrees—a whimpering of time-worn agony.

And it was as I sat thus that I became aware of a white figure that stole out from the castle by a door that I could not see, and, with hands clasped, ran swiftly across the terrace to the wood. I had but a momentary glance, but I felt convinced that the figure was that of Jessica Davenant.

And instinctively I knew that some great danger was imminent. It was, I think, the suggestion of despair conveyed by those clasped hands. At any rate, I did not hesitate. My window was some height from the ground, but the wall below was ivy-clad and afforded good foothold. The descent was quite easy. I achieved it, and was just in time to take up the pursuit in the right direction, which was into the thickness of the wood that clung to the slope of the hill.

I shall never forget that wild chase. There was just sufficient room to enable me to follow the rough path, which, luckily, since I had now lost sight of my quarry, was the only possible way that she could have taken; there were no intersecting tracks, and the wood was too thick on either side to permit of deviation.

And the wood seemed full of dreadful sounds—moaning and wailing and hideous laughter.

The wind, of course, and the screaming of night birds—once I felt the fluttering of wings in close proximity to my face. But I could not rid myself of the thought that I, in my turn, was being pursued, that the forces of hell were combined against me.

The path came to an abrupt end on the border of the sombre lake that I have already mentioned. And now I realized that I was indeed only just in time, for before me, plunging knee deep in the water, I recognized the white-clad figure of the woman I had been pursuing. Hearing my footsteps, she turned her head, and then threw up her arms and screamed. Her red hair fell in heavy masses about her shoulders, and her face, as I saw it in that moment, was hardly human for the agony of remorse that it depicted.

'Go!' she screamed. 'For God's sake let me die!'

But I was by her side almost as she spoke. She struggled with me—sought vainly to tear herself from my clasp—implored me, with panting breath, to let her drown.

'It's the only way to save him!' she gasped. 'Don't you understand that I am a thing accursed? For it is I—I—who have sapped his life blood! I know it now, the truth has been revealed to me tonight! I am a vampire, without hope in this world or the next, so for his sake—for the sake of his unborn child—let me die—let me die!' Was ever so terrible an appeal made? Yet I—what could I do? Gently I overcame her resistance and drew her back to shore. By the time I reached it she was lying a dead weight upon my arm. I laid her down upon a mossy bank, and, kneeling by her side, gazed intently into her face.

And then I knew that I had done well. For the face I looked upon was not that of Jessica the vampire, as I had seen it that afternoon, it was the face of Jessica, the woman whom Paul Davenant had loved.

And later Aylmer Vance had his tale to tell.

'I waited', he said, 'until I knew that Davenant was asleep, and then I stole into his room to watch by his bedside. And presently she came, as I guessed she would, the vampire, the accursed thing that has preyed upon the souls of her kin, making them like to herself when they too have passed into Shadowland, and gathering sustenance for her horrid task from the blood of those who are alien to her race. Paul's body and Jessica's soul—it is for one and the other, Dexter, that we have fought.'

'You mean,' I hesitated, 'Zaida the witch?'

'Even so,' he agreed. 'Hers is the evil spirit that has fallen like a blight upon the house of MacThane. But now I think she may be exorcized for ever.'

'Tell me.'

'She came to Paul Davenant last night, as she must have done before, in the guise of his wife.

'You know that Jessica bears a strong resemblance to her ancestress. He opened his arms, but she was foiled of her prey, for I had taken my precautions; I had placed that upon Davenant's breast while he slept which robbed the vampire of her power of ill. She sped wailing from the room—a shadow—she who a minute before had looked at him with Jessica's eyes and spoken to him with Jessica's voice. Her red lips were Jessica's lips, and they were close to his when his eyes were opened and he saw her as she was—a hideous phantom of the corruption of the ages. And so the spell was removed, and she fled away to the place whence she had come —'

He paused. 'And now?' I inquired.

'Blackwick Castle must be razed to the ground,' he replied. 'That is the only way. Every stone of it, every brick, must be ground to powder and burnt with fire, for therein is the cause of all the evil. Davenant has consented.'

'And Mrs Davenant?'

'I think,' Vance answered cautiously, 'that all may be well with her. The curse will be removed with the destruction of the castle. She has not—thanks to you—perished under its influence. She was less guilty than she imagined—herself preyed upon rather than preying. But can't you understand her remorse when she realized, as she was bound to realize, the part she had played? And the knowledge of the child to come—its fatal inheritance—'

'I understand.' I muttered with a shudder. And then, under my breath, I whispered, 'Thank God!'

The Tomb of Sarah

by F. G. Loring

My father was the head of a celebrated firm of church restorers and decorators about sixty years ago. He took a keen interest in his work, and made an especial study of any old legends or family histories that came under his observation. He was necessarily very well read and thoroughly well posted in all questions of folklore and medieval legend. As he kept a careful record of every case he investigated the manuscripts he left at his death have a special interest. From amongst them I have selected the following, as being a particularly weird and extraordinary experience. In presenting it to the public I feel it is superfluous to apologize for its supernatural character.

My Father's Diary

1841. — June 17th. Received a commission from my old friend Peter Grant to enlarge and restore the chancel of his church at Hagarstone, in the wilds of the West Country.

July 5th. Went down to Hagarstone with my' head man, Somers. A very long and tiring journey.

July 7th. Got the work well started. The old church is one of special interest to the antiquarian, and I shall endeavour while restoring it to alter the existing arrangements as little as possible. One large tomb, however, must be moved bodily ten feet at least to the southward. Curiously enough, there is a somewhat forbidding inscription upon it in Latin, and I am sorry that this particular tomb should have to be moved. It stands amongst the graves of the Kenyons, an old family which has been extinct in these parts for centuries. The inscription on it runs thus:

Sarah.
1630.
For the Sake of the Dead and the Welfare
Of the Living, Let this Sepulchre Remain
Untouched and its Occupant Undisturbed till the Coming of Christ.
In the Name of the Father, the Son, and The Holy Ghost.

July 8th. Took counsel with Grant concerning the 'Sarah Tomb'. We are both very loth to disturb it, but the ground has sunk so beneath it that the safety of the church is in danger; thus we have no choice. However, the work shall be done as reverently as possible under our own direction.

Grant says there is a legend in the neighbourhood that it is the tomb of the last of the Kenyons, the evil Countess Sarah, who was murdered in 1630. She lived quite alone in the old castle, whose ruins still stand three miles from here on the road to Bristol. Her reputation was an evil one even for those days. She was a witch or were-woman, the only companion of her solitude being a familiar in the shape of a huge Asiatic wolf. This creature was reputed to seize upon children, or failing these, sheep and other small animals, and convey them to the castle, where the Countess used to suck their blood, It was popularly supposed that she could never be killed. This, however, proved a fallacy, since she was strangled one day by a mad peasant woman who had lost two children, she declaring that they had both been seized and carried off by the Countess's familiar, This is a very interesting story, since it points to a local superstition very similar to that of the Vampire, existing in Slavonic and Hungarian Europe.

The tomb is built of black marble, surmounted by an enormous slab of the same material. On the slab is a magnificent group of figures. A young and handsome woman reclines upon a couch; round her neck is a piece of rope, the end of which she holds in her hand. At her side is a gigantic dog with bared fangs and lolling tongue. The face of the reclining figure is a cruel one: the corners of the mouth are curiously lifted, showing the sharp points of long canine or dog teeth. The whole group, though magnificently executed, leaves a most unpleasant sensation.

If we move the tomb it will have to be done in two pieces, the covering slab first and then the tomb proper. We have decided to remove the covering slab tomorrow.

July 9th. 6 p.m. A very strange day.

By noon everything was ready for lifting off the covering stone, and after the men's dinner we started the jacks and pulley's. The slab lifted easily enough, though if fitted closely into its seat and was further secured by some sort of mortar or putty, which must have kept the interior perfectly air-tight.

None of us were prepared for the horrible rush of foul, mouldy air that escaped as the cover lifted clear of its seating. And the contents that gradually came into view were more startling still. There lay the fully dressed body of a woman, wizened and shrunk and ghastly pale as if from starvation. Round her neck was a loose cord, and, judging by the scars still visible, the story of death of strangulation was true enough.

The most horrible part, however, was the extraordinary freshness of the body. Except for the appearance of starvation, life might have been only just extinct. The flesh was soft and white, the eyes were wide open and seemed to stare at us with a fearful understanding in them. The body itself lay on mould, without any pretence to coffin or shell.

For several moments we gazed with horrible curiosity, and then it became too much for my workmen, who implored us to replace the covering slab. That, of course, we would not do; but I set the carpenters to work at once to make a temporary cover while we moved the tomb to its new position. This is a long job, and will take two or three days at least.

July 9th. 9 p.m. Just at sunset we were startled by the howling of, seemingly, every dog in the village. It lasted for ten minutes or a quarter of an hour, and then ceased as suddenly as it began. This, and a curious mist that has risen round the church, makes me feel rather anxious about the 'Sarah Tomb'. According to the best-established traditions of the Vampire-haunted countries, the disturbance of dogs or wolves at sunset is supposed to indicate the presence of one of these fiends, and local fog is always considered to be a certain sign. The Vampire has the power of producing it for the purpose of concealing its movements near its hiding-place at any time.

I dare not mention or even hint my fears to the Rector, for he is, not unnaturally perhaps, a rank disbeliever in many things that I know, from experience, are not only possible but even probable. I must work this out alone at first, and get his aid without his knowing in what direction he is helping me. I shall now watch till midnight at least.

10:15 p.m. As I feared and half expected. Just before ten there was another outburst of the hideous howling. It was commenced most distinctly by a particularly horrible and blood-curdling wail from the vicinity of the churchyard. The chorus lasted only a few minutes, however, and at the end of it I saw a large dark shape, like a huge dog, emerge from the fog and lope away at a rapid canter towards the open country. Assuming this to be what I fear, I shall see it return soon after midnight.

12.30 p.m. I was right. Almost as midnight struck I saw the beast returning. It stopped at the spot where the fog seemed to commence, and lifting up its head, gave tongue to that particularly horrible long-drawn wail that I had noticed as preceding the outburst earlier in the evening.

Tomorrow I shall tell the Rector what I have seen; and if, as I expect, we hear of some neighbouring sheepfold having been raided, I shall get him to watch with me for this nocturnal marauder. I shall also examine the 'Sarah Tomb' for something which he may notice without any previous hint from me.

July 10th. I found the workmen this morning much disturbed in mind about the howling of the dogs. 'We doan't like it, zur,' one of them said to me — 'we doan't like it; there was summat abroad last night that was unholy.' They were still more uncomfortable when the news came round that a large dog had made a raid upon a flock of sheep, scattering them far and wide, and leaving three of them dead with torn throats in the field.

When I told the Rector of what I had seen and what was being said in the village, he immediately decided that we must try and catch or at least identify the beast I had seen. 'Of course,' said he, 'it is some dog lately imported into the neighbourhood, for I know of nothing about here nearly as large as the animal you describe, though its size may be due to the deceptive moonlight.'

This afternoon I asked the Rector, as a favour, to assist me in lifting the temporary cover that was on the tomb, giving as an excuse the reason that I wished to obtain a portion of the curious mortar with which it had been sealed. After a slight demur he consented, and we raised the lid. If the sight that met our eyes gave me a shock, at least it appalled Grant.

'Great God!' he exclaimed; 'the woman is alive!'

And so it seemed for a moment. The corpse had lost much of its starved appearance and looked hideously fresh and alive. It was still wrinkled and shrunken, but the lips were firm, and of the rich red hue of health. The eyes, if possible, were more appalling than ever, though fixed and staring. At one corner of the mouth I thought I noticed a slight dark-coloured froth, but I said nothing about it then.

'Take your piece of mortar, Harry,' gasped Grant, 'and let us shut the tomb again. God help me! Parson though I am, such dead faces frighten me!'

Nor was I sorry to hide that terrible face again; but I got my bit of mortar, and I have advanced a step towards the solution of the mystery.

This afternoon the tomb was moved several feet towards its new position, but it will be two or three days yet before we shall be ready to replace the slab.

10.15 p.m. Again the same howling at sunset, the same fog enveloping the church, and at ten o'clock the same great beast slipping silently out into the open country. I must get the Rector's help and watch for its return. But precautions we must take, for if things are as I believe, we take our lives in our hands when we venture out into the night to waylay the — Vampire. Why not admit it at once? For that the beast I have seen is the Vampire of that evil thing in the tomb I can have no reasonable doubt.

Not yet come to its full strength, thank Heaven! after the starvation of nearly two centuries, for at present it can only maraud as wolf apparently. But, in a day or two, when full power returns, that dreadful woman in new strength and beauty will be able to leave her refuge. Then it would not be sheep merely that would satisfy her disgusting lust for blood, but victims that would yield their life-blood without a murmur to her caressing touch — victims that, dying of her foul embrace, themselves must become Vampires in their turn to prey on others.

Mercifully my knowledge gives me a safeguard; for that little piece of mortar that I rescued today from the tomb contains a portion of the Sacred Host, and who holds it, humbly and firmly believing in its virtue, may pass safely through such an ordeal as I intend to submit myself and the Rector to tonight.

12.30 p.m. Our adventure is over for the present, and we are back safe.

After writing the last entry recorded above, I went off to find Grant and tell him that the marauder was out on the prowl again. 'But, Grant,' I said, 'before we start out tonight I must insist that you will let me prosecute this affair in my own way; you must promise to put yourself completely under my orders, without asking any questions as to the why and wherefore.'

After a little demur, and some excusable chaff on his part at the serious view I was taking of what he called a 'dog hunt', he gave me his promise. I then told him that we were to watch tonight and try and track the mysterious beast, but not to interfere with it in any wax. I think, in spite of his jests, that I impressed him with the fact that there might be, after all, good reason for my precautions.

It was just after eleven when we stepped out into the still night.

Our first move was to try and penetrate the dense fog round the church, but there was something so chilly about it, and a faint smell so disgustingly rank and loathsome, that neither our nerves nor our stomachs were proof against it. Instead, we stationed ourselves in the dark shadow of a yew tree that commanded a good view of the wicket entrance to the churchyard.

At midnight the howling of the dogs began again, and in a few minutes we saw a large grey shape, with green eyes shining like lamps, shamble swiftly down the path towards us.

The Rector started forward, but I laid a firm hand upon his arm and whispered a warning 'Remember!' Then we both stood very still and watched as the great beast cantered swiftly by. It was real enough, for we could hear the clicking of its nails on the stone flags. It passed within a few yards of us, and seemed to be nothing more nor less than a great grey wolf, thin and gaunt, with bristling hair and dripping jaws. It stopped where the mist commenced, and turned round. It was truly a horrible sight, and made one's blood run cold. The eyes burnt like fires, the upper lip was snarling and raised, showing the great canine teeth, while round the mouth clung and dripped a dark-coloured froth.

It raised its head and gave tongue to its long wailing howl, which was answered from afar by the village dogs. After standing for a few moments it turned and disappeared into the thickest part of the fog.

Very shortly afterwards the atmosphere began to clear, and within ten minutes the mist was all gone, the dogs in the village were silent, and the night seemed to reassume its normal aspect. We examined the spot where the beast had been standing and found, plainly enough upon the stone flags, dark spots of froth and saliva.

'Well, Rector,' I said, 'will you admit now, in view of the things you have seen today, in consideration of the legend, the woman in the tomb, the fog, the howling dogs, and, last but not least, the mysterious beast you have seen so close, that there is something not quite normal in it all? Will you put yourself unreservedly in my hands and help me, whatever I may do, to first make assurance doubly sure, and finally take the necessary steps for putting an end to this horror of the night?' I saw that the uncanny influence of the night was strong upon him, and wished to impress it as much as possible.

'Needs must,' he replied, 'when the Devil drives: and in the face of what I have seen I must believe that some unholy forces are at work. Yet, how can they work in the sacred precincts of a church? Shall we not call rather upon Heaven to assist us in our need.'

'Grant,' I said solemnly, 'that we must do, each in his own way. God helps those who help themselves, and by His help and the light of my knowledge we must fight this battle for Him and the poor lost soul within.'

We then returned to the rectory and to our rooms, though I have sat up to write this account while the scene is fresh in my mind.

July 11th. Found the workmen again very much disturbed in their minds, and full of a strange dog that had been seen during the night by several people, who had hunted it. Farmer Stotman, who had been watching his sheep (the same flock that had been raided the night before), had surprised it over a fresh carcass and tried to drive it off, but its size and fierceness so alarmed him that he had beaten a hasty retreat for a gun. When he returned the animal was gone, though he found that three more sheep from his flock were dead and torn.

The 'Sarah Tomb' was moved today to its new position; but it was a long, heavy business, and there was not time to replace the covering slab. For this I was glad, as in the prosaic light of day the Rector almost disbelieves the events of the night, and is prepared to think everything to have been magnified and distorted by our imagination.

As, however, I could not possibly proceed with my war of extermination against this foul thing without assistance, and as there is nobody else I can rely upon, I appealed to him for one more night — to convince him that it was no delusion, but a ghastly, horrible truth, which must be fought and conquered for our own sakes, as well as that of all those living in the neighbourhood.

'Put yourself my hands, Rector,' I said, 'for tonight at least. Let us take those precautions which my study of the subject tells me are the right ones. Tonight you and I must watch in the church; and I feel assured that tomorrow you will be as convinced as I am, and be equally prepared to take those awful steps which I know to be proper, and I must warn you that we shall find a more startling change in the body lying there than you noticed yesterday.'

My words came true; for on raising the wooden cover once more the rank stench of a slaughterhouse arose, making us feel positively sick. There lay the Vampire, but how changed from the starved and shrunken corpse we saw two days ago for the first time! The wrinkles had almost disappeared, the flesh was firm and full, the crimson lips grinned horribly over the long pointed teeth, and a distinct smear of blood had trickled down one corner of the mouth. We set our teeth, however, and hardened our hearts, Then we replaced the cover and put what we had collected into a safe place in the vestry. Yet even now Grant could not believe that there was any real or pressing danger concealed in that awful tomb, as he raised strenuous objections to any apparent desecration of the body without further proof. This he shall have tonight. God grant that I am not taking too much on myself! If there is any truth in old legends it would be easy enough to destroy the Vampire now; but Grant will not have it.

I hope for the best of this night's work, but the danger in waiting is very great.

6 p.m. I have prepared everything: the sharp knives, the pointed stake, fresh garlic, and the wild dog-roses. All these I have taken and concealed in the vestry, where we can get at them when our solemn vigil commences.

If either or both of us die with our fearful task undone, let those reading my record see that this is done. I lay it upon them as a solemn obligation. 'That the Vampire be pierced through the heart with the stake, then let the Burial Service be read over the poor clay at last released from its doom. Thus shall the Vampire cease to be, and a lost soul rest.

July 12th. All is over. After the most terrible night of watching and horror one Vampire at least will trouble the world no more. But how thankful should we be to a merciful Providence that that awful tomb was not disturbed by anyone not having the knowledge necessary to deal with its dreadful occupant! I write this with no feelings of self-complacency, but simply with a great gratitude for the years of study I have been able to devote to this special subject.

And now to my tale.

Just before sunset last night the Rector and I locked ourselves into the church, and took up our position in the pulpit. It was one of those pulpits, to be found in some churches, which is entered from the vestry, the preacher appearing at a good height through an arched opening in the wall. This gave us a sense of security (which we felt we needed), a good view of the interior, and direct access to the implements which I had concealed in the vestry.

The sun set and the twilight gradually deepened and faded. There was, so far, no sign of the usual fog, nor any howling of the dogs. At nine o'clock the moon rose, and her pale light gradually flooded the aisles, and still no sign of any kind from the 'Sarah Tomb'. The Rector had asked me several times what he might expect, but I was determined that no words or thought of mine should influence him, and that he should be convinced by his own senses alone.

By half-past ten we were both getting very tired, and I began to think that perhaps after all we should see nothing that night. However, soon after eleven we observed a light mist rising from the 'Sarah Tomb'. It seemed to scintillate and sparkle as it rose, and curled in a sort of pillar or spiral.

I said nothing, but I heard the Rector give a sort of gasp as he clutched my arm feverishly. 'Great Heaven!' he whispered, 'it is taking shape.'

And, true enough, in a very few moments we saw standing erect by the tomb the ghastly figure of the Countess Sarah!

She looked thin and haggard still, and her face was deadly white; but the crimson lips looked like a hideous gash in the pale cheeks, and her eyes glared like red coals in the gloom of the church.

It was a fearful thing to watch as she stepped unsteadily down the aisle, staggering a little as if from weakness and exhaustion. This was perhaps natural, as her body must have suffered much physically from her long incarceration, in spite of the unholy forces which kept it fresh and well.

We watched her to the door, and wondered what would happen; but it appeared to present no difficulty, for she melted through it and disappeared.

'Now, Grant,' I said, 'do you believe?'

'Yes,' he replied, 'I must. Everything is in your hands, and I will obey your commands to the letter, if you can only instruct me how to rid my poor people of this unnameable terror.'

'By God's help I will,' said I; 'but you shall be yet more convinced first, for we have a terrible work to do, and much to answer for in the future, before we leave the church again this morning. And now to work, for in its present weak state the Vampire will not wander far, but may return at any time, and must not find us unprepared.'

We stepped down from the pulpit and, taking dog-roses and garlic from the vestry, proceeded to the tomb. I arrived first and, throwing off the wooden cover, cried, 'Look! it is empty!' There was nothing there! Nothing except the impress of the body in the loose damp mould!

I took the flowers and laid them in a circle round the tomb, for legend teaches us that Vampires will not pass over these particular blossoms if they can avoid it.

Then, eight or ten feet away, I made a circle on the stone pavement, large enough for the Rector and myself to stand in, and within the circle I placed the implements that I had brought into the church with me.

'Now,' I said, 'from this circle, which nothing unholy can step across, you shall see the Vampire face to face, and see her afraid to cross that other circle of garlic and dog-roses to regain her unholy refuge. But on no account step beyond the holy place you stand in, for the Vampire has a fearful strength not her own, and, like a snake, can draw her victim willingly to his own destruction.'

Now so far my work was done, and, calling the Rector, we stepped into the Holy Circle to await the Vampire's return.

Nor was this long delayed. Presently a damp, cold odour seemed to pervade the church, which made our hair bristle and flesh to creep. And then, down the aisle with noiseless feet came That which we watched for.

I heard the Rector mutter a prayer, and I held him tightly by the arm, for he was shivering violently.

Long before we could distinguish the features we saw the glowing eyes and the crimson sensual mouth. She went straight to her tomb, but stopped short when she encountered my flowers. She walked right round the tomb seeking a place to enter, and as she walked she saw us.

A spasm of diabolical hate and fury passed over her face; but it quickly vanished, and a smile of love, more devilish still, took its place. She stretched out her arms towards us. Then we saw that round her mouth gathered a bloody froth, and from under her lips long pointed teeth gleamed and champed.

She spoke: a soft soothing voice, a voice that carried a spell with it, and affected us both strangely, particularly the Rector. I wished to test as far as possible, without endangering our lives, the Vampire's power.

Her voice had a soporific effect, which I resisted easily enough, but which seemed to throw the Rector into a sort of trance. More than this: it seemed to compel him to her in spite of his efforts to resist.

'Come!' she said — 'come! I give sleep and peace — sleep and peace — sleep and peace.'

She advanced a little towards us; but not far, for I noted that the Sacred Circle seemed to keep her back like an iron hand.

My companion seemed to become demoralized and spellbound. He tried to step forward and, finding me detain him, whispered, 'Harry, let go! I must go! She is calling me! I must! I must! Oh, help me! help me!' And he began to struggle.

It was time to finish.

'Grant!' I cried, in a loud, firm voice, 'in the name of all that you hold sacred, have done and play the man!' He shuddered violently and gasped, 'Where am I?' Then he remembered, and clung to me convulsively for a moment.

At this a look of damnable hate changed the smiling face before us, and with a sort of shriek she staggered back.

'Back!' I cried: 'back to your unholy tomb! No longer shall you molest the suffering world! Your end is near.'

It was fear that now showed itself in her beautiful face (for it was beautiful in spite of its horror) as she shrank back, back and over the circlet of flowers, shivering as she did so. At last, with a low mournful cry, she appeared to melt back again into her tomb.

As she did so the first gleams of the rising sun lit up the world, and I knew all danger was over for the day.

Taking Grant by the arm, I drew him with me out of the circle and led him to the tomb. There lay the Vampire once more, still in her living death as we had a moment before seen her in her devilish life. But in the eyes remained that awful expression of hate, and cringing, appalling fear.

Grant has pulling himself together.

'Now, I said, 'will you dare the last terrible act and rid the world for ever of this horror?'

'By God!' he said solemnly, 'I will. Tell me what to do.'

'Help me to lift her out of her tomb. She can harm us no more,' I replied.

With averted faces we set to our terrible task, and laid her out upon the flags.

'Now,' I said, 'read the Burial Service over the poor body, and then let us give it its release from this living hell that holds it.'

Reverently the Rector read the beautiful words, and reverently I made the necessary responses.

When it was over I took the stake and, without giving myself time to think, plunged it with all my strength through the heart.

As though really alive, the body for a moment writhed and kicked convulsively, and an awful heart-rending shriek woke the silent church, then all was still.

Then we lifted the poor body back; and, thank God! the consolation that legend tells is never denied to those who have to do such awful work as ours came at last. Over the face stole a great and solemn peace; the lips lost their crimson hue, the prominent sharp teeth sank back into the mouth, and for a moment we saw before us the calm, pale face of a most beautiful woman, who smiled as she slept. A few minutes more, and she faded away to dust before our eyes as we watched. We set to work and cleaned up every trace of our work, and then departed for the rectory. Most thankful were we to step out of the church, with its horrible associations, into the rosy warmth of the summer morning.

With the above end the notes in my father's diary, though a few days later this further entry occurs:

July 15th. Since the 12th everything has been quiet and as usual. We replaced and sealed up the 'Sarah Tomb' this morning. The workmen were surprised to find the body had disappeared, but took it to be the natural result of exposing it to the air.

One odd thing came to my ears today. It appears that the child of one of the villagers strayed from home the night of the 11th inst., and was found asleep in a coppice near the church, very pale and quite exhausted. There were two small marks on her throat, which have since disappeared.

What does this mean? I have, however, kept it to myself, as, now that the Vampire is no more, no further danger either to that child or any other is to be apprehended. It is only those who die of the Vampire's embrace that become Vampires at death in their turn.

The Vampire Maid

by Hume Nisbet

It was the exact kind of abode that I had been looking after for weeks, for I was in that condition of mind when absolute renunciation of society was a necessity. I had become diffident of myself, and wearied of my kind. A strange unrest was in my blood; a barren dearth in my brains. Familiar objects and faces had grown distasteful to me. I wanted to be alone.

This is the mood which comes upon every sensitive and artistic mind when the possessor has been overworked or living too long in one groove. It is Nature's hint for him to seek pastures new; the sign that a retreat has become needful.

If he does not yield, he breaks down and becomes whimsical and hypochondriacal, as well as hypercritical. It is always a bad sign when a man becomes over-critical and censorious about his own or other people's work, for it means that he is losing the vital portions of work, freshness and enthusiasm.

Before I arrived at the dismal stage of criticism I hastily packed up my knapsack, and taking the train to Westmorland, I began my tramp in search of solitude, bracing air and romantic surroundings.

Many places I came upon during that early summer wandering that appeared to have almost the required conditions, yet some petty drawback prevented me from deciding. Sometimes it was the scenery that I did not take kindly to. At other places I took sudden antipathies to the landlady or landlord, and felt I would abhor them before a week was spent under their charge. Other places which might have suited me I could not have, as they did not want a lodger. Fate was driving me to this Cottage on the Moor, and no one can resist destiny.

One day I found myself on a wide and pathless moor near the sea. I had slept the night before at a small hamlet, but that was already eight miles in my rear, and since I had turned my back upon it I had not seen any signs of humanity; I was alone with a fair sky above me, a balmy ozone-filled wind blowing over the stony and heather-clad mounds, and nothing to disturb my meditations.

How far the moor stretched I had no knowledge; I only knew that by keeping in a straight line I would come to the ocean cliffs, then perhaps after a time arrive at some fishing village.

I had provisions in my knapsack, and being young did not fear a night under the stars. I was inhaling the delicious summer air and once more getting back the vigour and happiness I had lost; my city-dried brains were again becoming juicy.

Thus hour after hour slid past me, with the paces, until I had covered about fifteen miles since morning, when I saw before me in the distance a solitary stone-built cottage with roughly slated roof. 'I'll camp there if possible,' I said to myself as I quickened my steps towards it.

To one in search of a quiet, free life, nothing could have possibly been more suitable than this cottage. It stood on the edge of lofty cliffs, with its front door facing the moor and the back-yard wall overlooking the ocean. The sound of the dancing waves struck upon my ears like a lullaby as I drew near; how they would thunder when the autumn gales came on and the seabirds fled shrieking to the shelter of the sedges.

A small garden spread in front, surrounded by a dry-stone wall just high enough for one to lean lazily upon when inclined. This garden was a flame of colour, scarlet predominating, with those other soft shades that cultivated poppies take on in their blooming, for this was all that the garden grew.

As I approached, taking notice of this singular assortment of poppies, and the orderly cleanness of the windows, the front door opened and a woman appeared who impressed me at once favourably as she leisurely came along the pathway to the gate, and drew it back as if to welcome me.

She was of middle age, and when young must have been remarkably good-looking. She was tall and still shapely, with smooth clear skin, regular features and a calm expression that at once gave me a sensation of rest.

To my inquiries she said that she could give me both a sitting and bedroom, and invited me inside to see them. As I looked at her smooth black hair, and cool brown eyes, I felt that I would not be too particular about the accomodation. With such a landlady, I was sure to find what I was after here.

The rooms surpassed my expectation, dainty white curtains and bedding with the perfume of lavender about them, a sitting-room homely yet cosy without being crowded. With a sigh of infinite relief I flung down my knapsack and clinched the bargain.

She was a widow with one daughter, whom I did not see the first day, as she was unwell and confined to her own room, but on the next day she was somewhat better, and then we met.

The fare was simple, yet it suited me exactly for the time, delicious milk and butter with home-made scones, fresh eggs and bacon; after a hearty tea I went early to bed in a condition of perfect content with my quarters.

Yet happy and tired out as I was I had by no means a comfortable night. This I put down to the strange bed. I slept certainly, but my sleep was filled with dreams so that I woke late and unrefreshed; a good walk on the moor, however, restored me, and I returned with a fine appetite for breakfast.

Certain conditions of mind, with aggravating circumstances, are required before even a young man can fall in love at first sight, as Shakespeare has shown in his Romeo and Juliet. In the city, where many fair faces passed me every hour, I had remained like a stoic, yet no sooner did I enter the cottage after that morning walk than I succumbed instantly before the weird charms of my landlady's daughter, Ariadne Brunnell.

She was somewhat better this morning and able to meet me at breakfast, for we had our meals together while I was their lodger. Ariadne was not beautiful in the strictly classical sense, her complexion being too lividly white and her expression too set to be quite pleasant at first sight; yet, as her mother had informed me, she had been ill for some time, which accounted for that defect. Her features were not regular, her hair and eyes seemed too black with that strangely white skin, and her lips too red for any except the decadent harmonies of an Aubrey Beardsley.

Yet my fantastic dreams of the preceding night, with my morning walk, had prepared me to be enthralled by this modern poster-like invalid.

The loneliness of the moor, with the singing of the ocean, had gripped my heart with a wistful longing. The incongruity of those flaunting and evanescent poppy flowers, dashing the giddy tints in the face of that sober heath, touched me with a shiver as I approached the cottage, and lastly that weird embodiment of startling contrasts completed my subjugation.

She rose from her chair as her mother introduced her, and smiled while she held out her hand. I clasped that soft snowflake, and as I did so a faint thrill tingled over me and rested on my heart, stopping for the moment its beating.

This contact seemed also to have affected her as it did me; a clear flush, like a white flame, lighted up her face, so that it glowed as if an alabaster lamp had been lit; her black eyes became softer and more humid as our glances crossed, and her scarlet lips grew moist. She was a living woman now, while before she had seemed half a corpse.

She permitted her white slender hand to remain in mine longer than most people do at an introduction, and then she slowly withdrew it, still regarding me with steadfast eyes for a second or two afterwards.

Fathomless velvety eyes these were, yet before they were shifted from mine they appeared to have absorbed all my willpower and made me her abject slave. They looked like deep dark pools of clear water, yet they filled me with fire and deprived me of strength. I sank into my chair almost as languidly as I had risen from my bed that morning.

Yet I made a good breakfast, and although she hardly tasted anything, this strange girl rose much refreshed and with a slight glow of colour on her cheeks, which improved her so greatly that she appeared younger and almost beautiful.

I had come here seeking solitude, but since I had seen Ariadne it seemed as if I had come for her only. She was not very lively; indeed, thinking back, I cannot recall any spontaneous remark of hers; she answered my questions by monosyllables and left me to lead in words; yet she was insinuating and appeared to lead my thoughts in her direction and speak to me with her eyes. I cannot describe her minutely, I only know that from the first glance and touch she gave me I was bewitched and could think of nothing else.

It was a rapid, distracting, and devouring infatuation that possessed me; all day long I followed her about like a dog, every night I dreamed of that white glowing face, those steadfast black eyes, those moist scarlet lips, and each morning I rose more languid than I had been the day before. Sometimes I dreamt that she was kissing me with those red lips, while I shivered at the contact of her silky black tresses as they covered my throat; sometimes that we were floating in the air, her arms about me and her long hair enveloping us both like an inky cloud, while I lay supine and helpless.

She went with me after breakfast on that first day to the moor, and before we came back I had spoken my love and received her assent. I held her in my arms and had taken her kisses in answer to mine, nor did I think it strange that all this had happened so quickly. She was mine, or rather I was hers, without a pause. I told her it was fate that had sent me to her, for I had no doubts about my love, and she replied that I had restored her to life.

Acting upon Ariadne's advice, and also from a natural shyness, I did not inform her mother how quickly matters had progressed between us, yet although we both acted as circumspectly as possible, I had no doubt Mrs Brunnell could see how engrossed we were in each other. Lovers are not unlike ostriches in their modes of concealment. I was not afraid of asking Mrs Brunnell for her daughter, for she already showed her partiality towards me, and had bestowed upon me some confidences regarding her own position in life, and I therefore knew that, so far as social position was concerned, there could be no real objection to our marriage. They lived in this lonely spot for the sake of their health, and kept no servant because they could not get any to take service so far away from other humanity. My coming had been opportune and welcome to both mother and daughter.

For the sake of decorum, however, I resolved to delay my confession for a week or two and trust to some favourable opportunity of doing it discreetly.

Meantime Ariadne and I passed our time in a thoroughly idle and lotus-eating style. Each night I retired to bed meditating starting work next day, each morning I rose languid from those disturbing dreams with no thought for anything outside my love. She grew stronger every day, while I appeared to be taking her place as the invalid, yet I was more frantically in love than ever, and only happy when with her. She was my lone-star, my only joy—my life.

We did not go great distances, for I liked best to lie on the dry heath and watch her glowing face and intsense eyes while I listened to the surging of the distant waves. It was love made me lazy, I thought, for unless a man has all he longs for beside him, he is apt to copy the domestic cat and bask in the sunshine.

I had been enchanted quickly. My disenchantment came as rapidly, although it was long before the poison left my blood.

One night, about a couple of weeks after my coming to the cottage, I had returned after a delicious moonlight walk with Ariadne. The night was warm and the moon at the full, therefore I left my bedroom window open to let in what little air there was.

I was more than usually fagged out, so that I had only strength enough to remove my boots and coat before I flung myself wearily on the coverlet and fell almost instantly asleep without tasting the nightcap draught that was constantly placed on the table, and which I had always drained thirstily.

I had a ghastly dream this night. I thought I saw a monster bat, with the face and tresses of Ariadne, fly into the open window and fasten its white teeth and scarlet lips on my arm. I tried to beat the horror away, but could not, for I seemed chained down and thralled also with drowsy delight as the beast sucked my blood with a gruesome rapture.

I looked out dreamily and saw a line of dead bodies of young men lying on the floor, each with a red mark on their arms, on the same part where the vampire was then sucking me, and I remembered having seen and wondered at such a mark on my own arm for the past fortnight. In a flash I understood the reason for my strange weakness, and at the same moment a sudden prick of pain roused me from my dreamy pleasure.

The vampire in her eagerness had bitten a little too deeply that night, unaware that I had not tasted the drugged draught. As I woke I saw her fully revealed by the midnight moon, with her black tresses flowing loosely, and with her red lips glued to my arm. With a shriek of horror I dashed her backwards, getting one last glimpse of her savage eyes, glowing white face and blood-stained red lips; then I rushed out to the night, moved on by my fear and hatred, nor did I pause in my mad flight until I had left miles between me and that accursed Cottage on the Moor.

The Adventure of the Sussex Vampire

by Arthur Conan Doyle

Holmes had read carefully a note which the last post had brought him. Then, with the dry chuckle which was his nearest approach to a laugh, he tossed it over to me.

"For a mixture of the modern and the mediaeval, if the practical and of the wildly fanciful, I think this is surely the limit," said he. "What do you make of it, Watson?"

I read as follows:

46, OLD JEWRY,

Nov. 19th.

Re Vampires

SIR:

Our client, Mr. Robert Ferguson, of Ferguson and Muirhead, tea brokers, of Mincing Lane, has made some inquiry from us in a communication of even date concerning vampires. As our firm specializes entirely upon the assessment of machinery the matter hardly comes within our purview, and we have therefore recommended Mr. Ferguson to call upon you and lay the matter before you. We have not forgotten your successful action in the case of Matilda Briggs.

We are, sir,

Faithfully yours,

MORRISON, MORRISON, AND DODD.

per E. J. C.

"Matilda Briggs was not the name of a young woman, Watson," said Holmes in a reminiscent voice. "It was a ship which is associated with the giant rat of Sumatra, a story for which the world is not yet prepared. But what do we know about vampires? Does it come within our purview either? Anything is better than stagnation, but really we seem to have been switched on to a Grimms' fairy tale. Make a long arm, Watson, and see what V has to say."

I leaned back and took down the great index volume to which he referred. Holmes balanced it on his knee, and his eyes moved slowly and lovingly over the record of old cases, mixed with the accumulated information of a lifetime.

"Voyage of the Gloria Scott," he read. "That was a bad business. I have some recollection that you made a record of it, Watson, though I was unable to congratulate you upon the result. Victor Lynch, the forger. Venomous lizard or gila. Remarkable case, that! Vittoria, the circus belle. Vanderbilt and the Yeggman. Vipers. Vigor, the Hammersmith wonder. Hullo! Hullo! Good old index. You can't beat it. Listen to this, Watson. Vampirism in Hungary. And again, Vampires in Transylvania." He turned over the pages with eagerness, but after a short intent perusal he threw down the great book with a snarl of disappointment.

"Rubbish, Watson, rubbish! What have we to do with walking corpses who can only be held in their grave by stakes driven through their hearts? It's pure lunacy."

"But surely," said I, "the vampire was not necessarily a dead man? A living person might have the habit. I have read, for example, of the old sucking the blood of the young in order to retain their youth."

"You are right, Watson. It mentions the legend in one of these references. But are we to give serious attention to such things? This agency stands flat-footed upon the ground, and there it must remain. The world is big enough for us. No ghosts need apply. I fear that we cannot take Mr. Robert Ferguson very seriously. Possibly this note may be from him and may throw some light upon what is worrying him."

He took up a second letter which had lain unnoticed upon the table while he had been absorbed with the first. This he began to read with a smile of amusement upon his face which gradually faded away into an expression of intense interest and concentration. When he had finished he sat for some little time lost in thought with the letter dangling from his fingers. Finally, with a start, he aroused himself from his reverie.

"Cheeseman's, Lamberley. Where is Lamberley, Watson?"

"It is in Sussex, south of Horsham."

"Not very far, eh? And Cheeseman's?"

"I know that country, Holmes. It is full of old houses which are named after the men who built them centuries ago. You get Odley's and Harvey's and Carriton's - the folk are forgotten but their names live in their houses."

"Precisely," said Holmes coldly. It was one of the peculiarities of his proud, self-contained nature that though he docketed any fresh information very quietly and accurately in his brain, he seldom made any acknowledgment to the giver. "I rather fancy we shall know a good deal more about Cheeseman's, Lamberley, before we are through. The letter is, as I had hoped, from Robert Ferguson. By the way, he claims acquaintance with you."

"With me!"

"You had better read it."

He handed the letter across. It was headed with the address quoted.

DEAR MR. HOLMES [it said]:

I have been recommended to you by my lawyers, but indeed the matter is so extraordinarily delicate that it is most difficult to discuss. It concerns a friend for whom I am acting. This gentleman married some five years ago a Peruvian lady, the daughter of a Peruvian merchant, whom he had met in connection with the importation of nitrates. The lady was very beautiful, but the fact of her foreign birth and of her alien religion always caused a separation of interests and of feelings between husband and wife, so that after a time his love may have cooled towards her and he may have come to regard their union as a mistake. He felt there were sides of her character which he could never explore or understand. This was the more painful as she was as loving a wife as a man could have - to all appearance absolutely devoted.

Now for the point which I will make more plain when we meet. Indeed, this note is merely to give you a general idea of the situation and to ascertain whether you would care to interest yourself in the matter. The lady began to show some curious traits quite alien to her ordinarily sweet and gentle disposition. The gentleman had been married twice and he had one son by the first wife. This boy was now fifteen, a very charming and affectionate youth, though unhappily injured through an accident in childhood. Twice the wife was caught in the act of assaulting this poor lad in the most unprovoked way. Once she struck him with a stick and left a great weal on his arm.

This was a small matter, however, compared with her conduct to her own child, a dear boy just under one year of age. On one occasion about a month ago this child had been left by its nurse for a few minutes. A loud cry from the baby, as of pain, called the nurse back. As she ran into the room she saw her employer, the lady, leaning over the baby and apparently biting his neck. There was a small wound in the neck from which a stream of blood had escaped. The nurse was so horrified that she wished to call the husband, but the lady implored her not to do so and actually gave her five pounds as a price for her silence. No explanation was ever given, and for the moment the matter was passed over.

It left, however, a terrible impression upon the nurse's mind, and from that time she began to watch her mistress closely and to keep a closer guard upon the baby, whom she tenderly loved. It seemed to her that even as she watched the mother, so the mother watched her, and that every time she was compelled to leave the baby alone the mother was waiting to get at it. Day and night the nurse covered the child, and day and night the silent, watchful mother seemed to be lying in wait as a wolf waits for a lamb. It must read most incredible to you, and yet I beg you to take it seriously, for a child's life and a man's sanity may depend upon it.

At last there came one dreadful day when the facts could no longer be concealed from the husband. The nurse's nerve had given way; she could stand the strain no longer, and she made a clean breast of it all to the man. To him it seemed as wild a tale as it may now seem to you. He knew his wife to be a loving wife, and, save for the assaults upon her stepson, a loving mother. Why, then, should she wound her own dear little baby? He told the nurse that she was dreaming, that her suspicions were those of a lunatic, and that such libels upon her mistress were not to be tolerated. While they were talking a sudden cry of pain was heard. Nurse and master rushed together to the nursery. Imagine his feelings, Mr. Holmes, as he saw his wife rise from a kneeling position beside the cot and saw blood upon the child's exposed neck and upon the sheet. With a cry of horror, he turned his wife's face to the light and saw blood all round her lips. It was she - she beyond all question - who had drunk the poor baby's blood.

So the matter stands. She is now confined to her room. There has been no explanation. The husband is half demented. He knows, and I know, little of vampirism beyond the name. We had thought it was some wild tale of foreign parts. And yet here in the very heart of the English Sussex - well, all this can be discussed with you in the morning. Will you see me? Will you use your great powers in aiding a distracted man? If so, kindly wire to Ferguson, Cheeseman's, Lamberley, and I will be at your rooms by ten o'clock.

Yours faithfully,

ROBERT FERGUSON.

P. S. I believe your friend Watson played Rugby for Blackheath when I was three-quarter for Richmond. It is the only personal introduction which I can give.

"Of course I remembered him," said I as I laid down the letter. "Big Bob Ferguson, the finest three-quarter Richmond ever had. He was always a good-natured chap. It's like him to be so concerned over a friend's case."

Holmes looked at me thoughtfully and shook his head.

"I never get your limits, Watson," said he. "There are unexplored possibilities about you. Take a wire down, like a good fellow. 'Will examine your case with pleasure.'"

"Your case!"

"We must not let him think that this agency is a home for the weak-minded. Of course it is his case. Send him that wire and let the matter rest till morning."

Promptly at ten o'clock next morning Ferguson strode into our room. I had remembered him as a long, slab-sided man with loose limbs and a fine turn of speed which had carried him round many an opposing back. There is surely nothing in life more painful than to meet the wreck of a fine athlete whom one has known in his prime. This great frame had fallen in, his flaxen hair was scanty, and his shoulders were bowed. I fear that I roused corresponding emotions in him.

"Hullo, Watson," said he, and his voice was still deep and hearty. "You don't look quite the man you did when I threw you over the ropes into the crowd at the Old Deer Park. I expect I have changed a bit also. But it's this last day or two that has aged me. I see by your telegram, Mr. Holmes, that it is no use my pretending to be anyone's deputy."

"It is simpler to deal direct," said Holmes.

"Of course it is. But you can imagine how difficult it is when you are speaking of the one woman whom you are bound to protect and help. What can I do? How am I to go to the police with such a story? And yet the kiddies have got to be protected. Is it madness, Mr. Holmes? Is it something in the blood? Have you any similar case in your experience? For God's sake, give me some advice, for I am at my wit's end."

"Very naturally, Mr. Ferguson. Now sit here and pull yourself together and give me a few clear answers. I can assure you that I am very far from being at my wit's end, and that I am confident we shall find some solution. First of all, tell me what steps you have taken. Is your wife still near the children?"

"We had a dreadful scene. She is a most loving woman, Mr. Holmes. If ever a woman loved a man with all her heart and soul, she loves me. She was cut to the heart that I should have discovered this horrible, this incredible, secret. She would not even speak. She gave no answer to my reproaches, save to gaze at me with a sort of wild, despairing look in her eyes. Then she rushed to her room and locked herself in. Since then she has refused to see me. She has a maid who was with her before her marriage, Dolores by name - a friend rather than a servant. She takes her food to her."

"Then the child is in no immediate danger?"

"Mrs. Mason, the nurse, has sworn that she will not leave it night or day. I can absolutely trust her. I am more uneasy about poor little Jack, for, as I told you in my note, he has twice been assaulted by her."

"But never wounded?"

"No, she struck him savagely. It is the more terrible as he is a poor little inoffensive cripple." Ferguson's gaunt features softened as he spoke of his boy. "You would think that the dear lad's condition would soften anyone's heart. A fall in childhood and a twisted spine, Mr. Holmes. But the dearest, most loving heart within."

Holmes had picked up the letter of yesterday and was reading it over. "What other inmates are there in your house, Mr. Ferguson?"

"Two servants who have not been long with us. One stable-hand, Michael, who sleeps in the house. My wife, myself, my boy Jack, baby, Dolores, and Mrs. Mason. That is all."

"I gather that you did not know your wife well at the time of your marriage?"

"I had only known her a few weeks."

"How long had this maid Dolores been with her?"

"Some years."

"Then your wife's character would really be better known by Dolores than by you?"

"Yes, you may say so."

Holmes made a note.

"I fancy," said he, "that I may be of more use at Lamberley than here. It is eminently a case for personal investigation. If the lady remains in her room, our presence could not annoy or inconvenience her. Of course, we would stay at the inn."

Ferguson gave a gesture of relief.

"It is what I hoped, Mr. Holmes. There is an excellent train at two from Victoria if you could come."

"Of course we could come. There is a lull at present. I can give you my undivided energies. Watson, of course, comes with us. But there are one or two points upon which I wish to be very sure before I start. This unhappy lady, as I understand it, has appeared to assault both the children, her own baby and your little son?"

"That is so."

"But the assaults take different forms, do they not? She has beaten your son."

"Once with a stick and once very savagely with her hands."

"Did she give no explanation why she struck him?"

"None save that she hated him. Again and again she said so."

"Well, that is not unknown among stepmothers. A posthumous jealousy, we will say. Is the lady jealous by nature?"

"Yes, she is very jealous - jealous with all the strength of her fiery tropical love."

"But the boy - he is fifteen, I understand, and probably very developed in mind, since his body has been circumscribed in action. Did he give you no explanation of these assaults?"

"No, he declared there was no reason."

"Were they good friends at other times?"

"No, there was never any love between them."

"Yet you say he is affectionate?"

"Never in the world could there be so devoted a son. My life is his life. He is absorbed in what I say or do."

Once again Holmes made a note. For some time he sat lost in thought.

"No doubt you and the boy were great comrades before this second marriage. You were thrown very close together, were you not?"

"Very much so."

"And the boy, having so affectionate a nature, was devoted, no doubt, to the memory of his mother?"

"Most devoted."

"He would certainly seem to be a most interesting lad. There is one other point about these assaults. Were the strange attacks upon the baby and the assaults upon your son at the same period?"

"In the first case it was so. It was is if some frenzy had seized her, and she had vented her rage upon both. In the second case it was only Jack who suffered. Mrs. Mason had no complaint to make about the baby."

"That certainly complicates matters."

"I don't quite follow you, Mr. Holmes."

"Possibly not. One forms provisional theories and waits for time or fuller knowledge to explode them. A bad habit, Mr. Ferguson, but human nature is weak. I fear that your old friend here has given an exaggerated view of my scientific methods. However, I will only say at the present stage that your problem does not appear to me to be insoluble, and that you may expect to find us at Victoria at two o'clock."

It was evening of a dull, foggy November day when, having left our bags at the Chequers, Lamberley, we drove through the Sussex clay of a long winding lane and finally reached the isolated and ancient farmhouse in which Ferguson dwelt. It was a large, straggling building, very old in the centre, very new at the wings with towering Tudor chimneys and a lichen-spotted, high-pitched roof of Horsham slabs. The doorsteps were worn into curves, and the ancient tiles which lined the porch were marked with the rebus of a cheese and a man after the original builder. Within, the ceilings were corrugated with heavy oaken beams, and the uneven floors sagged into sharp curves. An odour of age and decay pervaded the whole crumbling building.

There was one very large central room into which Ferguson led us. Here, in a huge old-fashioned fireplace with an iron screen behind it dated 1670, there blazed and spluttered a splendid log fire.

The room, as I gazed round, was a most singular mixture of dates and of places. The half-panelled walls may well have belonged to the original yeoman farmer of the seventeenth century. They were ornamented, however, on the lower part by a line of well-chosen modern water-colours; while above, where yellow plaster took the place of oak, there was hung a fine collection of South American utensils and weapons, which had been brought, no doubt, by the Peruvian lady upstairs. Holmes rose, with that quick curiosity which sprang from his eager mind, and examined them with some care. He returned with his eyes full of thought.

"Hullo!" he cried. "Hullo!"

A spaniel had lain in a basket in the corner. It came slowly forward towards its master, walking with difficulty. Its hind legs moved irregularly and its tail was on the ground. It licked Ferguson's hand.

"What is it, Mr. Holmes?"

"The dog. What's the matter with it?"

"That's what puzzled the vet. A sort of paralysis. Spinal meningitis, he thought. But it is passing. He'll be all right soon - won't you, Carlo?"

A shiver of assent passed through the drooping tail. The dog's mournful eyes passed from one of us to the other. He knew that we were discussing his case.

"Did it come on suddenly?"

"In a single night."

"How long ago?"

"It may have been four months ago."

"Very remarkable. Very suggestive."

"What do you see in it, Mr. Holmes?"

"A confirmation of what I had already thought."

"For God's sake, what do you think, Mr. Holmes? It may be a mere intellectual puzzle to you, but it is life and death to me! My wife a would-be murderer - my child in constant danger! Don't play with me, Mr. Holmes. It is too terribly serious."

The big Rugby three-quarter was trembling all over. Holmes put his hand soothingly upon his arm.

"I fear that there is pain for you, Mr. Ferguson, whatever the solution may be," said he. "I would spare you all I can. I cannot say more for the instant, but before I leave this house I hope I may have something definite."

"Please God you may! If you will excuse me, gentlemen, I will go up to my wife's room and see if there has been any change."

He was away some minutes, during which Holmes resumed his examination of the curiosities upon the wall. When our host returned it was clear from his downcast face that he had made no progress. He brought with him a tall, slim, brownfaced girl.

"The tea is ready, Dolores," said Ferguson. "See that your mistress has everything she can wish."

"She verra ill," cried the girl, looking with indignant eyes at her master. "She no ask for food. She verra ill. She need doctor. I frightened stay alone with her without doctor."

Ferguson looked at me with a question in his eyes.

"I should be so glad if I could be of use."

"Would your mistress see Dr. Watson?"

"I take him. I no ask leave. She needs doctor."

"Then I'll come with you at once."

I followed the girl, who was quivering with strong emotion, up the staircase and down an ancient corridor. At the end was an iron-clamped and massive door. It struck me as I looked at it that if Ferguson tried to force his way to his wife he would find it no easy matter. The girl drew a key from her pocket, and the heavy oaken planks creaked upon their old hinges. I passed in and she swiftly followed, fastening the door behind her.

On the bed a woman was lying who was clearly in a high fever. She was only half conscious, But as I entered she raised a pair of frightened but beautiful eyes and glared at me in apprehension. Seeing a stranger, she appeared to be relieved and sank back with a sigh upon the pillow. I stepped up to her with a few reassuring words, and she lay still while I took her pulse and temperature. Both were high, and yet my impression was that the condition was rather that of mental and nervous excitement than of any actual seizure.

"She lie like that one day, two day. I 'fraid she die," said the girl.

The woman turned her flushed and handsome face towards me.

"Where is my husband?"

"He is below and would wish to see you."

"I will not see him. I will not see him." Then she seemed to wander off into delirium. "A fiend! A fiend! Oh, what shall I do with this devil?"

"Can I help you in any way?"

"No. No one can help. It is finished. All is destroyed. Do what I will, all is destroyed."

The woman must have some strange delusion. I could not see honest Bob Ferguson in the character of fiend or devil.

"Madame," I said, "your husband loves you dearly. He is deeply grieved at this happening."

Again she turned on me those glorious eyes.

"He loves me. Yes. But do I not love him? Do I not love him even to sacrifice myself rather than break his dear heart? That is how I love him. And yet he could think of me - he could speak of me so."

"He is full of grief, but he cannot understand."

"No, he cannot understand. But he should trust."

"Will you not see him?" I suggested.

"No, no, I cannot forget those terrible words nor the look upon his face. I will not see him. Go now. You can do nothing for me. Tell him only one thing. I want my child. I have a right to my child. That is the only message I can send him." She turned her face to the wall and would say no more.

I returned to the room downstairs, where Ferguson and Holmes still sat by the fire. Ferguson listened moodily to my account of the interview.

"How can I send her the child?" he said. "How do I know what strange impulse might come upon her? How can I ever forget how she rose from beside it with its blood upon her lips?" He shuddered at the recollection. "The child is safe with Mrs. Mason, and there he must remain."

A smart maid, the only modern thing which we had seen in the house, had brought in some tea. As she was serving it the door opened and a youth entered the room. He was a remarkable lad, pale-faced and fair-haired, with excitable light blue eyes which blazed into a sudden flame of emotion and joy as they rested upon his father. He rushed forward and threw his arms round his neck with the abandon of a loving girl.

"Oh, daddy," he cried, "I did not know that you were due yet. I should have been here to meet you. Oh, I am so glad to see you!"

Ferguson gently disengaged himself from the embrace with some little show of embarrassment.

"Dear old chap," said he, patting the flaxen head with a very tender hand. "I came early because my friends, Mr. Holmes and Dr. Watson, have been persuaded to come down and spend an evening with us."

"Is that Mr. Holmes, the detective?"

"Yes."

The youth looked at us with a very penetrating and, as it seemed to me, unfriendly gaze.

"What about your other child, Mr. Ferguson?" asked Holmes. "Might we make the acquaintance of the baby?"

"Ask Mrs. Mason to bring baby down," said Ferguson. The boy went off with a curious, shambling gait which told my surgical eyes that he was suffering from a weak spine. Presently he returned, and behind him came a tall, gaunt woman bearing in her arms a very beautiful child, dark-eyed, golden-haired, a wonderful mixture of the Saxon and the Latin. Ferguson was evidently devoted to it, for he took it into his arms and fondled it most tenderly.

Fancy anyone having the heart to hurt him," he muttered as he glanced down at the small, angry red pucker upon the cherub throat.

It was at this moment that I chanced to glance at Holmes and saw a most singular intentness in his expression. His face was as set as if it had been carved out of old ivory, and his eyes, which had glanced for a moment at father and child, were now fixed with eager curiosity upon something at the other side of the room. Following his gaze I could only guess that he was looking out through the window at the melancholy, dripping garden. It is true that a shutter had half closed outside and obstructed the view, but none the less it was certainly at the window that Holmes was fixing his concentrated attention. Then he smiled, and his eyes came back to the baby. On its chubby neck there was this small puckered mark. Without speaking, Holmes examined it with care. Finally he shook one of the dimpled fists which waved in front of him.

"Good-bye, little man. You have made a strange start in life. Nurse, I should wish to have a word with you in private."

He took her aside and spoke earnestly for a few minutes. I only heard the last words, which were: "Your anxiety will soon, I hope, be set at rest." The woman, who seemed to be a sour, silent kind of creature, withdrew with the child.

"What is Mrs. Mason like?" asked Holmes.

"Not very prepossessing externally, as you can see, but a heart of gold, and devoted to the child."

"Do you like her, Jack?" Holmes turned suddenly upon the boy. His expressive mobile face shadowed over, and he shook his head.

"Jacky has very strong likes and dislikes," said Ferguson, putting his arm round the boy. "Luckily I am one of his likes."

The boy cooed and nestled his head upon his father's breast. Ferguson gently disengaged him.

"Run away, little Jacky," said he, and he watched his son with loving eyes until he disappeared. "Now, Mr. Holmes," he continued when the boy was gone, "I really feel that I have brought you on a fool's errand, for what can you possibly do save give me your sympathy? It must be an exceedingly delicate and complex affair from your point of view."

"It is certainly delicate," said my friend with an amused smile, "but I have not been struck up to now with its complexity. It has been a case for intellectual deduction, but when this original intellectual deduction is confirmed point by point by quite a number of independent incidents, then the subjective becomes objective and we can say confidently that we have reached our goal. I had, in fact, reached it before we left Baker Street, and the rest has merely been observation and confirmation."

Ferguson put his big hand to his furrowed forehead.

"For heaven's sake, Holmes," he said hoarsely; "if you can see the truth in this matter, do not keep me in suspense. How do I stand? What shall I do? I care nothing as to how you have found your facts so long as you have really got them."

"Certainly I owe you an explanation, and you shall have it. But you will permit me to handle the matter in my own way? Is the lady capable of seeing us, Watson?"

"She is ill, but she is quite rational."

"Very good. It is only in her presence that we can clear the matter up. Let us go up to her."

"She will not see me," cried Ferguson.

"Oh, yes, she will," said Holmes. He scribbled a few lines upon a sheet of paper. "You at least have the entree, Watson. Will you have the goodness to give the lady this note?"

I ascended again and handed the note to Dolores, who cautiously opened the door. A minute later I heard a cry from within, a cry in which joy and surprise seemed to be blended. Dolores looked out.

"She will see them. She will leesten," said she.

At my summons Ferguson and Holmes came up. As we entered the room Ferguson took a step or two towards his wife, who had raised herself in the bed, but she held out her hand to repulse him. He sank into an armchair, while

Holmes seated himself beside him, after bowing to the lady, who looked at him with wide-eyed amazement.

"I think we can dispense with Dolores," said Holmes. "Oh, very well, madame, if you would rather she stayed I can see no objection. Now, Mr. Ferguson, I am a busy man with many calls, and my methods have to be short and direct. The swiftest surgery is the least painful. Let me first say what will ease your mind. Your wife is a very good, a very loving, and a very ill-used woman."

Ferguson sat up with a cry of joy.

"Prove that, Mr. Holmes, and I am your debtor forever."

"I will do so, but in doing so I must wound you deeply in another direction."

"I care nothing so long as you clear my wife. Everything on earth is insignificant compared to that."

"Let me tell you, then, the train of reasoning which passed through my mind in Baker Street. The idea of a vampire was to me absurd. Such things do not happen in criminal practice in England. And yet your observation was precise. You had seen the lady rise from beside the child's cot with the blood upon her lips."

"I did."

"Did it not occur to you that a bleeding wound may be sucked for some other purpose than to draw the blood from it? Was there not a queen in English history who sucked such a wound to draw poison from it?"

"Poison!"

"A South American household. My instinct felt the presence of those weapons upon the wall before, my eyes ever saw them. It might have been other poison, but that was what occurred to me. When I saw that little empty quiver beside the small bird-bow, it was just what I expected to see. If the child were pricked with one of those arrows dipped in curare or some other devilish drug, it would mean death if the venom were not sucked out.

"And the dog! If one were to use such a poison, would one not try it first in order to see that it had not lost its power? I did not foresee the dog, but at least I understand him and he fitted into my reconstruction.

"Now do you understand? Your wife feared such all attack. She saw it made and saved the child's life, and yet she shrank from telling you all the truth, for she knew how you loved the boy and feared lest it break your heart."

"Jacky!"

"I watched him as you fondled the child just now. His face was clearly reflected in the glass of the window where the shutter formed a background. I saw such jealousy, such cruel hatred, as I have seldom seen in a human face."

"My Jacky!"

"You have to face it, Mr. Ferguson. It is the more painful because it is a distorted love, a maniacal exaggerated love for you, and possibly for his dead mother, which has prompted his action. His very soul is consumed with hatred for this splendid child, whose health and beauty are a contrast to his own weakness."

"Good God! It is incredible!"

"Have I spoken the truth, madame?"

The lady was sobbing, with her face buried in the pillows. Now she turned to her husband.

"How could I tell you, Bob? I felt the blow it would be to you. It was better that I should wait and that it should come from some other lips than mine. When this gentleman, who seems to have powers of magic, wrote that he knew all, I was glad."

"I think a year at sea would be my prescription for Master Jacky," said Holmes, rising from his chair. "Only one thing is still clouded, madame. We can quite understand your attacks upon Master Jacky. There is a limit to a mother's patience. But how did you dare to leave the child these last two days?"

"I had told Mrs. Mason. She knew."

"Exactly. So I imagined."

Ferguson was standing by the bed, choking, his hands outstretched and quivering.

"This, I fancy, is the time for our exit, Watson," said Holmes in a whisper. "If you will take one elbow of the too faithful Dolores, I will take the other. There, now," he added as he closed the door behind him, "I think we may leave them to settle the rest among themselves."

I have only one further note of this case. It is the letter which Holmes wrote in final answer to that with which the narrative begins. It ran thus:

BAKER STREET,

Nov. 21st.

Re Vampires

SIR:

Referring to your letter of the 19th, I beg to state that I have looked into the inquiry of your client, Mr. Robert Ferguson, of Ferguson and Muirhead, tea brokers, of Mincing Lane, and that the matter has been brought to a satisfactory conclusion. With thanks for your recommendation, I am, sir,

Faithfully yours,

SHERLOCK HOLMES.

Mrs. Amworth

by E. F. Benson

The village of Maxley, where, last summer and autumn, these strange events took place, lies on a heathery and pine-clad upland of Sussex. In all England you could not find a sweeter and saner situation. Should the wind blow from the south, it comes laden with the spices of the sea; to the east high downs protect it from the inclemencies of March; and from the west and north the breezes which reach it travel over miles of aromatic forest and heather. The village itself is insignificant enough in point of population, but rich in amenities and beauty. Half-way down the single street, with its broad road and spacious areas of grass on each side, stands the little Norman Church and the antique graveyard long disused: for the rest there are a dozen small, sedate Georgian houses, red-bricked and long-windowed, each with a square of flower-garden in front, and an ampler strip behind; a score of shops, and a couple of score of thatched cottages belonging to labourers on neighbouring estates, complete the entire cluster of its peaceful habitations. The general peace, however, is sadly broken on Saturdays and Sundays, for we lie on one of the main roads between London and Brighton and our quiet street becomes a race-course for flying motor-cars and bicycles.

A notice just outside the village begging them to go slowly only seems to encourage them to accelerate their speed, for the road lies open and straight, and there is really no reason why they should do otherwise. By way of protest, therefore, the ladies of Maxley cover their noses and mouths with their handkerchiefs as they see a motor-car approaching, though, as the street is asphalted, they need not really take these precautions against dust. But late on Sunday night the horde of scorchers has passed, and we settle down again to five days of cheerful and leisurely seclusion. Railway strikes which agitate the country so much leave us undisturbed because most of the inhabitants of Maxley never leave it at all.

I am the fortunate possessor of one of these small Georgian houses, and consider myself no less fortunate in having so interesting and stimulating a neighbour as Francis Urcombe, who, the most confirmed of Maxleyites, has not slept away from his house, which stands just opposite to mine in the village street, for nearly two years, at which date, though still in middle life, he resigned his Physiological Professorship at Cambridge University and devoted himself to the study of those occult and curious phenomena which seem equally to concern the physical and the psychical sides of human nature. Indeed his retirement was not unconnected with his passion for the strange uncharted places that lie on the confines and borders of science, the existence of which is so stoutly denied by the more materialistic minds, for he advocated that all medical students should be obliged to pass some sort of examination in mesmerism, and that one of the tripos papers should be designed to test their knowledge in such subjects as appearances at time of death, haunted houses, vampirism, automatic writing, and possession.

"Of course they wouldn't listen to me," ran his account of the matter, "for there is nothing that these seats of learning are so frightened of as knowledge, and the road to knowledge lies in the study of things like these. The functions of the human frame are, broadly speaking, known. They are a country, anyhow, that has been charted and mapped out. But outside that lie huge tracts of undiscovered country, which certainly exist, and the real pioneers of knowledge are those who, at the cost of being derided as credulous and superstitious, want to push on into those misty and probably perilous places. I felt that I could be of more use by setting out without compass or knapsack into the mists than by sitting in a cage like a canary and chirping about what was known. Besides, teaching is very bad for a man who knows himself only to be a learner: you only need to be a self-conceited ass to teach."

Here, then, in Francis Urcombe, was a delightful neighbour to one who, like myself, has an uneasy and burning curiosity about what he called the "misty and perilous places"; and this last spring we had a further and most welcome addition to our pleasant little community, in the person of Mrs. Amworth, widow of an Indian civil servant. Her husband had been a judge in the North-West Provinces, and after his death at Peshawar she came back to England, and after a year in London found herself starving for the ampler air and sunshine of the country to take the place of the fogs and griminess of town. She had, too, a special reason for settling in Maxley, since her ancestors up till a hundred years ago had long been native to the place, and in the old churchyard, now disused, are many gravestones bearing her maiden name of Chaston. Big and energetic, her vigorous and genial personality speedily woke Maxley up to a higher degree of sociality than it had ever known. Most of us were bachelors or spinsters or elderly folk not much inclined to exert ourselves in the expense and effort of hospitality, and hitherto the gaiety of a small tea-party, with bridge afterwards and goloshes (when it was wet) to trip home in again for a solitary dinner, was about the climax of our festivities. But Mrs. Amworth showed us a more gregarious way, and set an example of luncheon-parties and little dinners, which we began to follow. On other nights when no such hospitality was on foot, a lone man like myself found it pleasant to know that a call on the telephone to Mrs. Amworth's house not a hundred yards off, and an inquiry as to whether I might come over after dinner for a game of piquet before bed-time, would probably evoke a response of welcome. There she would be, with a comrade-like eagerness for companionship, and there was a glass of port and a cup of coffee and a cigarette and a game of piquet. She played the piano, too, in a free and exuberant manner, and had a charming voice and sang to her own accompaniment; and as the days grew long and the light lingered late, we played our game in her garden, which in the course of a few months she had turned from being a nursery for slugs and snails into a glowing patch of luxuriant blossoming. She was always cheery and jolly; she was interested in everything, and in music, in gardening, in games of all sorts was a competent performer. Everybody (with one exception) liked her, everybody felt her to bring with her the tonic of a sunny day. That one exception was Francis Urcombe; he, though he confessed he did not like her, acknowledged that he was vastly interested in her. This always seemed strange to me, for pleasant and jovial as she was, I could see nothing in her that could call forth conjecture or intrigued surmise, so healthy and unmysterious a figure did she present. But of the genuineness of Urcombe's interest there could be no doubt; one could see him watching and scrutinising her. In matter of age, she frankly volunteered the information that she was forty-five; but her briskness, her activity, her unravaged skin, her coal-black hair, made it difficult to believe that she was not adopting an unusual device, and adding ten years on to her age instead of subtracting them.

Often, also, as our quite unsentimental friendship ripened, Mrs. Amworth would ring me up and propose her advent. If I was busy writing, I was to give her, so we definitely bargained, a frank negative, and in answer I could hear her jolly laugh and her wishes for a successful evening of work. Sometimes, before her proposal arrived, Urcombe would already have stepped across from his house opposite for a smoke and a chat, and he, hearing who my intending visitor was, always urged me to beg her to come. She and I should play our piquet, said he, and he would look on, if we did not object, and learn something of the game. But I doubt whether he paid much attention to it, for nothing could be clearer than that, under that penthouse of forehead and thick eyebrows, his attention was fixed not on the cards, but on one of the players.

But he seemed to enjoy an hour spent thus, and often, until one particular evening in July, he would watch her with the air of a man who has some deep problem in front of him. She, enthusiastically keen about our game, seemed not to notice his scrutiny. Then came that evening, when, as I see in the light of subsequent events, began the first twitching of the veil that hid the secret horror from my eyes. I did not know it then, though I noticed that thereafter, if she rang up to propose coming round, she always asked not only if I was at leisure, but whether Mr. Urcombe was with me. If so, she said, she would not spoil the chat of two old bachelors, and laughingly wished me good night.

Urcombe, on this occasion, had been with me for some half-hour before Mrs. Amworth's appearance, and had been talking to me about the medizval beliefs concerning vampirism, one of those borderland subjects which he declared had not been sufficiently studied before it had been consigned by the medical profession to the dust-heap of exploded superstitions. There he sat, grim and eager, tracing, with that pellucid clearness which had made him in his Cambridge days so admirable a lecturer, the history of those mysterious visitations. In them all there were the same general features: one of those ghoulish spirits took up its abode in a living man or woman, conferring supernatural powers of bat-like flight and glutting itself with nocturnal blood-feasts. When its host died it continued to dwell in the corpse, which remained undecayed. By day it rested, by night it left the grave and went on its awful errands. No European country in the Middle Ages seemed to have escaped them; earlier yet, parallels were to be found, in Roman and Greek and in Jewish history.

"It's a large order to set all that evidence aside as being moonshine," he said. "Hundreds of totally independent witnesses in many ages have testified to the occurrence of these phenomena, and there's no explanation known to me which covers all the facts. And if you feel inclined to say 'Why, then, if these are facts, do we not come across them now?' there are two answers I can make you. One is that there were diseases known in the Middle Ages, such as the black death; which were certainly existent then and which have become extinct since, but for that reason we do not assert that such diseases never existed. Just as the black death visited England and decimated the population of Norfolk, so here in this very district about three hundred years ago there was certainly an outbreak of vampirism, and Maxley was the centre of it. My second answer is even more convincing, for I tell you that vampirism is by no means extinct now. An outbreak of it certainly occurred in India a year or two ago."

At that moment I heard my knocker plied in the cheerful and peremptory manner in which Mrs. Amworth is accustomed to announce her arrival, and I went to the door to open it.

"Come in at once," I said, "and save me from having my blood curdled. Mr. Urcombe has been trying to alarm me."

Instantly her vital, voluminous presence seemed to fill the room.

"Ah, but how lovely!" she said. "I delight in having my blood curdled. Go on with your ghost-story, Mr. Urcombe. I adore ghost-stories."

I saw that, as his habit was, he was intently observing her.

"It wasn't a ghost-story exactly," said he. "I was only telling our host how vampirism was not extinct yet. I was saying that there was an outbreak of it in India only a few years ago."

There was a more than perceptible pause, and I saw that, if Urcombe was observing her, she on her side was observing him with fixed eye and parted mouth. Then her jolly laugh invaded that rather tense silence.

"Oh, what a shame!" she said. "You're not going to curdle my blood at all. Where did you pick up such a tale, Mr. Urcombe? I have lived for years in India and never heard a rumour of such a thing. Some story-teller in the bazaars must have invented it: they are famous at that."

I could see that Urcombe was on the point of saying something further, but checked himself.

"Ah! very likely that was it," he said.

But something had disturbed our usual peaceful sociability that night, and something had damped Mrs. Amworth's usual high spirits. She had no gusto for her piquet, and left after a couple of games. Urcombe had been silent too, indeed he hardly spoke again till she departed.

"That was unfortunate," he said, "for the outbreak of — of a very mysterious disease, let us call it, took place at Peshawar, where she and her husband were. And— "

"Well?" I asked.

"He was one of the victims of it," said he. "Naturally I had quite forgotten that when I spoke."

The summer was unreasonably hot and rainless, and Maxley suffered much from drought, and also from a plague of big black night-flying gnats, the bite of which was very irritating and virulent. They came sailing in of an evening, settling on one's skin so quietly that one perceived nothing till the sharp stab announced that one had been bitten. They did not bite the hands or face, but chose always the neck and throat for their feeding-ground, and most of us, as the poison spread, assumed a temporary goitre. Then about the middle of August appeared the first of those mysterious cases of illness which our local doctor attributed to the long-continued heat coupled with the bite of these venomous insects. The patient was a boy of sixteen or seventeen, the son of Mrs. Amworth's gardener, and the symptoms were an anemic pallor and a languid prostration, accompanied by great drowsiness and an abnormal appetite. He had, too, on his throat two small punctures where, so Dr. Ross conjectured, one of these great gnats had bitten him. But the odd thing was that there was no swelling or inflammation round the place where he had been bitten. The heat at this time had begun to abate, but the cooler weather failed to restore him, and the boy, in spite of the quantity of good food which he so ravenously swallowed, wasted away to a skin-clad skeleton.

I met Dr. Ross in the street one afternoon about this time, and in answer to my inquiries about his patient he said that he was afraid the boy was dying. The case, he confessed, completely puzzled him: some obscure form of pernicious anemia was all he could suggest. But he wondered whether Mr. Urcombe would consent to see the boy, on the chance of his being able to throw some new light on the case, and since Urcombe was dining with me that night, I proposed to Dr. Ross to join us. He could not do this, but said he would look in later. When he came, Urcombe at once consented to put his skill at the other's disposal, and together they went off at once. Being thus shorn of my sociable evening, I telephoned to Mrs. Amworth to know if I might inflict myself on her for an hour. Her answer was a welcoming affirmative, and between piquet and music the hour lengthened itself into two. She spoke of the boy who was lying so desperately and mysteriously ill, and told me that she had often been to see him, taking him nourishing and delicate food. But to-day — and her kind eyes moistened as she spoke she was afraid she had paid her last visit. Knowing the antipathy between her and Urcombe, I did not tell her that he had been called into consultation; and when I returned home she accompanied me to my door, for the sake of a breath of night air, and in order to borrow a magazine which contained an article on gardening which she wished to read.

"Ah, this delicious night air," she said, luxuriously sniffing in the coolness. "Night air and gardening are the great tonics. There is nothing so stimulating as bare contact with rich mother earth. You are never so fresh as when you have been grubbing in the soil — black hands, black nails, and boots covered with mud." She gave her great jovial laugh. "I'm a glutton for air and earth," she said. "Positively I look forward to death, for then I shall be buried and have the kind earth all round me. No leaden caskets for me — I have given explicit directions.

But what shall I do about air? Well, I suppose one can't have everything. The magazine? A thousand thanks, I will faithfully return it. Good night: garden and keep your windows open, and you won't have anæmia."

"I always sleep with my windows open," said I.

I went straight up to my bedroom, of which one of the windows looks out over the street, and as I undressed I thought I heard voices talking outside not far away. But I paid no particular attention, put out my lights, and falling asleep plunged into the depths of a most horrible dream, distortedly suggested no doubt, by my last words with Mrs. Amworth. I dreamed that I woke, and found that both my bedroom windows were shut. Half-suffocating I dreamed that I sprang out of bed, and went across to open them. The blind over the first was drawn down, and pulling it up I saw, with the indescribable horror of incipient nightmare, Mrs. Amworth's face suspended close to the pane in the darkness outside, nodding and smiling at me. Pulling down the blind again to keep that terror out, I rushed to the second window on the other side of the room, and there again was Mrs. Amworth's face. Then the panic came upon me in full blast; here was I suffocating in the airless room, and whichever window I opened Mrs. Amworth's face would float in, like those noiseless black gnats that bit before one was aware. The nightmare rose to screaming point, and with strangled yells I awoke to find my room cool and quiet with both windows open and blinds up and a half-moon high in its course, casting an oblong of tranquil light on the floor. But even when I was awake the horror persisted, and I lay tossing and turning. I must have slept long before the nightmare seized me, for now it was nearly day, and soon in the east the drowsy eyelids of morning began to lift.

I was scarcely downstairs next morning — for after the dawn I slept late — when Urcombe rang up to know if he might see me immediately. He came in, grim and preoccupied, and I noticed that he was pulling on a pipe that was not even filled.

"I want your help," he said, "and so I must tell you first of all what happened last night. I went round with the little doctor to see his patient, and found him just alive, but scarcely more. I instantly diagnosed in my own mind what this anemia, unaccountable by any other explanation, meant. The boy is the prey of a vampire."

He put his empty pipe on the breakfast-table, by which I had just sat down, and folded his arms, looking at me steadily from under his overhanging brows.

"Now about last night," he said. "I insisted that he should be moved from his father's cottage into my house. As we were carrying him on a stretcher, whom should we meet but Mrs. Amworth? She expressed shocked surprise that we were moving him. Now why do you think she did that?"

With a start of horror, as I remembered my dream that night before, I felt an idea come into my mind so preposterous and unthinkable that I instantly turned it out again.

"I haven't the smallest idea," I said.

"Then listen, while I tell you about what happened later. I put out all light in the room where the boy lay, and watched. One window was a little open, for I had forgotten to close it, and about midnight I heard something outside, trying apparently to push it farther open. I guessed who it was — yes, it was full twenty feet from the ground —and I peeped round the corner of the blind. Just outside was the face of Mrs. Amworth and her hand was on the frame of the window. Very softly I crept close, and then banged the window down, and I think I just caught the tip of one of her fingers."

"But it's impossible," I cried. "How could she be floating in the air like that? And what had she come for? Don't tell me such—"

Once more, with closer grip, the remembrance of my nightmare seized me.

"I am telling you what I saw," said he. "And all night long, until it was nearly day, she was fluttering outside, like some terrible bat, trying to gain admittance. Now put together various things I have told you."

He began checking them off on his fingers.

"Number one," he said: "there was an outbreak of disease similar to that which this boy is suffering from at Peshawar, and her husband died of it. Number two: Mrs. Amworth protested against my moving the boy to my house. Number three: she, or the demon that inhabits her body, a creature powerful and deadly, tries to gain admittance. And add this, too: in medieval times there was an epidemic of vampirism here at Maxley. The vampire, so the accounts run, was found to be Elizabeth Chaston ... I see you remember Mrs. Amworth's maiden name. Finally, the boy is stronger this morning. He would certainly not have been alive if he had been visited again. And what do you make of it?"

There was a long silence, during which I found this incredible horror assuming the hues of reality.

"I have something to add," I said, "which may or may not bear on it. You say that the — the spectre went away shortly before dawn."

"Yes."

I told him of my dream, and he smiled grimly.

"Yes, you did well to awake," he said. "That warning came from your subconscious self, which never wholly slumbers, and cried out to you of deadly danger. For two reasons, then, you must help me: one to save others, the second to save yourself."

"What do you want me to do?" I asked.

"I want you first of all to help me in watching this boy, and ensuring that she does not come near him. Eventually I want you to help me in tracking the thing down, in exposing and destroying it. It is not human: it is an incarnate fiend. What steps we shall have to take I don't yet know."

It was now eleven of the forenoon, and presently I went across to his house for a twelve-hour vigil while he slept, to come on duty again that night, so that for the next twenty-four hours either Urcombe or myself was always in the room where the boy, now getting stronger every hour, was lying. The day following was Saturday and a morning of brilliant, pellucid weather, and already when I went across to his house to resume my duty the stream of motors down to Brighton had begun. Simultaneously I saw Urcombe with a cheerful face, which boded good news of his patient, coming out of his house, and Mrs. Amworth, with a gesture of salutation to me and a basket in her hand, walking up the broad strip of grass which bordered the road. There we all three met. I noticed (and saw that Urcombe noticed it too) that one finger of her left hand was bandaged.

"Good morning to you both," said she. "And I hear your patient is doing well, Mr. Urcombe. I have come to bring him a bowl of jelly, and to sit with him for an hour. He and I are great friends. I am overjoyed at his recovery."

Urcombe paused a moment, as if making up his mind, and then shot out a pointing finger at her.

"I forbid that," he said. "You shall not sit with him or see him. And you know the reason as well as I do."

I have never seen so horrible a change pass over a human face as that which now blanched hers to the colour of a grey mist. She put up her hand as if to shield herself from that pointing finger, which drew the sign of the cross in the air, and shrank back cowering on to the road. There was a wild hoot from a horn, a grinding of brakes, a shout — too late — from a passing car, and one long scream suddenly cut short. Her body rebounded from the roadway after the first wheel had gone over it, and the second followed. It lay there, quivering and twitching, and was still.

She was buried three days afterwards in the cemetery outside Maxley, in accordance with the wishes she had told me that she had devised about her interment, and the shock which her sudden and awful death had caused to the little community began by degrees to pass off. To two people only, Urcombe and myself, the horror of it was mitigated from the first by the nature of the relief that her death brought; but, naturally enough, we kept our own counsel, and no hint of what greater horror had been thus averted was ever let slip. But, oddly enough, so it seemed to me, he was still not satisfied about something in connection with her, and would give no answer to my questions on the subject. Then as the days of a tranquil mellow September and the October that followed began to drop away like the leaves of the yellowing trees, his uneasiness relaxed. But before the entry of November the seeming tranquillity broke into hurricane.

I had been dining one night at the far end of the village, and about eleven o'clock was walking home again. The moon was of an unusual brilliance, rendering all that it shone on as distinct as in some etching. I had just come opposite the house which Mrs. Amworth had occupied, where there was a board up telling that it was to let, when I heard the click of her front gate, and next moment I saw, with a sudden chill and quaking of my very spirit, that she stood there. Her profile, vividly illuminated, was turned to me, and I could not be mistaken in my identification of her. She appeared not to see me (indeed the shadow of the yew hedge in front of her garden enveloped me in its blackness) and she went swiftly across the road, and entered the gate of the house directly opposite. There I lost sight of her completely.

My breath was coming in short pants as if I had been running - and now indeed I ran, with fearful backward glances, along the hundred yards that separated me from my house and Urcombe's. It was to his that my flying steps took me, and next minute I was within.

"What have you come to tell me?" he asked. "Or shall I guess?" "You can't guess," said I.

"No; it's no guess. She has come back and you have seen her. Tell me about it."

I gave him my story.

"That's Major Pearsall's house," he said. "Come back with me there at once."

"But what can we do?" I asked.

"I've no idea. That's what we have got to find out."

A minute later, we were opposite the house. When I had passed it before, it was all dark; now lights gleamed from a couple of windows upstairs. Even as we faced it, the front door opened, and next moment Major Pearsall emerged from the gate. He saw us and stopped.

"I'm on my way to Dr. Ross," he said quickly, "My wife has been taken suddenly ill. She had been in bed an hour when I came upstairs, and I found her white as a ghost and utterly exhausted. She had been to sleep, it seemed — but you will excuse me."

"One moment, Major," said Urcombe. "Was there any mark on her throat?"

"How did you guess that?" said he. "There was: one of those beastly gnats must have bitten her twice there. She was streaming with blood."

"And there's someone with her?" asked Urcombe.

"Yes, I roused her maid."

He went off, and Urcombe turned to me. "I know now what we have to do," he said. "Change your clothes, and I'll join you at your house."

"What is it?" I asked.

"I'll tell you on our way. We're going to the cemetery." He carried a pick, a shovel, and a screwdriver when he rejoined me, and wore round his shoulders a long coil of rope. As we walked, he gave me the outlines of the ghastly hour that lay before us.

"What I have to tell you," he said, "will seem to you now too fantastic for credence, but before dawn we shall see whether it outstrips reality. By a most fortunate happening, you saw the spectre, the astral body, whatever you choose to call it, of Mrs. Amworth, going on its grisly business, and therefore, beyond doubt, the vampire spirit which abode in her during life animates her again in death. That is not exceptional — indeed, all these weeks since her death I have been expecting it. If I am right, we shall find her body undecayed and untouched by corruption."

"But she has been dead nearly two months," said I.

"If she had been dead two years it would still be so, if the vampire has possession of her. So remember: whatever you see done, it will be done not to her, who in the natural course would now be feeding the grasses above her grave, but to a spirit of untold evil and malignancy, which gives a phantom life to her body."

"But what shall I see done?" said I.

"I will tell you. We know that now, at this moment, the vampire clad in her mortal semblance is out; dining out. But it must get back before dawn, and it will pass into the material form that lies in her grave. We must wait for that, and then with your help I shall dig up her body. If I am right, you will look on her as she was in life, with the full vigour of the dreadful nutriment she has received pulsing in her veins. And then, when dawn has come, and the vampire cannot leave the lair of her body, I shall strike her with this" — and he pointed to his pick — "through the heart, and she, who comes to life again only with the animation the fiend gives her, she and her hellish partner will be dead indeed. Then we must bury her again, delivered at last."

We had come to the cemetery, and in the brightness of the moonshine there was no difficulty in identifying her grave. It lay some twenty yards from the small chapel, in the porch of which, obscured by shadow, we concealed ourselves. From there we had a clear and open sight of the grave, and now we must wait till its infernal visitor returned home. The night was warm and windless, yet even if a freezing wind had been raging I think I should have felt nothing of it, so intense was my preoccupation as to what the night and dawn would bring. There was a bell in the turret of the chapel, that struck the quarters of the hour, and it amazed me to find how swiftly the chimes succeeded one another.

The moon had long set, but a twilight of stars shone in a clear sky, when five o'clock of the morning sounded from the turret. A few minutes more passed, and then I felt Urcombe's hand softly nudging me; and looking out in the direction of his pointing finger, I saw that the form of a woman, tall and large in build, was approaching from the right. Noiselessly, with a motion more of gliding and floating than walking, she moved across the cemetery to the grave which was the centre of our observation. She moved round it as if to be certain of its identity, and for a moment stood directly facing us. In the greyness to which now my eyes had grown accustomed, I could easily see her face, and recognise its features.

She drew her hand across her mouth as if wiping it, and broke into a chuckle of such laughter as made my hair stir on my head. Then she leaped on to the grave, holding her hands high above her head, and inch by inch disappeared into the earth. Urcombe's hand was laid on my arm, in an injunction to keep still, but now he removed it.

"Come," he said.

With pick and shovel and rope we went to the grave. The earth was light and sandy, and soon after six struck we had delved down to the coffin lid. With his pick he loosened the earth round it, and, adjusting the rope through the handles by which it had been lowered, we tried to raise it. This was a long and laborious business, and the light had begun to herald day in the east before we had it out, and lying by the side of the grave. With his screw-driver he loosed the fastenings of the lid, and slid it aside, and standing there we looked on the face of Mrs. Amworth. The eyes, once closed in death, were open, the cheeks were flushed with colour, the red, full-lipped mouth seemed to smile.

"One blow and it is all over," he said. "You need not look."

Even as he spoke he took up the pick again, and, laying the point of it on her left breast, measured his distance. And though I knew what was coming I could not look away...

He grasped the pick in both hands, raised it an inch or two for the taking of his aim, and then with full force brought it down on her breast. A fountain of blood, though she had been dead so long, spouted high in the air, falling with the thud of a heavy splash over the shroud, and simultaneously from those red lips came one long, appalling cry, swelling up like some hooting siren, and dying away again. With that, instantaneous as a lightning flash, came the touch of corruption on her face, the colour of it faded to ash, the plump cheeks fell in, the mouth dropped.

"Thank God, that's over," said he, and without pause slipped the coffin lid back into its place.

Day was coming fast now, and, working like men possessed, we lowered the coffin into its place again, and shovelled the earth over it... The birds were busy with their earliest pipings as we went back to Maxley.

The Sad Story of a Vampire

by Stanislaus Eric, Count Stenbock

Vampire stories are generally located in Styria; mine is also. Styria is by no means the romantic kind of place described by those who have certainly never been there. It is a flat, uninteresting country, only celebrated by its turkeys, its capons, and the stupidity of its inhabitants. Vampires generally arrive at night, in carriages drawn by two black horses.

Our Vampire arrived by the commonplace means of the railway train, and in the afternoon. You must think I am joking, or perhaps that by the word "Vampire" I mean a financial vampire. No, I am quite serious. The Vampire of whom I am speaking, who laid waste our hearth and home, was a real vampire.

Vampires are generally described as dark, sinister-looking, and singularly handsome. Our Vampire was, on the contrary, rather fair, and certainly was not at first sight sinister-looking, and though decidedly attractive in appearance, not what one would call singularly handsome.

Yes, he desolated our home, killed my brother—the one object of my adoration—also my dear father. Yet, at the same time, I must say that I myself came under the spell of his fascination, and, in spite of all, have no ill-will towards him now.

Doubtless you have read in the papers passim of "the Baroness and her beasts." It is to tell how I came to spend most of my useless wealth on an asylum for stray animals that I am writing this.

I am old now; what happened then was when I was a little girl of about thirteen. I will begin by describing our household. We were Poles; our name was Wronski: we lived in Styria, where we had a castle. Our household was very limited. It consisted, with the exclusion of domestics, of only my father, out governessva worthy Belgian named Mademoiselle Vonnaert—my brother, and myself. Let me begin with my father: he was old, and both my brother and I were children of his old age. Of my mother I remember nothing: she died in giving birth to my brother, who is only one year, or not as much, younger than myself. Our father was studious, continually occupied in reading books, chiefly on recondite subjects and in all kinds of unknown languages. He had a long white beard, and wore habitually a black velvet skull-cap.

How kind he was to us! It was more than I could tell. Still it was not I who was the favorite. His whole heart went out to Gabriel—"Gabryel" as we spelled it in Polish. He was always called by the Russian abbreviation Gavril—I mean, of course, my brother, who had a resemblance to the only portrait of my mother, a slight chalk sketch which hung in my father's study. But Iwas by no means jealous: my brother was and has been the only love of my life. It is for his sake that I am now keeping in Westbourne Park a home for stray cats and dogs.

I was at that time, as I said before, a little girl; my name was Carmela. My long tangled hair was always all over the place, and never would be combed straight. I was not pretty—at least, looking at a photograph of me at that time, I do not think I could describe myself as such. Yet at the same time, when I look at the photograph, I think my expression may have been pleasing to some people: irregular features, large mouth, and large wild eyes.

I was by way of being naughty—not so naughty as Gabriel in the opinion of Mlle. Vonnaert. Mlle. Vonnaert, I may interpose, was a wholly excellent person, middle-aged, who really did speak good French, although she was a Belgian, and could also make herself understood in German, which, as you may or may not know, is the current language of Styria.

I find it difficult to describe my brother Gabriel; there was something about him strange and superhuman, or perhaps I should rather say praeter-human, something between the animal and the divine. Perhaps the Greek idea of the Faun might illustrate what I mean; but that will not do either. He had large, wild, gazelle-like eyes: his hair, like mine, was in a perpetual tangle—that point he had in common with me, and indeed, as I afterwards heard, our mother having been of gypsy race, it will account for much of the innate wildness there was in our natures. I was wild enough, but Gabriel was much wilder. Nothing would induce him to put on shoes and socks, except on Sundays—when he also allowed his hair to be combed, but only by me. How shall I describe the grace of that lovely mouth, shaped verily "en arc d'amour." I always think of the text in the Psalm, "Grace is shed forth on thy lips, therefore has God blessed thee eternally"—lips that seemed to exhale the very breath of life. Then that beautiful, lithe, living, elastic form!

He could run faster than any deer: spring like a squirrel to the topmost branch of a tree: he might have stood for the sign and symbol of vitality itself. But seldom could he be induced by Mlle. Vonnaert to learn lessons; but when he did so, he learned with extraordinary quickness. He would play upon every conceivable instrument, holding a violin here, there, and everywhere except the right place: manufacturing instruments for himself out of reeds—even sticks. Mlle. Vonnaert made futile efforts to induce him to learn to play the piano. I suppose he was what was called spoiled, though merely in the superficial sense of the word. Our father allowed him to indulge in every caprice.

One of his peculiarities, when quite a little child, was horror at the sight of meat. Nothing on earth would induce him to taste it. Another thing which was particularly remarkable about him was his extraordinary power over animals. Everything seemed to come tame to his hand. Birds would sit on his shoulder. Then sometimes Mlle. Vonnaert and I would lose him in the woods—he would suddenly dart away. Then we would find him singing softly or whistling to himself, with all manner of woodland creatures around him,—hedgehogs, little foxes, wild rabbits, marmots, squirrels, and such like. He would frequently bring these things home with him and insist on keeping them. This strange menagerie was the terror of poor Mlle. Vonnaert's heart. He chose to live in a little room at the top of a turret; but which, instead of going upstairs, he chose to reach by means of a very tall chestnut tree, through the window. But in contradiction to all this, it was his custom to serve every Sunday Mass in the parish church, with hair nicely combed and with white surplice and red cassock. He looked as demure and tamed as possible. Then came the element of the divine. What an expression of ecstasy there was in those glorious eyes!

Thus far I have not been speaking about the Vampire. However, let me begin with my narrative at last. One day my father had to go to the neighboring town—as he frequently had. This time he returned accompanied by a guest. The gentleman, he said, had missed his train, through the late arrival of another at our station, which was a junction, and he would therefore, as trains were not frequent in our parts, have had to wait there all night. He had joined in conversation with my father in the too-late-arriving train from the town: and had consequently accepted my father's invitation to stay the night at our house. But of course, you know, in those out-of-the-way parts we are almost patriarchal in our hospitality.

He was announced under the name of Count Vardalek—the name being Hungarian. But he spoke German well enough: not with the monotonous accentuation of Hungarians, but rather, if anything, with a slight Slavonic intonation. His voice was peculiarly soft and insinuating. We soon afterwards found out he could talk Polish, and Mlle. Vonnaert vouched for his good French. Indeed he seemed to know all languages. But let me give my first impressions. He was rather tall, with fair wavy hair, rather long, which accentuated a certain effeminacy about his smooth face. His figure had something—I cannot say what—serpentine about it. The features were refined; and he had long, slender, subtle, magnetic-looking hands, a somewhat long sinuous nose, a graceful mouth, and an attractive smile, which belied the intense sadness of the expression of the eyes. When he arrived his eyes were half closed—indeed they were habitually so—so that I could not decide their color. He looked worn and wearied. I could not possibly guess his age.

Suddenly Gabriel burst into the room: a yellow butterfly was clinging to his hair. He was carrying in his arms a little squirrel. Of course he was bare-legged as usual. The stranger looked up at his approach; then I noticed his eyes. They were green: they seemed to dilate and grow larger. Gabriel stood stock-still, with a startled look, like that of a bird fascinated by a serpent. But nevertheless he held out his hand to the newcomer. Vardalek, taking his hand—I don't know why I noticed this trivial thing—pressed the pulse with his forefinger. Suddenly Gabriel darted from the room and rushed upstairs, going to his turret-room this time by the staircase instead of the tree. I was in terror what the Count might think of him. Great was my relief when he came down in his velvet Sunday suit, and shoes and stockings. I combed his hair, and set him generally right.

When the stranger came down to dinner his appearance had somewhat altered; he looked much younger. There was an elasticity of the skin, combined with a delicate complexion, rarely to be found in a man. Before, he had struck me as being very pale.

Well, at dinner we were all charmed with him, especially my father. He seemed to be thoroughly acquainted with all my father's particular hobbies. Once, when my father was relating some of his military experiences, he said something about a drummer-boy who was wounded in battle. His eyes opened completely again and dilated: this time with a particularly disagreeable expression, dull and dead, yet at the same time animated by some horrible excitement. But this was only momentary.

The chief subject of his conversation with my father was about certain curious mystical books which my father had just lately picked up, and which he could not make out, but Vardalek seemed completely to understand. At dessert-time my father asked him if he were in a great hurry to reach his destination: if not, would he not stay with us a little while: though our place was out of the way, he would find much that would interest him in his library.

He answered, "I am in no hurry. I have no particular reason for going to that place at all, and if I can be of service to you in deciphering these books, I shall be only too glad." He added with a smile which was bitter, very very bitter:

"'You see I am a cosmopolitan, a wanderer on the face of the earth."

After dinner my father asked him if he played the piano. He said, "Yes, I can a little," and he sat down at the piano. Then he played a Hungarian csardas-wild, rhapsodic, wonderful.

That is the music which makes men mad. He went on in the same strain.

Gabriel stood stock-still by the piano, his eyes dilated and fixed, his form quivering. At last he said very slowly, at one particular motive—for want of a better word you may call it the relâche of a csardas, by which I mean that point where the original quasi-slow movement begins again—"Yes, I think I could play that."

Then he quickly fetched his fiddle and self-made xylophone, and did actually, alternating the instruments, render the same very well indeed.

Vardalek looked at him, and said in a very sad voice, "Poor child! you have the soul of music within you."

I could not understand why he should seem to commiserate instead of congratulate Gabriel on what certainly showed an extraordinary talent.

Gabriel was shy even as the wild animals who were tame to him. Never before had he taken to a stranger. Indeed, as a rule, if any stranger came to the house by any chance, he would hide himself, and I had to bring him up his food to the turret chamber. You may imagine what was my surprise when I saw him walking about hand in hand with Vardalek the next morning, in the garden, talking livelily with him, and showing his collection of pet animals, which he had gathered from the woods, and for which we had had to fit up a regular Zoological gardens. He seemed utterly under the domination of Vardalek. What surprised us was (for otherwise we liked the stranger, especially for being kind to him) that he seemed, though not noticeably at first—except perhaps to me, who noticed everything with regard to him—to be gradually losing his general health and vitality. He did not become pale as yet; but there was a certain languor about his movements which certainly there was by no means before.

My father got more and more devoted to Count Vardalek. He helped him in his studies: and my father would hardly allow him to go away, which he did sometimes—to Trieste, he said: he always came back, bringing us presents of strange Oriental jewelry or textures.

I knew all kinds of people came to Trieste, Orientals included. Still, there was a strangeness and magnificence about these things which I was sure even then could not possibly have come from such a place as Trieste, memorable to me chiefly for its necktie shops.

When Vardalek was away, Gabriel was continually asking for him and talking about him. Then at the same time he seemed to regain his old vitality and spirits. Vardalek always returned looking much older, wan, and weary. Gabriel would rush to meet him, and kiss him on the mouth. Then he gave a slight shiver: and after a little while began to look quite young again.

Things continued like this for some time. My father would not hear of Vardalek's going away permanently. He came to be an inmate of our house. I indeed, and Mlle. Vonnaert also, could not help noticing what a difference there was altogether about Gabriel. But my father seemed totally blind to it.

One night I had gone downstairs to fetch something which I had left in the drawing-room. As I was going up again I passed Vardalek's room. He was playing on a piano, which had been specially put there for him, one of Chopin's nocturnes, very beautifully: I stopped, learning on the banisters to listen.

Something white appeared on the dark staircase. We believed in ghosts in our part. I was transfixed with terror, and clung to the banisters. What was my astonishment to see Gabriel walking slowly down the staircase, his eyes fixed as though in a trance! This terrified me even more than a ghost would. Could I believe my senses? Could that be Gabriel?

I simply could not move. Gabriel, clad in his long white nightshirt, came downstairs and opened the door. He left it open. Vardalek still continued playing, but talked as he

played. He said-this time speaking in Polish—Nie umiem wyrazic jak ciehie kocham,—"My darling, I fain would spare thee; but thy life is my life, and I must live, I who would rather die. Will God not have any mercy on me? Oh! oh! life; oh the torture of lifel" Here he struck one agonized and strange chord, then continued playing softly, "O Gabriel, my beloved! my life, yes life—oh, why life? I am sure this is but a little that I demand of thee. Surely thy superabundance of life can spare a little to one who is already dead. No, stay," he said now almost harshly, "what must be, must be!"

Gabriel stood there quite still, with the same fixed vacant expression, in the room. He was evidently walking in his sleep. Vardalek played on: then said, "Ahl" with a sigh of terrible agony. Then very gently, "Go now, Gabriel; it is enough." And Gabriel went out of the room and ascended the staircase at the same slow pace, with the same unconscious stare. Vardalek struck the piano, and although he did not play loudly, it seemed as though the strings would break. You never heard music so strange and so heart-rending!

I only know I was found by Mlle. Vonnaert in the morning, in an unconscious state, at the foot of the stairs. Was it a dream after all? I am sure now that it was not. I thought then it might be, and said nothing to any one about it. Indeed, what could I say?

Well, to let me cut a long story short, Gabriel, who had never known a moment's sickness in his life, grew ill: and we had to send to Gratz for a doctor, who could give no explanation of Gabriel's strange illness. Gradual wasting away, he said: absolutely no organic complaint. What could this mean?

My father at last became conscious of the fact that Gabriel was ill. His anxiety was fearful. The last trace of grey faded from his hair, and it became quite white. We sent to Vienna for doctors. But all with the same result.

Gabriel was generally unconscious, and when conscious, only seemed to recognize Vardalek, who sat continually by his bedside, nursing him with the utmost tenderness.

One day I was alone in the room: and Vardalek cried suddenly, almost fiercely, "Send for a priest at once, at once," he repeated. "It is now almost too late!"

Gabriel stretched out his arms spasmodically,and put them round Vardalek's neck. This was the only movement he had made for some time. Vardalek bent down and kissed him on the lips. I rushed downstairs: and the priest was sent for. When I came back Vardalek was not there. The priest administered extreme unction. I think Gabriel was already dead, although we did not think so at the time.

Vardalek had utterly disappeared; and when we looked for him he was nowhere to be found; nor have I seen or heard of him since.

My father died very soon afterwards: suddenly aged, and bent down with grief. And so the whole of the Wronski property came into my sole possession. And here I am, an old woman, generally laughed at for keeping, in memory of Gabriel, an asylum for stray animals—and—people do not, as a rule, believe in Vampires!

The Hills of the Dead

by Robert E. Howard

Chapter I: Voodoo

The twigs which N'Longa flung on the fire broke and crackled. The upleaping flames lighted the countenances of the two men. N'Longa, voodoo man of the Slave Coast, was very old. His wizened and gnarled frame was stooped and brittle, his face creased by hundreds of wrinkles. The red firelight glinted on the human finger-bones which composed his necklace.

The other was an Englishman, and his name was Solomon Kane. He was tall and broad-shouldered, clad in black close garments, the garb of the Puritan. His featherless slouch hat was drawn low over his heavy brows, shadowing his darkly pallid face. His cold deep eyes brooded in the firelight.

"You come again, brother," droned the fetish-man, speaking in the jargon which passed for a common language of black man and white on the West Coast. "Many moons burn and die since we make blood-palaver. You go to the setting sun, but you come back!"

"Aye," Kane's voice was deep and almost ghostly. "Yours is a grim land, N'Longa, a red land barred with the black darkness of horror and the bloody shadows of death. Yet I have returned."

N'Longa stirred the fire, saying nothing, and after a pause Kane continued.

"Yonder in the unknown vastness"—his long finger stabbed at the black silent jungle which brooded beyond the firelight—"yonder lie mystery and adventure and nameless terror. Once I dared the jungle—once she nearly claimed my bones. Something entered into my blood, something stole into my soul like a whisper of unnamed sin. The jungle! Dark and brooding —over leagues of the blue salt sea she has drawn me and with the dawn I go to seek the heart of her. Mayhap I shall find curious adventure—mayhap my doom awaits me. But better death than the ceaseless and everlasting urge, the fire that has burned my veins with bitter longing."

"She call," muttered N'Longa. "At night she coil like serpent about my hut and whisper strange things to me. Ai ya! The jungle call. We be blood brothers, you and I. Me, N'Longa, mighty worker of nameless magic! You go to the jungle as all men go who hear her call. Maybe you live, morelike you die. You believe in my fetish work?"

"I understand it not," said Kane grimly, "but I have seen you send your soul forth from your body to animate a lifeless corpse."

"Aye! Me N'Longa! priest of the Black God! Now watch, I make magic."

Kane gazed at the old voodoo man who bent over the fire, making even motions with his hands mumbling incantations. Kane watched and he seemed to grow sleepy. A mist wavered in front of him, through which he saw dimly the form N'Longa, etched dark against the flames. Then faded out.

Kane awoke with a start, hand shooting to pistol in his belt. N'Longa grinned at him across the flame and there was a scent of early dawn the air. The fetish-man held a long stave of curious black wood in his hands. This stave was carved in a strange manner, and one end tapered to a sharp point.

"This voodoo staff," said N'Longa, putting it in the Englishman's hand. "Where your guns and long knife fail, this save you. When you want me lay this on your breast, fold your hands on it and sleep. I come to you in your dreams."

Kane weighed the thing in his hand, highly suspicious of witchcraft. It was not heavy, but seemed as hard as iron. A good weapon at least, he decided. Dawn was just beginning to steal over the jungle and the river.

Chapter II: Red Eyes

Solomon Kane shifted his musket from his shoulder and let the stock fall to the earth. Silence lay about him like a fog. Kane's lined face and tattered garments showed the effect of long bush travel. He looked about him.

Some distance behind him loomed the green, rank jungle, thinning out to low shrubs, stunted trees and tall grass. Some distance in front of him rose the first of a chain of bare, sombre hills, littered with boulders, shimmering in the merciless heat of the sun. Between the hills and the jungle lay a broad expanse of rough, uneven grasslands, dotted here and there by clumps of thorn trees.

An utter silence hung over the country. The only sign of life was a few vultures flapping heavily across the distant hills. For the last few days Kane had noticed the increasing number of these unsavoury birds. The sun was rocking westward but its heat was in no way abated.

Trailing his musket he started forward slowly. He had no objective in view. This was all unknown country and one direction was as good as another. Many weeks ago he had plunged into the jungle with the assurance born of courage and ignorance. Having by some miracle survived the first few weeks, he w coming hard and toughened, able to hold his own with any of the grim denizens of the fastness he dared.

As he progressed he noted an occasional lion spoor but there seemed to be no animals in the grasslands—none that left tracks, at any rate. Vultures sat like black, brooding images in some of the stunted trees, and suddenly he saw an activity among them some distance beyond. Several of the dusky birds circled about a clump of high grass, dipping, then rising again. Some beast of prey was defending his kill against them, Kane decided, and wondered at the lack of snarling and roaring which usually accompanied such scenes. His curiosity was roused and he turned his steps in that direction.

At last, pushing through the grass which rose about his shoulders, he saw, as through a corridor walled with the rank waving blades, a ghastly sight. The corpse of a black man lay, face down, and as the Englishman looked, a great dark snake rose and slid away into the grass, moving so quickly that Kane was unable to decide its nature. But it had a weird human-like suggestion about it.

Kane stood over the body, noting that while the limbs lay awry as if broken, the flesh was not torn as a lion or leopard would have torn it. He glanced up at the whirling vultures and was amazed to see several of them skimming along close to the earth, following a waving of the grass which marked the flight of the thing which had presumably slain the black man. Kane wondered what thing the carrion birds, which eat only the dead, were hunting through the grasslands. But Africa is full of never-explained mysteries.

Kane shrugged his shoulders and lifted his musket again. Adventures he had had in plenty since he parted from N'Longa some moons agone, but still that nameless paranoid urge had driven him on and on, deeper and deeper into those trackless ways. Kane could not have analysed this call; he would have attributed it to Satan, who lures men to their destruction. But it was but the restless turbulent spirit of the adventurer, the wanderer—the same urge which sends the gipsy caravans about the world, which drove the Viking galleys over unknown seas and which guides the flights of the wild geese.

Kane sighed. Here in this barren land seemed neither food nor water, but he had wearied unto death of the dank, rank venom of the thick jungle. Even a wilderness of bare hills was preferable, for a time at least. He glanced at them, where they lay brooding in the sun, and started forward again.

He held N'Longa's fetish stave in his left hand, and though his conscience still troubled him for keeping a thing so apparently diabolic in nature, he had never been able to bring himself to throw it away.

Now as he went toward the hills, a sudden commotion broke out in the tall grass in front of him, which was, in places, taller than a man. A thin, high-pitched scream sounded and on its heels an earth-shaking roar. The grass parted and a slim figure came flying toward him like a wisp of straw blown on the wind —a brown-skinned girl, clad only in a skirt-like garment. Behind her, some yards away but gaining swiftly, came a huge lion.

The girl fell at Kane's feet with a wail and a sob, and lay clutching at his ankles. The Englishman dropped the voodoo stave, raised his musket to his shoulder and sighted coolly at the ferocious feline face which neared him every instant. Crash! The girl screamed once and slumped on her face. The huge cat leaped high and wildly, to fall and lie motionless.

Kane reloaded hastily before he spared a glance at the form at his feet. The girl lay as still as the lion he had just slain, but a quick examination showed that she had only fainted.

He bathed her face with water from his canteen and presently she opened her eyes and sat up. Fear flooded her face as she looked at her rescuer, and she made to rise.

Kane held out a restraining hand and she cowered down, trembling. The roar of his heavy musket was enough to frighten any native who had never before seen a white man, Kane reflected.

The girl was slim and well-formed. Her nose was straight and thin- bridged. She was a deep brown in colour, perhaps with a strong Berber strain.

Kane spoke to her in a river dialect, a simple language he had learned during his wanderings and she replied haltingly. The inland tribe traded slaves and ivory to the river people and were familiar with their jargon.

"My village is there," she answered Kane's question, pointing to the southern jungle with a slim, rounded arm. "My name is Zunna. My mother whipped me for breaking a cooking-kettle and I ran away because I was angry. I am afraid; let me go back to my mother!"

"You may go," said Kane, "but I will take you, child. Suppose another lion came along? You were very foolish to run away."

She whimpered a little. "Are you not a god?"

"No. Zunna. I am only a man, though the colour of my skin is not as yours. Lead me now to your village."

She rose hesitantly, eyeing him apprehensively through the wild tangle of her hair. To Kane she seemed like some frightened young animal. She led the way and Kane followed. She indicated that her village lay to the southeast, and their route brought them nearer to the hills. The sun began to sink and the roaring of lions reverberated over grasslands. Kane glanced at the western sky; open country was no place in which to be caught by night. He glanced toward the hills and that they were within a few hundred yards of the nearest. He saw what seemed to be a cave.

"Zunna," said he haltingly, "we can never reach your village before nightfall. If we bide here the lions will take us. Yonder is a cavern where we may spend the night—"

She shrank and trembled.

"Not in the hills, master!" she whimpered. "Better the lions!"

"Nonsense!" His tone was impatient; he had had enough of native superstition. "We will spend the night in yonder cave."

She argued no further, but followed him. They went up a short slope and stood at the mouth of the cavern, a small affair, with sides of solid rock a floor of deep sand.

"Gather some dry grass, Zunna," commanded Kane, standing his musket against the wall at the mouth of the cave. "But go not far away, and listen for lions. I will build here a fire which shall keep us safe from beasts tonight. Bring some grass and twigs you may find, like a good child, and we will sup. I have dried meat in my pouch and water also."

She gave him a strange, long glance, then turned away without a word. Kane tore up grass near at hand, noting how it was seared and crisp from the sun, and heaping it up, struck flint and steel. Flame leaped up and devoured the heap in an instant. He was wondering how he could gather enough grass to keep a fire going all night, when he was aware that he had visitors.

Kane was used to grotesque sights, but at first glance he started and a slight coldness travelled down his spine. Two men stood before him in silence. They were tall and gaunt and entirely naked. Their skins were a dusty black, tinged with a grey, ashy hue, as of death. Their faces were different from any he had ever seen. The brows were high and narrow, the noses huge and snout-like; the eyes were inhumanly large and inhumanly red. As the two stood there it seemed to Kane that only their burning eyes lived.

He spoke to them, but they did not answer. He invited them to eat with a motion of his hand, and they silently squatted down near the cave mouth, as far from the dying embers of the fire as they could get.

Kane turned to his pouch and began taking out the strips of dried meat which he carried. Once he glanced at his silent guests; it seemed to him that they were watching the glowing ashes of his fire, rather than him.

The sun was about to sink behind the western horizon. A red, fierce glow spread over the grasslands, so that all seemed like a waving sea of blood. Kane knelt over his pouch, and glancing up, saw Zunna come around the shoulder of the hill with her arms full of grass and dry branches.

As he looked, her eyes flared wide; the branches dropped from her arms and her scream knifed the silence, fraught with terrible warning. Kane whirled on his knee. Two great forms loomed over him as he came up with the lithe motion of a springing leopard. The fetish stave was in his hand and he drove it through the body of the nearest foe with a force which sent its sharp point out between the man's shoulders. Then the long, lean arms of the other locked about him, and the two went down together.

The talon-like nails of the stranger were tearing at his face, the hideous red eyes staring into his with a terrible threat, as Kane writhed about and, fending off the clawing hands with one arm, drew a pistol. He pressed the muzzle close against the savage side and pulled the trigger. At the muffled report, the stranger's body jerked to the concussion of the bullet, but the thick lips merely gaped in a horrid grin.

One long arm slid under Kane's shoulders, the other hand gripped his hair. The Englishman felt his head being forced back irresistibly. He clutched at the other's wrists with both hands, but the flesh under his frantic fingers was as hard as wood. Kane's brain was reeling; his neck seemed ready to break with a little more pressure. He threw his body backward with one volcanic effort, breaking the deadly hold. The other was on him, and the talons were clutching again. Kane found and raised the empty pistol, and he felt the man's skull cave in like a shell as he brought down the long barrel with all his strength. And once again the writhing lips parted in fearful mockery.

And now a near panic clutched Kane. What sort of man was this, who still menaced his life with tearing fingers, after having been shot and mortally bludgeoned? No man, surely, but one of the sons of Satan! At the thought Kane wrenched and heaved explosively, and the close- locked combatants tumbled across the earth to come to a rest in the smouldering ashes before the cave mouth. Kane barely felt the heat, but the mouth of his foe gaped, this time in seeming agony. The frightful fingers loosened their hold and Kane sprang clear.

The savage creature with his shattered skull was rising on one hand and one knee when Kane struck, returning to the attack as a gaunt wolf returns to a wounded bison. From the side he leaped, landing full on the sinewy back, his steely arms seeking and finding a deadly wrestling hold; and as they went to the earth together he broke the other's neck, so that the hideous dead face looked back over one shoulder. The body lay still but to Kane it seemed that it was not dead even then, for the red eyes still burned with their grisly light.

The Englishman turned, to see the girl crouching against the cave wall. He looked for his stave; it lay in a heap of dust, among which were a few mouldering bones. He stared, his brain reeling. Then with one stride he caught up the voodoo staff and turned to the fallen man. His face set in grim lines as he raised it; then he drove it through the savage breast. And before his eyes, the great body crumbled, dissolving to dust as he watched horror-struck, even as the first opponent had crumbled when Kane had first thrust the stave.

Chapter III: Dream Magic

"Great God!" whispered Kane. "The men were dead! Vampires! This is Satan's handiwork manifested."

Zunna crawled to his knees and clung there.

"These be walking dead men, master," she whimpered. "I should have warned you."

"Why did they not leap on my back when they first came?" asked he.

"They feared the fire. They were waiting for the embers to die entirely."

"Whence came they?"

"From the hills. Hundreds of their kind swarm among the boulders and caverns of these hills, and they live on human life, for a man they will slay, devouring his ghost as it leaves his quivering body. Aye, they are suckers of souls!

"Master, among the greater of these hills there is a silent city of stone, and in the old times, in the days of my ancestors, these people lived there. They were human, but they were not as we, for they had ruled this land for ages and ages. The ancestors of my people made war on them and slew many, and their magicians made all the dead men as these were. At last all died.

"And for ages have they preyed on the tribes of the jungle, stalking down from the hills at mid-night and at sunset to haunt the jungle- ways and slay and slay. Men and beasts flee them and only fire will destroy them."

"Here is that which will destroy them," said Kane grimly, raising the voodoo stave. "Black magic must fight black magic, and I know not what spell N'Longa put hereon, but—"

"You are a god," Zunna decided aloud. "No man could overcome two of the walking dead men. Master, can you not lift this curse from my tribe? There is nowhere for us to flee and the monsters slay us at will, catching wayfarers outside the village wall. Death is on this land and we die helpless!"

Deep in Kane stirred the spirit of the crusader, the fire of the zealot—the fanatic who devotes his life to battling the powers of darkness.

"Let us eat," said he; "then we will build a great fire at the cave mouth. The fire which keeps away beasts shall also keep away fiends."

Later Kane sat just inside the cave, chin rested on clenched fist, eyes gazing unseeingly into the fire. Behind in the shadows, Zunna watched him, awed.

"God of Hosts," Kane muttered, "grant me aid! My hand it is which must lift the ancient curse from this dark land. How am I to fight these dead fiends, who yield not to mortal weapons? Fire will destroy them—a broken neck renders them helpless—the voodoo stave thrust through them crumbles them to dust—but of what avail? How may I prevail against the hundreds who haunt these hills, and to whom human life-essence is Life? Have not—as Zunna says—warriors come against them in the past, only to find them fled to their high-walled city where no man can come against them?"

The night wore on. Zunna slept, her cheek pillowed on her round, girlish arm. The roaring of the lions shook the hills and still Kane sat and gazed broodingly into the fire. Outside, the night was alive with whispers and rustlings and stealthily soft footfalls. And at times Kane, glancing up from his meditations, seemed to catch the gleam of great red eyes beyond the flickering light of the fire.

Grey dawn was stealing over the grasslands when Kane shook Zunna into wakefulness.

"God have mercy on my soul for delving in barbaric magic," said he, "but demonry must be fought with demonry, mayhap. Tend ye the fire and aware me if aught untoward occur."

Kane lay down on his back on the sand floor and laid the voodoo staff on his breast, folding his hands upon it. He fell asleep instantly. And sleeping, he dreamed. To his slumbering self it seemed that he walked through a thick fog and in this fog he met N'Longa, true to life. N'Longa spoke, and the words were clear and vivid, impressing themselves on his consciousness so deeply as to span the gap between sleeping and waking.

"Send this girl to her village soon after sun-up when the lions have gone to their lairs," said N'Longa, "and bid her bring her lover to you at this cave. There make him lie down as if to slumber, holding the voodoo stave."

The dream faded and Kane awoke suddenly, wondering. How strange and vivid had been the vision, and how strange to hear N'Longa talking in English, without the jargon! Kane shrugged his shoulders. He knew that N'Longa claimed to possess the power of sending his spirit through space, and he himself had seen the voodoo man animate a dead man's body. Still—

"Zunna," said Kane, giving the problem up, "I will go with you as far as the edge of the jungle and you must go on to your village and return here to this cave with your lover."

"Kran?" she asked naively.

"Whatever his name is. Eat and we will go."

Again the sun slanted toward the west. Kane sat in the cave, waiting. He had seen the girl safely to the place where the jungle thinned to the grasslands, and though his conscience stung him at the thought of the dangers which might confront her, he sent her on alone and returned to the cave. He sat now, wondering if he would not be damned to everlasting flames for tinkering with the magic of a black sorcerer, blood-brother or not.

Light footfalls sounded, and as Kane reached for his musket, Zunna entered, accompanied by a tall, splendidly proportioned youth whose brown skin showed that he was of the same race as the girl. His soft dreamy eyes were fixed on Kane in a sort of awesome worship. Evidently the girl had not minimized this new god's glory in her telling.

He bade the youth lie down as he directed and placed the voodoo stave in his hands. Zunna crouched at one side, wide-eyed. Kane stepped back, half ashamed of this mummery and wondering what, if anything, would come of it. Then to his horror, the youth gave one gasp and stiffened!

Zunna screamed, bounding erect, "You have killed Kran!" she shrieked, flying at the Englishman who stood struck speechless.

Then she halted suddenly, wavered, drew a hand languidly across her brow—she slid down to lie with her arms about the motionless body of her lover.

And this body moved suddenly, made aimless motions with hands and feet, then sat up, disengaging itself from the clinging arms of the still senseless girl.

Kran looked up at Kane and grinned, a sly, knowing grin which seemed out of place on his face somehow. Kane started. Those soft eyes had changed in expression and were now hard and glittering and snaky— N'Longa's eyes!

"Ai ya," said Kran in a grotesquely familiar voice. "Blood-brother, you got no greeting for N'Longa?"

Kane was silent. His flesh crawled in spite of himself—Kran rose and stretched his arms in an unfamiliar sort of way, as if his limbs were new to him. He slapped his breast approvingly.

"Me N'Longa!" said he in the old boastful manner. "Mighty ju-ju man! Blood-brother, not you know me, eh?"

"You are Satan," said Kane sincerely. "Are you Kran or are you N'Longa?"

"Me N'Longa," assured the other. "My body sleep in ju-ju hut on Coast many treks from here. I borrow Kran's body for while. My ghost travel ten days march in one breath; twenty days march in same time. My ghost go out from my body and drive out Kran's."

"And Kran is dead?"

"No, he no dead. I send his ghost to shadow-land for a while—send the girl's ghost too, to keep him company; bimeby come back."

"This is the work of the Devil," said Kane frankly, "but I have seen you do even fouler magic—shall I call you N'Longa or Kran?"

"Kran—kah! Me N'Longa—bodies like clothes! Me N'Longa, in here now!" he rapped his breast. "Bimeby Kran live along here—then he be Kran and I be N'Longa, same like before. Kran no live along now; N'Longa live along this one fellow body. Blood-brother, I am N'Longa!"

Kane nodded. This was in truth a land of horror and enchantment; anything was possible, even that the thin voice of N'Longa should speak to him from the great chest of Kran, and the snaky eyes of N'Longa should blink at him from the handsome young face of Kran.

"This land I know long time," said N'Longa, getting down to business. "Mighty ju-ju, these dead people! No need to waste one fellow time—I know—I talk to you in sleep. My blood-brother want to kill out these dead fellows, eh?"

"Tis a thing opposed to nature," said Kane sombrely. "They are known in my land as vampires I never expected to come upon a whole nation of them."

Chapter IV: The Silent City

"Now we find this stone city," said N'Longa.

"Yes? Why not send your ghost out to kill these vampires?" Kane asked idly.

"Ghost got to have one fellow body to work in," N'Longa answered. "Sleep now. Tomorrow we start."

The sun had set; the fire glowed and flickered in the cave mouth. Kane glanced at the still form of the girl, who lay where she had fallen, and prepared himself for slumber.

"Awake me at midnight," he admonished, "and I will watch from then until dawn."

But when N'Longa finally shook his arm, Kane awoke to see the first light of dawn reddening the land.

"Time we start," said the fetish-man.

"But the girl—are you sure she lives?"

"She live, blood-brother."

"Then in God's name, we can not leave her here at the mercy of any prowling fiend who might chance upon her. Or some lion might—"

"No lion come. Vampire scent still linger, mixed with man scent. One fellow lion he no like man scent and he fear the walking dead men. No beast come, and"—lifting the voodoo stave and laying it across the cave entrance—"no dead man come now."

Kane watched him sombrely and without enthusiasm.

"How will that rod safeguard her?"

"That mighty ju-ju," said N'Longa. "You see how one fellow vampire go along dust alongside that stave! No vampire dare touch or come near it. I gave it to you, because outside Vampire Hills one fellow man sometimes meet a corpse walking in jungle when shadows be black. Not all walking dead men be here. And all must suck life from men—if not, they rot like dead wood."

"Then make many of these rods and arm me people with them."

"No can do!" N'Longa's skull shook violently. "That ju-ju rod be mighty magic! Old, old! No man live today can tell how old that fellow ju-ju stave be. I make my blood-brother sleep and do magic with it to guard him, that time we make palaver in Coast village. Today we scout and run, no need it. Leave it here to guard girl."

Kane shrugged his shoulders and followed the fetish-man, after glancing back at the still shape which lay in the cave. He would never have agreed to leave her so casually, had he not believed in his heart that she was dead. He had touched her, and her flesh was cold.

They went up among the barren hills as the sun was rising. Higher they climbed, up steep clay slopes, winding their way through ravines and between great boulders. The hills were honey-combed with dark, forbidding caves, and these they passed warily, and Kane's flesh crawled as he thought of the grisly occupants therein. For N'Longa said:

"Them vampires, he sleep in caves most all day till sunset. Them caves, he be full of one fellow dead man."

The sun rose higher, baking down on the bare slopes with an intolerable heat. Silence brooded like an evil monster over the land. They had seen nothing, but Kane could have sworn at times that a black shadow drifted behind a boulder at their approach.

"Them vampires, they stay hid in daytime," said N'Longa with a low laugh. "They be afraid of one fellow vulture! No fool vulture! He know death when he see it! He pounce on one fellow dead man and tear and eat if he be lying or walking!"

A strong shudder shook his companion.

"Great God!" Kane cried, striking his thigh with his hat; "is there no end to the horror of this hideous land? Truly this land is dedicated to the powers of darkness!"

Kane's eyes burned with a dangerous light. The terrible heat, the solitude and the knowledge of the horrors lurking on either hand were shaking even his steely nerves.

"Keep on one fellow hat, blood-brother," admonished N'Longa with a low gurgle of amusement. "That fellow sun, he knock you dead, suppose you no look out."

Kane shifted the musket he had insisted on bringing and made no reply. They mounted an eminence at last and looked down on a sort of plateau. And in the centre of this plateau was a silent city of grey and crumbling stone. Kane was smitten by a sense of incredible age as he looked. The walls and houses were of great stone blocks, yet they were falling into ruin. Grass grew on the plateau, and high in the streets of that dead city. Kane saw no movement among the ruins.

"That is their city—why do they choose to asleep in the caves?"

"Maybe-so one fellow stone fall on them from roof and crush. Them stone huts, he fall down bimeby. Maybe-so they no like to stay together —maybe-so they eat each other, too."

"Silence!" whispered Kane; "how it hangs over all!"

"Them vampires no talk nor yell; they dead. They sleep in caves, wander at sunset and at night. Maybe-so them fellow bush tribes come with spears, them vampires go to stone kraal and fight behind walls."

Kane nodded. The crumbling walls which surrounded that dead city were still high and solid enough to resist the attack of spearmen— especially when defended by these snout-nosed fiends.

"Blood-brother," said N'Longa solemnly, "I have mighty magic thought! Be silent a little while."

Kane seated himself on a boulder, and gazed broodingly at the bare crags and slopes which surrounded them. Far away to the south he saw the leafy green ocean that was the jungle. Distance lent a certain enchantment to the scene. Closer at hand loomed the dark blotches that were the mouths of the caves of horror.

N'Longa was squatting, tracing some strange pattern in the clay with a dagger point. Kane watched him, thinking how easy they might fall victim to the vampires if even three or four of the fiends should come out of their caverns.

And even as he thought it, a black and horrific shadow fell across the crouching fetish-man.

Kane acted without conscious thought. He shot from the boulder where he sat—like a stone hurled from a catapult, and his musket stock shattered the face of the hideous thing who had stolen upon them. Back and back Kane drove his inhuman foe staggering, never giving him time to halt or launch an offensive, battering him with the onslaught of a frenzied tiger.

At the very edge of the cliff the vampire wavered, then pitched back over, to fall for a hundred feet and lie writhing on the rocks of the plateau below. N'Longa was on his feet pointing; the hills were giving up their dead.

Out of the caves they were swarming, the terrible black silent shapes; up the slopes they came charging and over the boulders they came clambering, and their red eyes were all turned toward the two humans who stood above the silent city. The caves belched them forth in an unholy judgment day.

N'Longa pointed to a crag some distance away and with a shout started running fleetly toward it. Kane followed. From behind boulders taloned hands clawed at them, tearing their garments. They raced past caves, and mummied monsters came lurching out of the dark, gibbering silently, to join in the pursuit.

The dead hands were close at their back when they scrambled up the last slope and stood on a ledge which was the top of the crag. The fiends halted silently a moment, then came clambering after them. Kane clubbed his musket and smashed down into the red-eyed faces, knocking aside the upleaping hands. They surged up like a great wave; he swung his musket in a silent fury that matched theirs. The wave broke and wavered back; came on again.

He—could—not—kill—them! These words beat on his brain like a sledge on an anvil as he shattered wood-like flesh and dead bone with his smashing swings. He knocked them down, hurled them back, but they rose and came on again. This could not last—what in God's name was N'Longa doing? Kane spared one swift, tortured glance over his shoulder. The fetish-man stood on the highest part of the ledge, head thrown back, arms lifted as if in invocation.

Kane's vision blurred to the sweep of hideous faces with red, staring eyes. Those in front were horrible to see now, for their skulls were shattered, their faces caved in and their limbs broken. But still they came on and those behind reached across their shoulders to clutch at the man who defied them.

Kane was red but the blood was all his. From the long-withered veins of those monsters no single drop of warm red blood trickled. Suddenly from behind him came a long piercing wail—N'Longa! Over the crash of the flying musket-stock and the shattering of bones it sounded high and clear—the only voice lifted in that hideous fight.

The wave of vampires washed about Kane's feet, dragging him down. Keen talons tore at him, flaccid lips sucked at his wounds. He reeled up again, dishevelled and bloody, clearing a space with a shattering sweep of his splintered musket. Then they closed in again and he went down.

"This is the end!" he thought, but even at that instant the press slackened and the sky was suddenly filled with the beat of great wings.

Then he was free and staggered up, blindly and dizzily, ready to renew the strife. He halted, frozen. Down the slope the vampire horde was fleeing and over their heads and close at their shoulders flew huge vultures, tearing and rending avidly, sinking their beaks in the dead flesh, devouring the creatures as they fled.

Kane laughed, almost insanely.

"Defy man and God, but you may not deceive the vultures, sons of Satan! They know whether a man be alive or dead!"

N'Longa stood like a prophet on the pinnacle, and the great blackbirds soared and wheeled about him. His arms still waved and his voice still wailed out across the hills. And over the skylines they came, hordes on endless hordes—vultures, vultures, vultures! come to the feast so long denied them. They blackened the sky with their numbers, blotted out the sun; a strange darkness fell on the land. They settled in long dusky lines, diving into the caverns with a whir of wings and a clash of beaks. Their talons tore at the evil horrors which these caves disgorged.

Now all the vampires were fleeing to their city. The vengeance held back for ages had come down on them and their last hope was the heavy walls which had kept back the desperate human foes. Under those crumbling roofs they might find shelter. And N'Longa watched them stream into the city, and he laughed until the crags re-echoed.

Now all were in and the birds settled like a cloud over the doomed city, perching in solid rows along the walls, sharpening their beaks and claws on the towers.

And N'Longa struck flint and steel to a bundle of dry leaves he had brought with him. The bundle leaped into instant flame and he straightened and flung the blazing thing far out over the cliffs. It fell like a meteor to the plateau beneath, showering sparks. The tall grass of the plateau leaped aflame.

From the silent city beneath them fear flowed in unseen waves, like a white fog. Kane smiled grimly.

"The grass is sere and brittle from the drought," he said; "there has been even less rain than usual this season; it will burn swiftly."

Like a crimson serpent the fire ran through high dead grass. It spread and it spread and Kane, standing high above, yet felt the fearful intensity of the hundreds of red eyes which watched from the stone city.

Now the scarlet snake had reached the walls and was rearing as if to coil and writhe over them. The vultures rose on heavily flapping wings and soared reluctantly. A vagrant gust of wind whipped the blaze about and drove it in a long red sheet around the wall. Now the city was hemmed in on all sides by a solid barricade of flame. The roar came up to the two men on the high crag.

Sparks flew across the wall, lighting in the high grass in the streets. A score of flames leaped up and grew with terrifying speed. A veil of red cloaked streets and buildings, and through this crimson, whirling mist Kane and N'Longa saw hundreds of dark shapes scamper and writhe, to vanish suddenly in red bursts of flame. There rose an intolerable scent of decayed flesh burning.

Kane gazed, awed. This was truly a hell on earth. As in a nightmare he looked into the roaring red cauldron where dark insects fought against their doom and perished. The flames leaped a hundred feet into the air, and suddenly above their roar sounded one bestial, inhuman scream like a shriek from across nameless gulfs of cosmic apace, as one vampire, dying, broke the chains of silence which had held him for untold centuries. High and haunting it rose, the death cry of a vanishing race.

Then the flames dropped suddenly. The conflagration had been a typical grass fire, short and fierce. Now the plateau showed a blackened expanse and the city a charred and smoking mass of crumbling stone. Not one corpse lay in view, not even a charred bone. Above all whirled the dark swarms of the vultures, but they, too, were beginning to scatter.

Kane gazed hungrily at the clean blue sky. Like a strong sea wind clearing a fog of horror was the sight to him. From somewhere sounded the faint and far-off roaring of a distant lion. The vultures were flapping away in black, straggling lines.

Chapter V: Palaver Set!

Kane sat in the mouth of the cave where Zunna lay, submitting to the fetish-man's bandaging.

The Puritan's garments hung in tatters about his frame; his limbs and breast were deeply gashed and darkly bruised, but he had had no mortal wound in that deathly fight on the cliff.

"Mighty men, we be!" declared N'Longa with deep approval. "Vampire city be silent now, sure 'nough! No walking dead man live along these hills."

"I do not understand," said Kane, resting chin on hand. "Tell me, N'Longa, how have you done things? How talked you with me in my dreams; how came you into the body of Kran; and how summoned you the vultures?"

"My blood-brother," said N'Longa, discarding his pride in his pidgin English, to drop into the river language understood by Kane, "I am so old that you would call me a liar if I told you my age. All my life I have worked magic, sitting first at the feet of mighty ju-ju men of the south and the east; then I was a slave to the Buckra and learned more. My brother, shall I span all these years in a moment and make you understand with a word, what has taken me so long to learn? I could not even make you understand how these vampires have kept their bodies from decay by drinking the lives of men.

"I sleep and my spirit goes out over the jungle and the rivers to talk with the sleeping spirits of my friends. There is a mighty magic on the voodoo staff I gave you—a magic out of the Old Land which draws my ghost to it as a white man's magnet draws metal."

Kane listened unspeaking, seeing for the first time in N'Longa's glittering eyes something stronger and deeper than the avid gleam of the worker in black magic. To Kane it seemed almost as if he looked into the far-seeing and mystic eyes of a prophet of old.

"I spoke to you in dreams," N'Longa went on, "and I made a deep sleep come over the souls of Kran and of Zunna, and remove them to a far dim land, whence they shall soon return, unremembering. All things bow to magic, blood-brother, and beasts and birds obey the master words. I worked strong voodoo, vulture-magic, and flying people of the air gathered at my call.

"These things I know and am a part of, but how shall I tell you of them? Blood-brother, you are a mighty warrior, but in the ways of magic you are as a little child lost. And what has taken me long dark years to know, I may not divulge to you so you would understand. My friend, you think only of bad spirits, but were my magic always bad, should I not take this fine young body in place of my old wrinkled one and keep it? But Kran shall have his body back safely.

"Keep the voodoo staff, blood-brother. It has mighty power against all sorcerers and serpents and evil things. Now I return to the village on the Coast where my true body sleeps. And what of you, my blood- brother?"

Kane pointed silently eastward.

"The call grows no weaker. I go."

N'Longa nodded, held out his hand. Kane grasped it. The mystical expression had gone from the fetish-man's face and the eyes twinkled snakily with a sort of reptilian mirth.

"Me go now, blood-brother," said the fetish-man, returning to his beloved jargon, of which knowledge he was prouder man all his conjuring tricks. "You take care—that one fellow jungle, she pluck your bones yet! Remember that voodoo stave, brother. Ai ya, palaver set!"

He fell back on the sand, and Kane saw the keen, sly expression of N'Longa fading from the face of Kran. His flesh crawled again. Somewhere back on the Slave Coast, the body of N'Longa, withered and wrinkled, was stirring in the ju-ju hut, was rising as if from a deep sleep. Kane shuddered.

Kran sat up, yawned, stretched and smiled. Beside him the girl Zunna rose, rubbing, her eyes.

"Master," said Kran apologetically, "we must have slumbered."

Good Lady Ducayne

by Mary E. Braddon

I

Bella Rolleston had made up her mind that her only chance of earning her bread and helping her mother to an occasional crust was by going out into the great unknown world as companion to a lady. She was willing to go to any lady rich enough to pay her a salary and so eccentric as to wish for a hired companion. Five shillings told off reluctantly from one of those sovereigns which were so rare with the mother and daughter, and which melted away so quickly, five solid shillings, had been handed to a smartly-dressed lady in an office in Harbeck Street, W., in the hope that this very Superior Person would find a situation and a salary for Miss Rolleston.

The Superior Person glanced at the two half-crowns as they lay on the table where Bella's hand had placed them, to make sure they were neither of them forms, before she wrote a description of Bella's qualifications and requirements in a formidable-looking ledger.

"Age?" she asked curtly.

"Eighteen, last July."

"Any accomplishments?"

"No; I am not at all accomplished. If I were I should want to be a governess—a companion seems the lowest stage."

"We have some highly accomplished ladies on our books as companions, or chaperon companions."

"Oh, I know!" babbled Bella, loquacious in her youthful candour. "But that is quite a different thing. Mother hasn't been able to afford a piano since I was twelve years old, so I'm afraid I've forgotten how to play. And I have had to help mother with her needlework, so there hasn't been much time to study."

"Please don't waste time upon explaining what you can't do, but kindly tell me anything you can do," said the Superior Person, crushingly, with her pen poised between delicate fingers waiting to write. "Can you read aloud for two or three hours at a stretch? Are you active and handy, an early riser, a good walker, sweet tempered, and obliging?"

"I can say yes to all those questions except about the sweetness. I think I have a pretty good temper, and I should be anxious to oblige anybody who paid for my services. I should want them to feel that I was really earning my salary."

"The kind of ladies who come to me would not care for a talkative companion," said the Person, severely, having finished writing in her book. "My connection lies chiefly among the aristocracy, and in that class considerable deference is expected."

"Oh, of course," said Bella; "but it's quite different when I'm talking to you. I want to tell you all about myself once and for ever."

"I am glad it is to be only once!" said the Person, with the edges of her lips.

The Person was of uncertain age, tightly laced in a black silk gown. She had a powdery complexion and a handsome clump of somebody else's hair on the top of her head. It may be that Bella's girlish freshness and vivacity had an irritating effect upon nerves weakened by an eight hours day in that over-heated second floor in Harbeck Street. To Bella the official apartment, with its Brussels carpet, velvet curtains and velvet chairs, and French clock, ticking loud on the marble chimney-piece, suggested the luxury of a palace, as compared with another second floor in Walworth where Mrs Rolleston and her daughter had managed to exist for the last six years.

"Do you think you have anything on your books that would suit me?" faltered Bella, after a pause.

"Oh, dear, no; I have nothing in view at present," answered the Person, who had swept Bella's half-crowns into a drawer, absentmindedly, with the tips of her fingers. "You see, you are so very unformed—so much too young to be companion to a lady of position. It is a pity you have not enough education for a nursery governess; that would be more in your line."

"And do you think it will be very long before you can get me a situation?" asked Bella, doubtfully.

"I really cannot say. Have you any particular reason for being so impatient—not a love affair, I hope?"

"A love affair!" cried Bella, with flaming cheeks. "What utter nonsense. I want a situation because mother is poor, and I hate being a burden to her. I want a salary that I can share with her."

"There won't be much margin for sharing in the salary you are likely to get at your age—and with your—very—unformed manners," said the Person, who found Bella's peony cheeks, bright eyes, and unbridled vivacity more and more oppressive.

"Perhaps if you'd be kind enough to give me back the fee I could take it to an agency where the connection isn't quite so aristocratic," said Bella, who—as she told her mother in her recital of the interview—was determined not to be sat upon.

"You will find no agency that can do more for you than mine," replied the Person, whose harpy fingers never relinquished coin. "You will have to wait for your opportunity. Yours is an exceptional case: but I will bear you in mind, and if anything suitable offers I will write to you. I cannot say more than that."

The half-contemptuous bend of the stately head, weighted with borrowed hair, indicated the end of the interview. Bella went back to Walworth—tramped sturdily every inch of the way in the September afternoon—and "took off" the Superior Person for the amusement of her mother and the landlady, who lingered in the shabby little sitting-room after bringing in the tea-tray, to applaud Miss Rolleston's "taking off".

"Dear, dear, what a mimic she is!" said the landlady. "You ought to have let her go on the stage, mum. She might have made her fortune as a hactress."

II

Bella waited and hoped, and listened for the postman's knocks which brought such store of letters for the parlours and the first floor, and so few for that humble second floor, where mother and daughter sat sewing with hand and with wheel and treadle, for the greater part of the day. Mrs Rolleston was a lady by birth and education; but it had been her bad fortune to marry a scoundrel; for the last half—dozen years she had been that worst of widows, a wife whose husband had deserted her. Happily, she was courageous, industrious, and a clever needle-woman; and she had been able just to earn a living for herself and her only child, by making mantles and cloaks for a West-end house. It was not a luxurious living. Cheap lodgings in a shabby street off the Walworth Road, scanty dinners, homely food, well-worn raiment, had been the portion of mother and daughter; but they loved each other so dearly, and Nature had made them both so light-hearted, that they had contrived somehow to be happy.

But now this idea of going out into the world as companion to some fine lady had rooted itself into Bella's mind, and although she idolized her mother, and although the parting of mother and daughter must needs tear two loving hearts into shreds, the girl longed for enterprise and change and excitement, as the pages of old longed to be knights, and to start for the Holy Land to break a lance with the infidel.

She grew tired of racing downstairs every time the postman knocked, only to be told "nothing for you, miss," by the smudgy-faced drudge who picked up the letters from the passage floor. "Nothing for you, miss," grinned the lodging-house drudge, till at last Bella took heart of grace and walked up to Harbeck Street, and asked the Superior Person how it was that no situation had been found for her.

"You are too young," said the Person, "and you want a salary."

"Of course I do," answered Bella; "don't other people want salaries?"

"Young ladies of your age generally want a comfortable home.

"I don't," snapped Bella; "I want to help mother."

"You can call again this day week," said the Person; "or, if I hear of anything in the meantime, I will write to you.

No letter came from the Person, and in exactly a week Bella put on her neatest hat, the one that had been seldomest caught in the rain, and trudged off to Harbeck Street.

It was a dull October afternoon, and there was a greyness in the air which might turn to fog before night. The Walworth Road shops gleamed brightly through that grey atmosphere, and though to a young lady reared in Mayfair or Belgravia such shop-windows would have been unworthy of a glance, they were a snare and temptation for Bella. There were so many things that she longed for, and would never be able to buy.

Harbeck Street is apt to be empty at this dead season of the year, a long, long street, an endless perspective of eminently respectable houses. The Person's office was at the further end, and Bella looked down that long, grey vista almost despairingly, more tired than usual with the trudge from Walworth. As she looked, a carriage passed her, an old-fashioned, yellow chariot, on cee springs, drawn by a pair of high grey horses, with the stateliest of coachmen driving them, and a tall footman sitting by his side.

"It looks like the fairy god-mother's coach," thought Bella. "I shouldn't wonder if it began by being a pumpkin."

It was a surprise when she reached the Person's door to find the yellow chariot standing before it, and the tall footman waiting near the doorstep. She was almost afraid to go in and meet the owner of that splendid carriage. She had caught only a glimpse of its occupant as the chariot rolled by, a plumed bonnet, a patch of ermine.

The Person's smart page ushered her upstairs and knocked at the official door. "Miss Rolleston," he announced, apologetically, while Bella waited outside.

"Show her in," said the Person, quickly; and then Bella heard her murmuring something in a low voice to her client.

Bella went in fresh, blooming, a living image of youth and hope, and before she looked at the Person her gaze was riveted by the owner of the chariot.

Never had she seen anyone as old as the old lady sitting by the Person's fire: a little old figure, wrapped from chin to feet in an ermine mantle; a withered, old face under a plumed bonnet—a face so wasted by age that it seemed only a pair of eyes and a peaked chin. The nose was peaked, too, but between the sharply pointed chin and the great, shining eyes, the small, aquiline nose was hardly visible.

"This is Miss Rolleston, Lady Ducayne."

Claw-like fingers, flashing with jewels, lifted a double eyeglass to Lady Ducayne's shining black eyes, and through the glasses Bella saw those unnaturally bright eyes magnified to a gigantic size, and glaring at her awfully.

"Miss Torpinter has told me all about you," said the old voice that belonged to the eyes. "Have you good health? Are you strong and active, able to eat well, sleep well, walk well, able to enjoy all that there is good in life?"

"I have never known what it is to be ill, or idle," answered Bella.

"Then I think you will do for me."

"Of course, in the event of references being perfectly satisfactory," put in the Person.

"I don't want references. The young woman looks frank and innocent. I'll take her on trust."

"So like you, dear Lady Ducayne," murmured Miss Torpinter.

"I want a strong young woman whose health will give me no trouble."

"You have been so unfortunate in that respect," cooed the Person, whose voice and manner were subdued to a melting sweetness by the old woman's presence.

"Yes, I've been rather unlucky," grunted Lady Ducayne.

"But I am sure Miss Rolleston will not disappoint you, though certainly after your unpleasant experience with Miss Tomson, who looked the picture of health—and Miss Blandy, who said she had never seen a doctor since she was vaccinated—"

"Lies, no doubt," muttered Lady Ducayne, and then turning to Bella, she asked, curtly, "You don't mind spending the winter in Italy, I suppose?"

In Italy! The very word was magical. Bella's fair young face flushed crimson.

"It has been the dream of my life to see Italy," she gasped.

From Walworth to Italy! How far, how impossible such a journey had seemed to that romantic dreamer.

"Well, your dream will be realized. Get yourself ready to leave Charing Cross by the train deluxe this day week at eleven. Be sure you are at the station a quarter before the hour. My people will look after you and your luggage."

Lady Ducayne rose from her chair, assisted by her crutch-stick, and Miss Torpinter escorted her to the door.

"And with regard to salary?" questioned the Person on the way.

"Salary, oh, the same as usual—and if the young woman wants a quarter's pay in advance you can write to me for a cheque," Lady Ducayne answered, carelessly.

Miss Torpinter went all the way downstairs with her client, and waited to see her seated in the yellow chariot. When she came upstairs again she was slightly out of breath, and she had resumed that superior manner which Bella had found so crushing.

"You may think yourself uncommonly lucky, Miss Rolleston," she said. "I have dozens of young ladies on my books whom I might have recommended for this situation—but I remembered having told you to call this afternoon—and I thought I would give you a chance. Old Lady Ducayne is one of the best people on my books. She gives her companion a hundred a year, and pays all travelling expenses. You will live in the lap of luxury."

"A hundred a year! How too lovely! Shall I have to dress very grandly? Does Lady Ducayne keep much company?"

"At her age! No, she lives in seclusion—in her own apartments—her French maid, her footman, her medical attendant, her courier."

"Why did those other companions leave her?" asked Bella.

"Their health broke down!"

"Poor things, and so they had to leave?"

"Yes, they had to leave. I suppose you would like a quarter's salary in advance?"

"Oh, yes, please. I shall have things to buy."

"Very well, I will write for Lady Ducayne's cheque, and I will send you the balance—after deducting my commission for the year."

"To be sure, I had forgotten the commission."

"You don't suppose I keep this office for pleasure."

"Of course not," murmured Bella, remembering the five shillings entrance fee; but nobody could expect a hundred a year and a winter in Italy for five shillings.

III

"From Miss Rolleston, at Cap Ferrino, to Mrs Rolleston, in Beresford Street, Walworth.

"How I wish you could see this place, dearest; the blue sky, the olive woods, the orange and lemon orchards between the cliffs and the sea—sheltering in the hollow of the great hills—and with summer waves dancing up to the narrow ridge of pebbles and weeds which is the Italian idea of a beach! Oh, how I wish you could see it all, mother dear, and bask in this sunshine, that makes it so difficult to believe the date at the head of this paper. November! The air is like an English June-the sun is so hot that I can't walk a few yards without an umbrella. And to think of you at Walworth while I am here! I could cry at the thought that perhaps you will never see this lovely coast, this wonderful sea, these summer flowers that bloom in winter. There is a hedge of pink geraniums under my window, mother—a thick, rank hedge, as if the flowers grew wild—and there are Dijon roses climbing over arches and palisades all along the terrace-a rose garden full of bloom in November! Just picture it all! You could never imagine the luxury of this hotel. It is nearly new, and has been built and decorated regardless of expense. Our rooms are upholstered in pale blue satin, which shows up Lady Ducayne's parchment complexion; but as she sits all day in a corner of the balcony basking in the sun, except when she is in her carriage, and all the evening in her armchair close to the fire, and never sees anyone but her own people, her complexion matters very little.

"She has the handsomest suite of rooms in the hotel. My bedroom is inside hers, the sweetest room—all blue satin and white lace—white enamelled furniture, looking-glasses on every wall, till I know my pert little profile as I never knew it before. The room was really meant for Lady Ducayne's dressing-room, but she ordered one of the blue satin couches to be arranged as a bed for me-the prettiest little bed, which I can wheel near the window on sunny mornings, as it is on castors and easily moved about. I feel as if Lady Ducayne were a funny old grandmother, who had suddenly appeared in my life, very, very rich, and very, very kind.

"She is not at all exacting. I read aloud to her a good deal, and she dozes and nods while I read. Sometimes I hear her moaning in her sleep—as if she had troublesome dreams. When she is tired of my reading she orders Francine, her maid, to read a French novel to her, and I hear her chuckle and groan now and then, as if she were more interested in those books than in Dickens or Scott. My French is not good enough to follow Francine, who reads very quickly. I have a great deal of liberty, for Lady Ducayne often tells me to run away and amuse myself; I roam about the hills for hours. Everything is so lovely. I lose myself in olive woods, always climbing up and up towards the pine woods above—and above the pines there are the snow mountains that just show their white peaks above the dark hills. Oh, you poor dear, how can I ever make you understand what this place is like—you, whose poor, tired eyes have only the opposite side of Beresford Street? Sometimes I go no farther than the terrace in front of the hotel, which is a favourite lounging-place with everybody. The gardens lie below, and the tennis courts where I sometimes play with a very nice girl, the only person in the hotel with whom I have made friends. She is a year older than I, and has come to Cap Ferrino with her brother, a doctor—or a medical student, who is going to be a doctor. He passed his M.B. exam at Edinburgh just before they left home, Lotta told me. He came to Italy entirely on his sister's account. She had a troublesome chest attack last summer and was ordered to winter abroad. They are orphans, quite alone in the world, and so fond of each other. It is very nice for me to have such a friend as Lotta. She is so thoroughly respectable. I can't help using that word, for some of the girls in this hotel go on in a way that I know you would shudder at. Lotta was brought up by an aunt, deep down in the country, and knows hardly anything about life. Her brother won't allow her to read a novel, French or English, that he has not read and approved.

" 'He treats me like a child,' she told me, 'but I don't mind, for it's nice to know somebody loves me, and cares about what I do, and even about my thoughts.'

"Perhaps this is what makes some girls so eager to marry—the want of someone strong and brave and honest and true to care for them and order them about. I want no one, mother darling, for I have you, and you are all the world to me. No husband could ever come between us two. If I ever were to marry he would have only the second place in my heart. But I don't suppose I ever shall marry, or even know what it is like to have an offer of marriage. No young man can afford to marry a penniless girl nowadays. Life is too expensive.

"Mr Stafford, Lotta's brother, is very clever, and very kind. He thinks it is rather hard for me to have to live with such an old woman as Lady Ducayne, but then he does not know how poor we are-you and I—and what a wonderful life this seems to me in this lovely place. I feel a selfish wretch for enjoying all my luxuries, while you, who want them so much more than I, have none of them—hardly know what they are like—do you, dearest?—for my scamp of a father began to go to the dogs soon after you were married, and since then life has been all trouble and care and struggle for you."

This letter was written when Bella had been less than a month at Cap Ferrino, before the novelty had worn off the landscape, and before the pleasure of luxurious surroundings had begun to cloy. She wrote to her mother every week, such long letters as girls who have lived in closest companionship with a mother alone can write; letters that are like a diary of heart and mind. She wrote gaily always; but when the new year began Mrs Rolleston thought she detected a note of melancholy under all those lively details about the place and the people.

"My poor girl is getting homesick," she thought. "Her heart is in Beresford Street."

It might be that she missed her new friend and companion, Lotta Stafford, who had gone with her brother for a little tour to Genoa and Spezzia, and as far as Pisa. They were to return before February; but in the meantime Bella might naturally feel very solitary among all those strangers, whose manners and doings she described so well.

The mother's instinct had been true. Bella was not so happy as she had been in that first flush of wonder and delight which followed the change from Walworth to the Riviera. Somehow, she knew not how, lassitude had crept upon her. She no longer loved to climb the hills, no longer flourished her orange stick in sheer gladness of heart as her light feet skipped over the rough ground and the coarse grass on the mountain side. The odour of rosemary and thyme, the fresh breath of the sea, no longer filled her with rapture. She thought of Beresford Street and her mother's face with a sick longing. They were so far—so far away! And then she thought of Lady Ducayne, sitting by the heaped-up olive logs in the over-heated salon—thought of that wizened-nut-cracker profile, and those gleaming eyes, with an invincible horror.

Visitors at the hotel had told her that the air of Cap Ferrino was relaxing—better suited to age than to youth, to sickness than to health. No doubt it was so. She was not so well as she had been at Walworth; but she told herself that she was suffering only from the pain of separation from the dear companion of her girlhood, the mother who had been nurse, sister, friend, flatterer, all things in this world to her. She had shed many tears over that parting, had spent many a melancholy hour on the marble terrace with yearning eyes looking westward, and with her heart's desire a thousand miles away.

She was sitting in her favourite spot, an angle at the eastern end of the terrace, a quiet little nook sheltered by orange trees, when she heard a couple of Riviera habitués talking in the garden below. They were sitting on a bench against the terrace wall.

She had no idea of listening to their talk, till the sound of Lady Ducayne's name attracted her, and then she listened without any thought of wrong-doing. They were talking no secrets—just casually discussing an hotel acquaintance.

They were two elderly people whom Bella only knew by sight. An English clergyman who had wintered abroad for half his lifetime; a stout, comfortable, well-to-do spinster, whose chronic bronchitis obliged her to migrate annually.

"I have met her about Italy for the last ten years," said the lady; "but have never found out her real age.

"I put her down at a hundred—not a year less," replied the parson. "Her reminiscences all go back to the Regency. She was evidently then in her zenith; and I have heard her say things that showed she was in Parisian society when the First Empire was at its best—before Josephine was divorced."

"She doesn't talk much now."

"No; there's not much life left in her. She is wise in keeping herself secluded. I only wonder that wicked old quack, her Italian doctor, didn't finish her off years ago."

"I should think it must be the other way, and that he keeps her alive."

"My dear Miss Manders, do you think foreign quackery ever kept anybody alive?"

"Well, there she is—and she never goes anywhere without him. He certainly has an unpleasant countenance."

"Unpleasant," echoed the parson, "I don't believe the foul fiend himself can beat him in ugliness. I pity that poor young woman who has to live between old Lady Ducayne and Dr Parravicini."

"But the old lady is very good to her companions."

"No doubt. She is very free with her cash; the servants call her good Lady Ducayne. She is a withered old female Crœsus, and knows she'll never be able to get through her money, and doesn't relish the idea of other people enjoying it when she's in her coffin. People who live to be as old as she is become slavishly attached to life. I daresay she's generous to those poor girls—but she can't make them happy. They die in her service."

"Don't say they, Mr Carton; I know that one poor girl died at Mentone last spring."

"Yes, and another poor girl died in Rome three years ago. I was there at the time. Good Lady Ducayne left her there in an English family. The girl had every comfort. The old woman was very liberal to her—but she died. I tell you, Miss Manders, it is not good for any young woman to live with two such horrors as Lady Ducayne and Parravicini.

They talked of other things—but Bella hardly heard them. She sat motionless, and a cold wind seemed to come down upon her from the mountains and to creep up to her from the sea, till she shivered as she sat there in the sunshine, in the shelter of the orange trees in the midst of all that beauty and brightness.

Yes, they were uncanny, certainly, the pair of them—she so like an aristocratic witch in her withered old age; he of no particular age, with a face that was more like a waxen mask than any human countenance Bella had ever seen. What did it matter? Old age is venerable, and worthy of all reverence; and Lady Ducayne had been very kind to her. Dr Parravicini was a harmless, inoffensive student, who seldom looked up from the book he was reading. He had his private sitting-room, where he made experiments in chemistry and natural science-perhaps in alchemy. What could it matter to Bella? He had always been polite to her, in his far-off way. She could not be more happily placed than she was—in this palatial hotel, with this rich old lady.

No doubt she missed the young English girl who had been so friendly, and it might be that she missed the girl's brother, for Mr Stafford had talked to her a good deal—had interested himself in the books she was reading, and her manner of amusing herself when she was not on duty.

"You must come to our little salon when you are 'off,' as the hospital nurses call it, and we can have some music. No doubt you play and sing?" upon which Bella had to own with a blush of shame that she had forgotten how to play the piano ages ago.

"Mother and I used to sing duets sometimes between the lights, without accompaniment," she said, and the tears came into her eyes as she thought of the humble room, the half-hour's respite from work, the sewing-machine standing where a piano ought to have been, and her mother's plaintive voice, so sweet, so true, so dear.

Sometimes she found herself wondering whether she would ever see that beloved mother again. Strange forebodings came into her mind. She was angry with herself for giving way to melancholy thoughts.

One day she questioned Lady Ducayne's French maid about those two companions who had died within three years.

"They were poor, feeble creatures," Francine told her. "They looked fresh and bright enough when they came to Miladi; but they ate too much and they were lazy. They died of luxury and idleness. Miladi was too kind to them. They had nothing to do; and so they took to fancying things; fancying the air didn't suit them, that they couldn't sleep."

"I sleep well enough, but I have had a strange dream several times since I have been in Italy."

"Ah, you had better not begin to think about dreams, or you will be like those other girls. They were dreamers—and they dreamt themselves into the cemetery."

The dream troubled her a little, not because it was a ghastly or frightening dream, but on account of sensations which she had never felt before in sleep—a whirring of wheels that went round in her brain, a great noise like a whirlwind, but rhythmical like the ticking of a gigantic clock: and then in the midst of this uproar as of winds and waves she seemed to sink into a gulf of unconsciousness, out of sleep into far deeper sleep—total extinction. And then, after that blank interval, there had come the sound of voices, and then again the whirr of wheels, louder and louder—and again the blank—and then she knew no more till morning, when she awoke, feeling languid and oppressed.

She told Dr Parravicini of her dream one day, on the only occasion when she wanted his professional advice. She had suffered rather severely from the mosquitoes before Christmas—and had been almost frightened at finding a wound upon her arm which she could only attribute to the venomous sting of one of these torturers. Parravicini put on his glasses, and scrutinized the angry mark on the round, white arm, as Bella stood before him and Lady Ducayne with her sleeve rolled up above her elbow.

"Yes, that's rather more than a joke," he said, "he has caught you on the top of a vein. What a vampire! But there's no harm done, signorina, nothing that a little dressing of mine won't heal. You must always show me any bite of this nature. It might be dangerous if neglected. These creatures feed on poison and disseminate it."

"And to think that such tiny creatures can bite like this," said Bella; "my arm looks as if it had been cut by a knife."

"If I were to show you a mosquito's sting under my microscope you wouldn't be surprised at that," replied Parravicini.

Bella had to put up with the mosquito bites, even when they came on the top of a vein, and produced that ugly wound. The wound recurred now and then at longish intervals, and Bella found Dr Parravicini's dressing a speedy cure. If he were the quack his enemies called him, he had at least a light hand and a delicate touch in performing this small operation.

"Bella Rolleston to Mrs Rolleston—April 14th.

"Ever Dearest,—Behold the cheque for my second quarter's salary—five and twenty pounds. There is no one to pinch off a whole tenner for a year's commission as there was last time, so it is all for you, mother, dear. I have plenty of pocket-money in hand from the cash I brought away with me, when you insisted on my keeping more than I wanted. It isn't possible to spend money here—except on occasional tips to servants, or sous to beggars and children—unless one had lots to spend, for everything one would like to buy—tortoise-shell, coral, lace-is so ridiculously dear that only a millionaire ought to look at it. Italy is a dream of beauty: but for shopping, give me Newington Causeway.

"You ask me so earnestly if I am quite well that I fear my letters must have been very dull lately. Yes, dear, I am well—but I am not quite so strong as I was when I used to trudge to the West-end to buy half a pound of tea—just for a constitutional walk—or to Dulwich to look at the pictures. Italy is relaxing; and I feel what the people here call 'slack.' But I fancy I can see your dear face looking worried as you read this. Indeed, and indeed, I am not ill. I am only a little tired of this lovely scene—as I suppose one might get tired of looking at one of Turner's pictures if it hung on a wall that was always opposite one. I think of you every hour in every day—think of you and our homely little room—our dear little shabby parlour, with the armchairs from the wreck of your old home, and Dick singing in his cage over the sewing-machine. Dear, shrill, maddening Dick, who, we flattered ourselves, was so passionately fond of us. Do tell me in your next that he is well.

"My friend Lotta and her brother never came back after all. They went from Pisa to Rome. Happy mortals! And they are to be on the Italian lakes in May; which lake was not decided when Lotta last wrote to me. She has been a charming correspondent, and has confided all her little flirtations to me. We are all to go to Bellaggio next week—by Genoa and Milan. Isn't that lovely? Lady Ducayne travels by the easiest stages—except when she is bottled up in the train deluxe. We shall stop two days at Genoa and one at Milan. What a bore I shall be to you with my talk about Italy when I come home.

"Love and love-and ever more love from your adoring, Bella."

IV

Herbert Stafford and his sister had often talked of the pretty English girl with her fresh complexion, which made such a pleasant touch of rosy colour among all those sallow faces at the Grand Hotel. The young doctor thought of her with a compassionate tenderness—her utter loneliness in that great hotel where there were so many people, her bondage to that old, old woman, where everybody else was free to think of nothing but enjoying life. It was a hard fate;

and the poor child was evidently devoted to her mother, and felt the pain of separation-only two of them, and very poor, and all the world to each other," he thought.

Lotta told him one morning that they were to meet again at Bellaggio. "The old thing and her court are to be there before we are," she said. "I shall be charmed to have Bella again. She is so bright and gay—in spite of an occasional touch of homesickness. I never took to a girl on a short acquaintance as I did to her."

"I like her best when she is homesick," said Herbert; "for then I am sure she has a heart."

"What have you to do with hearts, except for dissection? Don't forget that Bella is an absolute pauper. She told me in confidence that her mother makes mantles for a West-end shop. You can hardly have a lower depth than that."

"I shouldn't think any less of her if her mother made match-boxes."

"Not in the abstract—of course not. Match-boxes are honest labour. But you couldn't marry a girl whose mother makes mantles."

"We haven't come to the consideration of that question yet," answered Herbert, who liked to provoke his sister.

In two years' hospital practice he had seen too much of the grim realities of life to retain any prejudices about rank. Cancer, phthisis, gangrene, leave a man with little respect for the outward differences which vary the husk of humanity. The kernel is always the same—fearfully and wonderfully made—a subject for pity and terror.

Mr Stafford and his sister arrived at Bellaggio in a fair May evening. The sun was going down as the steamer approached the pier; and all that glory of purple bloom which curtains every wall at this season of the year flushed and deepened in the glowing light. A group of ladies were standing on the pier watching the arrivals, and among them Herbert saw a pale face that startled him out of his wonted composure.

"There she is," murmured Lotta, at his elbow, "but how dreadfully changed. She looks a wreck."

They were shaking hands with her a few minutes later, and a flush had lighted up her poor pinched face in the pleasure of meeting.

"I thought you might come this evening," she said. "We have been here a week."

She did not add that she had been there every evening to watch the boat in, and a good many times during the day. The Grand Bretagne was close by, and it had been easy for her to creep to the pier when the boat bell rang. She felt a joy in meeting these people again; a sense of being with friends; a confidence which Lady Ducayne's goodness had never inspired in her.

"Oh, you poor darling, how awfully ill you must have been, exclaimed Lotta, as the two girls embraced.

Bella tried to answer, but her voice was choked with tears.

"What has been the matter, dear? That horrid influenza, I suppose?"

"No, no, I have not been ill—I have only felt a little weaker than I used to be. 1 don't think the air of Cap Ferrino quite agreed with me."

"It must have disagreed with you abominably. I never saw such a change in anyone. Do let Herbert doctor you. He is fully qualified, you know. He prescribed for ever so many influenza patients at the Londres. They were glad to get advice from an English doctor in a friendly way."

"I am sure he must be very clever!" faltered Bella, "but there is really nothing the matter. I am not ill, and if I were ill, Lady Ducayne's physician—"

"That dreadful man with the yellow face? I would as soon one of the Borgias prescribed for me. I hope you haven't been taking any of his medicines."

"No, dear, I have taken nothing. I have never complained of being ill."

This was said while they were all three walking to the hotel. The Staffords' rooms had been secured in advance, pretty ground-floor rooms, opening into the garden. Lady Ducayne's statelier apartments were on the floor above.

"I believe these rooms are just under ours," said Bella.

"Then it will be all the easier for you to run down to us," replied Lotta, which was not really the case, as the grand staircase was in the centre of the hotel.

"Oh, I shall find it easy enough," said Bella. "I'm afraid you'll have too much of my society. Lady Ducayne sleeps away half the day in this warm weather, so I have a good deal of idle time; and I get awfully moped thinking of mother and home."

Her voice broke upon the last word. She could not have thought of that poor lodging which went by the name of home more tenderly had it been the most beautiful that art and wealth ever created. She moped and pined in this lovely garden, with the sunlit lake and the romantic hills spreading out their beauty before her. She was homesick and she had dreams: or, rather, an occasional recurrence of that one bad dream with all its strange sensations—it was more like a hallucination than dreaming—the whirring of wheels; the sinking into an abyss; the struggling back to consciousness. She had the dream shortly before she left Cap Ferrino, but not since she had come to Bellaggio, and she began to hope the air in this lake district suited her better, and that those strange sensations would never return.

Mr Stafford wrote a prescription and had it made up at the chemist's near the hotel. It was a powerful tonic, and after two bottles, and a row or two on the lake, and some rambling over the hills and in the meadows where the spring flowers made earth seem paradise, Bella's spirits and looks improved as if by magic.

"It is a wonderful tonic," she said, but perhaps in her heart of hearts she knew that the doctor's kind voice and the friendly hand that helped her in and out of the boat, and the watchful care that went with her by land and lake, had something to do with her cure.

"I hope you don't forget that her mother makes mantles," Lotta said, warningly.

"Or match-boxes: it is just the same thing, so far as I am concerned."

"You mean that in no circumstances could you think of marrying her?"

"I mean that if ever I love a woman well enough to think of marrying her, riches or rank will count for nothing with me. But I fear—I fear your poor friend may not live to be any man's wife."

"Do you think her so very ill?"

He sighed, and left the question unanswered.

One day, while they were gathering wild hyacinths in an upland meadow, Bella told Mr Stafford about her bad dream.

"It is curious only because it is hardly like a dream," she said. "I daresay you could find some common-sense reason for it. The position of my head on my pillow, or the atmosphere, or something."

And then she described her sensations; how in the midst of sleep there came a sudden sense of suffocation; and then those whirring wheels, so loud, so terrible; and then a blank, and then a coming back to waking consciousness.

"Have you ever had chloroform given you—by a dentist, for instance?"

"Never—Dr Parravicini asked me that question one day.

"Lately?"

"No, long ago, when we were in the train de luxe."

"Has Dr Parravicini prescribed for you since you began to feel weak and ill?"

"Oh, he has given me a tonic from time to time, but I hate medicine, and took very little of the stuff. And then I am not ill, only weaker than I used to be. I was ridiculously strong and well when I lived at Walworth, and used to take long walks every day. Mother made me take those tramps to Dulwich or Norwood, for fear I should suffer from too much sewing-machine; sometimes—but very seldom—she went with me. She was generally toiling at home while I was enjoying fresh air and exercise. And she was very careful about our food—that, however plain it was, it should be always nourishing and ample. I owe at to her care that I grew up such a great, strong creature."

"You don't look great or strong now, you poor dear," said Lotta.

"I'm afraid Italy doesn't agree with me."

"Perhaps it is not Italy, but being cooped up with Lady Ducayne that has made you ill."

"But I am never cooped up. Lady Ducayne is absurdly kind, and lets me roam about or sit in the balcony all day if I like. I have read more novels since I have been with her than in all the rest of my life."

"Then she is very different from the average old lady, who is usually a slave-driver," said Stafford. "I wonder why she carries a companion about with her if she has so little need of society."

"Oh, I am only part of her state. She is inordinately rich—and the salary she gives me doesn't count. Apropos of Dr Parravicini, I know he is a clever doctor, for he cures my horrid mosquito bites."

"A little ammonia would do that, in the early stage of the mischief. But there are no mosquitoes to trouble you now."

"Oh, yes, there are, I had a bite just before we left Cap Ferrino.

She pushed up her loose lawn sleeve, and exhibited a scar, which he scrutinized intently, with a surprised and puzzled look.

"This is no mosquito bite," he said.

"Oh, yes it is—unless there are snakes or adders at Cap Ferrino."

"It is not a bite at all. You are trifling with me. Miss Rolleston—you have allowed that wretched Italian quack to bleed you. They killed the greatest man in modern Europe that way, remember. How very foolish of you."

"I was never bled in my life, Mr Stafford."

"Nonsense! Let me look at your other arm. Are there any more mosquito bites?"

"Yes; Dr Parravicini says I have a bad skin for healing, and that the poison acts more virulently with me than with most people."

Stafford examined both her arms in the broad sunlight, scars new and old.

"You have been very badly bitten, Miss Rolleston," he said, "and if ever I find the mosquito I shall make him smart. But, now tell me, my dear girl, on your word of honour, tell me as you would tell a friend who is sincerely anxious for your health and happiness—as you would tell your mother if she were here to question you—have you no knowledge of any cause for these scars except mosquito bites—no suspicion even?"

"No, indeed! No, upon my honour! I have never seen a mosquito biting my arm. One never does see the horrid little fiends. But I have heard them trumpeting under the curtains, and I know that I have often had one of the pestilent wretches buzzing about me."

Later in the day Bella and her friends were sitting at tea in the garden, while Lady Ducayne took her afternoon drive with her doctor.

"How long do you mean to stop with Lady Ducayne, Miss Rolleston?" Herbert Stafford asked, after a thoughtful silence, breaking suddenly upon the trivial talk of the two girls.

"As long as she will go on paying me twenty-five pounds a quarter."

"Even if you feel your health breaking down in her service?"

"It is not the service that has injured my health. You can see that I have really nothing to do—to read aloud for an hour or so once or twice a week; to write a letter once in a way to a London tradesman. I shall never have such an easy time with anybody else. And nobody else would give me a hundred a year."

"Then you mean to go on till you break down; to die at your post?"

"Like the other two companions? No! If ever I feel seriously ill—really ill—I shall put myself in a train and go back to Walworth without stopping."

"What about the other two companions?"

"They both died. It was very unlucky for Lady Ducayne. That's why she engaged me; she chose me because I was ruddy and robust. She must feel rather disgusted at my having grown white and weak. By-the-bye, when I told her about the good your tonic had done me, she said she would like to see you and have a little talk with you about her own case."

"And I should like to see Lady Ducayne. When did she say this?"

"The day before yesterday."

"Will you ask her if she will see me this evening?"

"With pleasure I wonder what you will think of her? She looks rather terrible to a stranger; but Dr Parravicini says she was once a famous beauty."

It was nearly ten o'clock when Mr Stafford was summoned by message from Lady Ducayne, whose courier came to conduct him to her ladyship's salon. Bella was reading aloud when the visitor was admitted; and he noticed the languor in the low, sweet tones, the evident effort.

"Shut up the book," said the querulous old voice. "You are beginning to drawl like Miss Blandy."

Stafford saw a small, bent figure crouching over the piled-up olive logs; a shrunken old figure in a gorgeous garment of black and crimson brocade, a skinny throat emerging from a mass of old Venetian lace, clasped with diamonds that flashed like fire-flies as the trembling old head turned towards him.

The eyes that looked at him out of the face were almost as bright as the diamonds—the only living feature in that narrow parchment mask. He had seen terrible faces in the hospital—faces on which disease had set dreadful marks—but he had never seen a face that impressed him so painfully as this withered countenance, with its indescribable horror of death outlived, a face that should have been hidden under a coffin-lid years and years ago.

The Italian physician was standing on the other side of the fireplace, smoking a cigarette, and looking down at the little old woman brooding over the hearth as if he were proud of her.

"Good evening, Mr Stafford; you can go to your room, Bella, and write your everlasting letter to your mother at Walworth," said Lady Ducayne. "I believe she writes a page about every wild flower she discovers in the woods and meadows. I don't know what else she can find to write about," she added, as Bella quietly withdrew to the pretty little bedroom opening out of Lady Ducayne's spacious apartment. Here, as at Cap Ferrino, she slept in a room adjoining the old lady's.

"You are a medical man, I understand, Mr Stafford."

"I am a qualified practitioner, but I have not begun to practise."

"You have begun upon my companion, she tells me."

"I have prescribed for her, certainly, and I am happy to find my prescription has done her good; but I look upon that improvement as temporary. Her case will require more drastic treatment. "Never mind her case. There is nothing the matter with the girl—absolutely nothing—except girlish nonsense; too much liberty and not enough work."

"I understand that two of your ladyship's previous companions died of the same disease," said Stafford, looking first at Lady Ducayne, who gave her tremulous old head an impatient jerk, and then at Parravicini, whose yellow complexion had paled a little under Stafford's scrutiny.

"Don't bother me about my companions, sir," said Lady Ducayne. "I sent for you to consult you about myself—not about a parcel of anæmic girls. You are young, and medicine is a progressive science, the newspapers tell me. Where have you studied?"

"In Edinburgh—and in Paris."

"Two good schools. And you know all the new-fangled theories, the modem discoveries—that remind one of the mediæval witchcraft, of Albertus Magnus, and George Ripley; you have studied hypnotism—electricity?"

"And the transfusion of blood," said Stafford, very slowly, looking at Parravicini.

"Have you made any discovery that teaches you to prolong human life—any elixir—any mode of treatment? I want my life prolonged, young man. That man there has been my physician for thirty years. He does all he can to keep me alive—after his lights. He studies all the new theories of all the scientists—but he is old; he gets older every day—his brain-power is going—he is bigoted—prejudiced—can't receive new ideas—can't grapple with new systems. He will let me die if I am not on my guard against him."

"You are of an unbelievable ingratitude, Ecclenza," said Parravicini.

"Oh, you needn't complain. I have paid you thousands to keep me alive. Every year of my life has swollen your hoards; you know there is nothing to come to you when I am gone. My whole fortune is left to endow a home for indigent women of quality who have reached their ninetieth year. Come, Mr Stafford, I am a rich woman. Give me a few years more in the sunshine, a few years more above ground, and I will give you the price of a fashionable London practice—I will set you up at the West-end."

"How old are you, Lady Ducayne?"

"I was born the day Louis XVI was guillotined."

"Then I think you have had your share of the sunshine and the pleasures of the earth, and that you should spend your few remaining days in repenting your sins and trying to make atonement for the young lives that have been sacrificed to your love of life."

"What do you mean by that, sir?"

"Oh, Lady Ducayne, need I put your wickedness and your physician's still greater wickedness in plain words? The poor girl who is now in your employment has been reduced from robust health to a condition of absolute danger by Dr Parravicini's experimental surgery; and I have no doubt those other two young women who broke down in your service were treated by him in the same manner. I could take upon myself to demonstrate—by most convincing evidence, to a jury of medical men—that Dr Parravicini has been bleeding Miss Rolleston, after putting her under chloroform, at intervals, ever since she has been in your service. The deterioration in the girl's health speaks for itself; the lancet marks upon the girl's arms are unmistakable; and her description of a series of sensations, which she calls a dream, points unmistakably to the administration of chloroform while she was sleeping. A practice so nefarious, so murderous, must, if exposed, result in a sentence only less severe than the punishment of murder."

"I laugh," said Parravicini, with an airy motion of his skinny fingers; "I laugh at once at your theories and at your threats. I, Parravicini Leopold, have no fear that the law can question anything I have done."

"Take the girl away, and let me hear no more of her," cried Lady Ducayne, in the thin, old voice, which so poorly matched the energy and fire of the wicked old brain that guided its utterances. "Let her go back to her mother—I want no more girls to die in my service. There are girls enough and to spare in the world, God knows."

"If you ever engage another companion—or take another English girl into your service, Lady Ducayne, I will make all England ring with the story of your wickedness."

"I want no more girls. I don't believe in his experiments. They have been full of danger for me as well as for the girl—an air bubble, and I should be gone. I'll have no more of his dangerous quackery. I'll find some new man—a better man than you, sir, a discoverer like Pasteur, or Virchow, a genius—to keep me alive. Take your girl away, young man. Marry her if you like. I'll write her a cheque for a thousand pounds, and let her go and live on beef and beer, and get strong and plump again. I'll have no more such experiments. Do you hear, Parravicini?" she screamed, vindictively, the yellow, wrinkled face distorted with fury, the eyes glaring at him.

The Staffords carried Bella Rolleston off to Varese next day, she very loth to leave Lady Ducayne, whose liberal salary afforded such help for the dear mother. Herbert Stafford insisted, however, treating Bella as coolly as if he had been the family physician, and she had been given over wholly to his care.

"Do you suppose your mother would let you stop here to die?" he asked. "If Mrs Rolleston knew how ill you are, she would come post haste to fetch you. "I shall never be well again till I get back to Walworth," answered Bella, who was low-spirited and inclined to tears this morning, a reaction after her good spirits of yesterday.

"We'll try a week or two at Varese first," said Stafford. "When you can walk half-way up Monte Generoso without palpitation of the heart, you shall go back to Walworth."

"Poor mother, how glad she will be to see me, and how sorry that I've lost such a good place."

This conversation took place on the boat when they were leaving Bellaggio. Lotta had gone to her friend's room at seven o'clock that morning, long before Lady Ducayne's withered eyelids had opened to the daylight, before even

Francine, the French maid, was astir, and had helped to pack a Gladstone bag with essentials, and hustled Bella downstairs and out of doors before she could make any strenuous resistance.

"It's all right." Lotta assured her. "Herbert had a good talk with Lady Ducayne last night and it was settled for you to leave this morning. She doesn't like invalids, you see."

"No," sighed Bella, "she doesn't like invalids. It was very unlucky that I should break down, just like Miss Tomson and Miss Blandy."

"At any rate, you are not dead, like them," answered Lotta, "and my brother says you are not going to die."

It seemed rather a dreadful thing to be dismissed in that off-hand way, without a word of farewell from her employer.

"I wonder what Miss Torpinter will say when I go to her for another situation," Bella speculated, ruefully, while she and her friends were breakfasting on board the steamer.

"Perhaps you may never want another situation," said Stafford.

"You mean that I may never be well enough to be useful to anybody?"

"No, I don't mean anything of the kind."

It was after dinner at Varese, when Bella had been induced to take a whole glass of Chianti, and quite sparkled after that unaccustomed stimulant, that Mr Stafford produced a letter from his pocket.

"I forgot to give you Lady Ducayne's letter of adieu" he said.

"What, did she write to me? I am so glad—I hated to leave her in such a cool way; for after all she was very kind to me, and if I didn't like her it was only because she was too dreadfully old."

She tore open the envelope. The letter was short and to the point:

"Goodbye, child. Go and marry your doctor. I enclose a farewell gift for your trousseau.—Adeline Ducayne."

"A hundred pounds, a whole year's salary—no—why, it's for a—A cheque for a thousand!" cried Bella. "What a generous old soul! She really is the dearest old thing."

"She just missed being very dear to you, Bella," said Stafford.

He had dropped into the use of her Christian name while they were on board the boat. It seemed natural now that she was to be in his charge till they all three went back to England.

"I shall take upon myself the privileges of an elder brother till we land at Dover," he said; "after that—well, it must be as you please."

The question of their future relations must have been satisfactorily settled before they crossed the Channel, for Bella's next letter to her mother communicated three startling facts.

First, that the enclosed cheque for £1,000 was to be invested in debenture stock in Mrs Rolleston's name, and was to be her very own, income and principal, for the rest of her life.

Next, that Bella was going home to Walworth immediately.

And last, that she was going to be married to Mr Herbert Stafford in the following autumn.

"And I am sure you will adore him, mother, as much as I do," wrote Bella. "It is all good Lady Ducayne's doing. I never could have married if I had not secured that little nest-egg for you. Herbert says we shall be able to add to it as the years go by, and that wherever we live there shall be always a room in our house for you. The word 'mother-in-law' has no terrors for him."

Dracula's Guest

by Bram Stoker

When we started for our drive the sun was shining brightly on Munich, and the air was full of the joyousness of early summer. Just as we were about to depart, Herr Delbrück (the maître d'hôtel of the Quatre Saisons, where I was staying) came down, bareheaded, to the carriage and, after wishing me a pleasant drive, said to the coachman, still holding his hand on the handle of the carriage door:

'Remember you are back by nightfall. The sky looks bright but there is a shiver in the north wind that says there may be a sudden storm. But I am sure you will not be late.' Here he smiled, and added, 'for you know what night it is.'

Johann answered with an emphatic, 'Ja, mein Herr,' and, touching his hat, drove off quickly. When we had cleared the town, I said, after signalling to him to stop:

'Tell me, Johann, what is tonight?'

He crossed himself, as he answered laconically: 'Walpurgis nacht.' Then he took out his watch, a great, old-fashioned German silver thing as big as a turnip, and looked at it, with his eyebrows gathered together and a little impatient shrug of his shoulders. I realised that this was his way of respectfully protesting against the unnecessary delay, and sank back in the carriage, merely motioning him to proceed. He started off rapidly, as if to make up for lost time. Every now and then the horses seemed to throw up their heads and sniffed the air suspiciously. On such occasions I often looked round in alarm. The road was pretty bleak, for we were traversing a sort of high, wind-swept plateau. As we drove, I saw a road that looked but little used, and which seemed to dip through a little, winding valley. It looked so inviting that, even at the risk of offending him, I called Johann to stop—and when he had pulled up, I told him I would like to drive down that road. He made all sorts of excuses, and frequently crossed himself as he spoke. This somewhat piqued my curiosity, so I asked him various questions. He answered fencingly, and repeatedly looked at his watch in protest. Finally I said:

'Well, Johann, I want to go down this road. I shall not ask you to come unless you like; but tell me why you do not like to go, that is all I ask.' For answer he seemed to throw himself off the box, so quickly did he reach the ground. Then he stretched out his hands appealingly to me, and implored me not to go. There was just enough of English mixed with the German for me to understand the drift of his talk. He seemed always just about to tell me something—the very idea of which evidently frightened him; but each time he pulled himself up, saying, as he crossed himself: 'Walpurgis-Nacht!'

I tried to argue with him, but it was difficult to argue with a man when I did not know his language. The advantage certainly rested with him, for although he began to speak in English, of a very crude and broken kind, he always got excited and broke into his native tongue—and every time he did so, he looked at his watch. Then the horses became restless and sniffed the air. At this he grew very pale, and, looking around in a frightened way, he suddenly jumped forward, took them by the bridles and led them on some twenty feet. I followed, and asked why he had done this. For answer he crossed himself, pointed to the spot we had left and drew his carriage in the direction of the other road, indicating a cross, and said, first in German, then in English: 'Buried him—him what killed themselves.'

I remembered the old custom of burying suicides at cross-roads: 'Ah! I see, a suicide. How interesting!' But for the life of me I could not make out why the horses were frightened.

Whilst we were talking, we heard a sort of sound between a yelp and a bark. It was far away; but the horses got very restless, and it took Johann all his time to quiet them. He was pale, and said, 'It sounds like a wolf—but yet there are no wolves here now.'

'No?' I said, questioning him; 'isn't it long since the wolves were so near the city?'

'Long, long,' he answered, 'in the spring and summer; but with the snow the wolves have been here not so long.'

Whilst he was petting the horses and trying to quiet them, dark clouds drifted rapidly across the sky. The sunshine passed away, and a breath of cold wind seemed to drift past us. It was only a breath, however, and more in the nature of a warning than a fact, for the sun came out brightly again. Johann looked under his lifted hand at the horizon and said:

'The storm of snow, he comes before long time.' Then he looked at his watch again, and, straightway holding his reins firmly—for the horses were still pawing the ground restlessly and shaking their heads—he climbed to his box as though the time had come for proceeding on our journey.

I felt a little obstinate and did not at once get into the carriage.

'Tell me,' I said, 'about this place where the road leads,' and I pointed down.

Again he crossed himself and mumbled a prayer, before he answered, 'It is unholy.'

'What is unholy?' I enquired.

'The village.'

'Then there is a village?'

'No, no. No one lives there hundreds of years.' My curiosity was piqued, 'But you said there was a village.'

'There was.'

'Where is it now?'

Whereupon he burst out into a long story in German and English, so mixed up that I could not quite understand exactly what he said, but roughly I gathered that long ago, hundreds of years, men had died there and been buried in their graves; and sounds were heard under the clay, and when the graves were opened, men and women were found rosy with life, and their mouths red with blood. And so, in haste to save their lives (aye, and their souls!—and here he crossed himself) those who were left fled away to other places, where the living lived, and the dead were dead and not—not something. He was evidently afraid to speak the last words. As he proceeded with his narration, he grew more and more excited. It seemed as if his imagination had got hold of him, and he ended in a perfect paroxysm of fear—white-faced, perspiring, trembling and looking round him, as if expecting that some dreadful presence would manifest itself there in the bright sunshine on the open plain. Finally, in an agony of desperation, he cried:

'Walpurgis nacht!' and pointed to the carriage for me to get in. All my English blood rose at this, and, standing back, I said:

'You are afraid, Johann—you are afraid. Go home; I shall return alone; the walk will do me good.' The carriage door was open. I took from the seat my oak walking-stick—which I always carry on my holiday excursions—and closed the door, pointing back to Munich, and said, 'Go home, Johann—Walpurgis-nacht doesn't concern Englishmen.'

The horses were now more restive than ever, and Johann was trying to hold them in, while excitedly imploring me not to do anything so foolish. I pitied the poor fellow, he was deeply in earnest; but all the same I could not help laughing. His English was quite gone now. In his anxiety he had forgotten that his only means of making me understand was to talk my language, so he jabbered away in his native German. It began to be a little tedious. After giving the direction, 'Home!' I turned to go down the cross-road into the valley.

With a despairing gesture, Johann turned his horses towards Munich. I leaned on my stick and looked after him. He went slowly along the road for a while: then there came over the crest of the hill a man tall and thin. I could see so much in the distance. When he drew near the horses, they began to jump and kick about, then to scream with terror. Johann could not hold them in; they bolted down the road, running away madly. I watched them out of sight, then looked for the stranger, but I found that he, too, was gone.

With a light heart I turned down the side road through the deepening valley to which Johann had objected. There was not the slightest reason, that I could see, for his objection; and I daresay I tramped for a couple of hours without thinking of time or distance, and certainly without seeing a person or a house. So far as the place was concerned, it was desolation, itself. But I did not notice this particularly till, on turning a bend in the road, I came upon a scattered fringe of wood; then I recognised that I had been impressed unconsciously by the desolation of the region through which I had passed.

I sat down to rest myself, and began to look around. It struck me that it was considerably colder than it had been at the commencement of my walk—a sort of sighing sound seemed to be around me, with, now and then, high overhead, a sort of muffled roar. Looking upwards I noticed that great thick clouds were drifting rapidly across the sky from North to South at a great height. There were signs of coming storm in some lofty stratum of the air. I was a little chilly, and, thinking that it was the sitting still after the exercise of walking, I resumed my journey.

The ground I passed over was now much more picturesque. There were no striking objects that the eye might single out; but in all there was a charm of beauty. I took little heed of time and it was only when the deepening twilight forced itself upon me that I began to think of how I should find my way home. The brightness of the day had gone. The air was cold, and the drifting of clouds high overhead was more marked. They were accompanied by a sort of far-away rushing sound, through which seemed to come at intervals that mysterious cry which the driver had said came from a wolf. For a while I hesitated. I had said I would see the deserted village, so on I went, and presently came on a wide stretch of open country, shut in by hills all around. Their sides were covered with trees which spread down to the plain, dotting, in clumps, the gentler slopes and hollows which showed here and there. I followed with my eye the winding of the road, and saw that it curved close to one of the densest of these clumps and was lost behind it.

As I looked there came a cold shiver in the air, and the snow began to fall. I thought of the miles and miles of bleak country I had passed, and then hurried on to seek the shelter of the wood in front. Darker and darker grew the sky, and faster and heavier fell the snow, till the earth before and around me was a glistening white carpet the further edge of which was lost in misty vagueness. The road was here but crude, and when on the level its boundaries were not so marked, as when it passed through the cuttings; and in a little while I found that I must have strayed from it, for I missed underfoot the hard surface, and my feet sank deeper in the grass and moss. Then the wind grew stronger and blew with ever increasing force, till I was fain to run before it. The air became icy-cold, and in spite of my exercise I began to suffer. The snow was now falling so thickly and whirling around me in such rapid eddies that I could hardly keep my eyes open. Every now and then the heavens were torn asunder by vivid lightning, and in the flashes I could see ahead of me a great mass of trees, chiefly yew and cypress all heavily coated with snow.

I was soon amongst the shelter of the trees, and there, in comparative silence, I could hear the rush of the wind high overhead. Presently the blackness of the storm had become merged in the darkness of the night By-and-by the storm seemed to be passing away: it now only came in fierce puffs or blasts. At such moments the weird sound of the wolf appeared to be echoed by many similar sounds around me.

Now and again, through the black mass of drifting cloud, came a straggling ray of moonlight, which lit up the expanse, and showed me that I was at the edge of a dense mass of cypress and yew trees. As the snow had ceased to fall, I walked out from the shelter and began to investigate more closely. It appeared to me that, amongst so many old foundations as I had passed, there might be still standing a house in which, though in ruins, I could find some sort of shelter for a while. As I skirted the edge of the copse, I found that a low wall encircled it, and following this I presently found an opening. Here the cypresses formed an alley leading up to a square mass of some kind of building. Just as I caught sight of this, however, the drifting clouds obscured the moon, and I passed up the path in darkness. The wind must have grown colder, for I felt myself shiver as I walked; but there was hope of shelter, and I groped my way blindly on.

I stopped, for there was a sudden stillness. The storm had passed; and, perhaps in sympathy with nature's silence, my heart seemed to cease to beat. But this was only momentarily; for suddenly the moonlight broke through the clouds, showing me that I was in a graveyard, and that the square object before me was a great massive tomb of marble, as white as the snow that lay on and all around it. With the moonlight there came a fierce sigh of the storm, which appeared to resume its course with a long, low howl, as of many dogs or wolves. I was awed and shocked, and felt the cold perceptibly grow upon me till it seemed to grip me by the heart. Then while the flood of moonlight still fell on the marble tomb, the storm gave further evidence of renewing, as though it was returning on its track. Impelled by some sort of fascination, I approached the sepulchre to see what it was, and why such a thing stood alone in such a place. I walked around it, and read, over the Doric door, in German:

Countess Dolingen of Gratzin Styria
Sought and Found Death
1801

On the top of the tomb, seemingly driven through the solid marble—for the structure was composed of a few vast blocks of stone—was a great iron spike or stake. On going to the back I saw, graven in great Russian letters:

'The dead travel fast.'

There was something so weird and uncanny about the whole thing that it gave me a turn and made me feel quite faint. I began to wish, for the first time, that I had taken Johann's advice. Here a thought struck me, which came under almost mysterious circumstances and with a terrible shock. This was Walpurgis Night!

Walpurgis Night, when, according to the belief of millions of people, the devil was abroad—when the graves were opened and the dead came forth and walked. When all evil things of earth and air and water held revel. This very place the driver had specially shunned. This was the depopulated village of centuries ago. This was where the suicide lay; and this was the place where I was alone—unmanned, shivering with cold in a shroud of snow with a wild storm gathering again upon me! It took all my philosophy, all the religion I had been taught, all my courage, not to collapse in a paroxysm of fright.

And now a perfect tornado burst upon me. The ground shook as though thousands of horses thundered across it; and this time the storm bore on its icy wings, not snow, but great hailstones which drove with such violence that they might have come from the thongs of Balearic slingers—hailstones that beat down leaf and branch and made the shelter of the cypresses of no more avail than though their stems were standing-corn. At the first I had rushed to the nearest tree; but I was soon fain to leave it and seek the only spot that seemed to afford refuge, the deep Doric doorway of the marble tomb. There, crouching against the massive bronze door, I gained a certain amount of protection from the beating of the hailstones, for now they only drove against me as they ricocheted from the ground and the side of the marble.

As I leaned against the door, it moved slightly and opened inwards. The shelter of even a tomb was welcome in that pitiless tempest, and I was about to enter it when there came a flash of forked-lightning that lit up the whole expanse of the heavens. In the instant, as I am a living man, I saw, as my eyes were turned into the darkness of the tomb, a beautiful woman, with rounded cheeks and red lips, seemingly sleeping on a bier. As the thunder broke overhead, I was grasped as by the hand of a giant and hurled out into the storm. The whole thing was so sudden that, before I could realise the shock, moral as well as physical, I found the hailstones beating me down. At the same time I had a strange, dominating feeling that I was not alone. I looked towards the tomb. Just then there came another blinding flash, which seemed to strike the iron stake that surmounted the tomb and to pour through to the earth, blasting and crumbling the marble, as in a burst of flame. The dead woman rose for a moment of agony, while she was lapped in the flame, and her bitter scream of pain was drowned in the thundercrash. The last thing I heard was this mingling of dreadful sound, as again I was seized in the giant-grasp and dragged away, while the hailstones beat on me, and the air around seemed reverberant with the howling of wolves. The last sight that I remembered was a vague, white, moving mass, as if all the graves around me had sent out the phantoms of their sheeted-dead, and that they were closing in on me through the white cloudiness of the driving hail.

Gradually there came a sort of vague beginning of consciousness; then a sense of weariness that was dreadful. For a time I remembered nothing; but slowly my senses returned. My feet seemed positively racked with pain, yet I could not move them. They seemed to be numbed. There was an icy feeling at the back of my neck and all down my spine, and my ears, like my feet, were dead, yet in torment; but there was in my breast a sense of warmth which was, by comparison, delicious. It was as a nightmare—a physical nightmare, if one may use such an expression; for some heavy weight on my chest made it difficult for me to breathe.

This period of semi-lethargy seemed to remain a long time, and as it faded away I must have slept or swooned. Then came a sort of loathing, like the first stage of sea-sickness, and a wild desire to be free from something—I knew not what. A vast stillness enveloped me, as though all the world were asleep or dead—only broken by the low panting as of some animal close to me. I felt a warm rasping at my throat, then came a consciousness of the awful truth, which chilled me to the heart and sent the blood surging up through my brain. Some great animal was lying on me and now licking my throat. I feared to stir, for some instinct of prudence bade me lie still; but the brute seemed to realise that there was now some change in me, for it raised its head. Through my eyelashes I saw above me the two great flaming eyes of a gigantic wolf. Its sharp white teeth gleamed in the gaping red mouth, and I could feel its hot breath fierce and acrid upon me.

For another spell of time I remembered no more. Then I became conscious of a low growl, followed by a yelp, renewed again and again. Then, seemingly very far away, I heard a 'Holloa! holloa!' as of many voices calling in unison. Cautiously I raised my head and looked in the direction whence the sound came; but the cemetery blocked my view. The wolf still continued to yelp in a strange way, and a red glare began to move round the grove of cypresses, as though following the sound. As the voices drew closer, the wolf yelped faster and louder. I feared to make either sound or motion. Nearer came the red glow, over the white pall which stretched into the darkness around me. Then all at once from beyond the trees there came at a trot a troop of horsemen bearing torches. The wolf rose from my breast and made for the cemetery. I saw one of the horsemen (soldiers by their caps and their long military cloaks) raise his carbine and take aim. A companion knocked up his arm, and I heard the ball whizz over my head. He had evidently taken my body for that of the wolf. Another sighted the animal as it slunk away, and a shot followed. Then, at a gallop, the troop rode forward—some towards me, others following the wolf as it disappeared amongst the snow-clad cypresses.

As they drew nearer I tried to move, but was powerless, although I could see and hear all that went on around me. Two or three of the soldiers jumped from their horses and knelt beside me. One of them raised my head, and placed his hand over my heart.

'Good news, comrades!' he cried. 'His heart still beats!'

Then some brandy was poured down my throat; it put vigour into me, and I was able to open my eyes fully and look around. Lights and shadows were moving among the trees, and I heard men call to one another. They drew together, uttering frightened exclamations; and the lights flashed as the others came pouring out of the cemetery pell-mell, like men possessed. When the further ones came close to us, those who were around me asked them eagerly:

'Well, have you found him?'

The reply rang out hurriedly:

'No! no! Come away quick—quick! This is no place to stay, and on this of all nights!'

'What was it?' was the question, asked in all manner of keys. The answer came variously and all indefinitely as though the men were moved by some common impulse to speak, yet were restrained by some common fear from giving their thoughts.

'It—it—indeed!' gibbered one, whose wits had plainly given out for the moment.

'A wolf—and yet not a wolf!' another put in shudderingly.

'No use trying for him without the sacred bullet,' a third remarked in a more ordinary manner.

'Serve us right for coming out on this night! Truly we have earned our thousand marks!' were the ejaculations of a fourth.

'There was blood on the broken marble,' another said after a pause —' the lightning never brought that there. And for him—is he safe? Look at his throat! See, comrades, the wolf has been lying on him and keeping his blood warm.'

The officer looked at my throat and replied:

'He is all right; the skin is not pierced. What does it all mean? We should never have found him but for the yelping of the wolf.'

'What became of it?' asked the man who was holding up my head, and who seemed the least panic-stricken of the party, for his hands were steady and without tremor. On his sleeve was the chevron of a petty officer.

'It went to its home,' answered the man, whose long face was pallid, and who actually shook with terror as he glanced around him fearfully. 'There are graves enough there in which it may lie. Come, comrades—come quickly! Let us leave this cursed spot.'

The officer raised me to a sitting posture, as he uttered a word of command; then several men placed me upon a horse. He sprang to the saddle behind me, took me in his arms, gave the word to advance; and, turning our faces away from the cypresses, we rode away in swift, military order.

As yet my tongue refused its office, and I was perforce silent. I must have fallen asleep; for the next thing I remembered was finding myself standing up, supported by a soldier on each side of me. It was almost broad daylight, and to the north a red streak of sunlight was reflected, like a path of blood, over the waste of snow. The officer was telling the men to say nothing of what they had seen, except that they found an English stranger, guarded by a large dog.

'Dog! that was no dog,' cut in the man who had exhibited such fear. 'I think I know a wolf when I see one.'

The young officer answered calmly: 'I said a dog.'

'Dog!' reiterated the other ironically. It was evident that his courage was rising with the sun; and, pointing to me, he said, 'Look at his throat. Is that the work of a dog, master?'

Instinctively I raised my hand to my throat, and as I touched it I cried out in pain. The men crowded round to look, some stooping down from their saddles; and again there came the calm voice of the young officer:

'A dog, as I said. If aught else were said we should only be laughed at.'

I was then mounted behind a trooper, and we rode on into the suburbs of Munich. Here we came across a stray carriage, into which I was lifted, and it was driven off to the Quatre Saisons—the young officer accompanying me, whilst a trooper followed with his horse, and the others rode off to their barracks.

When we arrived, Herr Delbrück rushed so quickly down the steps to meet me, that it was apparent he had been watching within. Taking me by both hands he solicitously led me in. The officer saluted me and was turning to withdraw, when I recognised his purpose, and insisted that he should come to my rooms. Over a glass of wine I warmly thanked him and his brave comrades for saving me. He replied simply that he was more than glad, and that Herr Delbrück had at the first taken steps to make all the searching party pleased; at which ambiguous utterance the maître d'hôtel smiled, while the officer pleaded duty and withdrew.

'But Herr Delbrück,' I enquired, 'how and why was it that the soldiers searched for me?'

He shrugged his shoulders, as if in depreciation of his own deed, as he replied:

'I was so fortunate as to obtain leave from the commander of the regiment in which I served, to ask for volunteers.'

'But how did you know I was lost?' I asked.

'The driver came hither with the remains of his carriage, which had been upset when the horses ran away.'

'But surely you would not send a search-party of soldiers merely on this account?'

'Oh, no!' he answered; 'but even before the coachman arrived, I had this telegram from the Boyar whose guest you are,' and he took from his pocket a telegram which he handed to me, and I read:

Bistritz.

Be careful of my guest—his safety is most precious to me. Should aught happen to him, or if he be missed, spare nothing to find him and ensure his safety. He is English and therefore adventurous. There are often dangers from snow and wolves and night. Lose not a moment if you suspect harm to him. I answer your zeal with my fortune.
—Dracula.

As I held the telegram in my hand, the room seemed to whirl around me; and, if the attentive maître d'hôtel had not caught me, I think I should have fallen. There was something so strange in all this, something so weird and impossible to imagine, that there grew on me a sense of my being in some way the sport of opposite forces—the mere vague idea of which seemed in a way to paralyse me. I was certainly under some form of mysterious protection. From a distant country had come, in the very nick of time, a message that took me out of the danger of the snow-sleep and the jaws of the wolf.

Each Man Kills
by Victoria Glad

"... to live you must feed on the living"—Vincent Napoli

Now that it's all over, it seems like a bad dream. But when I look at Maria's picture on my desk, I realize it couldn't have been a dream. Actually, it was only six months ago that I sat at this same desk, looking at her picture, wondering what could have happened to her. It had been six weeks since there had been any word from her, and she had promised to write as soon as she arrived in Europe. Considering that my future rested in her small hands, I had every right to be apprehensive.

We had grown up together, had lost our folks within a few years of each other and had been fond of each other the way kids are apt to be. Then the change came: It seemed I loved her, and she was still just "fond" of me. During our early college days I sort of let things ride, but once we went on to graduate school, I began to crowd her.

The next thing I knew, she had signed up with a student tour destined for Central Europe, and told me she would give me my answer when she returned. I had to be content with that, but couldn't help worrying. Maria was a strange girl—withdrawn, dreamy and soft-hearted. Knowing the section she was going to, I was inclined to be uneasy, since it is the realm of gypsies, fortune tellers and the like. It is also the birthplace of many strange legends, and Maria claimed to be strongly psychic. As a matter of fact, she had foretold one or two things which were probably coincidental, like the death of our parents, and which even made an impression on me—and you'd hardly call me a "believer."

This so-called talent of hers led her into trouble on more than one occasion. I remember in her senior year at college she fell under the spell of a short, fat, greasy spook-reader with a strictly phony accent and all but gave her eye teeth away, until I realized something was amiss, got to the bottom of it, and dispatched friend spook-reader pronto. If she should meet some unscrupulous person now, with no one around to get her out of the scrape—but I didn't want to think of that. I was sure this time everything would be all right.

When she didn't write at first, I let it go that she was busy. Finally, six weeks' silent treatment aroused my curiosity. It also aroused my nasty temper, and the next thing I knew I was on a plane bound for the Continent. Within two hours after landing, I found her at a little inn in Transylvania, a quaint little place that looked as if it were made of gingerbread, and was surrounded by the huge, craggy Transylvania Mountain range. I also found Tod Hunter.

"What's wrong, Maria? Why didn't you write?" I asked.

Her usually gay, shining brown eyes flashed angrily. "Why couldn't you leave me alone? I told you not to come after me. I came here so I could think this out. For God's sake, Bill, can't you see I wanted to think? To be by myself?"

"But you promised to write," I persisted, wondering at this change in her, this impatience. Wondered, too, at her wraithlike slimness. She'd always been curved in the right places.

"Maria has been studying much too diligently," Tod said slowly. "She's always tired lately. She hasn't been too well, either. Her throat bothers her."

I wanted to punch his head in. For some reason I didn't like him. Not because I sensed his rivalry; I was above that. God knows I wanted her to be happy, above everything. It was just something about him that irritated me. An attitude. Not supercilious; I could have coped with that. Rather, it was a calm imperturbability that seemed to speak his faith in his eventual success, regardless of any effort on my part.

I don't know how to fight that sort of strategy. I look like I am: blunt and obvious. Suddenly I didn't care if he was there.

"Maria. Ria, darling. This guy's no good for you, can't you see that? What do you know about him?"

She looked at me, her eyes surprised and a little hurt. Then she looked at him, seemed to be looking through him and into herself, if you know what I mean. A slow flush spread from the base of her throat, that thin, almost transparent throat.

"All I have to know," she said softly. "I love him."

She looked out the window. "I'm going up into Konigstein Mountain, to a small sanitarium for my health shortly; the doctor has told me I must go away, and Tod has suggested this place. There Tod and I shall be married."

I knew then how it felt to be on the receiving end of a monkey-punch. That she had come to this decision because of my objections, I had not the slightest doubt. She was going to marry someone about whom she knew absolutely nothing. She was much more ill than she knew. Hunter was undoubtedly after her money; she was considerably well-off. Obviously she was once more being influenced in the wrong direction.

"I won't let you!" I warned. "Give it some more time, if for nothing else, then for old times' sake."

"How about me, Morris?" Tod interrupted. "You haven't asked me my feelings on the subject. I happen to love Maria dearly. Have I no say just because you're a childhood friend of hers?"

"Childhood friend! I was her whole family for years before she ever heard of you! I'll see you in hell before I let her marry you!" I shouted. Looking back, I'm sure that had he said anything else, I would have killed him, if Ria hadn't come between us.

"That's enough, Bill Morris! I've heard all I want to from you. I'm twenty-three, and if I choose to marry Tod, I'll do so and there's nothing you can do about it. Now, please go."

"Okay, Ria," I said, "if that's the way you want it. But I'm not through. If you won't protect yourself, I'll do it for you. I'd like to know more about the mysterious Mr. Tod Hunter, American, and I do wish, for your own sake, you'd do the same. I wouldn't care if you married King Tut, so long as you knew all about him. People just don't marry strangers; not if they're smart. For God's sake, ask him about himself!"

"All right, Bill," she replied, smiling patiently. "I'll ask him. Now, do stop being childish."

"Okay, darling," I said sheepishly. "But do me one more favor. Don't marry him until I get back. Only a little while; give me a week. Just wait a little longer."

As I closed the door, I could still feel his smile, mocking—yet a little sad.

But Maria didn't wait. I was gone a week. I had walked my legs off trying to track down the elusive Mister Hunter and discovered exactly—nothing. All his landlady could tell me was that he was an American who had come to this climate for his health, and that he slept late mornings. I was licked and I knew it. If I had been a pup, I would have fitted my tail neatly between my legs and made for home. But I wasn't a pup, so I headed straight for Ria's flat to face the music.

They were waiting for me, she and Tod. When I saw her, I wished I were dead.

She lay in Tod's arms, her body a mere whisper of a body. White and cold she was, like frozen milk on a cold winter's day. They were both dead.

You know how it is when at a wake someone views the deceased and says kindly, "She's beautiful," and "she" isn't beautiful at all; just a made-up, lifeless handful of clay. Dead as dead, and frightening. Well, it wasn't that way this time. Their fair skins were faintly pink-tinted and their blonde heads, hers ashen and his a reddish cast, gleamed brightly. And they sat so close in the sofa before the fire, his head resting in the hollow of her throat. They looked—peaceful; no line marred their faces. I almost fancied I saw them breathe. And on her third finger, left hand, was the ring—a thin, platinum band. He had won, and in winning somehow he had lost. How they had died and why they found each other and death at the same time, I would probably never know. I only knew one thing: I had to get away from there—quickly. I almost ran the distance to my flat. Stumbled into the place and poured a triple Scotch which I could scarcely hold. The Scotch seared my throat and tasted bitter; someone must have poured salt in it. Then I realized that it was tears—my tears. I, Bill Morris, who hadn't cried since my fifth birthday—I was sobbing like a baby.

I didn't call the police. That would mean I would have to go back and watch them cover that lovely body, carry it away and submit it to untold indignities in order to ascertain the cause of death. The cleaning girl would find them in the morning and would notify the police.

But it wasn't so simple as that. In the morning I found I couldn't shake off the guilt which possessed me. Even two bottles of Scotch hadn't helped me to forget. I was dead drunk and cold sober at the same time.

I phoned Ria's landlady and told her I had failed to reach the Hunters by phone, that I was sure something was amiss. Would she please go to their flat and see if anything was wrong.

She was amused. "Really, Mr. Morris, you must be mistaken. Miss Maria went out just an hour ago with her new husband. Surely you are jesting. Why she has never looked better. So happy. They have left for Konigstein. They have also left you a note.

I told her I would be right over, and hopped a cab. I began to think I was losing my mind. I had seen them both—dead. The landlady had seen them this morning—alive!"

When I arrived, the landlady looked at me for a long moment, taking in my rough, dark-blue complexion, unpressed clothes, red-rimmed eyes, then wagged a finger playfully.

"You are playing a joke, no? A wedding joke, maybe. Here, too, we haze newlyweds. But of course I understood. Who could help loving Miss Maria? Be of good heart, young man. For you there will be another, some day. But I talk too much. Here is your letter."

I went where I would be undisturbed, to the reading room of the library on the same street as my flat. To the musty, oblong, dimly lit room whose threshold sunshine and fresh air dared not cross. Without the saving warmth of sunlight or the fresh, clean relief of sweet-smelling air, I read. Read, inhaling the pungent, sour smell of the Scotch I had consumed during the long, sleepless night. Read, and then doubted that I had read at all—but the blue ink on the white paper forced me to acknowledge its actuality. It had been written by Hunter, in a neat, scholar's script.

Dear Morris: (It began)

Why should I not have wanted Maria? You did; others doubtless did. Why then should she not be mine? There are many things worse than being married to me; she might have married a man who beat her!

With her I have known the two happiest days of my life. I want no more than that. I have no right to ask for more. Have we, any of us, a right to endless bliss on this earth? Hardly.

You thought of her welfare above all; for that I owe you some explanation. You must be patient, you must believe, and in the end, you must do as I ask. You must.

You wanted to know about me—of my life before Maria. Before Maria? It seems strange to think about it. There is no life without Maria. Still, there was a time when for me she didn't exist. I have been constantly going forward to the day when I would meet her, yet there was a time when I didn't know where I would find her, or even what her name would be!

It was chance that brought us together. For me, good chance; for you, possibly ill chance; for Maria? Only she can say. Some three years ago I was studying in England under a Rhodes Scholarship. The future held great things for me. I was a Yank like yourself, and damn proud of it. Life in England seemed strange and slow and sometimes utterly dismal under Austerity. Then, little by little I slipped into their slower ways, growing to love the people for their spunk, and finally coming to feel I was one of them, so to speak.

I have said everything slowed down: I was wrong. Studying intensified for me. The folklore of the British Isles intrigued me. I delved into the Black Welsh tales, the mischievous fancies of the Irish, the English legends of the prowling werewolf. For me it was a relief from political science, which suddenly palled and which smacked of treason in the light of current events. My extracurricular research consumed the better part of my evenings. My books were and always have been a part of me, and as was to be expected, I overdid it. I studied too hard with too little let-up. Sometimes it seemed to me there was more truth to what I read than myth. It became somewhat of an obsession. Suddenly, one night, everything blacked out.

I came to in a sanatorium. I didn't know how I got there, and when they explained it to me, I laughed. I thought they were joking. When I tried to get up, to walk, I collapsed. Then I knew how bad it had been. I knew, too, I would have to go slowly.

It was there I met Eve. She was beautiful. Not like Maria, who is like a fragile, fair, spun-sugar angel. Eve was more earthy, with skin like ivory, creamy and rich and pale. Her blue-black hair she wore long and gathered in the back. She looked about twenty-five, but a streak of pure white ran back from each of her temples. She was the most striking woman I have ever met. I had never known anyone like her, nor have I since I saw her last.

You know how it is: the air of mystery about a woman makes a man like a kid again. She reminded me of a sleek, black cat, with her large, hazel eyes. I bumped into her one day on the verandah, and spent every day with her after that.

The doctors wanted me to take exercise—short walks and the like, and Eve went with me, struggling to keep up with me. The slightest effort tired her. She suffered from a rather nasty case of anemia. She seldom smiled; the effort was probably too much for her. I saw her really smile only once.

We had been on one of our short hikes in the woods close by the grounds. She stumbled over a twig or a branch, I'm not sure which. Suddenly she was in my arms. Have you ever held a cloud in your arms, Morris? So light she was, although she was almost as tall as I. Warm and pulsating. Her eyes held mine; it was almost uncanny. I have never been affected like that by a woman. Then I was kissing her; then a sharp sting, and I winced. There was the warm, salt taste of blood on my lips. I never knew how it happened. But she was smiling, her full mouth parted in the strangest smile I have ever seen. And those small white teeth gleamed; and in her eyes, which were all black pupils now, with the iris quite hidden, was desire—or something beyond desire. I couldn't define it then; now, I think I can. Her small, pink tongue darted over her lips, tasting, seeming to savor.

I was frightened, for some indefinable reason. I wanted to get away from her, from the woods, from myself. I grasped her arm roughly and we started back for the grounds. We never mentioned the episode again, but we neither of us ever forgot. She intrigued me now, more than ever. The doctors were able to satisfy my curiosity somewhat. They told me she had been a patient for some four years. Some days she was better, some days worse. She needed rest—much rest.

Most days she slept past noon with their approval. Some days there was a faint flush beneath that ivory skin; other days it was pale and cool.

Just when we became lovers, I scarcely remember. Things were happening so fast I could barely keep pace with them. There was a magnetism about Eve which compelled. I couldn't have resisted if I'd wanted to—and I didn't.

I began to have long periods of lassitude, times when I would black out and remember nothing afterwards. And the dreams began. I would dream I was stroking a large, velvety-black cat, a cat with shining yellow eyes that looked at me as if they knew my every thought. I would stroke it continuously and it would nip me playfully. Then, one night the dream intensified: I was playing with the creature, caressing it gently, when of a sudden its lips drew back in a snarl, and without warning it sprang at my throat and buried its fangs deep! I thought I could feel life being drawn from me; I screamed.

The doctors told me afterwards that I was semi-conscious for days; that I had to be restrained.

When I was well again, Eve came to see me. She was gentle—soothing. She held me close to her and oh! it was good to be alive and to belong to someone.

I remember to this day what she wore. Black velvet lounging slacks, a low-necked amber satin blouse, caught at the "V" by a curiously wrought antique silver pin. It was round, about four inches in diameter. In its center was the carved figure of a serpent coiled to strike. Its eyes were deep amber topazes and its darting tongue was raised and set with a blood-red ruby.

"What an unusual pin, Eve," I said "I've never seen it before, have I?"

"No," she replied. "It belongs to the deep, dark, seldom discussed skeleton in the Orcaczy closet, Tod. You see, my great-great grandmother was quite a wicked lady, to hear tell. Went in for Witches' masses and the like. They say she poisoned her husband, a rather elderly and very childish man, for her lover, whom she subsequently married. Together they did away with relatives who stood in the way of their accumulating more money. This pin was the instrument of death."

Her slim fingers pressed the ruby tongue and the pin opened, revealing a space large enough to secrete powder.

"It's like those employed by the infamous Borgias, as you can see," she continued, shrugging. "Perhaps it was fate then, that her devoted new husband tired of her once her fortune was assured him, took a young mistress for himself, and disposed of the unfortunate wife, using her own pin to perpetrate her murder. She was excommunicated by her church, too, which must have made it most unpleasant for her, poor old dear." The slim shoulders straightened. "But let's not discuss such unpleasant things, my dear. The important thing now is for you to get well quickly. I've missed you terribly, you know."

It was then I asked her to marry me. I knew I didn't really love her, but there seemed nothing to prevent our marriage. And she had gotten under my skin. It was as elemental as that. She said she thought we should wait until I fully recovered.

"Don't say any more, darling," she said. "Rest your poor, sore throat."

She bent over me solicitously and I reached up to stroke that smooth black hair. It had a familiar feel to it that I couldn't quite place. Of course I had stroked it hundreds of times before, but it wasn't that. Then she looked straight at me, those large, glowing hazel eyes boring into mine, and I knew. Knew and disbelieved at the same time. I froze where I lay, paralyzed by my fear; unable to make a sound.

"So you know," she whispered. "It is well. I have marked you for my own these many months. Now that you know, you will not fight. You know what I am, or at least you can guess. This pin you admired so—it was mine three hundred years ago and it will always be mine!"

Her lips were on mine. She had never kissed me like this. It was like the touch of hot ice, freezing, then searing. Unendurable. I lay inert; I couldn't have moved if I wanted to. I could scarcely breathe. Then I felt the blood within me pounding, pulsing, beginning to answer in spite of myself. I tasted once more the warm, salty fluid on my lips. Eve's body was liquid in my arms; warm, heady, narcotizing. Once again I felt the agonizing, dagger sharp pain in my throat and—darkness.

Have you ever wakened to a bright, sunny afternoon and heard yourself pronounced dead? They spoke in low, hushed tones. How unfortunate. Young fellow only thirty, dying so far away from his homeland. No family. Good thing he was well-set in life. This sudden anemia was most extraordinary; fellow showed no signs of it previously. All he had really needed was rest. If he had recovered, that lovely Eve Orcaczy might have made both their lives happier, richer. Sad ending to what might have been an idyll. Good of her to claim the body. She said she was going to inter it in the family vault in Konigstein Mountain in Transylvania.

I heard them distinctly. I wanted to shout that I wasn't dead; I wanted to wake up from this horrible nightmare. I was as alive as they. I knew I had to get out of there, some way; to get away from Eve, whom I now feared. They left to make arrangements.

The lassitude crept through me without warning; I dozed in spite of myself. And I dreamed again. I was a cat running, leaping through windows, loping over the countryside, stopping for no one. I panted with my exertions. Towns and cities flew by; I had to get someplace and quickly. Then the dream ended.

"Tod," she said, "Get up, my dear." I heard Her and I hated Her. Hated Her while I was drawn to Her. There was a white mist before my eyes. I reached up to brush it away. It was not a mist; it was a cloth. I shivered.

"I must wake up," I whispered hoarsely, "I must! I'm going mad!"

There was a creaking sound and daylight descended upon me. When I saw where I was, I covered my face with my hands and sobbed. I tried to pray, but the words froze on my lips. I was sitting in a coffin in a mausoleum! I had been buried alive!

"What am I?" I shrieked. "Where am I and what have You done? I'm out of my mind; stark, staring mad!"

Eve's lips parted, showing the even white teeth—those slightly pointed teeth.

"You're quite sane, my dear," She said calmly. "You are now one of us; a revenant, even as I, and to live you must feed on the living."

"It's not true!" I shouted. "This is all a crazy nightmare, part of my illness! You're not real! Nothing is real!"

"I'm quite real, Tod. To be trite, I am what I am, and have accepted it calmly, as you shall in time. I have told you of my life. You have been a student of legends. Legends are often—more often than you think—reality. When one has been murdered, if one has lived a so-called wicked life, he is doomed to walk the earth battening on the living. My fate was sealed as I lay in my coffin. But that wasn't enough. As I lay there, my pet cat, Suma, slunk into the room and leapt over me. That was a double insurance of my life after death. Those whom I mark for my own must, too, live on. Accept it, my dear. You have no other choice."

"No!" I cried. "I'm an American! Things like this don't happen to us! It's only in stories, and then to foreigners!"

She chuckled drily. "I'm afraid these things do happen, and in this case, you're it, my dear. Make the best of it."

But I wouldn't; I refused to—for a while. I would not feast on the blood of the living. Something within me fought. For a time.

Then, the awful hunger began. The tearing pangs of hunger that ordinary food wouldn't arrest. I fought it as long as I could. I lost.

First it was small animals; animals that I loved. It was my life or theirs. Then there was a little girl; a dear little creature who might have been my child under different circumstances.

After the episode of the little girl, Eve left me. She had no further use for me; she had wanted the child, too, and I had got it. I was now competition to be shunned. I was alone once again alone and thoroughly miserable. I couldn't understand myself, my motives, so how could I expect someone else to understand?

I only knew what I was; nor could I rationalize on why I had become this way. I could only presume it had happened to others equally as innocent as myself of wrong-doing. In the daytime, when I was like others, I reproached myself; goodness knows I loathed myself and what I had to do in order to "live." I wished I might really die, for I was tired—so frightfully tired and sick of it all. But I knew of no way to accomplish this, so I had to bear it all, fasting until my voracious, disgusting appetites got the better of me.

I decided there must be some information on my kind, particularly in this area where vampire legends are rife, so I took to haunting reading rooms. It was there I met Maria. She told me, after we knew each other better, that she was doing graduate work in regional superstitions and had decided that her thesis would treat of the history of vampirism. She found it terribly amusing, but at the same time frightening: Didn't I? I fear I saw nothing laughable about it, but I held my peace. Why, I could have done a thesis for her that would have driven some mild-mannered prof completely out of his mind! I kept my knowledge to myself, though; I didn't want to scare Maria.

She was like a flash of sunshine in a darkened room. She made each day worth living. For the first time the hunger pangs ceased. Ceased for one week, then two. I was certain I was cured. Perhaps, I thought, the whole thing was just a dream and I am finally awake.

I felt then I had the right to tell her of my love. She looked infinitely sad. She wasn't certain, she said. She knew she was awfully fond of me, but she was confused. She had just come away from the States, trying to make up her mind about someone dear, whom she didn't want to hurt, and she wanted a breather. I said I would wait up to and through eternity, if she wished.

Things, went along peacefully then. We would walk for hours together, walk in complete silence and understanding. My strength seemed to be returning more day by day. We went far afield in search of material for her thesis. She would track down the most minute speck of hearsay, to get authenticity.

One day, in our wanderings, I thoughtlessly let myself be led too near my resting place. One of the locals mentioned a "place of horror" nearby and Maria wanted to investigate. I had no choice. We poked amid the still fustiness of the deserted mausoleum I knew so well. She thought it odd that the door was unlocked. I said, yes, wasn't it. Then she saw the box, that gleaming copper box which Eve had so thoughtfully provided. She stroked it gently, commenting on its beauty, and before I could prevent it or divert her attention, she had lifted the heavy lid exposing the disarranged shroud, the remains of one or two hapless small creatures, the horrible blood-stained satin lining. She screamed and dropped the lid, somehow pinching her finger. She hopped on one foot, as one usually does to fight down sudden pain. Then she was clinging to me, thoroughly frightened.

"What does it mean, Tod?"

I quieted her with the usual platitudes. Then I was kissing that poor, red little finger. Without warning to myself or her, I nipped it affectionately. A warm glow spread through me; there was a taste more delightful than fine old brandy, or vintage wine, and I knew irrevocably that I was not cured; no, nor ever should be! And I knew, too, that I wanted Maria—not just as a man longs for the woman he loves—but to drink of the fountain of her life, that warm, intoxicating fountain, greedily, joyously. She never knew what went through my mind at that moment. If I could have killed myself then, I would have, and with no compunction. But there is more to killing a revenant than that. The Church knows the procedure. I hurried Maria home as fast as I could and told her I had to go away for a week on business. She believed me and said she would miss me. But I didn't go away. That night I fought a losing battle with myself, and then and every night thereafter, I returned to her, partook of her and slunk away, loathing myself. I knew that I must soon kill the one being I loved above all others, kill, too, her immortal soul, and there was nothing I could do to prevent it.

She began to fade visibly. When I "returned" in a week, she was so ill that a few steps tired her. Her appetite all but vanished. She seemed genuinely glad to see me. She was beset by nightmares, she said. Could I help her get some rest? I took her to a physician who sagely prescribed a change in climate, rest and a diet rich in blood and iron, gave her a prescription for sedatives, and called it a day.

You know how she looked when you saw her. The day was approaching when she would have no more blood, when life as you know it would stop and she would become like me. Somehow I couldn't take her with me without some warning, but I didn't know how to do it. You see, since I was an innocent victim myself. I could speak, could warn my intended victim, because although my soul had all but died, there was still a spark that evil hadn't touched. I knew she would think it a joke if I told her about myself without warning.

Then, happily for me, you came along. I knew you would sense something amiss and I didn't care. I was almost certain of her love, and I decided to seize the few minutes left me and devil take the hindmost! When you told her to confront me, you gave me the happiest days of my life. For this I thank you sincerely. For what I have done and will ask you to do, forgive me!

Maria asked me directly, as you had known she would. I replied frankly, sparing her nothing. I told her that the fact that this life had been wished on me, as it were, gave me some rights, and that I could tell her how to rid herself of me, if she wished. Then she turned to me, her large, lovely eyes thoughtful.

"Tod, dearest," she said softly, "I must die some day, really die, so what difference does it make when? I only know that I love you. Why wait until I'm decrepit and alone, with only a few memories to look back on? Why not now, with you, where life doesn't really stop? With all I've read about this, don't you think I could free myself if I wished?"

I still wonder if she really believed me. We were married three days later. I never told her what her life with me would be like—that one day I would desert her, fearing and hating her rivalry for the very source of my life, and the ghastly chain would continue. I couldn't. I loved her so, Morris, can you understand that? I couldn't betray her then and I can't now.

On the second night of our marriage, she died as you know it, in my arms. I don't think she knows it yet. But it won't be long until she does discover it. We were quite alive when you found us; she was in an hypnotic state induced by her condition. She heard and saw nothing. But I knew. And I must keep my faith. I must, and you are the only one who can help me.

If you will show this to a priest, he will gladly accompany you to the place in Konigstein, where we rest during the morning in a new "bed" I had specially constructed for us. I couldn't bring Maria to that other bed of corruption. A map of how to get there is enclosed. There you will perform the ancient, effective rites, and you will lay us to rest together, as we wish. That is all I ask....

When I had finished reading I stared at nothing, trying to force myself to think. This was "all" he asked. In substance, he wished me to murder the girl I loved. I could refuse; I could ignore his request. I could even doubt the verity of his statements. He might be a madman. But I didn't doubt. I believed every word, and I knew I would do as he asked.

That she had gone willingly I didn't doubt. I no longer hated him so much; rather I pitied him, the hapless victim of a horrible chain of circumstance.

I found the priest, a venerable, gentle soul, after much searching. The younger men had looked at me searchingly, laughed and told me to read the Good Book for consolation, and to lay off the bottle. Father Kalman was understanding, with the wisdom of the very old.

"Yes, my son," he said, "I will go. Many might doubt, but I believe. Lucifer roams the earth in many guises and must be recognized and exorcised."

It was five o'clock in the morning when we approached the mausoleum. The Good Father explained that the "creatures of darkness" had to be back in their resting places before the cock crew. At night they drew sustenance; during the morning they slept.

There was a gleaming copper casket. Tod had not lied. We approached it warily. In it was nothing but grisly remains, bloodstains and dust. We drew back, fearful. Then we saw the other, newer casket in richest mahogany, almost twice the width of the copper box: Their bridal bed!

They lay together, his arm about her. She wore a gown of palest blue, but oh, that mockery of a gown! Stained it was with fresh blood which had seeped onto it from him. Obviously she had not taken to prowling yet. His mouth was dark, rich with blood, slightly open in a half-smile. His hand pressed her fair head close to his chest. She lay trustingly within the circle of his arm, like a small child. The priest crossed himself. The bodies twitched slightly.

"You know what you must do," Father Kalman whispered.

I nodded, the pit of my stomach churning madly. I couldn't do it! Not Maria, the lovely. But I knew I would; I had to. She must not wake again to see that blood-stained gown or to wonder at her husband's gory lips. She should know rest, eternal rest.

Father Kalman circled the box several times, ringing his small bell, and at one point laid a crucifix upon each of their chests. Their faces writhed and I felt my skin creep.

Then, chanting in a low, firm voice, the priest gave me the signal. Together we drove two long stakes, dipped first in Holy Water, home, piercing their hearts simultaneously.

The bodies leapt forward in the box, straining against the stake, and a horrible, drawn-out wail shattered the stillness of the tomb. The priest dropped to his knees and I clapped my hands over my ears, but the dreadful shriek penetrated. My stomach turned over and I retched. The Good Father followed suit. We were no supermen and our bodies and our very souls revolted against this monstrous thing.

"Let us finish, my son," the priest said slowly, after a time, his face the color of ashes. "We must bury these dead, that they may sleep in consecrated ground."

I couldn't. I had to see her again before it was done. She lay, small and fragile as ever, her face calm, only there was no trace of life now. She was still and white, as only the dead—the truly dead—are. Tod's arm was flung across her chest, as if to protect her. I made myself move the arm, resting her head upon his shoulder, where it belonged. Then, as I looked, there was just Maria. Tod was gone and only a handful of dust lay piled up around the stake. It was enough. I slammed the lid shut.

Looking back now, I can see it was all for the best. Ria was different—apart from other women. A dreamer, a mystic, too easily influenced by the bizarre and un-normal. I, on the other hand, am practical almost to a fault. Had she married me I might have crushed in her the very thing that drew me to her. In time she might have grown to hate me.

Hunter, on the other hand, was a student. Introspective, given to romanticizing. Susceptible to suggestion. Had I been confronted with an Eve, I should have run like hell. To him, though, she was cloaked in mystery; hence, more desirable. What better choice for him ultimately than Ria? That Ria had to die to achieve her happiness is of no real importance. Life is a transitory thing anyway.

Sometimes, though, when I look at Ria's picture, it's hard to be practical. She was everything I shall ever want.

I had never been to Europe before the summer of 1947. I went to find Maria, to marry her. Instead, I found and murdered her, and I will never go back again.

Isle of the Undead

by Lloyd Arthur Eshbach

1: A Horror from the Past

A drab gray sheet of cloud slipped stealthily from the moon's round face, like a shroud slipping from the face of one long dead, a coldly phosphorescent face from which the eyes had been plucked. Yellow radiance fell toward a calm, oily sea, seeking a narrow bank of fog lying low on the water, penetrating its somber mass like frozen yellow fingers.

Vilma Bradley shuddered and shrank against Clifford Darrell's brawny form. "It's — it's ghastly, Cliff!" she said.

"Ghastly?" Darrell leaned against the rail, laughing softly. "One cocktail too many — that's the answer. It's given you the jitters. Listen!" Faintly from the salon

came strains of dance music and the rhythmic shuffle of feet. "A nifty yacht, a South Sea moon, a radio dance orchestra, dancers — and little Clifford! And you call it ghastly!" Almost savagely his arms tightened about her, and the bantering note left his voice. "I'm crazy about you, Vilma."

She tried to laugh, but it was an unconvincing sound. "It's the moon, Cliff — I guess. I never saw it like that before. Something's going to happen — something dreadful. I just know it!"

"Oh — be sensible, Vilma!" There was a hint of impatience in Cliff's deep voice. A gorgeous girl in his arms — dark-haired, dark-eyed, made for love — and she talked of dreadful things which were going to happen because the moon looked screwy.

She released herself and glanced out over the sea. "I know I'm silly, but —" Her voice froze and her slender body stiffened. "Cliff — look!"

Darrell spun around, and as he stared, he felt a dryness seeping into his throat, choking him....

Out of the winding-sheet of fog into the moonlight crept a strange, strange craft, her crumbling timbers blackened and rotted with incredible age. The corpse of a ship, she seemed, resurrected from the grave of the sea. Her prow thrust upward like a scimitar bent backward, hovering over the gaunt ruin of a cabin whose seaward sides were formed by port and starboard bows. From a shallow pit amidships jutted the broken arm of a mast, its splintered tip pointing toward the blindly watching moon. The stern, thickly covered with the moldering encrustations of age, curved inward above the strange high poop, beneath which lay another cabin. And along either side of her worm-eaten freeboard ran a row of apertures like oblong portholes. Out of these projected great oars, long, unwieldy, as somberly black as the rest of the ancient hulk.

Now a sound drifted across the waters, the steady, rhythmic br-rr-oom, br-rr-oom, br-rr-oom of a drum beating time for the rowers. Its hollow thud checked the heart, set it to throbbing in tempo with its own weary pulse. Ghostly fingers, dripping dread, crawled up Darrell's spine.

Stiff-lipped, Vilma gasped: "What — what is it?"

Cliff answered in a dry husky voice, the words seeming to trip over an awkward tongue. "It's — it's — it can't be, damn it! — but it's a galley, a ship from the days of Alexander the Great! What's it doing — here — now?"

Closer she came through the moon-path, a frothing lip of brine curling away from her swelling prow. Closer — her course crossing that of the Ariel — and the watchers saw her crew! They gasped, and the blood ebbed from their faces.

Men of ancient Persia, clad in leather kirtles and rusted armor, and they were hideous! In the yellow moon-glow Cliff could see them clearly now — a lookout standing motionless in the stem, the steersman on the poop-deck, the drummer squatting beside the broken mast, the rowers in the pit — and all, all were a bloodless white, the skin of their faces puffed and bloated and horribly wrinkled, like flesh that had been under water a long time.

Dead men ... men whose movements were stiffly wooden ... as dead as their faces. But most horrible was the fact that they were there, that they moved at all!

"A queer mirage, isn't it?" A hollow voice spoke suavely behind them.

Vilma gasped at the sudden sound, and they whirled. A foot away stood the tall, lean figure of the Ariel's captain, Leon Corio. A queer smile twisted his thin lips.

"What's the idea — sneaking up on us?" Darrell demanded angrily. He didn't like this man, hadn't liked him from the moment he had approached Cliff to sell him the yacht. But Cliff had bought the craft because she was a bargain, and in accordance with their agreement he had hired Corio as captain.

The tall man's smile remained fixed, and he bowed gravely. "Sorry, sir. I always walk softly. A habit, I suppose." He gestured toward the galley. "It looks quite life-like, don't you think so?"

"Life-like?" Cliff spoke between his teeth as he again faced the black ship. "It looks dead to me!"

The galley had almost reached them now, veering sharply to draw up beside the Ariel. The drum quieted, and the oars trailed in the water, motionless except for the swaying imparted by the waves. A musty, age-old odor filtered through the air like a breath from a grave. The music and dancing had stopped. A fear-filled hush shrouded the yacht.

Vilma drew Cliff's arm about her shoulder. He glanced back at the motionless captain.

"Do something, Corio!" he rasped. "Don't stand there like a dummy!"

Corio nodded with his same queer smile. His hand darted to an inside pocket, came out bearing a curious instrument like four twisted cones of silver bound together with silver thongs. As he raised this to his mouth, his eyelids were slits behind which burned the embers of his eyes.

Out over the sea crept a single note, deep, hollow, laden with eery minor wailings — a sound that summoned imperatively, yet a sound that repelled. It was a moan, hideous as the moan of a dying demon. It raked the heart with fear-tipped claws. It rose, and fell, and rose again, and as it died, it awakened the crew of the ancient galley to motion, sweeping them in a horde to the rail of the yacht.

Cliff swung toward Corio in bursting fury, fury mingled with dread. His fist lashed out at that glittering silver instrument and the face behind it, but Corio avoided him like a wraith, still smiling fixedly, the horn again at his lips. Cliff cursed, and hurled himself through the air. One hand caught a bony shoulder; he felt fingers like hooks close on his own throat. He wrenched free, landing a stunning blow on Corio's face — saw him reel and crash to the deck — and then he heard Vilma scream!

He whirled. She was struggling between two of the flabby-faced things from the galley! In an instant he was upon them, his fist thudding against icy flesh, burying itself in something horribly soft and yielding. Startled, Cliff swung a second blow; and an arm, tomb-cold and strong as the tentacle of an octopus, wrapped itself around him — a vise of thin-covered bone! A dead, drowned face peered over his shoulder, staring blankly. Other arms seized his legs, and though he struggled and writhed with the strength of a mounting fear, he was borne to the rail. Over they went, and dropped to the rotting deck of the galley.

A numbness was creeping through him like a contagion, spreading from those crushing hands of ice. His struggles ceased. With eyes that turned stiffly in their sockets he looked for Vilma, saw her raised high above the heads of two other pallid creatures, saw them climb over the rail. Then the blackness of a dank and musty cabin enveloped him; and he was dropped with jarring force.

His captors bulked black against the moonlit doorway, treading soundlessly, and were gone.

Cliff lay in rigid paralysis, every sense keenly alive, his mind striving to clutch a single spar of reason in this chaotic whirlpool of the incredible. This couldn't be! Soon he'd awaken to laugh at his absurd nightmare.... Yet it seemed horribly real.... It was real!

From the Ariel boiled a fearful bedlam. Screams of terror. Curses. Then other shadows loomed in the doorway, and Vilma, motionless and rigid, was dropped brutally beside him on the spongy floor.

Furiously Cliff struggled against the maddening restraint of paralysis. He couldn't lie here helpless! Vilma needed him! He'd — he'd have to do something. With an effort that studded his forehead with rounded drops of sweat and sent the blood throbbing through the distended veins of his neck, he sought to move. And like a cord snapping, his invisible bonds fell from him.

He was crouching over Vilma, rubbing her wrists, calling to her, when again he heard the silver horn of Corio. A low droning utterly unlike the note that had awakened the galley's crew, it drifted languidly along a channel of endless sleep. It seeped through the ear-drums, touching every nerve-tip with resistless lassitude. Doggedly Cliff fought against the sound, pressing his hands over his ears, gritting his teeth, holding his eyelids wide. Yet he felt his muscles weaken, began to relax, knew dimly that his mind, sodden with drowsiness, was creeping toward the pits of slumber — and the vibrant drone ended!

His head cleared rapidly, and he bent over Vilma. As he touched a limp arm, he knew she had passed from paralysis into a deep, quiet sleep. He shook her. It was useless. He listened, heard her steady breathing; and at that instant realized that the noises from the yacht had ceased.

Rising, he strode toward the square of chalky moonlight. A foot away he halted, fell back. He had heard a faint footfall, had seen an armor-clad figure climbing over the rail! With silent haste he flung himself down beside Vilma.

And there he lay while the crew of the galley carried his friends from the Ariel, all slumped in that unnatural sleep, and stretched them out on the floor of the black cabin. Unmoving, he watched through narrow lids till all save Corio had been carried aboard, and the drowned things had gone back to their places in the rowers' pits. Again the hollow voice of the drum began throbbing through the silence, and the oars creaked a faint accompaniment. He could feel the galley cleaving the oily sea.

On his feet, he peered through the doorway. The backs of the rowers rose and fell with stiff, mechanical rhythm. Beyond the galley's stern came the yacht, slinking along like a thief, only one dim light showing, her Diesel engines purring almost soundlessly.

He turned and bent over Vilma, still in thrall to that strange deep slumber. As he traced the delicate outlines of her lovely face, now so lifeless and pale, bitter wrath flared within him, wrath and hatred for Leon Corio. But as he thought of the ghastly undead things out there in the galley pit, thought of this water-soaked anachronism which had no right to be afloat, his skin crisped with a sense of foreboding, a fear of what was yet to come. He must do something!

Stepping over the still forms of his friends, he moved to the forward wall where a beam of radiance crept fearfully through a gap between two boards. His hands touched the hull — and he jerked them away. Rotten, clammy, like a decayed corpse, partly frozen. Crouching, he peered through.

Far ahead, a blotch of evil blackness squatted on the horizon, an island crouching low like a black beast ready to spring. Around it the moonlight seemed to dim, as though it were striving to hide some nameless horror. Interminably Cliff watched while the shadowed mass drew closer ... closer....

They were headed for a towering wall of black basalt; and as the galley neared it, Cliff saw that it bore striking resemblance to a gigantic human skull, its rounded surface broken by caves that the sea had carved into hollow eye-sockets and an empty nasal cavity. The rock wall ended high above the water; beneath it lay a gaping chasm of pitchy darkness. And the galley, drum silenced, oars at rest, slid under the ledge, into the mouth of the skull!

Just before total blackness fell, Cliff sprang to Vilma's side and raised her in his arms. If he hoped to do anything, he must do it now! He groped his way to the starboard bow and moved one hand along the dank timbers, searching. He found what he sought, a wide gap at the edge of a board. Gently lowering Vilma to the floor, he gripped the slimy wood with both hands and thrust outward mightily. A wide strip of decayed timber burst free. He dropped it into the sea and attacked the next board. In moments a wide irregular opening yawned in the galley's hull.

Leaning out, Cliff looked down. He could see nothing. Then suddenly a faint light appeared, and he heard the hum of the Ariel's motors as she entered the cave. The humming ceased instantly, but the faint light persisted.

Now he could see the blackness of waters, a rock wall beyond. He drew back — and a he did so, he heard movements on deck! At any moment the rowers might enter! He'd have to risk a drop into the water with Vilma — there was nothing else to do. If only she were conscious!

He stooped and raised her, holding her firmly with one arm. Gripping the hull with the other, he climbed through the opening, inhaled deeply, and dropped! A heart-stopping plunge — and cold water closed over them. Down, down — then they shot upward, reached the surface; and even as Cliff gulped a single gasping breath, something struck his skull a blinding, stunning blow! The oars!

With rapidly numbing arms and legs Cliff kicked and flailed the water, striving for land. Dimly he knew he no longer held Vilma; dimly he visioned her as were those ghastly undead; then his body scraped on something hard, and a blackness that was not physical blotted out consciousness.

2: The Dreadful Isle

Red-hot hammers pounding against his temples wakened Cliff Darrell. He opened his eyes to stare into total darkness crawling with mental monsters spawned by his pain-stabbed brain. He lay half immersed in shallow brine, his head resting on a jagged stone just above the surface. Struggling to his hands and knees, he shook his head from side to side, dumbly, like an animal in pain. Something had hit him — and now he was in water — and there was no light. What had happened? Where was Vilma?

Vilma! He groaned. He remembered now. They had dropped — and his head had struck something — and — and — maybe she was floating out there even now, dead eyes staring upward.

"Vilma!" he cried, his voice pleading. "Vilma!"

Only a mocking echo answered him. There was no other sound, not even the whisper of waves swishing among the rocks.

Cliff pressed his hands fiercely against his throbbing head. The pain had become a madness, matched only by the agony of his own helplessness. He felt his reason reeling; he fought an insane desire to fling himself shrieking into that silent expanse of water to search for Vilma; then with a tremendous physical effort he jarred himself back to sanity.

He staggered to his feet, groped stumblingly over the rocks away from the water. His hand touched a rock wall broken and pitted by the action of the sea; and he crept slowly inland, feeling his way like a blind man. As he plodded on his thoughts blended into one fixed idea: he must get to light, must get light to search for Vilma.

Gradually the insensate pounding in his head abated, and strength returned to his body. When at last he saw light beyond a narrow fissure around an angle in the cavern, he had almost recovered. In moments he was gazing out over a plain bathed in the glow of a leprous moon. As he stared, he shivered; and it was not because of the cold draft drawing through the fissure, fanning his brine-drenched body.

Grim and starkly forbidding the plain lay before him, dead as the frozen landscape of the moon. Once there had been life there, but now only the skeletons of trees remained, lifting their wasted limbs in rigid pleading to an unresponsive sky. Some, there were, that had fallen, uprooted by the fury of passing hurricanes; these lay like the scattered bones of a dismembered giant, age-blackened, and painted with hoarfrost by the brushes of moonlight. Feebly the dead forest stirred under the touch of a moaning wind, and the gaunt shadows cast by the trees seemed to be multi-armed monsters slithering over the rocky earth.

He looked beyond the trees, and he saw light. Little squares of pale radiance cut high in the walls of an ancient black castle. Castle? Cliff frowned. He could liken it to nothing else, though he could not recall ever having seen a castle which thrust curving, needle-thin spires into the sky like a devil's horns.

Impatiently Cliff stepped from the wall of rock and glanced along a path that writhed through the forest; glanced — and crouched swiftly, a low cry escaping him. A single spot of water on a smooth, flat stone! A spot shaped like a woman's shoe! Vilma had passed this way!

But — might it not have been some other woman from the Ariel? No! They had been carried — and even if they had walked, their feet were dry!

Like a hound on the scent, Cliff Darrell sped along the serpentine path. The wind moaned above him, and the soughing branches seemed to whisper croaking warnings, but he ran on, his eyes constantly seeking signs of Vilma's course. Here a drop of water shaken from her drenched skirt, there another; and Cliff blessed the full moon whose light made possible his trailing of the almost invisible spoor.

Now he had passed beyond the dead forest and was moving toward the castle. The trail had been growing steadily fainter, but he managed to follow it. It led him toward a narrow stone stairway climbing crookedly to a misshapen opening in the wall. Light glowed faintly lurid somewhere deep within; and now Cliff heard a blasphemous sound belch from the depths of the castle — a wheezing, sardonic croaking like the moan of a demoniac organ, rumbling an obscene dirge. His hair bristled, and he stopped short.

He looked at the steps, searching for the fading trail — and he stiffened. There on the second step was an irregular blotch of moisture! What did it mean? Had Vilma crouched there? Had she ascended those steps? Entered?

With drawn face he began to skirt the base of the black building, searching every nook and cranny, scanning the bare walls. His heart lay like ballast in his breast. If — if something had lured Vilma into that demon-infested vault ... he checked the thought.

Suddenly he cursed. Mechanically he had begun to measure his stride in time with the doleful dirge from the castle. He stalked on with altered pace. As he rounded the corner at the rear of the structure, he saw a shadow outlined against the sky, crouching on a ledge below one of the little windows. He looked again — cried:

"Vilma!"

The figure above him stirred, looked down, then climbed hastily earthward. It was Vilma ... Vilma, with black hair hanging stringily about her head, face pale, eyes fixed in the wideness of fear ... Vilma, with her wet clothing clinging to the lovely contours of her symmetrical body.

"Oh, Cliff!" she gasped, a dry sob choking her. "Thank God — thank God!"

She clung to him, her face hidden against his shoulder, quivering uncontrollably. Then tears came, saving tears, relieving her pent-up emotions.

Cliff said nothing, only held her close, strongly protective. And gradually he felt the tempest of terror subside. At last she looked up. Some of the dread had gone from her face, and she tried to smile.

"I guess — I can't take it," she said.

Cliff shook his head solemnly. "You're a game girl, Vilma! You've nerve enough for two men. If you can, tell me what happened. Or if you'd rather let it wait, just say so."

"I'll feel better if I get it off my chest," she said. "You probably saw those — things — carry me from the yacht." Cliff nodded. "Well, I was just about paralyzed when they dropped me in their terrible boat. I remember, you tried to arouse me; then that horn blew, and I just seemed to float away in an ocean of sleep.

"After that I can remember nothing till I awoke with water filling my eyes and nose and mouth, choking me. Someone's arms were around me — it must have been you, Cliff — and then they weren't there any more, and I struggled wildly, out of my wits. I don't know how I got to shore, but I did, and I lay there in the shadow of the galley, choking and gagging, but afraid to cough. It wasn't altogether dark, and I could see those dreadful things with people hanging over their shoulders, carrying them along a narrow ledge close to the water's edge, heading inland. I thought maybe you were one of those limp bodies; and I — I almost died of fright. After a while the last one had gone, and the light went out. Then I heard another pair of feet moving over the rocks. Corio, I suppose. The sound died — and I was alone.

"That place was awful, Cliff. The blackness almost drove me mad. I wanted to scream, but I was afraid to. Some terrible weight seemed to be crushing my lungs. If I followed those undead things, they might capture me, but it seemed worse to stay there in that dreadful dark.

"I got out of there somehow, though it seemed to take hours. Then I didn't know what to do. I stood at the edge of the dead forest trying to decide; trying, too, to keep myself from shrieking and running — anywhere. Then Corio's horn blew again — a sound, Cliff, worse than anything I've ever heard. It — it was a wicked sound, promising to fulfill every foul desire that ever tainted a human mind. It repelled, yet it lured irresistibly. And — I answered!"

She stopped, and buried her face in her hands. After a moment she went on. "The sound stopped just as I found myself crawling on hands and knees up the stone stairway on the other side. Another started — that awful groaning — music — but it didn't draw me. I ran down the steps and scurried away like a rabbit trying to find a place to hide.

"After a while I came back — I thought you must be in there — and I climbed up to the window. And — and — Cliff, it's hellish!"

Her eyes, boring into his, widened in the same rigid terror he had seen in them when he joined her.

"We could go back to the cove and get away on the Ariel, Vilma," Cliff said stonily. "And if you think we should, we will. But — I brought our friends here, and — well, I want to get them out if I can."

With an effort Vilma nodded. "Of course. We can't do anything else."

He released her and stepped up to the wall.

"I'm going to see what's going on in there," he said. "You wait here till I come down."

In sudden dread Vilma seized his arm. "No, Cliff. I couldn't stand waiting here alone. I'll go with you."

He nodded understandingly. And together they began climbing the precipitous wall, fitting hands and feet in step-like crevices that made progress fairly rapid. Soon they were crouching on a wide stone ledge, clinging to thin, rusted bars, staring into the black castle.

3: The Steps of Torture

A gigantic hall lay before them, a single chamber whose walls were the walls of the castle, whose arched ceiling rose far above them. Directly below their window a stone platform jutted from the wall, spreading entirely across the chamber. A stone altar squatted in the center of the platform, a strangely phosphorescent fire smoldering on its top. And from the altar descended a wide, wide stairway ending in the middle of the hall. All this Cliff saw in a single sweeping glance; afterward he had eyes for nothing save the lethal horror of a mad, mad scene, revealed by the dim radiance of the altar fire.

Behind the altar stood five huge figures clad in long, hooded cloaks of scarlet. The central figure had arms raised wide, his cloak spread like the wings of some bloody bird of prey; and from his lips came a guttural incantation, a blasphemous chant in archaic Latin, in time with the wheeze of the buried organ. Now his arms dropped, and he was silent.

From the room below came a concerted whine of ceremonial devotion, a hollow, hungry wail. It rose from the bloodless lips of strangely assorted human figures ranging down the center of the long stairway in two facing columns. A hundred or more there must have been, representing half as many periods and countries, according to their strange and ancient costumes. Men in the armor of medieval Persia — the crew of the black galley; yellow-haired Vikings; hawk-faced Egyptians with leather-brown skins; half-naked islanders; red-sashed pirates from the Spanish main; men of today! And about all, like the dampness that clings to a tombstone, hovered a cloud of — death! The undead!

Cliff's gaze roved over the tensely waiting columns, then leaped to the foot of the stairs. There, cowering dumbly like sheep in a slaughter-pen, were his friends from the Ariel. All clothing had been stripped from them, and they stood waiting in waxen, statuesque stiffness. He saw then that three others lay prone before the stone altar, naked and ominously still.

And far down at the very end of the hall stood Leon Corio, draped in a hooded cape of unbroken black, a glint of silver in his hand — his horn of drugging sounds.

Now, as though at a silent command, a girl left the group and began to mount the stairs, as those motionless three must have mounted! Vivacious Ann — she had been the life of Cliff's yacht party; but now she was — changed. Her blanched face was rigid with inexpressible terror despite the semi-stupor which numbed her senses. Her nude body glowed like marble in the dim light. Horribly, her feet began their climb with a little catch step suggested by the moaning chant of that cracked organ note.

She reached the first of the undead, and Cliff saw light glint on a knife-blade. A crimson gash appeared in the flesh of her thigh; and dead lips touched that wound, drank thirstily. The girl strode on, blood gleaming darkly on the white skin. A second drank of the crimson flow — a third — and the blood ceased gushing forth.

Another knife flashed — and lips closed again and again on a redly dripping wound. And the girl with the unchanging pace of a robot climbed the stairway to its very top — climbed while fiendish corpses drank her life's blood — climbed, to sink down on the altar.

One of the red-clad figures stooped over her, lifted her, buried long teeth in her throat — and Cliff saw his face.... His own face paled, and talons of fear raked his brain. Those others on the stairs — they were abhorrent, zombies freed from the grave. But this monster! A vampire vested with the lust and cruelty and power of hell!

He lowered her, finally, and she sank down, lay still, beside the other three.

Another began the hellish climb, a giant of a man with a thickly muscled torso. Cliff knew him instantly; and his heart seemed to stop. Leslie Starke! They'd played football together. A brave man — a fighter. He mounted the stairway with the same little catch step, the same plodding stiffness. No resistance, no struggle — only a hell of fear on his face.

The marrow melted from Cliff Darrell's bones. What — what could he do against a power that did that to Les Starke? He tried to swallow, but the saliva had dried on his tongue. He wanted to turn to Vilma, but he could not wrench his eyes from the frightful spectacle.

Up the stone steps Starke strode. And no blade leaped toward him; no thirsty lips closed on his flesh! In an unwavering line he mounted toward the cowled monster in the center of the dais, like a puppet on the end of a string; mounted to pause before the stone altar, to lie on it, head bent back, throat bared.... Mercifully Cliff regained enough control to close his eyes.

He opened them at a gasp from Vilma; saw the vampire raise the flaccid body of Les Starke and hurl it far from him, to crash to the stone steps, to roll and thud and tumble, down and down, sickeningly, to lie awkwardly twisted on the floor before his companions!

And another began to climb the long stone steps....

All through the interminable night Cliff and Vilma crouched on the ledge, staring through the barred window. A hundred times they would have fled to escape the maddening scene, but they could not move. Senses reeled before the awful monotony of the ceaseless climbing, their eyes smarted with fixed staring, their tongues and throats were parched to desert dryness; yet only after hours of endless watching, only after the last victim had climbed the steps, did the edge of terror dull, and a modicum of control return to their bodies.

Stiffly Cliff looked over his shoulder. A faint tinge of gray rimmed the sea on the eastern horizon.

"Almost daylight," he whispered hoarsely.

Vilma nodded, her gaze still held by that chamber of horror. Cliff followed the direction of her eyes; and saw Corio standing like a great bat in his hooded cape close to the far wall. He raised his four-piped horn to his lips. And the instrument's fourth note crept through the room.

It was a doleful sound, a cry like the cry Death itself might possess; yet oddly — and horribly — it was soothing, promising the peace of endless sleep. And touched by its power, the columns of undead stiffened, thinned to wraiths, flowed as water flows down the stone steps, vanished!

The dead-alive — those five vampires in crimson cowls — looked upward uneasily. The shadows under the roof were graying with the light of dawn. Cliff could sense their thought. Before sunrise they must be in their tombs under the castle, to sleep until another night. With one accord they strode down the stairs, past Corio who had prostrated himself, and entered a black opening in the wall. With their departure the altar fire dimmed to a sullen ember.

Corio arose. He was alone in the chamber save for that dead, broken body lying in a twisted heap at the foot of the stairs, and those other half-alive wretches stretched out before the altar. Now, Cliff told himself, was the time for him to get in there at Corio; now was the time to rescue his friends — but he continued to crouch, unmoving.

Again Corio blew on his silver horn, and a faint cry leaped from Vilma's tensed lips. The luring note that had drawn her, Cliff thought hazily; then he thought of nothing save the sound, the sound that promised him all he could desire. Earth and its dominion, his for the taking — if he answered that call!... Then even the sound eluded his senses, and he heard only the promise.... He must answer, must claim what was rightfully his!

But those half-dead creatures — sight of their stirring steadied his staggering sanity. Here and there heads lifted and bloodless husks of bodies tried to rise. In the pallid light they seemed like corpses, freed from newly opened graves. Some could only reach their knees; others rose to uncertain limbs. And all moved down the stairway toward Corio, answering his summons; followed as he made his slow way toward the opening in the wall, still blowing the single note — the note that promised Earth and all it held....

Cliff glanced toward Vilma — and she was not there. He looked down, saw her far below, dropping from crack to crevice with amazing speed and daring, hastening toward — Corio!

The thought jarred any lingering taint of allurement from Cliff's mind. He must stop her. He swung around, ignoring the cramped stiffness of his legs, and started down the steep wall. Down, down, recklessly, with Corio's horn-note only a faintly heard sound fading behind him.

Now he saw Vilma reach the rocks below and dash around the corner of the castle, and he cursed, redoubling his speed. Down — down — and suddenly the ancient rock crumbled underfoot. For an instant he hung from straining fingertips — then dropped.

A smashing impact — a stone that slid beneath him — and his head crashed against the castle wall. Through a fiery mist of pain he pictured Vilma in the grasp of Corio. The mist thickened — grew black — engulfed him.

4: In Corio's Hands

Cliff awoke with the sun glaring down on his face. He opened his eyes, and stabbing lances of light pierced his eyeballs. Momentarily blinded, he pressed his hands across his face and struggled erect. There was a sick feeling in his stomach, and the back of his head throbbed incessantly. He touched the aching area, and winced. A lump like an egg thrust out his scalp; it was sticky with blood. He stood there, weaving from side to side, trying to recall something....

As memory came, he groaned. Vilma! He had last seen her racing madly toward Corio, lured by his damned horn. It was daylight now; the sun had risen at least an hour ago. An hour — with Vilma gone!

Shaking his head to clear it, and gritting his teeth at the pain, he stalked along the wall. Turning the corner he strode on toward the crooked steps. The lifeless terrain reeled dizzily, but he went on resolutely. The pain in his head was fading to a dull ache; and as he mounted the steps, strength seemed to flow back into his legs. With every sense taut he passed into the gloom of the castle.

A quick glance he cast about — saw the body of Starke lying where it had fallen. No use to examine it; there was no life there. His gaze swept up the slope of the stairway to the altar at its head, lingered on the phosphorescent eye of light still glowing there. Then he shrugged grimly and moved on to the doorway in the wall. Warily he peered in.

As his eyes adjusted themselves to the greater darkness, he saw a narrow stairway leading downward into a shadowy corridor. Somewhere in the tunnel's depths a faint light shone. He could see nothing more. He moved stealthily down the damp, dank stairs.

At the bottom he paused, listening. He could hear nothing. A hundred feet ahead, the corridor divided in two; a burning torch was thrust in the wall at the junction. Cliff nodded with satisfaction. Corio must be somewhere near by; for only a human needed light.

Silently Cliff strode along the corridor. At the fork he hesitated, then chose the right branch, for light glowed faintly along that passageway. The other led downward, black as the pits of hell.

A doorway appeared in the wall ahead, and he moved warily, with fists clenched. Flickering torchlight filtered into the corridor. There was no audible sound. Now Cliff peered into a small chamber, and gasped in sudden horror, his eyes staring unwinkingly at a spectacle incredibly pitiful.

Here were the passengers of the Ariel, whitely naked, and lying in little groups on the cold stone floor, huddled together for warmth. Their faces turned toward Darrell as he stood in the doorway, but there was no recognition in the vacuous eyes, no thought, no intelligence, and little life in the wide-mouthed stares. It seemed as though their souls had been drained from their bodies with their blood.

Sickened, Cliff turned away, cursing his own helplessness to aid them, cursing Leon Corio who was responsible for their plight. Black wrath gripped him as he moved on.

Again the corridor branched, and again he kept to the right. Suddenly he halted, ears straining. He heard the sound of a voice — the hollow voice of Corio! It came faintly but clearly from a room at the end of the passageway. Cliff went forward slowly.

"And so, my dear," Corio was saying, "we entered into a pact with the — Master, a pact sealed with blood. In exchange for our lives we three were to bring other humans to this island for the feasting of the dead-alive. Every third month each of us must return with our cargo when the moon is full; and since we come back on alternating months, they have a constant supply of fresh blood. Usually some of our captives live from full moon to full moon before they become like those of the galley — the undead. Some of these we waken when it suits our fancy; they are not like the Masters; they awaken only when we call them — we three or the Masters.

"More than life they give us for what we do. Centuries ago pirates used this island for refuge. They — died — and they left their treasure in this castle. It lies in the room where the Masters lie; and we three receive payment in gold and gems. Tonight I receive my pay, and tomorrow I leave on the Ariel — and you go with me!"

Cliff heard Vilma answer, and even while his heart leaped with relief, he marveled at the cool scorn in her voice.

"So I go with you, do I? I'd rather climb the stairs with the rest of your victims than have anything to do with you — you monster! When Cliff Darrell finds you —"

"Darrell!" Corio's voice was a frozen sneer. "He'll do nothing! I'll find him — and he'll wish he could climb the stairs of blood! As for you, you'll go with me, and like it! A drop of my blood in your veins, and you will belong to the Master, as I do. We shall attend to that; but first there is something else — more pleasant." His words fell to an indistinguishable purr.

Still moving stealthily, Cliff hastened forward. Suddenly Vilma screamed; and he launched himself madly across the remaining distance, stood crouching at the threshold.

Vilma lay on an ancient bed, her wrists and ankles bound with leather thongs drawn about the four tall bed-posts. Only the torn remnants of her under-garments covered the rounded contours of her body, and Corio crouched over her, caressing the pink flesh. Vilma writhed beneath his touch.

Cliff growled deep in his throat as he sprang. Corio spun around and leaped aside, but he was too slow to escape Cliff's powerful lunge. One hand closed on his thin neck, and the other, a rock-like fist, made a bloody ruin of his mouth. Howling with pain, Corio tried to sink his teeth in Cliff's arm.

Cliff flung him aside, following with the easy glide of a boxer. Corio crawled to his feet, cringing, dodging before the nemesis that stalked him. Again Cliff leaped, and Corio, yellow with fear, darted around the bed and ran wildly into the hallway. At the door Cliff checked himself, reason holding him. Corio could elude him with ease in this labyrinth of passages; and his first concern was Vilma's safety.

He returned to the bed. Vilma looked up at him with such relief and thankfulness on her face that Cliff, with a little choked cry, flung himself to his knees beside the bed and kissed her hungrily. For moments their lips clung; then Cliff straightened shakily, trying to laugh.

"We've got to get out of here, sweetheart," he said. "I'm not afraid of Corio, but he knows things about this place that we don't know. After you're safe on the yacht, I'll come back and get him."

He looked around for something with which to cut her bonds. On the wall above the bed were crossed a pair of murderous-looking cutlasses. Seizing one of these, Cliff wrenched it from its fastenings and drew it through the cords.... She stood beside him, free.

"Your clothing —" Cliff began, his eyes on her almost-nude body.

She blushed and pointed mutely to a heap of rags on the floor. Her eyes flamed wrathfully. "He — he ripped them from me!"

The muscles of Cliff's jaws knotted, and he scowled as he surveyed the room for a drape or hanging to cover her. For the first time he really saw the place. All the lavish splendor of royalty had been expended on this chamber. It might have been the bedroom of a king, except that the ancient furnishings belonged to no particular period; were, in fact, the loot of raids extended over centuries. Yet despite its splendor, everything was repulsive, cloaked with the same air of unearthly gloom that hovered about the galley.

He moved toward an intricately woven tapestry; but Vilma checked him, shuddering with revulsion.

"No, Cliff — it's too much like grave clothes. Everything about this place makes my flesh crawl. I'd rather stay as I am than touch any of it!"

Cliff nodded slowly. "Let's go then."

They hurried through the corridors toward the stairway, with Cliff holding the cutlas in readiness. As they passed the room in which lay the Ariel's passengers, he tried to divert Vilma's attention, but she looked in as though hypnotized.

"I saw them before," she whispered. "It's awful."

As they started up the stairway to the great hall, Cliff took the lead. He moved with utmost caution.

"It doesn't seem right," he said uneasily. "We should hear from Corio."

At that moment they did hear from him — literally. From somewhere in the maze of tunnels came the sound of his accursed horn — the note of sleep! It swirled insidiously about their heads, numbing their senses. Cliff felt his stride falter, saw Vilma stumble, and he hurled himself forward furiously, gripping her arm.

"Hurry!" he shouted, striving to pierce the fog of sleep. "We've got to get out! Damn him!"

Vilma rallied for an instant, and they reached the top of the stairs. On — across that wide, wide room, each step a struggle.... On while the droning sound floated languidly through every nerve cell.... On — till their muscles could no longer move, and they sagged to the hard stone, asleep.

Moments later Cliff opened his eyes to meet the hellish glare of Leon Corio. Corio smiled thinly.

"So — you awaken. Good! I would have you know the fate I have planned for you. You see this?" He held the cutlas high above Darrell's throat like the blade of a guillotine. "With this I could end your life quite painlessly and quickly. It really would prove entertaining for Miss Bradley, I'm sure." He chuckled faintly behind bruised and swollen lips.

Cliff squirmed, striving to rise, then subsided instantly. He was bound hand and foot.

"I could kill you," Corio repeated musingly, "but that would lack finesse." His teeth bared in a feline smile. "And it would be such a waste — of blood! Instead, I'll take you out to the galley and let you lie there till her crew awakens tonight. They have tasted blood, and after tonight will taste none again for another month. I imagine they'll — drain you dry!" The last phrase was a vicious snarl.

Cliff heard Vilma utter a suppressed sob, and he turned his head. She lay close by, bound like him with strips of leather. Furiously Cliff strained at his fetters, but they held.

"And while you wait for those gentle Persians to awaken," Corio continued in tones caressingly soft, "you can think of your sweetheart in my arms! It may teach you not to strike your betters — though you can never profit by your lesson."

Stooping, he raised Cliff's powerful form and managed to fling him over one shoulder. Then he moved from the great hall, down the stone steps, and across the dead plain with its sighing skeleton trees. He was panting jerkily by the time he came to the fissure leading to the cove, but he reached it, despite Cliff's two hundred pounds. Without pausing, he went on into the cavern, along the rock ledge, to step at last upon the deck of the black galley.

"Pleasant thoughts," he said gently as he dropped Cliff to the spongy boards. "You have only to wait till dark!"

Cliff listened to his rapid footfalls till they died in distance; then there was no sound save his own breathing.

Gradually his eyes became accustomed to the heavy gloom, and he saw that Corio had dropped him just at the edge of the rowers' pit. There were white things down there — bones, pale as marble, scattered about aimlessly. Could — could those bones join to make the rowers who would arise with the night? It seemed absurd — was absurd — yet he knew it was so! He had seen too much to doubt it.

He rolled over on his back and stared upward into the shadows. He must lie here helpless while Corio returned to Vilma — did with her as he pleased! Perhaps he might even transform her into a blood-tainted monster like himself! He saw her again in that room of ancient splendor, spread-eagled to the bed;

and the muscles corded in his arms, and his lips strained white in a futile effort to break free.

Interminably he lay there waiting. The galley was damp with the chilling dampness of a sepulcher, and the dampness penetrated deeper and deeper. Clamping his jaws together to prevent their quivering, he struggled against a rising tide of madness which gnawed at his reason. His mind began to crunch and jangle like a machine out of gear, threatening to destroy itself.

On and on in plodding indifference the stolid moments passed, till at last Cliff realized that it was growing darker. He rolled over on his side and stared into the galley pit, eyes fixed on the inert masses of white. Soon they would move! Soon the undead would rise! His thoughts, touched by the whips of dread, sped about like slaves seeking escape from a torture pit. And abruptly out of the welter of chaotic ideas came one straw of sanity; he seized it, his heart hammering with hope.

Those Persian sailors were armed! Their swords and knives were real, for they cut flesh! Somewhere among their bones must lie sharp-edged blades!

He struggled to the edge of the pit, let his feet drop over. As they touched, he balanced precariously for an instant, then fell to his knees. He peered feverishly about among white bones, moldering garments, and rusted armor — and saw a faint glimmer of light on pointed steel. He sank forward on his face in the direction of the gleam, turned over, squirmed and writhed till he felt the cold blade against his hands. He caught it between his fingers and began sawing back and forth.

It was heart-breaking work. Age had dulled the weapon, and long slivers of rust flaked off, but the leather which bound him was also ancient. Though progress was slow, and the effort laborious, Cliff knew his bonds were weakening.

But it was growing darker. Even now he could see only a suggestion of gray among the shadows. If those undead things materialized while he lay among them!... Sweat stood out on his forehead and he redoubled his efforts, straining at the leather as he sawed.

With a snap the cords parted and his hands were free. A single slash severed the thongs about his ankles, and he stood up, leaped to the deck. Not an instant too soon! There was movement in the pit — a hideous crawling of bones assembling themselves into skeletal form....

Cliff waited to see no more. There were limits to what one could see and remain sane. With a bound he crossed the rotting deck, and sprang ashore. Despite the dark, he almost ran from the madness of that cave, ran till he passed through the wall of rock, till he saw the rim of the moon gleaming behind the castle.

5: The End of the Island

Out on the plain he sprinted through the ghostly forest. He knew he had no time to spare — knew that soon the march of torture would begin — knew that if Vilma were within the castle, she must answer the summons of Corio's horn. Even now light glowed faintly in the high, square windows.

That horn! At the foot of the steps he stopped short. If he heard the horn, he too must answer! He dared not risk it. With impatient fingers he tore a strip of cloth from his shirt, rolled it into a cylinder, and thrust it into his ear. Another for the other ear — and he darted up into the castle.

A sweeping glance revealed no one, only the murky glow of the altar fire, and the wraiths of smoke pluming upward toward the shadowed roof. Wishing now that he had brought a weapon from the galley, Cliff crossed to the opening in the wall. He stood at the top of the steps, listening, then cursed silently as he remembered that he could hear none but very loud sounds. He saw nothing; so he hastened down into the corridor. His steps were swiftly stealthy as he moved toward Corio's room.

He was past the first branching passage, when a sixth sense warned him of someone's approach. He ran swiftly to the next fork, then paused within its shelter and glanced back, saw five red-cowled figures glide along the tunnel and vanish up the stairway. Cliff frowned. With the vampires in the great hall, Corio must soon follow, leading his victims to the blood-feast. He drew back deeper into the shadows.

His groping hands touched something in the dark — round and hard — like a keg. Curiously he investigated. It was a keg, and there were others. A sandy powder trailed to the floor from a crack in one of them. Thoughtfully Cliff let it run through his fingers. Gunpowder! Of course — he had heard Corio mention pirates and their treasure, and this had been their cache of explosive. An idea was forming....

He looked up to see a shadow pass the mouth of the tunnel; he crept forward and peered out. He saw the black-hooded figure of Leon Corio striding along, saw him enter the room where the passengers of the Ariel lay. In a breath Cliff was down the corridor to Corio's room. A tarnished silver candelabrum shed faint light through the chamber, and by its flickering glow he searched for Vilma, thoroughly, painstakingly — futilely.

He stood in the center of the room in indecision, his forehead creased with anxiety. If only he could find her, he'd know how to plan! He ran his hand through his hair helplessly, then heard very faintly the luring note of Corio's horn. She must answer that summons, unless Corio had her tied somewhere. His best chance of finding her lay in the hall above.

On the wall still hung the mate of the cutlas he had used to free Vilma; he wrenched it down and ran out into the corridor. The last of the naked marchers was disappearing up the stairway. Now the horn-note died, and he could feel more than hear the rumbling bass of the dirge from the depths below him.

He ran the rest of the distance along the passageway and mounted the steps two at a stride. He looked into the torture hall. As on the previous night, Corio stood far back, close to the wall in which Cliff crouched. The arms of the Master were raised high; raised, Cliff knew though he could not hear it, in a blasphemous incantation. And then he saw something that sent a crimson lance of fury crashing through his brain.

Vilma, stripped like the rest, stood with the other victims at the foot of the long steps! Her body gleamed pinkly, in contrast to the pallid drabness of the half-dead automatons, and she held her head proudly erect. But from where he stood Cliff could see the side of her face, and it bore a look of terror.

He could see Corio's face, too, and he was looking at the girl, baffled fury glaring from his eyes — as though she were there against his will.

Cliff's first impulse was to fling himself out there with his cutlas and hack a way to freedom for Vilma and himself, but cold reason checked this folly. Such a course could end only in death. Motionless he watched the scene before him, his brain frantically seeking a plan with even a ghost of a chance of succeeding.

The gunpowder! There was enough of the stuff below to blast this entire castle into the hell where it belonged! Hastily he retraced his steps to the tunnel in which he had found the kegs, plucking the torch from its niche in the wall as he passed it. He held it high above his head as he examined the contents of the broken keg. Unmistakably gunpowder!

Thrusting the cutlas beneath his belt, he clutched a handful of the black dust. Then, crouching close to the floor, he drew an irregular thread through the passageway toward the stairs. Once he returned for more powder, but in a few minutes the job was done. At the foot of the steps where the trail ended, he touched his torch to the black line and watched a hissing spark snake its white-smoked way back toward the powder kegs. An instant he watched it, then sprang up the stairs. He'd have to move fast!

With a hideous howl he darted into the hall, his cutlas above his head. Corio spun about — and it was his last living act. A single sweep of the great blade sheared his head from his neck, sent it rolling grotesquely along the floor. For three heart-beats the body stood with a fountain of blood spurting from severed arteries; then it crashed.

Coolly Cliff leaned over the twitching cadaver, ignoring the bedlam on the stairs, the horde sweeping down toward him, hurling aside the waiting humans. He pried open clutching fingers, seized a twisted silver instrument, and raised it to his lips.

The mass of undead were almost upon him, the murky light glinting on menacing blades, when Cliff blew the first note. The note of sleep! He tried again, hastily. And it was the right one!

At the doleful, soothing sound the undead halted in their tracks; halted — and melted into nothingness before his eyes!

But now those other five in their robes of bloody red — they were charging, and even though they were unarmed, Cliff felt a stab of fear. They possessed powers beyond the human, powers a mortal could not combat. He braced himself and waited.

At the bottom of the steps they stopped, ranging in a wide half-circle. The central monster — the Master — flung up his arms in a strangely terrifying gesture, and Cliff saw his carmine lips move in a chant which he could not hear. Something, a chilling Presence, hovered about him, seemed to settle upon him, cloaking him with the might of the devil himself. That unheard incantation continued, and Cliff felt a cold rigidity creeping through every fiber, slowly freezing his limbs into columns of ice.

With a mighty effort of will he flung himself toward that accursed drinker of blood — and at that instant a terrific detonation rocked the ancient building, and a cloud of smoke and flame burst from the opening in the wall. Cliff was hurled from his feet, rolled over and over, and crashed against the wall by the awful concussion, the cutlas and silver horn sent whirling through the air.

Dizzily he staggered to his feet, crouching defensively. Sounds came to him clearly now; the explosion must have jarred the plugs from his ears. He scanned the room; saw the unclad humans scattered everywhere, most of them lying still and unconscious. He saw Vilma rising slowly; then he looked for the monsters in red. Startled, he saw them rushing toward the opening in the wall, to vanish in its smoke-filled interior. Why did they — — ? Then he knew. Down there somewhere were their graves — graves rent and broken by the explosion —

graves threatened by the flames — and panic had seized the vampires, fear of the death which would result with exile from their tombs!

Unsteadily Cliff crossed to Vilma. She saw him coming and flung herself sobbing into his arms. He crushed her lithe form close — and another explosion, more violent than the first, sent a section of the stone floor leaping upward as though with life of its own. Clinging to Vilma, Cliff managed to maintain his footing, though the floor bucked and heaved. A snapping, booming roar — and a great chasm opened in the floor. A breathless instant — and a segment of the stone stairs, rumbling thunderously, dropped out of sight into a newly formed pit! With it went the blasphemous altar and its phosphorescent fire.

Deafened, stunned, momentarily powerless to move, Cliff's mind groped for an explanation. It seemed incredible that gunpowder could cause such havoc. And the swaying of the floor continued; the thick stone walls shook alarmingly. Suddenly he understood. An earthquake! The explosions had jarred the none-too-stable understrata of rock into spasmodic motion that must grind everything to bits! The island was doomed! And Earth would be better without it.

If only they could reach the Ariel first!

New strength flowed through him, and hugging Vilma close, he staggered toward the spot where he knew the door must be. Somehow he reached it, and reeled down the broken stone steps.

The plain of dead trees swayed like the deck of a ship in a storm as Cliff started across it. A gale had arisen and swept in from the sea, ripping dry branches from the skeleton growths and whirling them about like straws. Yet somehow Cliff reached the crevice in the rock wall with his burden, reached the deck of the galley, crossed it, and won to the safety of the Ariel. Minutes later, with Diesel engines purring, they crept out through the narrow channel into the open sea.

Ten minutes later the Isle of the Undead lay safely behind them. Vilma had dressed; and now they sat together in the pilot house. Cliff had one arm about her, and one hand on the wheel.

"And so," the girl was saying, "while Corio carried you to that terrible old boat, I got loose. He hadn't tied me very tightly, and I slipped my hands free. I had to hide, and I could think of only one place that might be safe, where he wouldn't think to look for me. I ran down to the room where those — those others lay; I undressed, and buried myself among them. It was horrible — the way they sucked each other's wounds...."

Cliff pressed a hand across her lips. "Forget that!" he said almost fiercely. "Forget all of it — d'you hear?"

She looked up at him and said simply: "I'll try."

They glanced back toward the black blotch on the horizon. The seismic disturbances continued unabated. At that moment they saw the barrier of rock like a skull split and sink into the sea. Beyond, cleansing tongues of flame licked the sky. They saw a single jagged wall of the castle still standing, one window glowing in its black expanse like a square, bloody moon against a bloody sky. It crumbled.

They turned away, and Cliff's arm circled the girl he loved. Their lips met and clung.... And the Ariel plowed on through the frothing brine, bearing them toward safety and forgetfulness.... Together.

The Vampire

by Jan Neruda

The excursion steamer brought us from Constantinople to the shore of the island of Prinkipo and we disembarked. The number of passengers was not large. There was one Polish family, a father, a mother, a daughter and her bridegroom, and then we two. Oh, yes, I must not forget that when we were already on the wooden bridge which crosses the Golden Horn to Constantinople, a Greek, a rather youthful man, joined us. He was probably an artist, judging by the portfolio he carried under his arm. Long black locks floated to his shoulders, his face was pale, and his black eyes were deeply set in their sockets. From the first moment he interested me, especially for his obligingness and for his knowledge of local conditions. But he talked too much, and I then turned away from him.

All the more agreeable was the Polish family. The father and mother were good-natured, fine people, the lover a handsome young fellow, of direct and refined manners. They had come to Prinkipo to spend the summer months for the sake of the daughter, who was slightly ailing. The beautiful pale girl was either just recovering from a severe illness or else a serious disease was just fastening its hold upon her. She leaned upon her lover when she walked and very often sat down to rest, while a frequent dry little cough interrupted her whispers. Whenever she coughed, her escort would considerately pause in their walk. He always cast upon her a glance of sympathetic suffering and she would look back at him as if she would say: "It is nothing. I am happy!" They believed in health and happiness.

On the recommendation of the Greek, who departed from us immediately at the pier, the family secured quarters in the hotel on the hill. The hotel-keeper was a Frenchman and his entire building was equipped comfortably and artistically, according to the French style.

We breakfasted together and when the noon heat had abated somewhat we all betook ourselves to the heights, where in the grove of Siberian stone-pines we could refresh ourselves with the view. Hardly had we found a suitable spot and settled ourselves when the Greek appeared again. He greeted us lightly, looked about and seated himself only a few steps from us. He opened his portfolio and began to sketch.

"I think he purposely sits with his back to the rocks so that we can't look at his sketch," I said.

"We don't have to," said the young Pole. "We have enough before us to look at." After a while he added, "It seems to me he's sketching us in as a sort of background. Well — let him!"

We truly did have enough to gaze at. There is not a more beautiful or more happy corner in the world than that very Prinkipo! The political martyr, Irene, contemporary of Charles the Great, lived there for a month as an exile. If I could live a month of my life there I would be happy for the memory of it for the rest of my days! I shall never forget even that one day spent at Prinkipo.

The air was as clear as a diamond, so soft, so caressing, that one's whole soul swung out upon it into the distance. At the right beyond the sea projected the brown Asiatic summits; to the left in the distance purpled the steep coasts of Europe. The neighboring Chalki, one of the nine islands of the "Prince's Archipelago," rose with its cypress forests into the peaceful heights like a sorrowful dream, crowned by a great structure—an asylum for those whose minds are sick.

The Sea of Marmora was but slightly ruffled and played in all colors like a sparkling opal. In the distance the sea was as white as milk, then rosy, between the two islands a glowing orange and below us it was beautifully greenish blue, like a transparent sapphire. It was resplendent in its own beauty. Nowhere were there any large ships— only two small craft flying the English flag sped along the shore. One was a steamboat as big as a watchman's booth, the second had about twelve oarsmen, and when their oars rose simultaneously molten silver dripped from them. Trustful dolphins darted in and out among them and dove with long, arching flights above the surface of the water. Through the blue heavens now and then calm eagles winged their way, measuring the space between two continents.

The entire slope below us was covered with blossoming roses whose fragrance filled the air. From the coffee-house near the sea music was carried up to us through the clear air, hushed somewhat by the distance.

The effect was enchanting. We all sat silent and steeped our souls completely in the picture of paradise. The young Polish girl lay on the grass with her head supported on the bosom of her lover. The pale oval of her delicate face was slightly tinged with soft color, and from her blue eyes tears suddenly gushed forth. The lover understood, bent down and kissed tear after tear. Her mother also was moved to tears, and I — even I — felt a strange twinge.

"Here mind and body both must get well," whispered the girl. "How happy a land this is!"

"God knows I haven't any enemies, but if I had I would forgive them here!" said the father in a trembling voice.

And again we became silent. We were all in such a wonderful mood — so unspeakably sweet it all was! Each felt for himself a whole world of happiness and each one would have shared his happiness with the whole world. All felt the same — and so no one disturbed another. We had scarcely even noticed the Greek, after an hour or so, had arisen, folded his portfolio and with a slight nod had taken his departure. We remained.

Finally after several hours, when the distance was becoming overspread with a darker violet, so magically beautiful in the south, the mother reminded us it was time to depart. We arose and walked down towards the hotel with the easy, elastic steps that characterize carefree children. We sat down in the hotel under the handsome veranda.

Hardly had we been seated when we heard below the sounds of quarreling and oaths. Our Greek was wrangling the hotel-keeper, and for the entertainment of it we listened.

The amusement did not last long. "If I didn't have other guests," growled the hotel-keeper, and ascended the steps towards us.

"I beg you to tell me, sir," asked the young Pole of the approaching hotel-keeper, "who is that gentleman? What's his name?"

"Eh — who knows what the fellow's name is?" grumbled the hotel-keeper, and he gazed venomously downwards. "We call him the Vampire."

"An artist?"

"Fine trade! He sketches only corpses. Just as soon as someone in Constantinople or here in the neighborhood dies, that very day he has a picture of the dead one completed. That fellow paints them beforehand — and he never makes a mistake — just like a vulture!"

The old Polish woman shrieked affrightedly. In her arms lay her daughter pale as chalk. She had fainted.

In one bound the lover had leaped down the steps. With one hand he seized the Greek and with the other reached for the portfolio.

We ran down after him. Both men were rolling in the sand. The contents of the portfolio were scattered all about. On one sheet, sketched with a crayon, was the head of the young Polish girl, her eyes closed and a wreath of myrtle on her brow.

The Vampire of Croglin Grange

by Augustus Hare

An intriguing account of vampirism was related by a certain Captain Fisher, to Augustus Hare, who who wrote of it in the Story of My Life.

"Fisher," said the Captain, "may sound a very plebeian name, but this family is of a very ancient lineage, and for many hundreds of years they have possessed a very curious old place in Cumberland, which bears the weird name of Croglin Grange. The great characteristic of the house is that never at any period of its very long existence has it been more than one story high, but it has a terrace from which large grounds sweep away towards the church in the hollow, and a fine distant view.

"When, in lapse of years, the Fishers outgrew Croglin Grange in family and fortune, they were wise enough not to destroy the long-standing characteristic of the place by adding another story to the house, but they went away to the south, to reside at Thorncombe near Guildford, and they let Croglin Grange.

"They were extremely fortunate in their tenants, two brothers and a sister. They heard their praises from all quarters. To their poorer neighbours they were all that is most kind and beneficent, and their neighbours of a higher class spoke of them as a most welcome addition to the little society of the neighbourhood. On their part, the tenants were greatly delighted with their new residence. The arrangement of the house, which would have been a trial to many, was not so to them. In every respect Croglin Grange was exactly suited to them.

"The winter was spent most happily by the new inmates of Croglin Grange, who shared in all the little social pleasures of the district, and made themselves very popular. In the following summer there was one day which was dreadfully, annihilatingly hot. The brothers lay under the trees with their books, for it was too hot for any active occupation. The sister sat in the veranda and worked, or tried to work, for in the intense sultriness of that summer day, work was next to impossible. They dined early, and after dinner they still sat out on the veranda, enjoying the cool air which came with the evening, and they watched the sun set, and the moon rise over the belt of trees which separated the grounds from the churchyard, seeing it mount the heavens till the whole lawn was bathed in silver light, across which the long shadows from the shrubbery fell as if embossed, so vivid and distinct were they.

"When they separated for the night, all retiring to their rooms on the ground floor (for, as I said, there was no upstairs in that house), the sister felt that the heat was still so great that she could not sleep, and having fastened her window, she did not close the shutters—in that very quiet place it was not necessary—and, propped against the pillows, she still watched the wonderful, the marvellous beauty of that summer night. Gradually she became aware of two lights, two lights which flickered in and out in the belt of trees which separated the lawn from the churchyard, and, as her gaze became fixed upon them, she saw them emerge, fixed in a dark substance, a definite ghastly something, which seemed every moment to become nearer, increasing in size and substance as it approached. Every now and then it was lost for a moment in the long shadows which stretched across the lawn from the trees, and then it emerged larger than ever, and still coming on. As she watched it, the most uncontrollable horror seized her. She longed to get away, but the door was close to the window, and the door was locked on the inside, and while she was unlocking it she must be for an instant nearer to it. She longed to scream, but her voice seemed paralysed, her tongue glued to the roof of her mouth.

"Suddenly—she could never explain why afterwards—the terrible object seemed to turn to one side, seemed to be going round the house, not to be coming to her at all, and immediately she jumped out of bed and rushed to the door, but as she was unlocking it she heard scratch, scratch, scratch upon the window, and saw a hideous brown face with flaming eyes glaring in at her. She rushed back to the bed, but the creature continued to scratch, scratch, scratch upon the window.

She felt a sort of mental comfort in the knowledge that the window was securely fastened on the inside. Suddenly the scratching sound ceased, and a kind of pecking sound took its place. Then, in her agony, she became aware that the creature was unpicking the lead! The noise continued, and a diamond pane of glass fell into the room. Then a long bony finger of the creature came in and turned the handle of the window, and the window opened, and the creature came in; and it came across the room, and her terror was so great that she could not scream, and it came up to the bed, and it twisted its long, bony fingers into her hair, and it dragged her head over the side of the bed, and—it bit her violently in the throat.

"As it bit her, her voice was released, and she screamed with all her might and main. Her brothers rushed out of their rooms, but the door was locked on the inside. A moment was lost while they got a poker and broke it open. Then the creature had already escaped through the window, and the sister, bleeding violently from a wound in the throat, was lying unconscious over the side of the bed. One brother pursued the creature, which fled before him through the moonlight with gigantic strides, and eventually seemed to disappear over the wall into the churchyard. Then he rejoined his brother by the sister's bedside. She was dreadfully hurt, and her wound was a very definite one, but she was of strong disposition, not even given to romance or superstition, and when she came to herself she said, 'What has happened is most extraordinary and I am very much hurt. It seems inexplicable, but of course there is an explanation, and we must wait for it. It will turn out that a lunatic has escaped from some asylum and found his way here.' The wound healed, and she appeared to get well, but the doctor who was sent for to her would not believe that she could bear so terrible a shock so easily, and insisted that she must have change, mental and physical; so her brothers took her to Switzerland.

"Being a sensible girl, when she went abroad she threw herself at once into the interests of the country she was in. She dried plants, she made sketches, she went up mountains, and as autumn came on, she was the person who urged that they should return to Croglin Grange. 'We have taken it,' she said, 'for seven years, and we have only been there one; and we shall always find it difficult to let a house which is only one story high, so we had better return there; lunatics do not escape every day.' As she urged it, her brothers wished nothing better, and the family returned to Cumberland. From there being no upstairs in the house it was impossible to make any great change in their arrangements. The sister occupied the same room, but it is unnecessary to say she always closed the shutters, which, however, as in many old houses, always left one top pane of the window uncovered. The brothers moved, and occupied a room together, exactly opposite that of their sister, and they always kept loaded pistols in their room.

"The winter passed most peacefully and happily. In the following March, the sister was suddenly awakened by a sound she remembered only too well—scratch, scratch, scratch upon the window, and, looking up, she saw, climbed up to the topmost pane of the window, the same hideous brown shrivelled face, with glaring eyes, looking in at her. This time she screamed as loud as she could. Her brothers rushed out of their room with pistols, and out of the front door.

The creature was already scudding away across the lawn. One of the brothers fired and hit it in the leg, but still with the other leg it continued to make way, scrambled over the wall into the churchyard, and seemed to disappear into a vault which belonged to a family long extinct.

"The next day the brothers summoned all the tenants of Croglin Grange, and in their presence the vault was opened. A horrible scene revealed itself. The vault was full of coffins; they had been broken open, and their contents, horribly mangled and distorted, were scattered over the floor. One coffin alone remained intact. Of that the lid had been lifted, but still lay loose upon the coffin. They raised it, and there, brown, withered, shrivelled, mummified, but quite entire, was the same hideous figure which had looked in at the windows of Croglin Grange, with the marks of a recent pistol-shot in the leg: and they did the only thing that can lay a vampire—they burnt it."

Told in a First-Class Smoker: A Modern Vampire

by T. F. Ridgwell

"I think the syndicate should be formed without delay."

It was Curzon who was responsible for this pronouncement. Need I say that we were comfortably established among the upholstery of a certain compartment forming an integral part of our beloved 4.30 p.m. train?

"A syndicate! What for?" challenged Briggs, who challenged most remarks not involving a self-evident proposition out of Euclid.

"Perhaps I should have said a club. I think a club should be established, restricted to a membership of six persons, for the purpose of promoting social intercourse en route over the iron road. It would be unique — a club in a train. The railway company provide the club premises for the price of six season tickets. Entrance fee, nil. Annual subscription, daily punctuality. It would be the most exclusive club in the world, and I vote Briggs be made perpetual secretary, steward, legal adviser, and chairman."

"What in the world are you chattering about?" I demanded, glancing up from a pocket edition of my favourite poet.

"Clubs," returned Curzon, sententiously.

"They're useful sometimes!" snapped the lawyer.

"Curzon is not alluding to the Indian nor to the New York police variety, I think," suggested Wilbraham. "But why a club?"

"The Raconteurs' Club would be a good name," pursued Curzon, unheedingly. "The only condition of membership is that a man shall be able to tell a good story."

"Oh, I begin to see. What do you think of the idea, Smith?" murmured Wilbraham.

"I raise no objection," I answered, "seeing that I am in the enviable position of the Irishman who wished to be hanged first that he might enjoy the spectacle of seeing his comrades strung up afterwards."

"Supposing we name it 'The Ananias Club'?" queried Wilbraham, quietly, looking at me.

"You funny man!" I retorted.

"I rather like Curzon's suggestion," remarked Briggs, "and we'll do it. Let's consider it done. Each man must tell a story. Smith lied most artistically about a month ago; now it's our turn. Five more stories, gentlemen. I think, however, the tales should have at least a substratum of truth —"

"I beg your pardon!" I interrupted, hotly. "Not at all, young man. Has not the Psalmist himself observed that 'All men are journalists' — or did he say 'liars'?"*

"Well, I'm not a journalist."

"You're not a bad amateur. But no offence — let it pass. I claim the right to call for the next story. Now, Wilbraham, you needn't be so interested in your 'First Special,' nor is it necessary, my dear Curzon, that you should make those elaborate preparations for the cleaning of your meerschaum. The Lancet will wait, doctor, till you have arrived at your third glass of after-dinner port. Why, hang me if you don't look for all the world like a class of youngsters called up for Latin grammar. No skulking, if you please. I call on Dr. Harley to minister to our present entertainment."

The doctor fidgeted in his seat, and eyed the lights of a local station through which we were spinning, as though meditating on the minimum of compound fractures, cuts, and bruises that might be involved in a wild leap from the train, but, under the disciplinary influence of our chairman's watchful gaze, finally responded to the invitation endorsed by our expectant silence.

"I have seen a good many wonderful things in the course of my experience as a medical practitioner," began the doctor, "but not so many as you would suppose of the sensational order.

"It were easy to tell you of extraordinary cures and successful operations wherein the element of luok has been combined with the most exact knowledge of modern medical and surgical science. Such relations are perhaps more suited to the columns of a scientific magazine than to the purpose of the raconteur.

"I am thinking, however, of one experience in my life that made a most profound impression upon me. I have never mentioned it to a living person since the event — not even to my own colleagues, for medical men are proverbially hard-headed and sceptical, having little in common with sentiment. The path of the physician is a straight and bare one, and he may not yield to the temptation of straying into the meadows of imagination to pluck fruit off enchanted ground. In short, physiology appeals to him more than psychology, pathology more than astrology, the materia medica more than metempsychosis."

"I think the doctor can go one better than you, Smith."

The interruption came from our humourist in the opposite corner, but observing that Briggs "held him up," so to speak, with his threatening optic "at full cock," I allowed the doctor to proceed.

"I might relate rather a startling anecdote about a case of hypnotic suggestion that recently came under my notice. In a novelist's skilful hands the tale might shape into a nucleus for a series of fine amateur detective stories, but such episodes are not uncommon, and have been treated in current literature. I might —"

"The story, man — the story! Never mind the exordium."

Our chairman's brow grew stormy. "One more such unseemly interruption," he said, sternly, "and I will order the court to be cleared — no, I mean — but wait, his punishment shall be exemplary. I'll call on him for a story the very next occasion."

Wilbraham turned pale, and, order being restored, the doctor this time got well under weigh.

"The lights of a local station, through which we were spinning"

"One morning, several years ago, I was summoned to attend a patient — a young lady whom I will call Miss Beatrice Varley (her real name might not be unknown to you).

"Miss Varley was the only child of Sir Connaught Varley, a gentleman of good family and distinguished character, and she had the reputation of being as good as she was beautiful — a combination of qualities that cannot always be taken for granted in this wicked world of ours. Beatrice Varley was an acknowledged Society belle, and rumour had it that she had lately become affianced to Mr. Francis Faversham, a young lieutenant in a crack cavalry corps.

"In response to the urgent call I drove rapidly to the fashionable square where Sir Connaught Varley leased a small mansion, well pleased with the distinction of having been called in to attend a patient in such a favoured locality.

"Alighting at the door, I rang, and, being admitted, presently found myself in a daintily-furnished room.

"All West-end apartments, whether drawing-rooms or morning-rooms, are, to my uneducated masculine eyes, pretty much alike. But this boudoir was a striking exception, and the charm of the surroundings unobtrusively forced itself upon me as I waited there. There were numerous accessories and ornaments that only cultured taste and womanly artistic impulse can suggest and contrive. A few rare paintings and some exquisite etchings and nocturnes adorned the walls. Books, water-colour sketches, bric-à-brac, and the hundred-and-one trifles that are found in the chamber of an educated woman whose means are commensurate with her desires were displayed in cases and on shelves, peeped out from cunningly-wrought receptacles, or lay in picturesque disorder around.

"But the charm of the place was not merely in the evidences of good taste on the part of its mistress — for conviction stole upon nie that this beautiful sanctum must be Miss Varley's very own — but rather a nameless atmosphere that pervaded all, an unnameable something suggesting a vague consciousness of what, for want of a better phrase, I will call spiritual inferiority.

"I was surprised to find that I had not been conducted to the patient's bedroom, but immediately reflected that her indisposition might simply be one of those neurotic affections to which Society ladies often lay themselves open.

"Presently an elderly lady appeared, and I bowed to her dignified salutation.

"Her niece, she explained, had been taken ill that morning early. The family doctor was sent for, but was discovered ill in bed with an attack of influenza. He had hastily given the addresses of several practitioners, mine among the number, and it appeared that I was first on the scene.

"With a few further words of explanation I was taken upstairs, and found myself at the bedside of my patient.

"It required but a glance to verify the report of Miss Varley's beauty, but the deadly pallor of her face, revealing the blue veins, the statuesqueness and immobility of her features, reminded me of a work of Florentine art in marble. Her pulse was feeble and intermittent. There was no sign of fever, and she lay, to all appearance, dying from general failure of the system. Had she shown the slightest animation, even so little as a quivering of the closed eyelids, I could have likened her to Niobe newly turned to living flesh. As it was she seemed a Niobe returning to her original dumb and pulseless stone.

"Making a brief examination, I questioned the aunt and nurse on several points, but got no inspiration; indeed, a growing feeling of incompetence and ignorance filled me with dismay, until at length a sensation of failure struck cold to my heart.

"Had she had any shock to the system! No; her life had been one round of quiet pleasure and usefulness, unruffled by any distracting cares. Had she usually good health! She had scarcely known a day's illness. I had satisfied myself that the heart and lungs were free from organic disease. What, then, ailed her? I tried again.

"Had she suffered any loss of blood? No, nothing of the sort had happened.

"I turned desperately to the aunt.

" 'Do you mean to say that you cannot account in any way for your niece's condition?'

" 'It is an absolute mystery to me,' she answered, 'and her father is well-nigh distracted.'

"I began to feel distracted too, but managed to sustain a professional demeanour, and, after prescribing some simple restoratives, took my leave, after promising to return in an hour or two's time.

"Entering my brougham, I drove straight to Sir Martyn Croker, the eminent specialist, and by good fortune found him at home. Sir Martyn had been an old friend of my father's, and I know that I could always count upon his experience and goodwill.

"In a few words I made him aware of my strange case and the difficulty I was in. The great man listened courteously, and, as I ran over point after point, detailing my attempts at diagnosis, his interest perceptibly quickened. To be brief, he promised to see Miss Varley in consultation with me, and with this assurance I hastened back to Sir Connaught's house full of enthusiasm, not unmingled with perplexity and misgiving.

"The father's consent having been readily obtained, the specialist duly arrived at the house, and the consultation was held.

"To my unutterable astonishment and, shall I say, to my secret professional gratification, Sir Martyn appeared as mystified as I had been. Miss Varley then seemed on the whole a trifle better. There was a alight improvement of pulse, and once she had opened her eyes and looked about her. Sir Martyn prescribed a highly concentrated form of diet and strong tonic remedies, and on the third day I had the satisfaction of seeing my interesting patient making slow but unmistakable progress towards convalescence.

"In a conversation I had with Sir Martyn Croker later, he confessed to me that he had never felt so nonplussed in the whole course of his career.

" 'I don't know,' he remarked, 'whether it is a case for the doctor or for the police.'

" 'Foul play?' I suggested.

"The deadly pallor of her face reminded me
of a work of Florentine art in marble"

"He leaned back in his arm-chair and puffed slowly at a cigar. Then, leaning towards me, he replied with deliberation:

" 'My dear boy, a score of theories, many of them fringed with suspicion, have flitted through my mind ever since I saw that pallid form simulating death, but I've been forced to dismiss one and all as untenable, and I'm no nearer the truth than when I first entered that chamber of mystery nearly a week ago. The recovery is almost as inexplicable as the malady. It isn't catalepsy, and the condition could not have been taken for death. I thought I knew a little about the ailments of the human body, and I'm not considered a novice on the subject of brain disease, but I am like a child groping in the dark, or a person who wakes from sleep striving to piece together the night's forgotten dream. There is something uncanny, devilish, in this affair, and — I'm going to sleep over it.'

"The hour was late, and, without reply, I rose and left the discomfited specialist to his own meditations.

"The following morning, 'at home' in my surgery, and still pondering the singular experience of the 'Varley case,' a card was brought in to me, inscribed

" 'Francis Faversham.

" '——th Hussars.'

"I nodded, and a moment after my servant opened the door again to admit a visitor.

"The young gentleman who confronted me was in the prime of early manhood. I have studied men in half-a-dozen countries in Europe, to say nothing of one or two out-of-the-way corners of the earth where civilisation has not yet begun to eat the core from physical strength and beauty, but never in my life have I seen such a perfect specimen of the human animal as stood before me. At least six feet four inches in height, his body was suitably proportioned, his limbs being grandly moulded. Possibly the head was rather small, and the face was wanting from an intellectual standpoint, but the features lacked neither dignity nor expression.

"With his incoming there seemed to burst into my dingy room a breath from the ocean, a suggestion of rude health almost unknown in these degenerate days. Stripped of his fashionable attire, this modern barbarian might have posed for Caractacus before the Romans.

"I am dwelling somewhat circumstantially on this young fellow's appearance, possibly at the risk of exciting your unspoken criticism. I do so with a reason, for it is necessary that you should see this man with your mind's eye. I guarantee that, if he could step into our midst at the present moment, you would all experience something of the feeling I had when we met face to face that day. He attracted, yet repelled. His flesh and blood were so pronounced that his physical presence positively jarred on my nerves as a powerful flood of light affects the eyes. It was aggressive, insistent, ever in evidence. Something from the man seemed to leap out and cause me the sensation of having received a blow.

"When he commenced speaking I found myself listening to the typical British officer and gentleman.

" 'You attended Miss Beatrice Varley in a recent illness. That young lady has promised to be my wife, which must plead as excuse for my unceremonious visit.'

"I bowed, and begged him to be seated.

" 'Dr. Harley, I am a most miserable man.'

" 'Your looks certainly don't pity you,' I said, with a smile.

" 'That's my cursed body,' he replied. 'I can't help feeling or looking well. Never knew an ache or pain in my life. I'm a mystery to myself. Do you know, sir, I sometimes fancy I'm a modern Wandering Jew, with a variation — instead of being unable to die, I find it impossible to contract an illness. It seems certain to me that I shall die only by violence. I've made marvellous demands upon my constitution, but nothing seems to hurt or tire me.'

"At that moment my professional interest awoke. The lust of science rioted in my veins. Here was a man indeed! Vivisection! Great heavens! what a subject for experiment! I could cheerfully have stretched him on the operating table then and there.

"He recommenced to speak, and I became a practical medical man again, vaguely wondering at my late extraordinary trend of thought.

" 'You will believe me when I say that I have the deepest affection for Miss Varley. Indeed, if anything were to happen to her I — ' He broke off with a sound like a sob.

"My man, then, had a heart. I was glad to find him not all flesh and blood.

" 'I scarcely know how to tell you all that troubles me, Doctor Harley, but, having made up my mind to ask your help, it's no good shirking the matter. In a word, I believe I am the cause of Miss Varley's malady.'

" 'You the cause?' I repeated, in astonishment.

" 'It seems to me that I am, and what confirms my extraordinary fancy is that my fiancée appears to entertain the same delusion. I want you to convince me that it is a delusion. She carries the conviction in her face. She loves me, but fears me.'

" 'But how on earth have you caused her illness?' I inquired, with an almost shivering sensation.

" 'I wish you could tell me,' answered the young hussar; 'I don't know. When we first met,' he went on after a moody silence, 'we were drawn unaccountably each to the other. When her eyes looked into mine for the first time they were familiar eyes. A consciousness as of pre-knowledge sprang into my brain.

Afterwards Beatrice told me that precisely the same idea took possession of her own mind. She felt that she had known me all her life, and thousands of years before. I remember how we fell to laughing at this strange conceit.

" 'Well, we became engaged, and I thought Heaven was opened to me; but as our friendship ripened I was more than once startled to note a change in my dear girl's appearance. Over and over again, when I called at her house, Miss Varley would look the picture of health. But if I stayed long at her side she grew pale and nervous, and on several occasions she has seemed on the point of fainting. Her friends appear to have seen nothing of these fluctuations in health, or, if they have noted anything, it has been attributed to excitement or an over-heated room, and the matter has called forth no further comment.

" 'So things went on until one day, when we had been thrown much into each other's society, the climax was reached. I shall never forget how ill, how worn, how transparently pale she grew, and — what stung me to the quick — how at last she avoided me. Deeply mortified and tortured with apprehension, I left her. The next morning she was taken ill, and the rest you know. Now, Dr. Harley, am I not the most miserable of men?'

"In five minutes' time I shall
shuffle off this mortal coil"

" 'My dear sir,' answered I, 'you have become morbid. The whole thing is absurd, paradoxical, unscientific. I take it that you haven't worried the young lady in any thoughtless mood?'

" 'Dr. Harley,' exclaimed the young man,' Beatrice Varley is a saint of Heaven in my thought, and rather than vex her or wound one susceptibility I would suffer nameless torment.'

" 'It is extraordinary,' I mused. 'All you have told me is the veriest nonsense, and my reason utterly rejects the conclusions you appear to have arrived at. Yet there must be a cause, and,' I added mentally, 'I would give a hundred pounds to find it.'

" 'Do you think, Dr. Harley, asked my visitor, slowly, 'it is possible that I can possess unconsciously any occult influence — mesmeric or something of the kind? And, supposing that I have some such power, is it possible for it to be exerted unknowingly?'

" 'No,' I answered, after a moment's reflection, 'it is not. Hypnotic or mesmeric force — a rare faculty, and one requiring a deal of cultivation — cannot be used without a particular volition — an effort of concentration upon a specified object. There must be a distinct outputting of strength. And, further, you would have to be endowed with very peculiar powers to reach a person unaware of your design.'

" 'I have never thought about the subject,' said Faversham, somewhat hopelessly; 'but once or twice it has flashed across me that I may have some power whose existence no one has ever suspected. I remember once, a few years ago, a party of us were at the Alhambra, and a wrestling competition formed part of the programme. There were professional wrestlers of several nationalities, and one fellow — a Turk, I believe — threw every opponent. He afterwards challenged any person in the audience to try conclusions with him. Well, my friends were on for a spree that night, and, after some persuasion, they induced me to enter the lists against this doughty champion. When I got on to the stage I was considerably impressed with his massive proportions, and realised that I had a very fair chance of making myself a laughingstock. We soon got to work, and I found my man knew three times as much about the game as I did. I am pretty strong,' pursued the young officer, modestly, stretching out an arm that Sandow might have envied, 'and as the professional tried trick after trick it was more luck and sheer weight and muscle than science that prevented my being thrown. I felt I must eventually go under unless I could bring off something startling. So I glared at the big Turk as though I was Argus-eyed, and I longed for victory. Our bodies swayed to and fro in a terrible embrace, wbile the audience held their breath. Presently my assailant began to smile — the smile of a man assured of success. That smile was his undoing. The dogged determination of a long line of fighting Favershams surged in my breast. Keeping my eyes on my opponent, I felt a rush of strength go through me like a fire. The man told me afterwards that my eyes burnt him; but, however that may have been, the smile died on his lips and his enormous muscles relaxed. A moment later the audience were clapping and shrieking with delight at the sight of my Turk on his back, both shoulders touching the floor. Now, sir, there was more than physical prowess in that.'

" 'No doubt,' I replied. 'It was a nice operation of mind acting upon highly trained matter. I have known even delicate women to become, under extraordinary excitement, as strong as a giant until the tension was relaxed. But all this proves nothing with regard to Miss Varley, inasmuch as your will has never been exercised designedly to her hurt.'

" 'Great heavens, no! I am like a little child in her presence.' And he relapsed into silence.

" 'Well, Mr. Faversham,' I said, after a pause, 'you don't look an imaginative man, and I cannot help thinking that your fiancée's condition has superinduced a morbid set of fancies in your usually healthy brain. But the facts of Miss Varley's illness are so mysterious that I cannot view your state of mind as wholly unreasonable.'

" 'Do you advise me to go and see Miss Varley — for the present?' inquired Faversham.

"I pondered the question for a moment or two. Instinct — blind, unreasoning intuition — whispered: Keep this man away from your patient at any cost! Science answered with a superior smile: How can a man's presence harm the woman he loves? Experience and common sense backed up the dictum, and, being a medical man, I smothered instinct.

" 'Certainly,' I assented, rising as I saw my visitor rise. 'By all means go and see her. Go and destroy this chimera of the brain, and I warrant you shall have many another good laugh together over your queer, fantastic notions.'

"We clasped hands, and as his strong fingers closed on mine I was again conscious of the masterfulness of his physical presence, so strangely at variance with the idle fancies of his brain.

"Singularly uncomfortable, and with an undefinable presentiment of coming evil, I led my visitor to the door and watched his tall figure disappear into the street.

"Mr. Faversham made straight for his sweetheart's house, and found her up and well. She greeted him affectionately. I am no hand at love stories, so you can imagine for yourselves what this happy couple had to say to each other.

"Faversham's joy, however, was soon turned to th« wildest terror, for scarcely an hour had passed in pleasant intercourse when the girl was stricken down for the second time, with all her former symptoms acutely present. Ringing the bell for assistance, and hurriedly leaving her in the care of her affrighted relatives and attendants, he strode to the door and hurried from the house like a madman.

"The girl's condition was precisely as before. Several of the most famous doctors in London were called in, and one or two muttered something about hysteria. Others looked solemn and used long Latin terms; but in my heart I knew that the mysterious affection baffled all their science and skill, bringing them face to face with a wall on which were traced strange cabalistic characters they lacked the ability to decipher.

"As for the hapless lover, I learnt from his own lips that he had planned to destroy himself, only being prevented in his design by one of those singular interpositions which some men attribute to chance and others to God.

"He had reasoned the whole thing out, and felt that Fate was too hard. So he determined to act. He sat in his favourite room and pondered the situation till (as he described it) a great horror confronted him. What strange delusion took possession of his brain I cannot say, or how much was delusion and how much dimly-apprehended truth. Rising quietly, he took a rerolver from a drawer and loaded it with ball cartridge.

" 'In five minutes' time,' thought he, 'I shall shuffle off this mortal coil. When the hand points to three I will die. Five minutes more of life, and then — well, I shall know something more about the supernatural At present I only dream of it.'

"Four minutes and three-quarters went by, and the suicide pressed the glittering barrel to his temple and waited for the signal.

"The clock struck three, and at the first musical chime this strong man threw away the deadly weapon and cried like a child. It appears the clock had been her gift, and — well, you can imagine the rest.

"Three months later Lieutenant Faversham perished in one of our small tribal wars abroad. He rescued a wounded comrade and carried him to safety, all the while exposed to a murderous fire. I learnt from good authority that his body contained no less than eleven wounds."

"Is that all?" asked our chairman, as the doctor paused and folded up his newspaper.

"Practically. Beatrice Varley is probably alive to-day, and, likely enough, married. She slowly recovered after Faversham went abroad, and, so far as I know, never had a repetition of her peculiar illness."

"Look here, Harley, I protest against your way of telling a tale," burst out the lawyer, excitedly. "We want to know something more about this affair. What the dickens was the matter with this girl?"

"I don't know," replied the doctor, seriously. "I have a theory, but it is so wild and extravagant that I dare not utter it — in fact, I don't really accept it myself. But sometimes, when I wake up in the night and think about it, then I believe it."

"Doctor," I cried, impulsively, "you shall not leave this train until you tell us what you think about this."

"Hear, hear!" came from two-thirds of our members.

"Well, if you will, you must Don't let the matter disturb our friendship. I solemnly believe — I mean," corrected the doctor, hastily, "I have sometimes imagined that Faversham was a sort of human vampire, affecting people more or less remotely as they were more or less in sympathy with him. Beatrice Varley was the one person in the whole world who could not bear the approximation of his strong vitality. It absorbed her. His touch to her was death. His presence robbed her of life as the sun steals water from the lake.

"I know the suggestion must appear extravagant even to the lay mind. Science, as we apprehend her teachings, makes no provision for such a ghastly theory. If you were to ask the guard of this train if he believed that mandrakes were endowed with some mysterious sense, seemingly human, and shrieked with pain when violently disrooted, he would probably grin and wonder why you were chaffing him."

"Well, I should too," volunteered Wilbraham. And the club endorsed the sentiment audibly. Only Densmore was silent.

"Precisely," agreed the doctor; "we belong to an age of materialism. Two and two make four, and can never make five. We believe only what we can understand — what our petty environments have permitted our minds to receive. 'Miracles cannot happen,' we say. But they do — every day. 'A nation of shopkeepers,' however, we keep the book of our life on the same principle as our ledger — by double entry. Imagination — all the rich purple glow of poetic fancy that has come to us as a splendid heritage from those 'wise men of the East' — is crushed out of our reckoning by what Keats calls

'The weariness, the fever, and the fret
Here where men sit and hear each other groan.' "

"That is very fine," I commented (I could appreciate the sentiment, being an amateur poet myself), "but what has it to do with Miss Varley's mysterious disease?"

"Everything, or nothing," replied the man of medicine, sententiously. "I have little more to say except to remind you that 'there are more things in Heaven and on earth, than are dreamt of in our philosophy.' There is a law of attraction and a law of repulsion. It has been said that every human being has his or her counterpart somewhere knocking about in the universe — some creature whose disposition exactly dovetails into the other. I see no reason why the reverse should not be true. Perhaps in China or Peru there is a human specimen who might prove a vampire to me, or I to him; and so with each one of us. I don't want to meet him. Luckily, the world is large. Two suoh repellent beings, such antipodean forces, might even live in the same street for fifty years and never come together. Fate shuffles the cards well. Combinations of musical sounds are infinite. So with many other affairs. We jostle up against a man one day and may never touch him again to all eternity. But I am afraid I bore you, and I'm thirsty enough to drink a whole bottle of that port Briggs alluded to so feelingly."

We thanked the doctor warmly; and, as I gathered up my traps, Wilbraham lightly kicked my shins and smiled.

I never did like Wilbraham's smile. It is older than his face. His smile must have been floating about somewhere before Nature gave him a face, though the one was evidently designed to fit the other. But he has no imagination, has Wilbraham.

Carmilla

by Joseph Sheridan Le Fanu

Prologue

Upon a paper attached to the Narrative which follows, Doctor Hesselius has written a rather elaborate note, which he accompanies with a reference to his Essay on the strange subject which the MS. illuminates.

This mysterious subject he treats, in that Essay, with his usual learning and acumen, and with remarkable directness and condensation. It will form but one volume of the series of that extraordinary man's collected papers.

As I publish the case, in this volume, simply to interest the "laity," I shall forestall the intelligent lady, who relates it, in nothing; and after due consideration, I have determined, therefore, to abstain from presenting any précis of the learned Doctor's reasoning, or extract from his statement on a subject which he describes as "involving, not improbably, some of the profoundest arcana of our dual existence, and its intermediates."

I was anxious on discovering this paper, to reopen the correspondence commenced by Doctor Hesselius, so many years before, with a person so clever and careful as his informant seems to have been. Much to my regret, however, I found that she had died in the interval.

She, probably, could have added little to the Narrative which she communicates in the following pages, with, so far as I can pronounce, such conscientious particularity.

I: An Early Fright

In Styria, we, though by no means magnificent people, inhabit a castle, or schloss. A small income, in that part of the world, goes a great way. Eight or nine hundred a year does wonders. Scantily enough ours would have answered among wealthy people at home. My father is English, and I bear an English name, although I never saw England. But here, in this lonely and primitive place, where everything is so marvelously cheap, I really don't see how ever so much more money would at all materially add to our comforts, or even luxuries.

My father was in the Austrian service, and retired upon a pension and his patrimony, and purchased this feudal residence, and the small estate on which it stands, a bargain.

Nothing can be more picturesque or solitary. It stands on a slight eminence in a forest. The road, very old and narrow, passes in front of its drawbridge, never raised in my time, and its moat, stocked with perch, and sailed over by many swans, and floating on its surface white fleets of water lilies.

Over all this the schloss shows its many-windowed front; its towers, and its Gothic chapel.

The forest opens in an irregular and very picturesque glade before its gate, and at the right a steep Gothic bridge carries the road over a stream that winds in deep shadow through the wood. I have said that this is a very lonely place. Judge whether I say truth. Looking from the hall door towards the road, the forest in which our castle stands extends fifteen miles to the right, and twelve to the left. The nearest inhabited village is about seven of your English miles to the left. The nearest inhabited schloss of any historic associations, is that of old General Spielsdorf, nearly twenty miles away to the right.

I have said "the nearest inhabited village," because there is, only three miles westward, that is to say in the direction of General Spielsdorf's schloss, a ruined village, with its quaint little church, now roofless, in the aisle of which are the moldering tombs of the proud family of Karnstein, now extinct, who once owned the equally desolate chateau which, in the thick of the forest, overlooks the silent ruins of the town.

Respecting the cause of the desertion of this striking and melancholy spot, there is a legend which I shall relate to you another time.

I must tell you now, how very small is the party who constitute the inhabitants of our castle. I don't include servants, or those dependents who occupy rooms in the buildings attached to the schloss. Listen, and wonder! My father, who is the kindest man on earth, but growing old; and I, at the date of my story, only nineteen. Eight years have passed since then.

I and my father constituted the family at the schloss. My mother, a Styrian lady, died in my infancy, but I had a good-natured governess, who had been with me from, I might almost say, my infancy. I could not remember the time when her fat, benignant face was not a familiar picture in my memory.

This was Madame Perrodon, a native of Berne, whose care and good nature now in part supplied to me the loss of my mother, whom I do not even remember, so early I lost her. She made a third at our little dinner party. There was a fourth, Mademoiselle De Lafontaine, a lady such as you term, I believe, a "finishing governess." She spoke French and German, Madame Perrodon French and broken English, to which my father and I added English, which, partly to prevent its becoming a lost language among us, and partly from patriotic motives, we spoke every day. The consequence was a Babel, at which strangers used to laugh, and which I shall make no attempt to reproduce in this narrative. And there were two or three young lady friends besides, pretty nearly of my own age, who were occasional visitors, for longer or shorter terms; and these visits I sometimes returned.

These were our regular social resources; but of course there were chance visits from "neighbors" of only five or six leagues distance. My life was, notwithstanding, rather a solitary one, I can assure you.

My gouvernantes had just so much control over me as you might conjecture such sage persons would have in the case of a rather spoiled girl, whose only parent allowed her pretty nearly her own way in everything.

The first occurrence in my existence, which produced a terrible impression upon my mind, which, in fact, never has been effaced, was one of the very earliest incidents of my life which I can recollect. Some people will think it so trifling that it should not be recorded here. You will see, however, by-and-by, why I mention it. The nursery, as it was called, though I had it all to myself, was a large room in the upper story of the castle, with a steep oak roof. I can't have been more than six years old, when one night I awoke, and looking round the room from my bed, failed to see the nursery maid. Neither was my nurse there; and I thought myself alone. I was not frightened, for I was one of those happy children who are studiously kept in ignorance of ghost stories, of fairy tales, and of all such lore as makes us cover up our heads when the door cracks suddenly, or the flicker of an expiring candle makes the shadow of a bedpost dance upon the wall, nearer to our faces. I was vexed and insulted at finding myself, as I conceived, neglected, and I began to whimper, preparatory to a hearty bout of roaring; when to my surprise, I saw a solemn, but very pretty face looking at me from the side of the bed. It was that of a young lady who was kneeling, with her hands under the coverlet. I looked at her with a kind of pleased wonder, and ceased whimpering. She caressed me with her hands, and lay down beside me on the bed, and drew me towards her, smiling; I felt immediately delightfully soothed, and fell asleep again. I was wakened by a sensation as if two needles ran into my breast very deep at the same moment, and I cried loudly. The lady started back, with her eyes fixed on me, and then slipped down upon the floor, and, as I thought, hid herself under the bed.

I was now for the first time frightened, and I yelled with all my might and main. Nurse, nursery maid, housekeeper, all came running in, and hearing my story, they made light of it, soothing me all they could meanwhile. But, child as I was, I could perceive that their faces were pale with an unwonted look of anxiety, and I saw them look under the bed, and about the room, and peep under tables and pluck open cupboards; and the housekeeper whispered to the nurse: "Lay your hand along that hollow in the bed; someone did lie there, so sure as you did not; the place is still warm."

I remember the nursery maid petting me, and all three examining my chest, where I told them I felt the puncture, and pronouncing that there was no sign visible that any such thing had happened to me.

The housekeeper and the two other servants who were in charge of the nursery, remained sitting up all night; and from that time a servant always sat up in the nursery until I was about fourteen.

I was very nervous for a long time after this. A doctor was called in, he was pallid and elderly. How well I remember his long saturnine face, slightly pitted with smallpox, and his chestnut wig. For a good while, every second day, he came and gave me medicine, which of course I hated.

The morning after I saw this apparition I was in a state of terror, and could not bear to be left alone, daylight though it was, for a moment.

I remember my father coming up and standing at the bedside, and talking cheerfully, and asking the nurse a number of questions, and laughing very heartily at one of the answers; and patting me on the shoulder, and kissing me, and telling me not to be frightened, that it was nothing but a dream and could not hurt me.

But I was not comforted, for I knew the visit of the strange woman was not a dream; and I was awfully frightened.

I was a little consoled by the nursery maid's assuring me that it was she who had come and looked at me, and lain down beside me in the bed, and that I must have been half-dreaming not to have known her face. But this, though supported by the nurse, did not quite satisfy me.

I remembered, in the course of that day, a venerable old man, in a black cassock, coming into the room with the nurse and housekeeper, and talking a little to them, and very kindly to me; his face was very sweet and gentle, and he told me they were going to pray, and joined my hands together, and desired me to say, softly, while they were praying, "Lord hear all good prayers for us, for Jesus' sake." I think these were the very words, for I often repeated them to myself, and my nurse used for years to make me say them in my prayers.

I remembered so well the thoughtful sweet face of that white-haired old man, in his black cassock, as he stood in that rude, lofty, brown room, with the clumsy furniture of a fashion three hundred years old about him, and the scanty light entering its shadowy atmosphere through the small lattice. He kneeled, and the three women with him, and he prayed aloud with an earnest quavering voice for, what appeared to me, a long time. I forget all my life preceding that event, and for some time after it is all obscure also, but the scenes I have just described stand out vivid as the isolated pictures of the phantasmagoria surrounded by darkness.

II: A Guest

I am now going to tell you something so strange that it will require all your faith in my veracity to believe my story. It is not only true, nevertheless, but truth of which I have been an eyewitness.

It was a sweet summer evening, and my father asked me, as he sometimes did, to take a little ramble with him along that beautiful forest vista which I have mentioned as lying in front of the schloss.

"General Spielsdorf cannot come to us so soon as I had hoped," said my father, as we pursued our walk.

He was to have paid us a visit of some weeks, and we had expected his arrival next day. He was to have brought with him a young lady, his niece and ward, Mademoiselle Rheinfeldt, whom I had never seen, but whom I had heard described as a very charming girl, and in whose society I had promised myself many happy days. I was more disappointed than a young lady living in a town, or a bustling neighborhood can possibly imagine. This visit, and the new acquaintance it promised, had furnished my day dream for many weeks.

"And how soon does he come?" I asked.

"Not till autumn. Not for two months, I dare say," he answered. "And I am very glad now, dear, that you never knew Mademoiselle Rheinfeldt."

"And why?" I asked, both mortified and curious.

"Because the poor young lady is dead," he replied. "I quite forgot I had not told you, but you were not in the room when I received the General's letter this evening."

I was very much shocked. General Spielsdorf had mentioned in his first letter, six or seven weeks before, that she was not so well as he would wish her, but there was nothing to suggest the remotest suspicion of danger.

"Here is the General's letter," he said, handing it to me. "I am afraid he is in great affliction; the letter appears to me to have been written very nearly in distraction."

We sat down on a rude bench, under a group of magnificent lime trees. The sun was setting with all its melancholy splendor behind the sylvan horizon, and the stream that flows beside our home, and passes under the steep old bridge I have mentioned, wound through many a group of noble trees, almost at our feet, reflecting in its current the fading crimson of the sky. General Spielsdorf's letter was so extraordinary, so vehement, and in some places so self-contradictory, that I read it twice over—the second time aloud to my father—and was still unable to account for it, except by supposing that grief had unsettled his mind.

It said "I have lost my darling daughter, for as such I loved her. During the last days of dear Bertha's illness I was not able to write to you.

Before then I had no idea of her danger. I have lost her, and now learn all, too late. She died in the peace of innocence, and in the glorious hope of a blessed futurity. The fiend who betrayed our infatuated hospitality has done it all. I thought I was receiving into my house innocence, gaiety, a charming companion for my lost Bertha. Heavens! what a fool have I been!

I thank God my child died without a suspicion of the cause of her sufferings. She is gone without so much as conjecturing the nature of her illness, and the accursed passion of the agent of all this misery. I devote my remaining days to tracking and extinguishing a monster. I am told I may hope to accomplish my righteous and merciful purpose. At present there is scarcely a gleam of light to guide me. I curse my conceited incredulity, my despicable affectation of superiority, my blindness, my obstinacy—all—too late. I cannot write or talk collectedly now. I am distracted. So soon as I shall have a little recovered, I mean to devote myself for a time to enquiry, which may possibly lead me as far as Vienna. Some time in the autumn, two months hence, or earlier if I live, I will see you—that is, if you permit me; I will then tell you all that I scarce dare put upon paper now. Farewell. Pray for me, dear friend."

In these terms ended this strange letter. Though I had never seen Bertha Rheinfeldt my eyes filled with tears at the sudden intelligence; I was startled, as well as profoundly disappointed.

The sun had now set, and it was twilight by the time I had returned the General's letter to my father.

It was a soft clear evening, and we loitered, speculating upon the possible meanings of the violent and incoherent sentences which I had just been reading. We had nearly a mile to walk before reaching the road that passes the schloss in front, and by that time the moon was shining brilliantly. At the drawbridge we met Madame Perrodon and Mademoiselle De Lafontaine, who had come out, without their bonnets, to enjoy the exquisite moonlight.

We heard their voices gabbling in animated dialogue as we approached. We joined them at the drawbridge, and turned about to admire with them the beautiful scene.

The glade through which we had just walked lay before us. At our left the narrow road wound away under clumps of lordly trees, and was lost to sight amid the thickening forest. At the right the same road crosses the steep and picturesque bridge, near which stands a ruined tower which once guarded that pass; and beyond the bridge an abrupt eminence rises, covered with trees, and showing in the shadows some grey ivy-clustered rocks.

Over the sward and low grounds a thin film of mist was stealing like smoke, marking the distances with a transparent veil; and here and there we could see the river faintly flashing in the moonlight.

No softer, sweeter scene could be imagined. The news I had just heard made it melancholy; but nothing could disturb its character of profound serenity, and the enchanted glory and vagueness of the prospect.

My father, who enjoyed the picturesque, and I, stood looking in silence over the expanse beneath us. The two good governesses, standing a little way behind us, discoursed upon the scene, and were eloquent upon the moon.

Madame Perrodon was fat, middle-aged, and romantic, and talked and sighed poetically. Mademoiselle De Lafontaine—in right of her father who was a German, assumed to be psychological, metaphysical, and something of a mystic—now declared that when the moon shone with a light so intense it was well known that it indicated a special spiritual activity. The effect of the full moon in such a state of brilliancy was manifold. It acted on dreams, it acted on lunacy, it acted on nervous people, it had marvelous physical influences connected with life. Mademoiselle related that her cousin, who was mate of a merchant ship, having taken a nap on deck on such a night, lying on his back, with his face full in the light on the moon, had wakened, after a dream of an old woman clawing him by the cheek, with his features horribly drawn to one side; and his countenance had never quite recovered its equilibrium.

"The moon, this night," she said, "is full of idyllic and magnetic influence—and see, when you look behind you at the front of the schloss how all its windows flash and twinkle with that silvery splendor, as if unseen hands had lighted up the rooms to receive fairy guests."

There are indolent styles of the spirits in which, indisposed to talk ourselves, the talk of others is pleasant to our listless ears; and I gazed on, pleased with the tinkle of the ladies' conversation.

"I have got into one of my moping moods tonight," said my father, after a silence, and quoting Shakespeare, whom, by way of keeping up our English, he used to read aloud, he said:

"'In truth I know not why I am so sad.
It wearies me: you say it wearies you;
But how I got it—came by it.'

"I forget the rest. But I feel as if some great misfortune were hanging over us. I suppose the poor General's afflicted letter has had something to do with it."

At this moment the unwonted sound of carriage wheels and many hoofs upon the road, arrested our attention.

They seemed to be approaching from the high ground overlooking the bridge, and very soon the equipage emerged from that point. Two horsemen first crossed the bridge, then came a carriage drawn by four horses, and two men rode behind.

It seemed to be the traveling carriage of a person of rank; and we were all immediately absorbed in watching that very unusual spectacle. It became, in a few moments, greatly more interesting, for just as the carriage had passed the summit of the steep bridge, one of the leaders, taking fright, communicated his panic to the rest, and after a plunge or two, the whole team broke into a wild gallop together, and dashing between the horsemen who rode in front, came thundering along the road towards us with the speed of a hurricane.

The excitement of the scene was made more painful by the clear, long-drawn screams of a female voice from the carriage window.

We all advanced in curiosity and horror; me rather in silence, the rest with various ejaculations of terror.

Our suspense did not last long. Just before you reach the castle drawbridge, on the route they were coming, there stands by the roadside a magnificent lime tree, on the other stands an ancient stone cross, at sight of which the horses, now going at a pace that was perfectly frightful, swerved so as to bring the wheel over the projecting roots of the tree.

I knew what was coming. I covered my eyes, unable to see it out, and turned my head away; at the same moment I heard a cry from my lady friends, who had gone on a little.

Curiosity opened my eyes, and I saw a scene of utter confusion. Two of the horses were on the ground, the carriage lay upon its side with two wheels in the air; the men were busy removing the traces, and a lady with a commanding air and figure had got out, and stood with clasped hands, raising the handkerchief that was in them every now and then to her eyes.

Through the carriage door was now lifted a young lady, who appeared to be lifeless. My dear old father was already beside the elder lady, with his hat in his hand, evidently tendering his aid and the resources of his schloss. The lady did not appear to hear him, or to have eyes for anything but the slender girl who was being placed against the slope of the bank.

I approached; the young lady was apparently stunned, but she was certainly not dead. My father, who piqued himself on being something of a physician, had just had his fingers on her wrist and assured the lady, who declared herself her mother, that her pulse, though faint and irregular, was undoubtedly still distinguishable. The lady clasped her hands and looked upward, as if in a momentary transport of gratitude; but immediately she broke out again in that theatrical way which is, I believe, natural to some people.

She was what is called a fine looking woman for her time of life, and must have been handsome; she was tall, but not thin, and dressed in black velvet, and looked rather pale, but with a proud and commanding countenance, though now agitated strangely.

"Who was ever being so born to calamity?" I heard her say, with clasped hands, as I came up. "Here am I, on a journey of life and death, in prosecuting which to lose an hour is possibly to lose all. My child will not have recovered sufficiently to resume her route for who can say how long. I must leave her: I cannot, dare not, delay. How far on, sir, can you tell, is the nearest village? I must leave her there; and shall not see my darling, or even hear of her till my return, three months hence."

I plucked my father by the coat, and whispered earnestly in his ear: "Oh! papa, pray ask her to let her stay with us—it would be so delightful. Do, pray."

"If Madame will entrust her child to the care of my daughter, and of her good gouvernante, Madame Perrodon, and permit her to remain as our guest, under my charge, until her return, it will confer a distinction and an obligation upon us, and we shall treat her with all the care and devotion which so sacred a trust deserves."

"I cannot do that, sir, it would be to task your kindness and chivalry too cruelly," said the lady, distractedly.

"It would, on the contrary, be to confer on us a very great kindness at the moment when we most need it. My daughter has just been disappointed by a cruel misfortune, in a visit from which she had long anticipated a great deal of happiness. If you confide this young lady to our care it will be her best consolation. The nearest village on your route is distant, and affords no such inn as you could think of placing your daughter at; you cannot allow her to continue her journey for any considerable distance without danger. If, as you say, you cannot suspend your journey, you must part with her tonight, and nowhere could you do so with more honest assurances of care and tenderness than here."

There was something in this lady's air and appearance so distinguished and even imposing, and in her manner so engaging, as to impress one, quite apart from the dignity of her equipage, with a conviction that she was a person of consequence.

By this time the carriage was replaced in its upright position, and the horses, quite tractable, in the traces again.

The lady threw on her daughter a glance which I fancied was not quite so affectionate as one might have anticipated from the beginning of the scene; then she beckoned slightly to my father, and withdrew two or three steps with him out of hearing; and talked to him with a fixed and stern countenance, not at all like that with which she had hitherto spoken.

I was filled with wonder that my father did not seem to perceive the change, and also unspeakably curious to learn what it could be that she was speaking, almost in his ear, with so much earnestness and rapidity.

Two or three minutes at most I think she remained thus employed, then she turned, and a few steps brought her to where her daughter lay, supported by Madame Perrodon. She kneeled beside her for a moment and whispered, as Madame supposed, a little benediction in her ear; then hastily kissing her she stepped into her carriage, the door was closed, the footmen in stately liveries jumped up behind, the outriders spurred on, the postilions cracked their whips, the horses plunged and broke suddenly into a furious canter that threatened soon again to become a gallop, and the carriage whirled away, followed at the same rapid pace by the two horsemen in the rear.

III: We Compare Notes

We followed the cortege with our eyes until it was swiftly lost to sight in the misty wood; and the very sound of the hoofs and the wheels died away in the silent night air.

Nothing remained to assure us that the adventure had not been an illusion of a moment but the young lady, who just at that moment opened her eyes. I could not see, for her face was turned from me, but she raised her head, evidently looking about her, and I heard a very sweet voice ask complainingly, "Where is mamma?"

Our good Madame Perrodon answered tenderly, and added some comfortable assurances.

I then heard her ask:

"Where am I? What is this place?" and after that she said, "I don't see the carriage; and Matska, where is she?"

Madame answered all her questions in so far as she understood them; and gradually the young lady remembered how the misadventure came about, and was glad to hear that no one in, or in attendance on, the carriage was hurt; and on learning that her mamma had left her here, till her return in about three months, she wept.

I was going to add my consolations to those of Madame Perrodon when Mademoiselle De Lafontaine placed her hand upon my arm, saying:

"Don't approach, one at a time is as much as she can at present converse with; a very little excitement would possibly overpower her now."

As soon as she is comfortably in bed, I thought, I will run up to her room and see her.

My father in the meantime had sent a servant on horseback for the physician, who lived about two leagues away; and a bedroom was being prepared for the young lady's reception.

The stranger now rose, and leaning on Madame's arm, walked slowly over the drawbridge and into the castle gate.

In the hall, servants waited to receive her, and she was conducted forthwith to her room. The room we usually sat in as our drawing room is long, having four windows, that looked over the moat and drawbridge, upon the forest scene I have just described.

It is furnished in old carved oak, with large carved cabinets, and the chairs are cushioned with crimson Utrecht velvet. The walls are covered with tapestry, and surrounded with great gold frames, the figures being as large as life, in ancient and very curious costume, and the subjects represented are hunting, hawking, and generally festive. It is not too stately to be extremely comfortable; and here we had our tea, for with his usual patriotic leanings he insisted that the national beverage should make its appearance regularly with our coffee and chocolate.

We sat here this night, and with candles lighted, were talking over the adventure of the evening.

Madame Perrodon and Mademoiselle De Lafontaine were both of our party. The young stranger had hardly lain down in her bed when she sank into a deep sleep; and those ladies had left her in the care of a servant.

"How do you like our guest?" I asked, as soon as Madame entered. "Tell me all about her?"

"I like her extremely," answered Madame, "she is, I almost think, the prettiest creature I ever saw; about your age, and so gentle and nice."

"She is absolutely beautiful," threw in Mademoiselle, who had peeped for a moment into the stranger's room.

"And such a sweet voice!" added Madame Perrodon.

"Did you remark a woman in the carriage, after it was set up again, who did not get out," inquired Mademoiselle, "but only looked from the window?"

"No, we had not seen her."

Then she described a hideous black woman, with a sort of colored turban on her head, and who was gazing all the time from the carriage window, nodding and grinning derisively towards the ladies, with gleaming eyes and large white eyeballs, and her teeth set as if in fury.

"Did you remark what an ill-looking pack of men the servants were?" asked Madame.

"Yes," said my father, who had just come in, "ugly, hang-dog looking fellows as ever I beheld in my life. I hope they mayn't rob the poor lady in the forest. They are clever rogues, however; they got everything to rights in a minute."

"I dare say they are worn out with too long traveling," said Madame.

"Besides looking wicked, their faces were so strangely lean, and dark, and sullen. I am very curious, I own; but I dare say the young lady will tell you all about it tomorrow, if she is sufficiently recovered."

"I don't think she will," said my father, with a mysterious smile, and a little nod of his head, as if he knew more about it than he cared to tell us.

This made us all the more inquisitive as to what had passed between him and the lady in the black velvet, in the brief but earnest interview that had immediately preceded her departure.

We were scarcely alone, when I entreated him to tell me. He did not need much pressing.

"There is no particular reason why I should not tell you. She expressed a reluctance to trouble us with the care of her daughter, saying she was in delicate health, and nervous, but not subject to any kind of seizure—she volunteered that—nor to any illusion; being, in fact, perfectly sane."

"How very odd to say all that!" I interpolated. "It was so unnecessary."

"At all events it was said," he laughed, "and as you wish to know all that passed, which was indeed very little, I tell you. She then said, 'I am making a long journey of vital importance—she emphasized the word—rapid and secret;

I shall return for my child in three months; in the meantime, she will be silent as to who we are, whence we come, and whither we are traveling.' That is all she said. She spoke very pure French. When she said the word 'secret,' she paused for a few seconds, looking sternly, her eyes fixed on mine. I fancy she makes a great point of that. You saw how quickly she was gone. I hope I have not done a very foolish thing, in taking charge of the young lady."

For my part, I was delighted. I was longing to see and talk to her; and only waiting till the doctor should give me leave. You, who live in towns, can have no idea how great an event the introduction of a new friend is, in such a solitude as surrounded us.

The doctor did not arrive till nearly one o'clock; but I could no more have gone to my bed and slept, than I could have overtaken, on foot, the carriage in which the princess in black velvet had driven away.

When the physician came down to the drawing room, it was to report very favorably upon his patient. She was now sitting up, her pulse quite regular, apparently perfectly well. She had sustained no injury, and the little shock to her nerves had passed away quite harmlessly. There could be no harm certainly in my seeing her, if we both wished it; and, with this permission I sent, forthwith, to know whether she would allow me to visit her for a few minutes in her room.

The servant returned immediately to say that she desired nothing more.

You may be sure I was not long in availing myself of this permission.

Our visitor lay in one of the handsomest rooms in the schloss. It was, perhaps, a little stately. There was a somber piece of tapestry opposite the foot of the bed, representing Cleopatra with the asps to her bosom; and other solemn classic scenes were displayed, a little faded, upon the other walls. But there was gold carving, and rich and varied color enough in the other decorations of the room, to more than redeem the gloom of the old tapestry.

There were candles at the bedside. She was sitting up; her slender pretty figure enveloped in the soft silk dressing gown, embroidered with flowers, and lined with thick quilted silk, which her mother had thrown over her feet as she lay upon the ground.

What was it that, as I reached the bedside and had just begun my little greeting, struck me dumb in a moment, and made me recoil a step or two from before her? I will tell you.

I saw the very face which had visited me in my childhood at night, which remained so fixed in my memory, and on which I had for so many years so often ruminated with horror, when no one suspected of what I was thinking.

It was pretty, even beautiful; and when I first beheld it, wore the same melancholy expression.

But this almost instantly lighted into a strange fixed smile of recognition.

There was a silence of fully a minute, and then at length she spoke; I could not.

"How wonderful!" she exclaimed. "Twelve years ago, I saw your face in a dream, and it has haunted me ever since."

"Wonderful indeed!" I repeated, overcoming with an effort the horror that had for a time suspended my utterances. "Twelve years ago, in vision or reality, I certainly saw you. I could not forget your face. It has remained before my eyes ever since."

Her smile had softened. Whatever I had fancied strange in it, was gone, and it and her dimpling cheeks were now delightfully pretty and intelligent.

I felt reassured, and continued more in the vein which hospitality indicated, to bid her welcome, and to tell her how much pleasure her accidental arrival had given us all, and especially what a happiness it was to me.

I took her hand as I spoke. I was a little shy, as lonely people are, but the situation made me eloquent, and even bold. She pressed my hand, she laid hers upon it, and her eyes glowed, as, looking hastily into mine, she smiled again, and blushed.

She answered my welcome very prettily. I sat down beside her, still wondering; and she said:

"I must tell you my vision about you; it is so very strange that you and I should have had, each of the other so vivid a dream, that each should have seen, I you and you me, looking as we do now, when of course we both were mere children. I was a child, about six years old, and I awoke from a confused and troubled dream, and found myself in a room, unlike my nursery, wainscoted clumsily in some dark wood, and with cupboards and bedsteads, and chairs, and benches placed about it. The beds were, I thought, all empty, and the room itself without anyone but myself in it; and I, after looking about me for some time, and admiring especially an iron candlestick with two branches, which I should certainly know again, crept under one of the beds to reach the window; but as I got from under the bed, I heard someone crying; and looking up, while I was still upon my knees, I saw you—most assuredly you—as I see you now; a beautiful young lady, with golden hair and large blue eyes, and lips—your lips—you as you are here.

"Your looks won me; I climbed on the bed and put my arms about you, and I think we both fell asleep. I was aroused by a scream; you were sitting up screaming. I was frightened, and slipped down upon the ground, and, it seemed to me, lost consciousness for a moment; and when I came to myself, I was again in my nursery at home. Your face I have never forgotten since. I could not be misled by mere resemblance. You are the lady whom I saw then."

It was now my turn to relate my corresponding vision, which I did, to the undisguised wonder of my new acquaintance.

"I don't know which should be most afraid of the other," she said, again smiling—"If you were less pretty I think I should be very much afraid of you, but being as you are, and you and I both so young, I feel only that I have made your acquaintance twelve years ago, and have already a right to your intimacy; at all events it does seem as if we were destined, from our earliest childhood, to be friends. I wonder whether you feel as strangely drawn towards me as I do to you; I have never had a friend—shall I find one now?" She sighed, and her fine dark eyes gazed passionately on me.

Now the truth is, I felt rather unaccountably towards the beautiful stranger. I did feel, as she said, "drawn towards her," but there was also something of repulsion. In this ambiguous feeling, however, the sense of attraction immensely prevailed. She interested and won me; she was so beautiful and so indescribably engaging.

I perceived now something of languor and exhaustion stealing over her, and hastened to bid her good night.

"The doctor thinks," I added, "that you ought to have a maid to sit up with you tonight; one of ours is waiting, and you will find her a very useful and quiet creature."

"How kind of you, but I could not sleep, I never could with an attendant in the room. I shan't require any assistance—and, shall I confess my weakness, I am haunted with a terror of robbers. Our house was robbed once, and two servants murdered, so I always lock my door. It has become a habit—and you look so kind I know you will forgive me. I see there is a key in the lock."

She held me close in her pretty arms for a moment and whispered in my ear, "Good night, darling, it is very hard to part with you, but good night; tomorrow, but not early, I shall see you again."

She sank back on the pillow with a sigh, and her fine eyes followed me with a fond and melancholy gaze, and she murmured again "Good night, dear friend."

Young people like, and even love, on impulse. I was flattered by the evident, though as yet undeserved, fondness she showed me. I liked the confidence with which she at once received me. She was determined that we should be very near friends.

Next day came and we met again. I was delighted with my companion; that is to say, in many respects.

Her looks lost nothing in daylight—she was certainly the most beautiful creature I had ever seen, and the unpleasant remembrance of the face presented in my early dream, had lost the effect of the first unexpected recognition.

She confessed that she had experienced a similar shock on seeing me, and precisely the same faint antipathy that had mingled with my admiration of her. We now laughed together over our momentary horrors.

IV: Her Habits—A Saunter

I told you that I was charmed with her in most particulars.

There were some that did not please me so well.

She was above the middle height of women. I shall begin by describing her.

She was slender, and wonderfully graceful. Except that her movements were languid—very languid—indeed, there was nothing in her appearance to indicate an invalid. Her complexion was rich and brilliant; her features were small and beautifully formed; her eyes large, dark, and lustrous; her hair was quite wonderful, I never saw hair so magnificently thick and long when it was down about her shoulders; I have often placed my hands under it, and laughed with wonder at its weight. It was exquisitely fine and soft, and in color a rich very dark brown, with something of gold. I loved to let it down, tumbling with its own weight, as, in her room, she lay back in her chair talking in her sweet low voice, I used to fold and braid it, and spread it out and play with it. Heavens! If I had but known all!

I said there were particulars which did not please me. I have told you that her confidence won me the first night I saw her; but I found that she exercised with respect to herself, her mother, her history, everything in fact connected with her life, plans, and people, an ever wakeful reserve. I dare say I was unreasonable, perhaps I was wrong; I dare say I ought to have respected the solemn injunction laid upon my father by the stately lady in black velvet. But curiosity is a restless and unscrupulous passion, and no one girl can endure, with patience, that hers should be baffled by another. What harm could it do anyone to tell me what I so ardently desired to know? Had she no trust in my good sense or honor? Why would she not believe me when I assured her, so solemnly, that I would not divulge one syllable of what she told me to any mortal breathing.

There was a coldness, it seemed to me, beyond her years, in her smiling melancholy persistent refusal to afford me the least ray of light.

I cannot say we quarreled upon this point, for she would not quarrel upon any. It was, of course, very unfair of me to press her, very ill-bred, but I really could not help it; and I might just as well have let it alone.

What she did tell me amounted, in my unconscionable estimation—to nothing.

It was all summed up in three very vague disclosures:

First—Her name was Carmilla.

Second—Her family was very ancient and noble.

Third—Her home lay in the direction of the west.

She would not tell me the name of her family, nor their armorial bearings, nor the name of their estate, nor even that of the country they lived in.

You are not to suppose that I worried her incessantly on these subjects. I watched opportunity, and rather insinuated than urged my inquiries. Once or twice, indeed, I did attack her more directly. But no matter what my tactics, utter failure was invariably the result. Reproaches and caresses were all lost upon her. But I must add this, that her evasion was conducted with so pretty a melancholy and deprecation, with so many, and even passionate declarations of her liking for me, and trust in my honor, and with so many promises that I should at last know all, that I could not find it in my heart long to be offended with her.

She used to place her pretty arms about my neck, draw me to her, and laying her cheek to mine, murmur with her lips near my ear, "Dearest, your little heart is wounded; think me not cruel because I obey the irresistible law of my strength and weakness; if your dear heart is wounded, my wild heart bleeds with yours. In the rapture of my enormous humiliation I live in your warm life, and you shall die—die, sweetly die—into mine. I cannot help it; as I draw near to you, you, in your turn, will draw near to others, and learn the rapture of that cruelty, which yet is love; so, for a while, seek to know no more of me and mine, but trust me with all your loving spirit."

And when she had spoken such a rhapsody, she would press me more closely in her trembling embrace, and her lips in soft kisses gently glow upon my cheek.

Her agitations and her language were unintelligible to me.

From these foolish embraces, which were not of very frequent occurrence, I must allow, I used to wish to extricate myself; but my energies seemed to fail me. Her murmured words sounded like a lullaby in my ear, and soothed my resistance into a trance, from which I only seemed to recover myself when she withdrew her arms.

In these mysterious moods I did not like her. I experienced a strange tumultuous excitement that was pleasurable, ever and anon, mingled with a vague sense of fear and disgust. I had no distinct thoughts about her while such scenes lasted, but I was conscious of a love growing into adoration, and also of abhorrence. This I know is paradox, but I can make no other attempt to explain the feeling.

I now write, after an interval of more than ten years, with a trembling hand, with a confused and horrible recollection of certain occurrences and situations, in the ordeal through which I was unconsciously passing; though with a vivid and very sharp remembrance of the main current of my story.

But, I suspect, in all lives there are certain emotional scenes, those in which our passions have been most wildly and terribly roused, that are of all others the most vaguely and dimly remembered.

Sometimes after an hour of apathy, my strange and beautiful companion would take my hand and hold it with a fond pressure, renewed again and again; blushing softly, gazing in my face with languid and burning eyes, and breathing so fast that her dress rose and fell with the tumultuous respiration. It was like the ardor of a lover; it embarrassed me; it was hateful and yet over-powering; and with gloating eyes she drew me to her, and her hot lips traveled along my cheek in kisses; and she would whisper, almost in sobs, "You are mine, you shall be mine, you and I are one for ever." Then she had thrown herself back in her chair, with her small hands over her eyes, leaving me trembling.

"Are we related," I used to ask; "what can you mean by all this? I remind you perhaps of someone whom you love; but you must not, I hate it; I don't know you—I don't know myself when you look so and talk so."

She used to sigh at my vehemence, then turn away and drop my hand.

Respecting these very extraordinary manifestations I strove in vain to form any satisfactory theory—I could not refer them to affectation or trick. It was unmistakably the momentary breaking out of suppressed instinct and emotion. Was she, notwithstanding her mother's volunteered denial, subject to brief visitations of insanity; or was there here a disguise and a romance? I had read in old storybooks of such things. What if a boyish lover had found his way into the house, and sought to prosecute his suit in masquerade, with the assistance of a clever old adventuress. But there were many things against this hypothesis, highly interesting as it was to my vanity.

I could boast of no little attentions such as masculine gallantry delights to offer. Between these passionate moments there were long intervals of commonplace, of gaiety, of brooding melancholy, during which, except that I detected her eyes so full of melancholy fire, following me, at times I might have been as nothing to her. Except in these brief periods of mysterious excitement her ways were girlish; and there was always a languor about her, quite incompatible with a masculine system in a state of health.

In some respects her habits were odd. Perhaps not so singular in the opinion of a town lady like you, as they appeared to us rustic people. She used to come down very late, generally not till one o'clock, she would then take a cup of chocolate, but eat nothing; we then went out for a walk, which was a mere saunter, and she seemed, almost immediately, exhausted, and either returned to the schloss or sat on one of the benches that were placed, here and there, among the trees. This was a bodily languor in which her mind did not sympathize. She was always an animated talker, and very intelligent.

She sometimes alluded for a moment to her own home, or mentioned an adventure or situation, or an early recollection, which indicated a people of strange manners, and described customs of which we knew nothing. I gathered from these chance hints that her native country was much more remote than I had at first fancied.

As we sat thus one afternoon under the trees a funeral passed us by. It was that of a pretty young girl, whom I had often seen, the daughter of one of the rangers of the forest. The poor man was walking behind the coffin of his darling; she was his only child, and he looked quite heartbroken.

Peasants walking two-and-two came behind, they were singing a funeral hymn.

I rose to mark my respect as they passed, and joined in the hymn they were very sweetly singing.

My companion shook me a little roughly, and I turned surprised.

She said brusquely, "Don't you perceive how discordant that is?"

"I think it very sweet, on the contrary," I answered, vexed at the interruption, and very uncomfortable, lest the people who composed the little procession should observe and resent what was passing.

I resumed, therefore, instantly, and was again interrupted. "You pierce my ears," said Carmilla, almost angrily, and stopping her ears with her tiny fingers. "Besides, how can you tell that your religion and mine are the same; your forms wound me, and I hate funerals. What a fuss! Why you must die—everyone must die; and all are happier when they do. Come home."

"My father has gone on with the clergyman to the churchyard. I thought you knew she was to be buried today."

"She? I don't trouble my head about peasants. I don't know who she is," answered Carmilla, with a flash from her fine eyes.

"She is the poor girl who fancied she saw a ghost a fortnight ago, and has been dying ever since, till yesterday, when she expired."

"Tell me nothing about ghosts. I shan't sleep tonight if you do."

"I hope there is no plague or fever coming; all this looks very like it," I continued. "The swineherd's young wife died only a week ago, and she thought something seized her by the throat as she lay in her bed, and nearly strangled her. Papa says such horrible fancies do accompany some forms of fever. She was quite well the day before. She sank afterwards, and died before a week."

"Well, her funeral is over, I hope, and her hymn sung; and our ears shan't be tortured with that discord and jargon. It has made me nervous. Sit down here, beside me; sit close; hold my hand; press it hard-hard-harder."

We had moved a little back, and had come to another seat.

She sat down. Her face underwent a change that alarmed and even terrified me for a moment. It darkened, and became horribly livid; her teeth and hands were clenched, and she frowned and compressed her lips, while she stared down upon the ground at her feet, and trembled all over with a continued shudder as irrepressible as ague. All her energies seemed strained to suppress a fit, with which she was then breathlessly tugging; and at length a low convulsive cry of suffering broke from her, and gradually the hysteria subsided. "There! That comes of strangling people with hymns!" she said at last. "Hold me, hold me still. It is passing away."

And so gradually it did; and perhaps to dissipate the somber impression which the spectacle had left upon me, she became unusually animated and chatty; and so we got home.

This was the first time I had seen her exhibit any definable symptoms of that delicacy of health which her mother had spoken of. It was the first time, also, I had seen her exhibit anything like temper.

Both passed away like a summer cloud; and never but once afterwards did I witness on her part a momentary sign of anger. I will tell you how it happened.

She and I were looking out of one of the long drawing room windows, when there entered the courtyard, over the drawbridge, a figure of a wanderer whom I knew very well. He used to visit the schloss generally twice a year.

It was the figure of a hunchback, with the sharp lean features that generally accompany deformity. He wore a pointed black beard, and he was smiling from ear to ear, showing his white fangs. He was dressed in buff, black, and scarlet, and crossed with more straps and belts than I could count, from which hung all manner of things. Behind, he carried a magic lantern, and two boxes, which I well knew, in one of which was a salamander, and in the other a mandrake. These monsters used to make my father laugh. They were compounded of parts of monkeys, parrots, squirrels, fish, and hedgehogs, dried and stitched together with great neatness and startling effect. He had a fiddle, a box of conjuring apparatus, a pair of foils and masks attached to his belt, several other mysterious cases dangling about him, and a black staff with copper ferrules in his hand. His companion was a rough spare dog, that followed at his heels, but stopped short, suspiciously at the drawbridge, and in a little while began to howl dismally.

In the meantime, the mountebank, standing in the midst of the courtyard, raised his grotesque hat, and made us a very ceremonious bow, paying his compliments very volubly in execrable French, and German not much better.

Then, disengaging his fiddle, he began to scrape a lively air to which he sang with a merry discord, dancing with ludicrous airs and activity, that made me laugh, in spite of the dog's howling.

Then he advanced to the window with many smiles and salutations, and his hat in his left hand, his fiddle under his arm, and with a fluency that never took breath, he gabbled a long advertisement of all his accomplishments, and the resources of the various arts which he placed at our service, and the curiosities and entertainments which it was in his power, at our bidding, to display.

"Will your ladyships be pleased to buy an amulet against the oupire, which is going like the wolf, I hear, through these woods," he said dropping his hat on the pavement. "They are dying of it right and left and here is a charm that never fails; only pinned to the pillow, and you may laugh in his face."

These charms consisted of oblong slips of vellum, with cabalistic ciphers and diagrams upon them.

Carmilla instantly purchased one, and so did I.

He was looking up, and we were smiling down upon him, amused; at least, I can answer for myself. His piercing black eye, as he looked up in our faces, seemed to detect something that fixed for a moment his curiosity,

In an instant he unrolled a leather case, full of all manner of odd little steel instruments.

"See here, my lady," he said, displaying it, and addressing me, "I profess, among other things less useful, the art of dentistry. Plague take the dog!" he interpolated. "Silence, beast! He howls so that your ladyships can scarcely hear a word. Your noble friend, the young lady at your right, has the sharpest tooth,—long, thin, pointed, like an awl, like a needle; ha, ha! With my sharp and long sight, as I look up, I have seen it distinctly; now if it happens to hurt the young lady, and I think it must, here am I, here are my file, my punch, my nippers; I will make it round and blunt, if her ladyship pleases; no longer the tooth of a fish, but of a beautiful young lady as she is. Hey? Is the young lady displeased? Have I been too bold? Have I offended her?"

The young lady, indeed, looked very angry as she drew back from the window.

"How dares that mountebank insult us so? Where is your father? I shall demand redress from him. My father would have had the wretch tied up to the pump, and flogged with a cart whip, and burnt to the bones with the cattle brand!"

She retired from the window a step or two, and sat down, and had hardly lost sight of the offender, when her wrath subsided as suddenly as it had risen, and she gradually recovered her usual tone, and seemed to forget the little hunchback and his follies.

My father was out of spirits that evening. On coming in he told us that there had been another case very similar to the two fatal ones which had lately occurred. The sister of a young peasant on his estate, only a mile away, was very ill, had been, as she described it, attacked very nearly in the same way, and was now slowly but steadily sinking.

"All this," said my father, "is strictly referable to natural causes. These poor people infect one another with their superstitions, and so repeat in imagination the images of terror that have infested their neighbors."

"But that very circumstance frightens one horribly," said Carmilla.

"How so?" inquired my father.

"I am so afraid of fancying I see such things; I think it would be as bad as reality."

"We are in God's hands: nothing can happen without his permission, and all will end well for those who love him. He is our faithful creator; He has made us all, and will take care of us."

"Creator! Nature!" said the young lady in answer to my gentle father. "And this disease that invades the country is natural. Nature. All things proceed from Nature—don't they? All things in the heaven, in the earth, and under the earth, act and live as Nature ordains? I think so."

"The doctor said he would come here today," said my father, after a silence. "I want to know what he thinks about it, and what he thinks we had better do."

"Doctors never did me any good," said Carmilla.

"Then you have been ill?" I asked.

"More ill than ever you were," she answered.

"Long ago?"

"Yes, a long time. I suffered from this very illness; but I forget all but my pain and weakness, and they were not so bad as are suffered in other diseases."

"You were very young then?"

"I dare say, let us talk no more of it. You would not wound a friend?"

She looked languidly in my eyes, and passed her arm round my waist lovingly, and led me out of the room. My father was busy over some papers near the window.

"Why does your papa like to frighten us?" said the pretty girl with a sigh and a little shudder.

"He doesn't, dear Carmilla, it is the very furthest thing from his mind."

"Are you afraid, dearest?"

"I should be very much if I fancied there was any real danger of my being attacked as those poor people were."

"You are afraid to die?"

"Yes, every one is."

"But to die as lovers may—to die together, so that they may live together. Girls are caterpillars while they live in the world, to be finally butterflies when the summer comes; but in the meantime there are grubs and larvae, don't you see—each with their peculiar propensities, necessities and structure. So says Monsieur Buffon, in his big book, in the next room."

Later in the day the doctor came, and was closeted with papa for some time. He was a skilful man, of sixty and upwards, he wore powder, and shaved his pale face as smooth as a pumpkin. He and papa emerged from the room together, and I heard papa laugh, and say as they came out:

"Well, I do wonder at a wise man like you. What do you say to hippogriffs and dragons?"

The doctor was smiling, and made answer, shaking his head—

"Nevertheless life and death are mysterious states, and we know little of the resources of either."

And so they walked on, and I heard no more. I did not then know what the doctor had been broaching, but I think I guess it now.

V: A Wonderful Likeness

This evening there arrived from Gratz the grave, dark-faced son of the picture cleaner, with a horse and cart laden with two large packing cases, having many pictures in each. It was a journey of ten leagues, and whenever a messenger arrived at the schloss from our little capital of Gratz, we used to crowd about him in the hall, to hear the news.

This arrival created in our secluded quarters quite a sensation. The cases remained in the hall, and the messenger was taken charge of by the servants till he had eaten his supper. Then with assistants, and armed with hammer, ripping chisel, and turnscrew, he met us in the hall, where we had assembled to witness the unpacking of the cases.

Carmilla sat looking listlessly on, while one after the other the old pictures, nearly all portraits, which had undergone the process of renovation, were brought to light. My mother was of an old Hungarian family, and most of these pictures, which were about to be restored to their places, had come to us through her.

My father had a list in his hand, from which he read, as the artist rummaged out the corresponding numbers. I don't know that the pictures were very good, but they were, undoubtedly, very old, and some of them very curious also. They had, for the most part, the merit of being now seen by me, I may say, for the first time; for the smoke and dust of time had all but obliterated them.

"There is a picture that I have not seen yet," said my father. "In one corner, at the top of it, is the name, as well as I could read, 'Marcia Karnstein,' and the date '1698'; and I am curious to see how it has turned out."

I remembered it; it was a small picture, about a foot and a half high, and nearly square, without a frame; but it was so blackened by age that I could not make it out.

The artist now produced it, with evident pride. It was quite beautiful; it was startling; it seemed to live. It was the effigy of Carmilla!

"Carmilla, dear, here is an absolute miracle. Here you are, living, smiling, ready to speak, in this picture. Isn't it beautiful, Papa? And see, even the little mole on her throat."

My father laughed, and said "Certainly it is a wonderful likeness," but he looked away, and to my surprise seemed but little struck by it, and went on talking to the picture cleaner, who was also something of an artist, and discoursed with intelligence about the portraits or other works, which his art had just brought into light and color, while I was more and more lost in wonder the more I looked at the picture.

"Will you let me hang this picture in my room, papa?" I asked.

"Certainly, dear," said he, smiling, "I'm very glad you think it so like.

It must be prettier even than I thought it, if it is."

The young lady did not acknowledge this pretty speech, did not seem to hear it. She was leaning back in her seat, her fine eyes under their long lashes gazing on me in contemplation, and she smiled in a kind of rapture.

"And now you can read quite plainly the name that is written in the corner.

It is not Marcia; it looks as if it was done in gold. The name is Mircalla, Countess Karnstein, and this is a little coronet over and underneath A.D.

1698. I am descended from the Karnsteins; that is, mamma was."

"Ah!" said the lady, languidly, "so am I, I think, a very long descent, very ancient. Are there any Karnsteins living now?"

"None who bear the name, I believe. The family were ruined, I believe, in some civil wars, long ago, but the ruins of the castle are only about three miles away."

"How interesting!" she said, languidly. "But see what beautiful moonlight!" She glanced through the hall door, which stood a little open. "Suppose you take a little ramble round the court, and look down at the road and river."

"It is so like the night you came to us," I said.

She sighed; smiling.

She rose, and each with her arm about the other's waist, we walked out upon the pavement.

In silence, slowly we walked down to the drawbridge, where the beautiful landscape opened before us.

"And so you were thinking of the night I came here?" she almost whispered.

"Are you glad I came?"

"Delighted, dear Carmilla," I answered.

"And you asked for the picture you think like me, to hang in your room," she murmured with a sigh, as she drew her arm closer about my waist, and let her pretty head sink upon my shoulder. "How romantic you are, Carmilla," I said. "Whenever you tell me your story, it will be made up chiefly of some one great romance."

She kissed me silently.

"I am sure, Carmilla, you have been in love; that there is, at this moment, an affair of the heart going on."

"I have been in love with no one, and never shall," she whispered, "unless it should be with you."

How beautiful she looked in the moonlight!

Shy and strange was the look with which she quickly hid her face in my neck and hair, with tumultuous sighs, that seemed almost to sob, and pressed in mine a hand that trembled.

Her soft cheek was glowing against mine. "Darling, darling," she murmured, "I live in you; and you would die for me, I love you so."

I started from her.

She was gazing on me with eyes from which all fire, all meaning had flown, and a face colorless and apathetic.

"Is there a chill in the air, dear?" she said drowsily. "I almost shiver; have I been dreaming? Let us come in. Come; come; come in."

"You look ill, Carmilla; a little faint. You certainly must take some wine," I said.

"Yes. I will. I'm better now. I shall be quite well in a few minutes. Yes, do give me a little wine," answered Carmilla, as we approached the door.

"Let us look again for a moment; it is the last time, perhaps, I shall see the moonlight with you."

"How do you feel now, dear Carmilla? Are you really better?" I asked.

I was beginning to take alarm, lest she should have been stricken with the strange epidemic that they said had invaded the country about us.

"Papa would be grieved beyond measure," I added, "if he thought you were ever so little ill, without immediately letting us know. We have a very skilful doctor near us, the physician who was with papa today."

"I'm sure he is. I know how kind you all are; but, dear child, I am quite well again. There is nothing ever wrong with me, but a little weakness.

People say I am languid; I am incapable of exertion; I can scarcely walk as far as a child of three years old: and every now and then the little strength I have falters, and I become as you have just seen me. But after all I am very easily set up again; in a moment I am perfectly myself. See how I have recovered."

So, indeed, she had; and she and I talked a great deal, and very animated she was; and the remainder of that evening passed without any recurrence of what I called her infatuations. I mean her crazy talk and looks, which embarrassed, and even frightened me.

But there occurred that night an event which gave my thoughts quite a new turn, and seemed to startle even Carmilla's languid nature into momentary energy.

VI: A Very Strange Agony

When we got into the drawing room, and had sat down to our coffee and chocolate, although Carmilla did not take any, she seemed quite herself again, and Madame, and Mademoiselle De Lafontaine, joined us, and made a little card party, in the course of which papa came in for what he called his "dish of tea."

When the game was over he sat down beside Carmilla on the sofa, and asked her, a little anxiously, whether she had heard from her mother since her arrival.

She answered "No."

He then asked whether she knew where a letter would reach her at present.

"I cannot tell," she answered ambiguously, "but I have been thinking of leaving you; you have been already too hospitable and too kind to me. I have given you an infinity of trouble, and I should wish to take a carriage tomorrow, and post in pursuit of her; I know where I shall ultimately find her, although I dare not yet tell you."

"But you must not dream of any such thing," exclaimed my father, to my great relief. "We can't afford to lose you so, and I won't consent to your leaving us, except under the care of your mother, who was so good as to consent to your remaining with us till she should herself return. I should be quite happy if I knew that you heard from her: but this evening the accounts of the progress of the mysterious disease that has invaded our neighborhood, grow even more alarming; and my beautiful guest, I do feel the responsibility, unaided by advice from your mother, very much. But I shall do my best; and one thing is certain, that you must not think of leaving us without her distinct direction to that effect. We should suffer too much in parting from you to consent to it easily."

"Thank you, sir, a thousand times for your hospitality," she answered, smiling bashfully. "You have all been too kind to me; I have seldom been so happy in all my life before, as in your beautiful chateau, under your care, and in the society of your dear daughter."

So he gallantly, in his old-fashioned way, kissed her hand, smiling and pleased at her little speech.

I accompanied Carmilla as usual to her room, and sat and chatted with her while she was preparing for bed.

"Do you think," I said at length, "that you will ever confide fully in me?"

She turned round smiling, but made no answer, only continued to smile on me.

"You won't answer that?" I said. "You can't answer pleasantly; I ought not to have asked you."

"You were quite right to ask me that, or anything. You do not know how dear you are to me, or you could not think any confidence too great to look for.

But I am under vows, no nun half so awfully, and I dare not tell my story yet, even to you. The time is very near when you shall know everything. You will think me cruel, very selfish, but love is always selfish; the more ardent the more selfish. How jealous I am you cannot know. You must come with me, loving me, to death; or else hate me and still come with me. and hating me through death and after. There is no such word as indifference in my apathetic nature."

"Now, Carmilla, you are going to talk your wild nonsense again," I said hastily.

"Not I, silly little fool as I am, and full of whims and fancies; for your sake I'll talk like a sage. Were you ever at a ball?"

"No; how you do run on. What is it like? How charming it must be."

"I almost forget, it is years ago."

I laughed.

"You are not so old. Your first ball can hardly be forgotten yet."

"I remember everything about it—with an effort. I see it all, as divers see what is going on above them, through a medium, dense, rippling, but transparent. There occurred that night what has confused the picture, and made its colours faint. I was all but assassinated in my bed, wounded here," she touched her breast, "and never was the same since."

"Were you near dying?"

"Yes, very—a cruel love—strange love, that would have taken my life. Love will have its sacrifices. No sacrifice without blood. Let us go to sleep now; I feel so lazy. How can I get up just now and lock my door?"

She was lying with her tiny hands buried in her rich wavy hair, under her cheek, her little head upon the pillow, and her glittering eyes followed me wherever I moved, with a kind of shy smile that I could not decipher.

I bid her good night, and crept from the room with an uncomfortable sensation.

I often wondered whether our pretty guest ever said her prayers. I certainly had never seen her upon her knees. In the morning she never came down until long after our family prayers were over, and at night she never left the drawing room to attend our brief evening prayers in the hall.

If it had not been that it had casually come out in one of our careless talks that she had been baptised, I should have doubted her being a Christian. Religion was a subject on which I had never heard her speak a word. If I had known the world better, this particular neglect or antipathy would not have so much surprised me.

The precautions of nervous people are infectious, and persons of a like temperament are pretty sure, after a time, to imitate them. I had adopted Carmilla's habit of locking her bedroom door, having taken into my head all her whimsical alarms about midnight invaders and prowling assassins. I had also adopted her precaution of making a brief search through her room, to satisfy herself that no lurking assassin or robber was "ensconced."

These wise measures taken, I got into my bed and fell asleep. A light was burning in my room. This was an old habit, of very early date, and which nothing could have tempted me to dispense with.

Thus fortifed I might take my rest in peace. But dreams come through stone walls, light up dark rooms, or darken light ones, and their persons make their exits and their entrances as they please, and laugh at locksmiths.

I had a dream that night that was the beginning of a very strange agony.

I cannot call it a nightmare, for I was quite conscious of being asleep.

But I was equally conscious of being in my room, and lying in bed, precisely as I actually was. I saw, or fancied I saw, the room and its furniture just as I had seen it last, except that it was very dark, and I saw something moving round the foot of the bed, which at first I could not accurately distinguish. But I soon saw that it was a sooty-black animal that resembled a monstrous cat. It appeared to me about four or five feet long for it measured fully the length of the hearthrug as it passed over it; and it continued to-ing and fro-ing with the lithe, sinister restlessness of a beast in a cage. I could not cry out, although as you may suppose, I was terrified. Its pace was growing faster, and the room rapidly darker and darker, and at length so dark that I could no longer see anything of it but its eyes. I felt it spring lightly on the bed. The two broad eyes approached my face, and suddenly I felt a stinging pain as if two large needles darted, an inch or two apart, deep into my breast. I waked with a scream. The room was lighted by the candle that burnt there all through the night, and I saw a female figure standing at the foot of the bed, a little at the right side. It was in a dark loose dress, and its hair was down and covered its shoulders. A block of stone could not have been more still. There was not the slightest stir of respiration. As I stared at it, the figure appeared to have changed its place, and was now nearer the door; then, close to it, the door opened, and it passed out.

I was now relieved, and able to breathe and move. My first thought was that Carmilla had been playing me a trick, and that I had forgotten to secure my door. I hastened to it, and found it locked as usual on the inside. I was afraid to open it—I was horrified. I sprang into my bed and covered my head up in the bedclothes, and lay there more dead than alive till morning.

VII: Descending

It would be vain my attempting to tell you the horror with which, even now, I recall the occurrence of that night. It was no such transitory terror as a dream leaves behind it. It seemed to deepen by time, and communicated itself to the room and the very furniture that had encompassed the apparition.

I could not bear next day to be alone for a moment. I should have told papa, but for two opposite reasons. At one time I thought he would laugh at my story, and I could not bear its being treated as a jest; and at another I thought he might fancy that I had been attacked by the mysterious complaint which had invaded our neighborhood. I had myself no misgiving of the kind, and as he had been rather an invalid for some time, I was afraid of alarming him.

I was comfortable enough with my good-natured companions, Madame Perrodon, and the vivacious Mademoiselle Lafontaine. They both perceived that I was out of spirits and nervous, and at length I told them what lay so heavy at my heart.

Mademoiselle laughed, but I fancied that Madame Perrodon looked anxious.

"By-the-by," said Mademoiselle, laughing, "the long lime tree walk, behind Carmilla's bedroom window, is haunted!"

"Nonsense!" exclaimed Madame, who probably thought the theme rather inopportune, "and who tells that story, my dear?"

"Martin says that he came up twice, when the old yard gate was being repaired, before sunrise, and twice saw the same female figure walking down the lime tree avenue."

"So he well might, as long as there are cows to milk in the river fields," said Madame.

"I daresay; but Martin chooses to be frightened, and never did I see fool more frightened."

"You must not say a word about it to Carmilla, because she can see down that walk from her room window," I interposed, "and she is, if possible, a greater coward than I."

Carmilla came down rather later than usual that day.

"I was so frightened last night," she said, so soon as were together, "and I am sure I should have seen something dreadful if it had not been for that charm I bought from the poor little hunchback whom I called such hard names. I had a dream of something black coming round my bed, and I awoke in a perfect horror, and I really thought, for some seconds, I saw a dark figure near the chimneypiece, but I felt under my pillow for my charm, and the moment my fingers touched it, the figure disappeared, and I felt quite certain, only that I had it by me, that something frightful would have made its appearance, and, perhaps, throttled me, as it did those poor people we heard of.

"Well, listen to me," I began, and recounted my adventure, at the recital of which she appeared horrified.

"And had you the charm near you?" she asked, earnestly.

"No, I had dropped it into a china vase in the drawing room, but I shall certainly take it with me tonight, as you have so much faith in it."

At this distance of time I cannot tell you, or even understand, how I overcame my horror so effectually as to lie alone in my room that night. I remember distinctly that I pinned the charm to my pillow. I fell asleep almost immediately, and slept even more soundly than usual all night.

Next night I passed as well. My sleep was delightfully deep and dreamless.

But I wakened with a sense of lassitude and melancholy, which, however, did not exceed a degree that was almost luxurious.

"Well, I told you so," said Carmilla, when I described my quiet sleep, "I had such delightful sleep myself last night; I pinned the charm to the breast of my nightdress. It was too far away the night before. I am quite sure it was all fancy, except the dreams. I used to think that evil spirits made dreams, but our doctor told me it is no such thing. Only a fever passing by, or some other malady, as they often do, he said, knocks at the door, and not being able to get in, passes on, with that alarm."

"And what do you think the charm is?" said I.

"It has been fumigated or immersed in some drug, and is an antidote against the malaria," she answered.

"Then it acts only on the body?"

"Certainly; you don't suppose that evil spirits are frightened by bits of ribbon, or the perfumes of a druggist's shop? No, these complaints, wandering in the air, begin by trying the nerves, and so infect the brain, but before they can seize upon you, the antidote repels them. That I am sure is what the charm has done for us. It is nothing magical, it is simply natural.

I should have been happier if I could have quite agreed with Carmilla, but I did my best, and the impression was a little losing its force.

For some nights I slept profoundly; but still every morning I felt the same lassitude, and a languor weighed upon me all day. I felt myself a changed girl. A strange melancholy was stealing over me, a melancholy that I would not have interrupted. Dim thoughts of death began to open, and an idea that I was slowly sinking took gentle, and, somehow, not unwelcome, possession of me. If it was sad, the tone of mind which this induced was also sweet.

Whatever it might be, my soul acquiesced in it.

I would not admit that I was ill, I would not consent to tell my papa, or to have the doctor sent for.

Carmilla became more devoted to me than ever, and her strange paroxysms of languid adoration more frequent. She used to gloat on me with increasing ardor the more my strength and spirits waned. This always shocked me like a momentary glare of insanity.

Without knowing it, I was now in a pretty advanced stage of the strangest illness under which mortal ever suffered. There was an unaccountable fascination in its earlier symptoms that more than reconciled me to the incapacitating effect of that stage of the malady. This fascination increased for a time, until it reached a certain point, when gradually a sense of the horrible mingled itself with it, deepening, as you shall hear, until it discolored and perverted the whole state of my life.

The first change I experienced was rather agreeable. It was very near the turning point from which began the descent of Avernus.

Certain vague and strange sensations visited me in my sleep. The prevailing one was of that pleasant, peculiar cold thrill which we feel in bathing, when we move against the current of a river. This was soon accompanied by dreams that seemed interminable, and were so vague that I could never recollect their scenery and persons, or any one connected portion of their action. But they left an awful impression, and a sense of exhaustion, as if I had passed through a long period of great mental exertion and danger.

After all these dreams there remained on waking a remembrance of having been in a place very nearly dark, and of having spoken to people whom I could not see; and especially of one clear voice, of a female's, very deep, that spoke as if at a distance, slowly, and producing always the same sensation of indescribable solemnity and fear. Sometimes there came a sensation as if a hand was drawn softly along my cheek and neck. Sometimes it was as if warm lips kissed me, and longer and longer and more lovingly as they reached my throat, but there the caress fixed itself. My heart beat faster, my breathing rose and fell rapidly and full drawn; a sobbing, that rose into a sense of strangulation, supervened, and turned into a dreadful convulsion, in which my senses left me and I became unconscious.

It was now three weeks since the commencement of this unaccountable state.

My sufferings had, during the last week, told upon my appearance. I had grown pale, my eyes were dilated and darkened underneath, and the languor which I had long felt began to display itself in my countenance.

My father asked me often whether I was ill; but, with an obstinacy which now seems to me unaccountable, I persisted in assuring him that I was quite well.

In a sense this was true. I had no pain, I could complain of no bodily derangement. My complaint seemed to be one of the imagination, or the nerves, and, horrible as my sufferings were, I kept them, with a morbid reserve, very nearly to myself.

It could not be that terrible complaint which the peasants called the oupire, for I had now been suffering for three weeks, and they were seldom ill for much more than three days, when death put an end to their miseries.

Carmilla complained of dreams and feverish sensations, but by no means of so alarming a kind as mine. I say that mine were extremely alarming. Had I been capable of comprehending my condition, I would have invoked aid and advice on my knees. The narcotic of an unsuspected influence was acting upon me, and my perceptions were benumbed.

I am going to tell you now of a dream that led immediately to an odd discovery.

One night, instead of the voice I was accustomed to hear in the dark, I heard one, sweet and tender, and at the same time terrible, which said,

"Your mother warns you to beware of the assassin." At the same time a light unexpectedly sprang up, and I saw Carmilla, standing, near the foot of my bed, in her white nightdress, bathed, from her chin to her feet, in one great stain of blood.

I wakened with a shriek, possessed with the one idea that Carmilla was being murdered. I remember springing from my bed, and my next recollection is that of standing on the lobby, crying for help.

Madame and Mademoiselle came scurrying out of their rooms in alarm; a lamp burned always on the lobby, and seeing me, they soon learned the cause of my terror.

I insisted on our knocking at Carmilla's door. Our knocking was unanswered.

It soon became a pounding and an uproar. We shrieked her name, but all was vain.

We all grew frightened, for the door was locked. We hurried back, in panic, to my room. There we rang the bell long and furiously. If my father's room had been at that side of the house, we would have called him up at once to our aid.

But, alas! he was quite out of hearing, and to reach him involved an excursion for which we none of us had courage.

Servants, however, soon came running up the stairs; I had got on my dressing gown and slippers meanwhile, and my companions were already similarly furnished. Recognizing the voices of the servants on the lobby, we sallied out together; and having renewed, as fruitlessly, our summons at Carmilla's door, I ordered the men to force the lock. They did so, and we stood, holding our lights aloft, in the doorway, and so stared into the room.

We called her by name; but there was still no reply. We looked round the room. Everything was undisturbed. It was exactly in the state in which I had left it on bidding her good night. But Carmilla was gone.

VIII: Search

At sight of the room, perfectly undisturbed except for our violent entrance, we began to cool a little, and soon recovered our senses sufficiently to dismiss the men. It had struck Mademoiselle that possibly Carmilla had been wakened by the uproar at her door, and in her first panic had jumped from her bed, and hid herself in a press, or behind a curtain, from which she could not, of course, emerge until the majordomo and his myrmidons had withdrawn. We now recommenced our search, and began to call her name again.

It was all to no purpose. Our perplexity and agitation increased. We examined the windows, but they were secured. I implored of Carmilla, if she had concealed herself, to play this cruel trick no longer—to come out and to end our anxieties. It was all useless. I was by this time convinced that she was not in the room, nor in the dressing room, the door of which was still locked on this side. She could not have passed it. I was utterly puzzled. Had Carmilla discovered one of those secret passages which the old housekeeper said were known to exist in the schloss, although the tradition of their exact situation had been lost? A little time would, no doubt, explain all—utterly perplexed as, for the present, we were.

It was past four o'clock, and I preferred passing the remaining hours of darkness in Madame's room. Daylight brought no solution of the difficulty.

The whole household, with my father at its head, was in a state of agitation next morning. Every part of the chateau was searched. The grounds were explored. No trace of the missing lady could be discovered. The stream was about to be dragged; my father was in distraction; what a tale to have to tell the poor girl's mother on her return. I, too, was almost beside myself, though my grief was quite of a different kind.

The morning was passed in alarm and excitement. It was now one o'clock, and still no tidings. I ran up to Carmilla's room, and found her standing at her dressing table. I was astounded. I could not believe my eyes. She beckoned me to her with her pretty finger, in silence. Her face expressed extreme fear.

I ran to her in an ecstasy of joy; I kissed and embraced her again and again. I ran to the bell and rang it vehemently, to bring others to the spot who might at once relieve my father's anxiety.

"Dear Carmilla, what has become of you all this time? We have been in agonies of anxiety about you," I exclaimed. "Where have you been? How did you come back?"

"Last night has been a night of wonders," she said.

"For mercy's sake, explain all you can."

"It was past two last night," she said, "when I went to sleep as usual in my bed, with my doors locked, that of the dressing room, and that opening upon the gallery. My sleep was uninterrupted, and, so far as I know, dreamless; but I woke just now on the sofa in the dressing room there, and I found the door between the rooms open, and the other door forced. How could all this have happened without my being wakened? It must have been accompanied with a great deal of noise, and I am particularly easily wakened; and how could I have been carried out of my bed without my sleep having been interrupted, I whom the slightest stir startles?"

By this time, Madame, Mademoiselle, my father, and a number of the servants were in the room. Carmilla was, of course, overwhelmed with inquiries, congratulations, and welcomes. She had but one story to tell, and seemed the least able of all the party to suggest any way of accounting for what had happened.

My father took a turn up and down the room, thinking. I saw Carmilla's eye follow him for a moment with a sly, dark glance.

When my father had sent the servants away, Mademoiselle having gone in search of a little bottle of valerian and salvolatile, and there being no one now in the room with Carmilla, except my father, Madame, and myself, he came to her thoughtfully, took her hand very kindly, led her to the sofa, and sat down beside her.

"Will you forgive me, my dear, if I risk a conjecture, and ask a question?"

"Who can have a better right?" she said. "Ask what you please, and I will tell you everything. But my story is simply one of bewilderment and darkness. I know absolutely nothing. Put any question you please, but you know, of course, the limitations mamma has placed me under."

"Perfectly, my dear child. I need not approach the topics on which she desires our silence. Now, the marvel of last night consists in your having been removed from your bed and your room, without being wakened, and this removal having occurred apparently while the windows were still secured, and the two doors locked upon the inside. I will tell you my theory and ask you a question."

Carmilla was leaning on her hand dejectedly; Madame and I were listening breathlessly.

"Now, my question is this. Have you ever been suspected of walking in your sleep?"

"Never, since I was very young indeed."

"But you did walk in your sleep when you were young?"

"Yes; I know I did. I have been told so often by my old nurse."

My father smiled and nodded.

"Well, what has happened is this. You got up in your sleep, unlocked the door, not leaving the key, as usual, in the lock, but taking it out and locking it on the outside; you again took the key out, and carried it away with you to some one of the five-and-twenty rooms on this floor, or perhaps upstairs or downstairs. There are so many rooms and closets, so much heavy furniture, and such accumulations of lumber, that it would require a week to search this old house thoroughly. Do you see, now, what I mean?"

"I do, but not all," she answered.

"And how, papa, do you account for her finding herself on the sofa in the dressing room, which we had searched so carefully?"

"She came there after you had searched it, still in her sleep, and at last awoke spontaneously, and was as much surprised to find herself where she was as any one else. I wish all mysteries were as easily and innocently explained as yours, Carmilla," he said, laughing. "And so we may congratulate ourselves on the certainty that the most natural explanation of the occurrence is one that involves no drugging, no tampering with locks, no burglars, or poisoners, or witches—nothing that need alarm Carmilla, or anyone else, for our safety."

Carmilla was looking charmingly. Nothing could be more beautiful than her tints. Her beauty was, I think, enhanced by that graceful languor that was peculiar to her. I think my father was silently contrasting her looks with mine, for he said:

"I wish my poor Laura was looking more like herself"; and he sighed.

So our alarms were happily ended, and Carmilla restored to her friends.

IX: The Doctor

As Carmilla would not hear of an attendant sleeping in her room, my father arranged that a servant should sleep outside her door, so that she would not attempt to make another such excursion without being arrested at her own door.

That night passed quietly; and next morning early, the doctor, whom my father had sent for without telling me a word about it, arrived to see me.

Madame accompanied me to the library; and there the grave little doctor, with white hair and spectacles, whom I mentioned before, was waiting to receive me.

I told him my story, and as I proceeded he grew graver and graver.

We were standing, he and I, in the recess of one of the windows, facing one another. When my statement was over, he leaned with his shoulders against the wall, and with his eyes fixed on me earnestly, with an interest in which was a dash of horror.

After a minute's reflection, he asked Madame if he could see my father.

He was sent for accordingly, and as he entered, smiling, he said:

"I dare say, doctor, you are going to tell me that I am an old fool for having brought you here; I hope I am."

But his smile faded into shadow as the doctor, with a very grave face, beckoned him to him.

He and the doctor talked for some time in the same recess where I had just conferred with the physician. It seemed an earnest and argumentative conversation. The room is very large, and I and Madame stood together, burning with curiosity, at the farther end. Not a word could we hear, however, for they spoke in a very low tone, and the deep recess of the window quite concealed the doctor from view, and very nearly my father, whose foot, arm, and shoulder only could we see; and the voices were, I suppose, all the less audible for the sort of closet which the thick wall and window formed.

After a time my father's face looked into the room; it was pale, thoughtful, and, I fancied, agitated.

"Laura, dear, come here for a moment. Madame, we shan't trouble you, the doctor says, at present."

Accordingly I approached, for the first time a little alarmed; for, although I felt very weak, I did not feel ill; and strength, one always fancies, is a thing that may be picked up when we please.

My father held out his hand to me, as I drew near, but he was looking at the doctor, and he said:

"It certainly is very odd; I don't understand it quite. Laura, come here, dear; now attend to Doctor Spielsberg, and recollect yourself."

"You mentioned a sensation like that of two needles piercing the skin, somewhere about your neck, on the night when you experienced your first horrible dream. Is there still any soreness?"

"None at all," I answered.

"Can you indicate with your finger about the point at which you think this occurred?"

"Very little below my throat—here," I answered.

I wore a morning dress, which covered the place I pointed to.

"Now you can satisfy yourself," said the doctor. "You won't mind your papa's lowering your dress a very little. It is necessary, to detect a symptom of the complaint under which you have been suffering."

I acquiesced. It was only an inch or two below the edge of my collar.

"God bless me!—so it is," exclaimed my father, growing pale.

"You see it now with your own eyes," said the doctor, with a gloomy triumph.

"What is it?" I exclaimed, beginning to be frightened.

"Nothing, my dear young lady, but a small blue spot, about the size of the tip of your little finger; and now," he continued, turning to papa, "the question is what is best to be done?"

Is there any danger?"I urged, in great trepidation.

"I trust not, my dear," answered the doctor. "I don't see why you should not recover. I don't see why you should not begin immediately to get better. That is the point at which the sense of strangulation begins?"

"Yes," I answered.

"And—recollect as well as you can—the same point was a kind of center of that thrill which you described just now, like the current of a cold stream running against you?"

"It may have been; I think it was."

"Ay, you see?" he added, turning to my father. "Shall I say a word to Madame?"

"Certainly," said my father.

He called Madame to him, and said:

"I find my young friend here far from well. It won't be of any great consequence, I hope; but it will be necessary that some steps be taken, which I will explain by-and-by; but in the meantime, Madame, you will be so good as not to let Miss Laura be alone for one moment. That is the only direction I need give for the present. It is indispensable."

"We may rely upon your kindness, Madame, I know," added my father.

Madame satisfied him eagerly.

"And you, dear Laura, I know you will observe the doctor's direction."

"I shall have to ask your opinion upon another patient, whose symptoms slightly resemble those of my daughter, that have just been detailed to you—very much milder in degree, but I believe quite of the same sort. She is a young lady—our guest; but as you say you will be passing this way again this evening, you can't do better than take your supper here, and you can then see her. She does not come down till the afternoon."

"I thank you," said the doctor. "I shall be with you, then, at about seven this evening."

And then they repeated their directions to me and to Madame, and with this parting charge my father left us, and walked out with the doctor; and I saw them pacing together up and down between the road and the moat, on the grassy platform in front of the castle, evidently absorbed in earnest conversation.

The doctor did not return. I saw him mount his horse there, take his leave, and ride away eastward through the forest.

Nearly at the same time I saw the man arrive from Dranfield with the letters, and dismount and hand the bag to my father.

In the meantime, Madame and I were both busy, lost in conjecture as to the reasons of the singular and earnest direction which the doctor and my father had concurred in imposing. Madame, as she afterwards told me, was afraid the doctor apprehended a sudden seizure, and that, without prompt assistance, I might either lose my life in a fit, or at least be seriously hurt.

The interpretation did not strike me; and I fancied, perhaps luckily for my nerves, that the arrangement was prescribed simply to secure a companion, who would prevent my taking too much exercise, or eating unripe fruit, or doing any of the fifty foolish things to which young people are supposed to be prone.

About half an hour after my father came in—he had a letter in his hand—and said:

"This letter had been delayed; it is from General Spielsdorf. He might have been here yesterday, he may not come till tomorrow or he may be here today."

He put the open letter into my hand; but he did not look pleased, as he used when a guest, especially one so much loved as the General, was coming.

On the contrary, he looked as if he wished him at the bottom of the Red Sea. There was plainly something on his mind which he did not choose to divulge.

"Papa, darling, will you tell me this?" said I, suddenly laying my hand on his arm, and looking, I am sure, imploringly in his face.

"Perhaps," he answered, smoothing my hair caressingly over my eyes.

"Does the doctor think me very ill?"

"No, dear; he thinks, if right steps are taken, you will be quite well again, at least, on the high road to a complete recovery, in a day or two," he answered, a little dryly. "I wish our good friend, the General, had chosen any other time; that is, I wish you had been perfectly well to receive him."

"But do tell me, papa," I insisted, "what does he think is the matter with me?"

"Nothing; you must not plague me with questions," he answered, with more irritation than I ever remember him to have displayed before; and seeing that I looked wounded, I suppose, he kissed me, and added, "You shall know all about it in a day or two; that is, all that I know. In the meantime you are not to trouble your head about it."

He turned and left the room, but came back before I had done wondering and puzzling over the oddity of all this; it was merely to say that he was going to Karnstein, and had ordered the carriage to be ready at twelve, and that I and Madame should accompany him; he was going to see the priest who lived near those picturesque grounds, upon business, and as Carmilla had never seen them, she could follow, when she came down, with Mademoiselle, who would bring materials for what you call a picnic, which might be laid for us in the ruined castle.

At twelve o'clock, accordingly, I was ready, and not long after, my father, Madame and I set out upon our projected drive.

Passing the drawbridge we turn to the right, and follow the road over the steep Gothic bridge, westward, to reach the deserted village and ruined castle of Karnstein.

No sylvan drive can be fancied prettier. The ground breaks into gentle hills and hollows, all clothed with beautiful wood, totally destitute of the comparative formality which artificial planting and early culture and pruning impart.

The irregularities of the ground often lead the road out of its course, and cause it to wind beautifully round the sides of broken hollows and the steeper sides of the hills, among varieties of ground almost inexhaustible.

Turning one of these points, we suddenly encountered our old friend, the General, riding towards us, attended by a mounted servant. His portmanteaus were following in a hired wagon, such as we term a cart.

The General dismounted as we pulled up, and, after the usual greetings, was easily persuaded to accept the vacant seat in the carriage and send his horse on with his servant to the schloss.

X: Bereaved

It was about ten months since we had last seen him: but that time had sufficed to make an alteration of years in his appearance. He had grown thinner; something of gloom and anxiety had taken the place of that cordial serenity which used to characterize his features. His dark blue eyes, always penetrating, now gleamed with a sterner light from under his shaggy grey eyebrows. It was not such a change as grief alone usually induces, and angrier passions seemed to have had their share in bringing it about.

We had not long resumed our drive, when the General began to talk, with his usual soldierly directness, of the bereavement, as he termed it, which he had sustained in the death of his beloved niece and ward; and he then broke out in a tone of intense bitterness and fury, inveighing against the "hellish arts" to which she had fallen a victim, and expressing, with more exasperation than piety, his wonder that Heaven should tolerate so monstrous an indulgence of the lusts and malignity of hell.

My father, who saw at once that something very extraordinary had befallen, asked him, if not too painful to him, to detail the circumstances which he thought justified the strong terms in which he expressed himself.

"I should tell you all with pleasure," said the General, "but you would not believe me."

"Why should I not?" he asked.

"Because," he answered testily, "you believe in nothing but what consists with your own prejudices and illusions. I remember when I was like you, but I have learned better."

"Try me," said my father; "I am not such a dogmatist as you suppose.

Besides which, I very well know that you generally require proof for what you believe, and am, therefore, very strongly predisposed to respect your conclusions."

"You are right in supposing that I have not been led lightly into a belief in the marvelous—for what I have experienced is marvelous—and I have been forced by extraordinary evidence to credit that which ran counter, diametrically, to all my theories. I have been made the dupe of a preternatural conspiracy."

Notwithstanding his professions of confidence in the General's penetration, I saw my father, at this point, glance at the General, with, as I thought, a marked suspicion of his sanity.

The General did not see it, luckily. He was looking gloomily and curiously into the glades and vistas of the woods that were opening before us.

"You are going to the Ruins of Karnstein?" he said. "Yes, it is a lucky coincidence; do you know I was going to ask you to bring me there to inspect them. I have a special object in exploring. There is a ruined chapel, ain't there, with a great many tombs of that extinct family?"

"So there are—highly interesting," said my father. "I hope you are thinking of claiming the title and estates?"

My father said this gaily, but the General did not recollect the laugh, or even the smile, which courtesy exacts for a friend's joke; on the contrary, he looked grave and even fierce, ruminating on a matter that stirred his anger and horror.

"Something very different," he said, gruffly. "I mean to unearth some of those fine people. I hope, by God's blessing, to accomplish a pious sacrilege here, which will relieve our earth of certain monsters, and enable honest people to sleep in their beds without being assailed by murderers. I have strange things to tell you, my dear friend, such as I myself would have scouted as incredible a few months since."

My father looked at him again, but this time not with a glance of suspicion—with an eye, rather, of keen intelligence and alarm.

"The house of Karnstein," he said, "has been long extinct: a hundred years at least. My dear wife was maternally descended from the Karnsteins. But the name and title have long ceased to exist. The castle is a ruin; the very village is deserted; it is fifty years since the smoke of a chimney was seen there; not a roof left."

"Quite true. I have heard a great deal about that since I last saw you; a great deal that will astonish you. But I had better relate everything in the order in which it occurred," said the General. "You saw my dear ward—my child, I may call her. No creature could have been more beautiful, and only three months ago none more blooming."

"Yes, poor thing! when I saw her last she certainly was quite lovely," said my father. "I was grieved and shocked more than I can tell you, my dear friend; I knew what a blow it was to you."

He took the General's hand, and they exchanged a kind pressure. Tears gathered in the old soldier's eyes. He did not seek to conceal them. He said:

"We have been very old friends; I knew you would feel for me, childless as I am. She had become an object of very near interest to me, and repaid my care by an affection that cheered my home and made my life happy. That is all gone. The years that remain to me on earth may not be very long; but by God's mercy I hope to accomplish a service to mankind before I die, and to subserve the vengeance of Heaven upon the fiends who have murdered my poor child in the spring of her hopes and beauty!"

"You said, just now, that you intended relating everything as it occurred," said my father. "Pray do; I assure you that it is not mere curiosity that prompts me."

By this time we had reached the point at which the Drunstall road, by which the General had come, diverges from the road which we were traveling to Karnstein.

"How far is it to the ruins?" inquired the General, looking anxiously forward.

"About half a league," answered my father. "Pray let us hear the story you were so good as to promise."

XI: The Story

With all my heart," said the General, with an effort; and after a short pause in which to arrange his subject, he commenced one of the strangest narratives I ever heard.

"My dear child was looking forward with great pleasure to the visit you had been so good as to arrange for her to your charming daughter." Here he made me a gallant but melancholy bow. "In the meantime we had an invitation to my old friend the Count Carlsfeld, whose schloss is about six leagues to the other side of Karnstein. It was to attend the series of fetes which, you remember, were given by him in honor of his illustrious visitor, the Grand Duke Charles."

"Yes; and very splendid, I believe, they were," said my father.

"Princely! But then his hospitalities are quite regal. He has Aladdin's lamp. The night from which my sorrow dates was devoted to a magnificent masquerade. The grounds were thrown open, the trees hung with colored lamps. There was such a display of fireworks as Paris itself had never witnessed. And such music—music, you know, is my weakness—such ravishing music! The finest instrumental band, perhaps, in the world, and the finest singers who could be collected from all the great operas in Europe. As you wandered through these fantastically illuminated grounds, the moon-lighted chateau throwing a rosy light from its long rows of windows, you would suddenly hear these ravishing voices stealing from the silence of some grove, or rising from boats upon the lake. I felt myself, as I looked and listened, carried back into the romance and poetry of my early youth.

"When the fireworks were ended, and the ball beginning, we returned to the noble suite of rooms that were thrown open to the dancers. A masked ball, you know, is a beautiful sight; but so brilliant a spectacle of the kind I never saw before.

"It was a very aristocratic assembly. I was myself almost the only 'nobody' present.

"My dear child was looking quite beautiful. She wore no mask. Her excitement and delight added an unspeakable charm to her features, always lovely. I remarked a young lady, dressed magnificently, but wearing a mask, who appeared to me to be observing my ward with extraordinary interest. I had seen her, earlier in the evening, in the great hall, and again, for a few minutes, walking near us, on the terrace under the castle windows, similarly employed. A lady, also masked, richly and gravely dressed, and with a stately air, like a person of rank, accompanied her as a chaperon.

Had the young lady not worn a mask, I could, of course, have been much more certain upon the question whether she was really watching my poor darling.

I am now well assured that she was.

"We were now in one of the salons. My poor dear child had been dancing, and was resting a little in one of the chairs near the door; I was standing near. The two ladies I have mentioned had approached and the younger took the chair next my ward; while her companion stood beside me, and for a little time addressed herself, in a low tone, to her charge.

"Availing herself of the privilege of her mask, she turned to me, and in the tone of an old friend, and calling me by my name, opened a conversation with me, which piqued my curiosity a good deal. She referred to many scenes where she had met me—at Court, and at distinguished houses. She alluded to little incidents which I had long ceased to think of, but which, I found, had only lain in abeyance in my memory, for they instantly started into life at her touch.

"I became more and more curious to ascertain who she was, every moment. She parried my attempts to discover very adroitly and pleasantly. The knowledge she showed of many passages in my life seemed to me all but unaccountable; and she appeared to take a not unnatural pleasure in foiling my curiosity, and in seeing me flounder in my eager perplexity, from one conjecture to another.

"In the meantime the young lady, whom her mother called by the odd name of Millarca, when she once or twice addressed her, had, with the same ease and grace, got into conversation with my ward.

"She introduced herself by saying that her mother was a very old acquaintance of mine. She spoke of the agreeable audacity which a mask rendered practicable; she talked like a friend; she admired her dress, and insinuated very prettily her admiration of her beauty. She amused her with laughing criticisms upon the people who crowded the ballroom, and laughed at my poor child's fun. She was very witty and lively when she pleased, and after a time they had grown very good friends, and the young stranger lowered her mask, displaying a remarkably beautiful face. I had never seen it before, neither had my dear child. But though it was new to us, the features were so engaging, as well as lovely, that it was impossible not to feel the attraction powerfully. My poor girl did so. I never saw anyone more taken with another at first sight, unless, indeed, it was the stranger herself, who seemed quite to have lost her heart to her.

"In the meantime, availing myself of the license of a masquerade, I put not a few questions to the elder lady.

"'You have puzzled me utterly,' I said, laughing. 'Is that not enough?

Won't you, now, consent to stand on equal terms, and do me the kindness to remove your mask?'

"'Can any request be more unreasonable?' she replied. 'Ask a lady to yield an advantage! Beside, how do you know you should recognize me? Years make changes.'

"'As you see,' I said, with a bow, and, I suppose, a rather melancholy little laugh.

"'As philosophers tell us,' she said; 'and how do you know that a sight of my face would help you?'

"'I should take chance for that,' I answered. 'It is vain trying to make yourself out an old woman; your figure betrays you.'

"'Years, nevertheless, have passed since I saw you, rather since you saw me, for that is what I am considering. Millarca, there, is my daughter; I cannot then be young, even in the opinion of people whom time has taught to be indulgent, and I may not like to be compared with what you remember me.

You have no mask to remove. You can offer me nothing in exchange.'

"'My petition is to your pity, to remove it.'

"'And mine to yours, to let it stay where it is,' she replied.

"'Well, then, at least you will tell me whether you are French or German; you speak both languages so perfectly.'

"'I don't think I shall tell you that, General; you intend a surprise, and are meditating the particular point of attack.'

"'At all events, you won't deny this,' I said, 'that being honored by your permission to converse, I ought to know how to address you. Shall I say Madame la Comtesse?'

"She laughed, and she would, no doubt, have met me with another evasion—if, indeed, I can treat any occurrence in an interview every circumstance of which was prearranged, as I now believe, with the profoundest cunning, as liable to be modified by accident.

"'As to that,' she began; but she was interrupted, almost as she opened her lips, by a gentleman, dressed in black, who looked particularly elegant and distinguished, with this drawback, that his face was the most deadly pale I ever saw, except in death. He was in no masquerade—in the plain evening dress of a gentleman; and he said, without a smile, but with a courtly and unusually low bow:—

"'Will Madame la Comtesse permit me to say a very few words which may interest her?'

"The lady turned quickly to him, and touched her lip in token of silence; she then said to me, 'Keep my place for me, General; I shall return when I have said a few words.'

"And with this injunction, playfully given, she walked a little aside with the gentleman in black, and talked for some minutes, apparently very earnestly. They then walked away slowly together in the crowd, and I lost them for some minutes.

"I spent the interval in cudgeling my brains for a conjecture as to the identity of the lady who seemed to remember me so kindly, and I was thinking of turning about and joining in the conversation between my pretty ward and the Countess's daughter, and trying whether, by the time she returned, I might not have a surprise in store for her, by having her name, title, chateau, and estates at my fingers' ends. But at this moment she returned, accompanied by the pale man in black, who said:

"'I shall return and inform Madame la Comtesse when her carriage is at the door.'

"He withdrew with a bow."

XII. A Petition

"'Then we are to lose Madame la Comtesse, but I hope only for a few hours,' I said, with a low bow.

"'It may be that only, or it may be a few weeks. It was very unlucky his speaking to me just now as he did. Do you now know me?'

"I assured her I did not.

"'You shall know me,' she said, 'but not at present. We are older and better friends than, perhaps, you suspect. I cannot yet declare myself. I shall in three weeks pass your beautiful schloss, about which I have been making enquiries. I shall then look in upon you for an hour or two, and renew a friendship which I never think of without a thousand pleasant recollections. This moment a piece of news has reached me like a thunderbolt. I must set out now, and travel by a devious route, nearly a hundred miles, with all the dispatch I can possibly make. My perplexities multiply. I am only deterred by the compulsory reserve I practice as to my name from making a very singular request of you. My poor child has not quite recovered her strength. Her horse fell with her, at a hunt which she had ridden out to witness, her nerves have not yet recovered the shock, and our physician says that she must on no account exert herself for some time to come. We came here, in consequence, by very easy stages—hardly six leagues a day. I must now travel day and night, on a mission of life and death—a mission the critical and momentous nature of which I shall be able to explain to you when we meet, as I hope we shall, in a few weeks, without the necessity of any concealment.'

"She went on to make her petition, and it was in the tone of a person from whom such a request amounted to conferring, rather than seeking a favor.

This was only in manner, and, as it seemed, quite unconsciously. Than the terms in which it was expressed, nothing could be more deprecatory. It was simply that I would consent to take charge of her daughter during her absence.

"This was, all things considered, a strange, not to say, an audacious request. She in some sort disarmed me, by stating and admitting everything that could be urged against it, and throwing herself entirely upon my chivalry. At the same moment, by a fatality that seems to have predetermined all that happened, my poor child came to my side, and, in an undertone, besought me to invite her new friend, Millarca, to pay us a visit. She had just been sounding her, and thought, if her mamma would allow her, she would like it extremely.

"At another time I should have told her to wait a little, until, at least, we knew who they were. But I had not a moment to think in. The two ladies assailed me together, and I must confess the refined and beautiful face of the young lady, about which there was something extremely engaging, as well as the elegance and fire of high birth, determined me; and, quite overpowered, I submitted, and undertook, too easily, the care of the young lady, whom her mother called Millarca.

"The Countess beckoned to her daughter, who listened with grave attention while she told her, in general terms, how suddenly and peremptorily she had been summoned, and also of the arrangement she had made for her under my care, adding that I was one of her earliest and most valued friends.

"I made, of course, such speeches as the case seemed to call for, and found myself, on reflection, in a position which I did not half like.

"The gentleman in black returned, and very ceremoniously conducted the lady from the room.

"The demeanor of this gentleman was such as to impress me with the conviction that the Countess was a lady of very much more importance than her modest title alone might have led me to assume.

"Her last charge to me was that no attempt was to be made to learn more about her than I might have already guessed, until her return. Our distinguished host, whose guest she was, knew her reasons.

"'But here,' she said, 'neither I nor my daughter could safely remain for more than a day. I removed my mask imprudently for a moment, about an hour ago, and, too late, I fancied you saw me. So I resolved to seek an opportunity of talking a little to you. Had I found that you had seen me, I would have thrown myself on your high sense of honor to keep my secret some weeks. As it is, I am satisfied that you did not see me; but if you now suspect, or, on reflection, should suspect, who I am, I commit myself, in like manner, entirely to your honor. My daughter will observe the same secrecy, and I well know that you will, from time to time, remind her, lest she should thoughtlessly disclose it.'

"She whispered a few words to her daughter, kissed her hurriedly twice, and went away, accompanied by the pale gentleman in black, and disappeared in the crowd.

"'In the next room,' said Millarca, 'there is a window that looks upon the hall door. I should like to see the last of mamma, and to kiss my hand to her.'

"We assented, of course, and accompanied her to the window. We looked out, and saw a handsome old-fashioned carriage, with a troop of couriers and footmen. We saw the slim figure of the pale gentleman in black, as he held a thick velvet cloak, and placed it about her shoulders and threw the hood over her head. She nodded to him, and just touched his hand with hers. He bowed low repeatedly as the door closed, and the carriage began to move.

"'She is gone,' said Millarca, with a sigh.

"'She is gone,' I repeated to myself, for the first time—in the hurried moments that had elapsed since my consent—reflecting upon the folly of my act.

"'She did not look up,' said the young lady, plaintively.

"'The Countess had taken off her mask, perhaps, and did not care to show her face,' I said; 'and she could not know that you were in the window.'

"She sighed, and looked in my face. She was so beautiful that I relented. I was sorry I had for a moment repented of my hospitality, and I determined to make her amends for the unavowed churlishness of my reception.

"The young lady, replacing her mask, joined my ward in persuading me to return to the grounds, where the concert was soon to be renewed. We did so, and walked up and down the terrace that lies under the castle windows.

Millarca became very intimate with us, and amused us with lively descriptions and stories of most of the great people whom we saw upon the terrace. I liked her more and more every minute. Her gossip without being ill-natured, was extremely diverting to me, who had been so long out of the great world. I thought what life she would give to our sometimes lonely evenings at home.

"This ball was not over until the morning sun had almost reached the horizon. It pleased the Grand Duke to dance till then, so loyal people could not go away, or think of bed.

"We had just got through a crowded saloon, when my ward asked me what had become of Millarca. I thought she had been by her side, and she fancied she was by mine. The fact was, we had lost her.

"All my efforts to find her were vain. I feared that she had mistaken, in the confusion of a momentary separation from us, other people for her new friends, and had, possibly, pursued and lost them in the extensive grounds which were thrown open to us.

"Now, in its full force, I recognized a new folly in my having undertaken the charge of a young lady without so much as knowing her name; and fettered as I was by promises, of the reasons for imposing which I knew nothing, I could not even point my inquiries by saying that the missing young lady was the daughter of the Countess who had taken her departure a few hours before.

"Morning broke. It was clear daylight before I gave up my search. It was not till near two o'clock next day that we heard anything of my missing charge.

"At about that time a servant knocked at my niece's door, to say that he had been earnestly requested by a young lady, who appeared to be in great distress, to make out where she could find the General Baron Spielsdorf and the young lady his daughter, in whose charge she had been left by her mother.

"There could be no doubt, notwithstanding the slight inaccuracy, that our young friend had turned up; and so she had. Would to heaven we had lost her!

"She told my poor child a story to account for her having failed to recover us for so long. Very late, she said, she had got to the housekeeper's bedroom in despair of finding us, and had then fallen into a deep sleep which, long as it was, had hardly sufficed to recruit her strength after the fatigues of the ball.

"That day Millarca came home with us. I was only too happy, after all, to have secured so charming a companion for my dear girl."

XIII: The Woodman

"There soon, however, appeared some drawbacks. In the first place, Millarca complained of extreme languor—the weakness that remained after her late illness—and she never emerged from her room till the afternoon was pretty far advanced. In the next place, it was accidentally discovered, although she always locked her door on the inside, and never disturbed the key from its place till she admitted the maid to assist at her toilet, that she was undoubtedly sometimes absent from her room in the very early morning, and at various times later in the day, before she wished it to be understood that she was stirring. She was repeatedly seen from the windows of the schloss, in the first faint grey of the morning, walking through the trees, in an easterly direction, and looking like a person in a trance. This convinced me that she walked in her sleep. But this hypothesis did not solve the puzzle. How did she pass out from her room, leaving the door locked on the inside? How did she escape from the house without unbarring door or window?

"In the midst of my perplexities, an anxiety of a far more urgent kind presented itself.

"My dear child began to lose her looks and health, and that in a manner so mysterious, and even horrible, that I became thoroughly frightened.

"She was at first visited by appalling dreams; then, as she fancied, by a specter, sometimes resembling Millarca, sometimes in the shape of a beast, indistinctly seen, walking round the foot of her bed, from side to side.

Lastly came sensations. One, not unpleasant, but very peculiar, she said, resembled the flow of an icy stream against her breast. At a later time, she felt something like a pair of large needles pierce her, a little below the throat, with a very sharp pain. A few nights after, followed a gradual and convulsive sense of strangulation; then came unconsciousness."

I could hear distinctly every word the kind old General was saying, because by this time we were driving upon the short grass that spreads on either side of the road as you approach the roofless village which had not shown the smoke of a chimney for more than half a century.

You may guess how strangely I felt as I heard my own symptoms so exactly described in those which had been experienced by the poor girl who, but for the catastrophe which followed, would have been at that moment a visitor at my father's chateau. You may suppose, also, how I felt as I heard him detail habits and mysterious peculiarities which were, in fact, those of our beautiful guest, Carmilla!

A vista opened in the forest; we were on a sudden under the chimneys and gables of the ruined village, and the towers and battlements of the dismantled castle, round which gigantic trees are grouped, overhung us from a slight eminence.

In a frightened dream I got down from the carriage, and in silence, for we had each abundant matter for thinking; we soon mounted the ascent, and were among the spacious chambers, winding stairs, and dark corridors of the castle.

"And this was once the palatial residence of the Karnsteins!" said the old General at length, as from a great window he looked out across the village, and saw the wide, undulating expanse of forest. "It was a bad family, and here its bloodstained annals were written," he continued. "It is hard that they should, after death, continue to plague the human race with their atrocious lusts. That is the chapel of the Karnsteins, down there."

He pointed down to the grey walls of the Gothic building partly visible through the foliage, a little way down the steep. "And I hear the axe of a woodman," he added, "busy among the trees that surround it; he possibly may give us the information of which I am in search, and point out the grave of Mircalla, Countess of Karnstein. These rustics preserve the local traditions of great families, whose stories die out among the rich and titled so soon as the families themselves become extinct."

"We have a portrait, at home, of Mircalla, the Countess Karnstein; should you like to see it?" asked my father.

"Time enough, dear friend," replied the General. "I believe that I have seen the original; and one motive which has led me to you earlier than I at first intended, was to explore the chapel which we are now approaching."

"What! see the Countess Mircalla," exclaimed my father; "why, she has been dead more than a century!"

"Not so dead as you fancy, I am told," answered the General.

"I confess, General, you puzzle me utterly," replied my father, looking at him, I fancied, for a moment with a return of the suspicion I detected before. But although there was anger and detestation, at times, in the old General's manner, there was nothing flighty.

"There remains to me," he said, as we passed under the heavy arch of the Gothic church—for its dimensions would have justified its being so styled—"but one object which can interest me during the few years that remain to me on earth, and that is to wreak on her the vengeance which, I thank God, may still be accomplished by a mortal arm."

"What vengeance can you mean?" asked my father, in increasing amazement.

"I mean, to decapitate the monster," he answered, with a fierce flush, and a stamp that echoed mournfully through the hollow ruin, and his clenched hand was at the same moment raised, as if it grasped the handle of an axe, while he shook it ferociously in the air.

"What?" exclaimed my father, more than ever bewildered.

"To strike her head off."

"Cut her head off!"

"Aye, with a hatchet, with a spade, or with anything that can cleave through her murderous throat. You shall hear," he answered, trembling with rage. And hurrying forward he said:

"That beam will answer for a seat; your dear child is fatigued; let her be seated, and I will, in a few sentences, close my dreadful story."

The squared block of wood, which lay on the grass-grown pavement of the chapel, formed a bench on which I was very glad to seat myself, and in the meantime the General called to the woodman, who had been removing some boughs which leaned upon the old walls; and, axe in hand, the hardy old fellow stood before us.

He could not tell us anything of these monuments; but there was an old man, he said, a ranger of this forest, at present sojourning in the house of the priest, about two miles away, who could point out every monument of the old Karnstein family; and, for a trifle, he undertook to bring him back with him, if we would lend him one of our horses, in little more than half an hour.

"Have you been long employed about this forest?" asked my father of the old man.

"I have been a woodman here," he answered in his patois, "under the forester, all my days; so has my father before me, and so on, as many generations as I can count up. I could show you the very house in the village here, in which my ancestors lived."

"How came the village to be deserted?" asked the General.

"It was troubled by revenants, sir; several were tracked to their graves, there detected by the usual tests, and extinguished in the usual way, by decapitation, by the stake, and by burning; but not until many of the villagers were killed.

"But after all these proceedings according to law," he continued—"so many graves opened, and so many vampires deprived of their horrible animation—the village was not relieved. But a Moravian nobleman, who happened to be traveling this way, heard how matters were, and being skilled—as many people are in his country—in such affairs, he offered to deliver the village from its tormentor. He did so thus: There being a bright moon that night, he ascended, shortly after sunset, the towers of the chapel here, from whence he could distinctly see the churchyard beneath him; you can see it from that window. From this point he watched until he saw the vampire come out of his grave, and place near it the linen clothes in which he had been folded, and then glide away towards the village to plague its inhabitants.

"The stranger, having seen all this, came down from the steeple, took the linen wrappings of the vampire, and carried them up to the top of the tower, which he again mounted. When the vampire returned from his prowlings and missed his clothes, he cried furiously to the Moravian, whom he saw at the summit of the tower, and who, in reply, beckoned him to ascend and take them. Whereupon the vampire, accepting his invitation, began to climb the steeple, and so soon as he had reached the battlements, the Moravian, with a stroke of his sword, clove his skull in twain, hurling him down to the churchyard, whither, descending by the winding stairs, the stranger followed and cut his head off, and next day delivered it and the body to the villagers, who duly impaled and burnt them.

"This Moravian nobleman had authority from the then head of the family to remove the tomb of Mircalla, Countess Karnstein, which he did effectually, so that in a little while its site was quite forgotten."

"Can you point out where it stood?" asked the General, eagerly.

The forester shook his head, and smiled.

"Not a soul living could tell you that now," he said; "besides, they say her body was removed; but no one is sure of that either."

Having thus spoken, as time pressed, he dropped his axe and departed, leaving us to hear the remainder of the General's strange story.

XIV: The Meeting

"My beloved child," he resumed, "was now growing rapidly worse. The physician who attended her had failed to produce the slightest impression on her disease, for such I then supposed it to be. He saw my alarm, and suggested a consultation. I called in an abler physician, from Gratz.

Several days elapsed before he arrived. He was a good and pious, as well as a learned man. Having seen my poor ward together, they withdrew to my library to confer and discuss. I, from the adjoining room, where I awaited their summons, heard these two gentlemen's voices raised in something sharper than a strictly philosophical discussion. I knocked at the door and entered. I found the old physician from Gratz maintaining his theory. His rival was combating it with undisguised ridicule, accompanied with bursts of laughter. This unseemly manifestation subsided and the altercation ended on my entrance.

"'Sir,' said my first physician,'my learned brother seems to think that you want a conjuror, and not a doctor.'

"'Pardon me,' said the old physician from Gratz, looking displeased, 'I shall state my own view of the case in my own way another time. I grieve, Monsieur le General, that by my skill and science I can be of no use.

Before I go I shall do myself the honor to suggest something to you.'

"He seemed thoughtful, and sat down at a table and began to write.

Profoundly disappointed, I made my bow, and as I turned to go, the other doctor pointed over his shoulder to his companion who was writing, and then, with a shrug, significantly touched his forehead.

"This consultation, then, left me precisely where I was. I walked out into the grounds, all but distracted. The doctor from Gratz, in ten or fifteen minutes, overtook me. He apologized for having followed me, but said that he could not conscientiously take his leave without a few words more. He told me that he could not be mistaken; no natural disease exhibited the same symptoms; and that death was already very near. There remained, however, a day, or possibly two, of life. If the fatal seizure were at once arrested, with great care and skill her strength might possibly return. But all hung now upon the confines of the irrevocable. One more assault might extinguish the last spark of vitality which is, every moment, ready to die.

"'And what is the nature of the seizure you speak of?' I entreated.

"'I have stated all fully in this note, which I place in your hands upon the distinct condition that you send for the nearest clergyman, and open my letter in his presence, and on no account read it till he is with you; you would despise it else, and it is a matter of life and death. Should the priest fail you, then, indeed, you may read it.'

"He asked me, before taking his leave finally, whether I would wish to see a man curiously learned upon the very subject, which, after I had read his letter, would probably interest me above all others, and he urged me earnestly to invite him to visit him there; and so took his leave.

"The ecclesiastic was absent, and I read the letter by myself. At another time, or in another case, it might have excited my ridicule. But into what quackeries will not people rush for a last chance, where all accustomed means have failed, and the life of a beloved object is at stake?

"Nothing, you will say, could be more absurd than the learned man's letter. It was monstrous enough to have consigned him to a madhouse. He said that the patient was suffering from the visits of a vampire! The punctures which she described as having occurred near the throat, were, he insisted, the insertion of those two long, thin, and sharp teeth which, it is well known, are peculiar to vampires; and there could be no doubt, he added, as to the well-defined presence of the small livid mark which all concurred in describing as that induced by the demon's lips, and every symptom described by the sufferer was in exact conformity with those recorded in every case of a similar visitation.

"Being myself wholly skeptical as to the existence of any such portent as the vampire, the supernatural theory of the good doctor furnished, in my opinion, but another instance of learning and intelligence oddly associated with some one hallucination. I was so miserable, however, that, rather than try nothing, I acted upon the instructions of the letter.

"I concealed myself in the dark dressing room, that opened upon the poor patient's room, in which a candle was burning, and watched there till she was fast asleep. I stood at the door, peeping through the small crevice, my sword laid on the table beside me, as my directions prescribed, until, a little after one, I saw a large black object, very ill-defined, crawl, as it seemed to me, over the foot of the bed, and swiftly spread itself up to the poor girl's throat, where it swelled, in a moment, into a great, palpitating mass.

"For a few moments I had stood petrified. I now sprang forward, with my sword in my hand. The black creature suddenly contracted towards the foot of the bed, glided over it, and, standing on the floor about a yard below the foot of the bed, with a glare of skulking ferocity and horror fixed on me, I saw Millarca. Speculating I know not what, I struck at her instantly with my sword; but I saw her standing near the door, unscathed. Horrified, I pursued, and struck again. She was gone; and my sword flew to shivers against the door.

"I can't describe to you all that passed on that horrible night. The whole house was up and stirring. The specter Millarca was gone. But her victim was sinking fast, and before the morning dawned, she died."

The old General was agitated. We did not speak to him. My father walked to some little distance, and began reading the inscriptions on the tombstones; and thus occupied, he strolled into the door of a side chapel to prosecute his researches. The General leaned against the wall, dried his eyes, and sighed heavily. I was relieved on hearing the voices of Carmilla and Madame, who were at that moment approaching. The voices died away.

In this solitude, having just listened to so strange a story, connected, as it was, with the great and titled dead, whose monuments were moldering among the dust and ivy round us, and every incident of which bore so awfully upon my own mysterious case—in this haunted spot, darkened by the towering foliage that rose on every side, dense and high above its noiseless walls—a horror began to steal over me, and my heart sank as I thought that my friends were, after all, not about to enter and disturb this triste and ominous scene.

The old General's eyes were fixed on the ground, as he leaned with his hand upon the basement of a shattered monument.

Under a narrow, arched doorway, surmounted by one of those demoniacal grotesques in which the cynical and ghastly fancy of old Gothic carving delights, I saw very gladly the beautiful face and figure of Carmilla enter the shadowy chapel.

I was just about to rise and speak, and nodded smiling, in answer to her peculiarly engaging smile; when with a cry, the old man by my side caught up the woodman's hatchet, and started forward. On seeing him a brutalized change came over her features. It was an instantaneous and horrible transformation, as she made a crouching step backwards. Before I could utter a scream, he struck at her with all his force, but she dived under his blow, and unscathed, caught him in her tiny grasp by the wrist. He struggled for a moment to release his arm, but his hand opened, the axe fell to the ground, and the girl was gone.

He staggered against the wall. His grey hair stood upon his head, and a moisture shone over his face, as if he were at the point of death.

The frightful scene had passed in a moment. The first thing I recollect after, is Madame standing before me, and impatiently repeating again and again, the question, "Where is Mademoiselle Carmilla?"

I answered at length, "I don't know—I can't tell—she went there," and I pointed to the door through which Madame had just entered; "only a minute or two since."

"But I have been standing there, in the passage, ever since Mademoiselle Carmilla entered; and she did not return."

She then began to call "Carmilla," through every door and passage and from the windows, but no answer came.

"She called herself Carmilla?" asked the General, still agitated.

"Carmilla, yes," I answered.

"Aye," he said; "that is Millarca. That is the same person who long ago was called Mircalla, Countess Karnstein. Depart from this accursed ground, my poor child, as quickly as you can. Drive to the clergyman's house, and stay there till we come. Begone! May you never behold Carmilla more; you will not find her here."

XV: Ordeal and Execution

As he spoke one of the strangest looking men I ever beheld entered the chapel at the door through which Carmilla had made her entrance and her exit. He was tall, narrow-chested, stooping, with high shoulders, and dressed in black. His face was brown and dried in with deep furrows; he wore an oddly-shaped hat with a broad leaf. His hair, long and grizzled, hung on his shoulders. He wore a pair of gold spectacles, and walked slowly, with an odd shambling gait, with his face sometimes turned up to the sky, and sometimes bowed down towards the ground, seemed to wear a perpetual smile; his long thin arms were swinging, and his lank hands, in old black gloves ever so much too wide for them, waving and gesticulating in utter abstraction.

"The very man!" exclaimed the General, advancing with manifest delight. "My dear Baron, how happy I am to see you, I had no hope of meeting you so soon." He signed to my father, who had by this time returned, and leading the fantastic old gentleman, whom he called the Baron to meet him. He introduced him formally, and they at once entered into earnest conversation. The stranger took a roll of paper from his pocket, and spread it on the worn surface of a tomb that stood by. He had a pencil case in his fingers, with which he traced imaginary lines from point to point on the paper, which from their often glancing from it, together, at certain points of the building, I concluded to be a plan of the chapel. He accompanied, what I may term, his lecture, with occasional readings from a dirty little book, whose yellow leaves were closely written over.

They sauntered together down the side aisle, opposite to the spot where I was standing, conversing as they went; then they began measuring distances by paces, and finally they all stood together, facing a piece of the sidewall, which they began to examine with great minuteness; pulling off the ivy that clung over it, and rapping the plaster with the ends of their sticks, scraping here, and knocking there. At length they ascertained the existence of a broad marble tablet, with letters carved in relief upon it.

With the assistance of the woodman, who soon returned, a monumental inscription, and carved escutcheon, were disclosed. They proved to be those of the long lost monument of Mircalla, Countess Karnstein.

The old General, though not I fear given to the praying mood, raised his hands and eyes to heaven, in mute thanksgiving for some moments.

"Tomorrow," I heard him say; "the commissioner will be here, and the Inquisition will be held according to law."

Then turning to the old man with the gold spectacles, whom I have described, he shook him warmly by both hands and said:

"Baron, how can I thank you? How can we all thank you? You will have delivered this region from a plague that has scourged its inhabitants for more than a century. The horrible enemy, thank God, is at last tracked."

My father led the stranger aside, and the General followed. I know that he had led them out of hearing, that he might relate my case, and I saw them glance often quickly at me, as the discussion proceeded.

My father came to me, kissed me again and again, and leading me from the chapel, said:

"It is time to return, but before we go home, we must add to our party the good priest, who lives but a little way from this; and persuade him to accompany us to the schloss."

In this quest we were successful: and I was glad, being unspeakably fatigued when we reached home. But my satisfaction was changed to dismay, on discovering that there were no tidings of Carmilla. Of the scene that had occurred in the ruined chapel, no explanation was offered to me, and it was clear that it was a secret which my father for the present determined to keep from me.

The sinister absence of Carmilla made the remembrance of the scene more horrible to me. The arrangements for the night were singular. Two servants, and Madame were to sit up in my room that night; and the ecclesiastic with my father kept watch in the adjoining dressing room.

The priest had performed certain solemn rites that night, the purport of which I did not understand any more than I comprehended the reason of this extraordinary precaution taken for my safety during sleep.

I saw all clearly a few days later.

The disappearance of Carmilla was followed by the discontinuance of my nightly sufferings.

You have heard, no doubt, of the appalling superstition that prevails in Upper and Lower Styria, in Moravia, Silesia, in Turkish Serbia, in Poland, even in Russia; the superstition, so we must call it, of the Vampire.

If human testimony, taken with every care and solemnity, judicially, before commissions innumerable, each consisting of many members, all chosen for integrity and intelligence, and constituting reports more voluminous perhaps than exist upon any one other class of cases, is worth anything, it is difficult to deny, or even to doubt the existence of such a phenomenon as the Vampire.

For my part I have heard no theory by which to explain what I myself have witnessed and experienced, other than that supplied by the ancient and well-attested belief of the country.

The next day the formal proceedings took place in the Chapel of Karnstein.

The grave of the Countess Mircalla was opened; and the General and my father recognized each his perfidious and beautiful guest, in the face now disclosed to view. The features, though a hundred and fifty years had passed since her funeral, were tinted with the warmth of life. Her eyes were open; no cadaverous smell exhaled from the coffin. The two medical men, one officially present, the other on the part of the promoter of the inquiry, attested the marvelous fact that there was a faint but appreciable respiration, and a corresponding action of the heart. The limbs were perfectly flexible, the flesh elastic; and the leaden coffin floated with blood, in which to a depth of seven inches, the body lay immersed.

Here then, were all the admitted signs and proofs of vampirism. The body, therefore, in accordance with the ancient practice, was raised, and a sharp stake driven through the heart of the vampire, who uttered a piercing shriek at the moment, in all respects such as might escape from a living person in the last agony. Then the head was struck off, and a torrent of blood flowed from the severed neck. The body and head was next placed on a pile of wood, and reduced to ashes, which were thrown upon the river and borne away, and that territory has never since been plagued by the visits of a vampire.

My father has a copy of the report of the Imperial Commission, with the signatures of all who were present at these proceedings, attached in verification of the statement. It is from this official paper that I have summarized my account of this last shocking scene.

XVI: Conclusion

I write all this you suppose with composure. But far from it; I cannot think of it without agitation. Nothing but your earnest desire so repeatedly expressed, could have induced me to sit down to a task that has unstrung my nerves for months to come, and reinduced a shadow of the unspeakable horror which years after my deliverance continued to make my days and nights dreadful, and solitude insupportably terrific.

Let me add a word or two about that quaint Baron Vordenburg, to whose curious lore we were indebted for the discovery of the Countess Mircalla's grave.

He had taken up his abode in Gratz, where, living upon a mere pittance, which was all that remained to him of the once princely estates of his family, in Upper Styria, he devoted himself to the minute and laborious investigation of the marvelously authenticated tradition of Vampirism. He had at his fingers' ends all the great and little works upon the subject.

"Magia Posthuma," "Phlegon de Mirabilibus," "Augustinus de cura pro Mortuis," "Philosophicae et Christianae Cogitationes de Vampiris," by John Christofer Herenberg; and a thousand others, among which I remember only a few of those which he lent to my father. He had a voluminous digest of all the judicial cases, from which he had extracted a system of principles that appear to govern—some always, and others occasionally only—the condition of the vampire. I may mention, in passing, that the deadly pallor attributed to that sort of revenants, is a mere melodramatic fiction. They present, in the grave, and when they show themselves in human society, the appearance of healthy life. When disclosed to light in their coffins, they exhibit all the symptoms that are enumerated as those which proved the vampire-life of the long-dead Countess Karnstein.

How they escape from their graves and return to them for certain hours every day, without displacing the clay or leaving any trace of disturbance in the state of the coffin or the cerements, has always been admitted to be utterly inexplicable. The amphibious existence of the vampire is sustained by daily renewed slumber in the grave. Its horrible lust for living blood supplies the vigor of its waking existence. The vampire is prone to be fascinated with an engrossing vehemence, resembling the passion of love, by particular persons. In pursuit of these it will exercise inexhaustible patience and stratagem, for access to a particular object may be obstructed in a hundred ways. It will never desist until it has satiated its passion, and drained the very life of its coveted victim. But it will, in these cases, husband and protract its murderous enjoyment with the refinement of an epicure, and heighten it by the gradual approaches of an artful courtship. In these cases it seems to yearn for something like sympathy and consent. In ordinary ones it goes direct to its object, overpowers with violence, and strangles and exhausts often at a single feast.

The vampire is, apparently, subject, in certain situations, to special conditions. In the particular instance of which I have given you a relation, Mircalla seemed to be limited to a name which, if not her real one, should at least reproduce, without the omission or addition of a single letter, those, as we say, anagrammatically, which compose it.

Carmilla did this; so did Millarca.

My father related to the Baron Vordenburg, who remained with us for two or three weeks after the expulsion of Carmilla, the story about the Moravian nobleman and the vampire at Karnstein churchyard, and then he asked the Baron how he had discovered the exact position of the long-concealed tomb of the Countess Mircalla? The Baron's grotesque features puckered up into a mysterious smile; he looked down, still smiling on his worn spectacle case and fumbled with it. Then looking up, he said:

"I have many journals, and other papers, written by that remarkable man; the most curious among them is one treating of the visit of which you speak, to Karnstein. The tradition, of course, discolors and distorts a little. He might have been termed a Moravian nobleman, for he had changed his abode to that territory, and was, beside, a noble. But he was, in truth, a native of Upper Styria. It is enough to say that in very early youth he had been a passionate and favored lover of the beautiful Mircalla, Countess Karnstein. Her early death plunged him into inconsolable grief. It is the nature of vampires to increase and multiply, but according to an ascertained and ghostly law.

"Assume, at starting, a territory perfectly free from that pest. How does it begin, and how does it multiply itself? I will tell you. A person, more or less wicked, puts an end to himself. A suicide, under certain circumstances, becomes a vampire. That specter visits living people in their slumbers; they die, and almost invariably, in the grave, develop into vampires. This happened in the case of the beautiful Mircalla, who was haunted by one of those demons. My ancestor, Vordenburg, whose title I still bear, soon discovered this, and in the course of the studies to which he devoted himself, learned a great deal more.

"Among other things, he concluded that suspicion of vampirism would probably fall, sooner or later, upon the dead Countess, who in life had been his idol. He conceived a horror, be she what she might, of her remains being profaned by the outrage of a posthumous execution. He has left a curious paper to prove that the vampire, on its expulsion from its amphibious existence, is projected into a far more horrible life; and he resolved to save his once beloved Mircalla from this.

"He adopted the stratagem of a journey here, a pretended removal of her remains, and a real obliteration of her monument. When age had stolen upon him, and from the vale of years, he looked back on the scenes he was leaving, he considered, in a different spirit, what he had done, and a horror took possession of him. He made the tracings and notes which have guided me to the very spot, and drew up a confession of the deception that he had practiced. If he had intended any further action in this matter, death prevented him; and the hand of a remote descendant has, too late for many, directed the pursuit to the lair of the beast."

We talked a little more, and among other things he said was this:

"One sign of the vampire is the power of the hand. The slender hand of Mircalla closed like a vice of steel on the General's wrist when he raised the hatchet to strike. But its power is not confined to its grasp; it leaves a numbness in the limb it seizes, which is slowly, if ever, recovered from."

The following Spring my father took me a tour through Italy. We remained away for more than a year. It was long before the terror of recent events subsided; and to this hour the image of Carmilla returns to memory with ambiguous alternations—sometimes the playful, languid, beautiful girl; sometimes the writhing fiend I saw in the ruined church; and often from a reverie I have started, fancying I heard the light step of Carmilla at the drawing room door.

Clarimonde

by Théophile Gautier

Brother, you ask me if I have ever loved. Yes. My story is a strange and terrible one; and though I am sixty-six years of age, I scarcely dare even now to disturb the ashes of that memory. To you I can refuse nothing; but I should not relate such a tale to any less experienced mind. So strange were the circumstances of my story, that I can scarcely believe myself to have ever actually been a party to them. For more than three years I remained the victim of a most singular and diabolical illusion. Poor country priest though I was, I led every night in a dream—would to God it had been all a dream!—a most worldly life, a damning life, a life of Sardanapalus. One single look too freely cast upon a woman well-nigh caused me to lose my soul; but finally by the grace of God and the assistance of my patron saint, I succeeded in casting out the evil spirit that possessed me. My daily life was long interwoven with a nocturnal life of a totally different character. By day I was a priest of the Lord, occupied with prayer and sacred things; by night, from the instant that I closed my eyes I became a young nobleman, a fine connoisseur in women, dogs, and horses; gambling, drinking, and blaspheming; and when I awoke at early daybreak, it seemed to me, on the other hand, that I had been sleeping, and had only dreamed that I was a priest. Of this somnambulistic life there now remains to me only the recollection of certain scenes and words which I cannot banish from my memory; but although I never actually left the walls of my presbytery, one would think to hear me speak that I were a man who, weary of all worldly pleasures, had become a religious, seeking to end a tempestuous life in the service of God, rather than a humble seminarist who has grown old in this obscure curacy, situated in the depths of the woods and even isolated from the life of the century.

Yes, I have loved as none in the world ever loved—with an insensate and furious passion—so violent that I am astonished it did not cause my heart to burst asunder. Ah, what nights—what nights!

From my earliest childhood I had felt a vocation to the priesthood, so that all my studies were directed with that idea in view. Up to the age of twenty-four my life had been only a prolonged novitiate. Having completed my course of theology I successively received all the minor orders, and my superiors judged me worthy, despite my youth, to pass the last awful degree. My ordination was fixed for Easter week.

I had never gone into the world. My world was confined by the walls of the college and the seminary. I knew in a vague sort of a way that there was something called Woman, but I never permitted my thoughts to dwell on such a subject, and I lived in a state of perfect innocence. Twice a year only I saw my infirm and aged mother, and in those visits were comprised my sole relations with the outer world.

I regretted nothing; I felt not the least hesitation at taking the last irrevocable step; I was filled with joy and impatience. Never did a betrothed lover count the slow hours with more feverish ardour; I slept only to dream that I was saying mass; I believed there could be nothing in the world more delightful than to be a priest; I would have refused to be a king or a poet in preference. My ambition could conceive of no loftier aim.

I tell you this in order to show you that what happened to me could not have happened in the natural order of things, and to enable you to understand that I was the victim of an inexplicable fascination.

At last the great day came. I walked to the church with a step so light that I fancied myself sustained in air, or that I had wings upon my shoulders. I believed myself an angel, and wondered at the sombre and thoughtful faces of my companions, for there were several of us. I had passed all the night in prayer, and was in a condition wellnigh bordering on ecstasy. The bishop, a venerable old man, seemed to me God the Father leaning over His Eternity, and I beheld Heaven through the vault of the temple.

You well know the details of that ceremony—the benediction, the communion under both forms, the anointing of the palms of the hands with the Oil of Catechumens, and then the holy sacrifice offered in concert with the bishop.

Ah, truly spake Job when he declared that the imprudent man is one who hath not made a covenant with his eyes! I accidentally lifted my head, which until then I had kept down, and beheld before me, so close that it seemed that I could have touched her—although she was actually a considerable distance from me and on the further side of the sanctuary railing—a young woman of extraordinary beauty, and attired with royal magnificence. It seemed as though scales had suddenly fallen from my eyes. I felt like a blind man who unexpectedly recovers his sight. The bishop, so radiantly glorious but an instant before, suddenly vanished away, the tapers paled upon their golden candlesticks like stars in the dawn, and a vast darkness seemed to fill the whole church. The charming creature appeared in bright relief against the background of that darkness, like some angelic revelation. She seemed herself radiant, and radiating light rather than receiving it.

I lowered my eyelids, firmly resolved not to again open them, that I might not be influenced by external objects, for distraction had gradually taken possession of me until I hardly knew what I was doing.

In another minute, nevertheless, I reopened my eyes, for through my eyelashes I still beheld her, all sparkling with prismatic colours, and surrounded with such a penumbra as one beholds in gazing at the sun.

Oh, how beautiful she was! The greatest painters, who followed ideal beauty into heaven itself, and thence brought back to earth the true portrait of the Madonna, never in their delineations even approached that wildly beautiful reality which I saw before me. Neither the verses of the poet nor the palette of the artist could convey any conception of her. She was rather tall, with a form and bearing of a goddess. Her hair, of a soft blonde hue, was parted in the midst and flowed back over her temples in two rivers of rippling gold; she seemed a diademed queen. Her forehead, bluish-white in its transparency, extended its calm breadth above the arches of her eyebrows, which by a strange singularity were almost black, and admirably relieved the effect of sea-green eyes of unsustainable vivacity and brilliancy. What eyes! With a single flash they could have decided a man's destiny. They had a life, a limpidity, an ardour, a humid light which I have never seen in human eyes; they shot forth rays like arrows, which I could distinctlysee enter my heart. I know not if the fire which illumined them came from heaven or from hell, but assuredly it came from one or the other. That woman was either an angel or a demon, perhaps both. Assuredly she never sprang from the flank of Eve, our common mother. Teeth of the most lustrous pearl gleamed in her ruddy smile, and at every inflection of her lips little dimples appeared in the satiny rose of her adorable cheeks. There was a delicacy and pride in the regal outline of her nostrils bespeaking noble blood. Agate gleams played over the smooth lustrous skin of her half-bare shoulders, and strings of great blonde pearls—almost equal to her neck in beauty of colour—descended upon her bosom. From time to time she elevated her head with the undulating grace of a startled serpent or peacock, thereby imparting a quivering motion to the high lace ruff which surrounded it like a silver trellis-work.

She wore a robe of orange-red velvet, and from her wide ermine-lined sleeves there peeped forth patrician hands of infinite delicacy, and so ideally transparent that, like the fingers of Aurora, they permitted the light to shine through them.

All these details I can recollect at this moment as plainly as though they were of yesterday, for notwithstanding I was greatly troubled at the time, nothing escaped me; the faintest touch of shading, the little dark speck at the point of the chin, the imperceptible down at the corners of the lips, the velvety floss upon the brow, the quivering shadows of the eyelashes upon the cheeks—I could notice everything with astonishing lucidity of perception.

And gazing I felt opening within me gates that had until then remained closed; vents long obstructed became all clear, permitting glimpses of unfamiliar perspectives within; life suddenly made itself visible to me under a totally novel aspect. I felt as though I had just been born into a new world and a new order of things. A frightful anguish commenced to torture-my heart as with red-hot pincers. Every successive minute seemed to me at once but a second and yet a century. Meanwhile the ceremony was proceeding, and I shortly found myself transported far from that world of which my newly born desires were furiously besieging the entrance. Nevertheless I answered 'Yes' when I wished to say 'No,' though all within me protested against the violence done to my soul by my tongue. Some occult power seemed to force the words from my throat against my will. Thus it is, perhaps, that so many young girls walk to the altar firmly resolved to refuse in a startling manner the husband imposed upon them, and that yet not one ever fulfils her intention. Thus it is, doubtless, that so many poor novices take the veil, though they have resolved to tear it into shreds at the moment when called upon to utter the vows. One dares not thus cause so great a scandal to all present, nor deceive the expectation of so many people. All those eyes, all those wills seem to weigh down upon you like a cope of lead, and, moreover, measures have been so well taken, everything has been so thoroughly arranged beforehand and after a fashion so evidently irrevocable, that the will yields to the weight of circumstances and utterly breaks down.

As the ceremony proceeded the features of the fair unknown changed their expression. Her look had at first been one of caressing tenderness; it changed to an air of disdain and of mortification, as though at not having been able to make itself understood.

With an effort of will sufficient to have uprooted a mountain, I strove to cry out that I would not be a priest, but I could not speak; my tongue seemed nailed to my palate, and I found it impossible to express my will by the least syllable of negation. Though fully awake, I felt like one under the influence of a nightmare, who vainly strives to shriek out the one word upon which life depends.

She seemed conscious of the martyrdom I was undergoing, and, as though to encourage me, she gave me a look replete with divinest promise. Her eyes were a poem; their every glance was a song.

She said to me:

'If thou wilt be mine, I shall make thee happier than God Himself in His paradise. The angels themselves will be jealous of thee. Tear off that funeral shroud in which thou art about to wrap thyself. I am Beauty, I am Youth, I am Life. Come to me! Together we shall be Love. Can Jehovah offer thee aught in exchange? Our lives will flow on like a dream, in one eternal kiss.

'Fling forth the wine of that chalice, and thou art free. I will conduct thee to the Unknown Isles. Thou shalt sleep in my bosom upon a bed of massy gold under a silver pavilion, for I love thee and would take thee away from thy God, before whom so many noble hearts pour forth floods of love which never reach even the steps of His throne!'

These words seemed to float to my ears in a rhythm of infinite sweetness, for her look was actually sonorous, and the utterances of her eyes were reechoed in the depths of my heart as though living lips had breathed them into my life. I felt myself willing to renounce God, and yet my tongue mechanically fulfilled all the formalities of the ceremony. The fair one gave me another look, so beseeching, so despairing that keen blades seemed to pierce my heart, and I felt my bosom transfixed by more swords than those of Our Lady of Sorrows.

All was consummated; I had become a priest.

Never was deeper anguish painted on human face than upon hers. The maiden who beholds her affianced lover suddenly fall dead at her side, the mother bending over the empty cradle of her child, Eve seated at the threshold of the gate of Paradise, the miser who finds a stone substituted for his stolen treasure, the poet who accidentally permits the only manuscript of his finest work to fall into the fire, could not wear a look so despairing, so inconsolable. All the blood had abandoned her charming face, leaving it whiter than marble; her beautiful arms hung lifelessly on either side of her body as though their muscles had suddenly relaxed, and she sought the support of a pillar, for her yielding limbs almost betrayed her. As for myself, I staggered toward the door of the church, livid as death, my forehead bathed with a sweat bloodier than that of Calvary; I felt as though I were being strangled; the vault seemed to have flattened down upon my shoulders, and it seemed to me that my head alone sustained the whole weight of the dome.

As I was about to cross the threshold a hand suddenly caught mine—a woman's hand! I had never till then touched the hand of any woman. It was cold as a serpent's skin, and yet its impress remained upon my wrist, burnt there as though branded by a glowing iron. It was she. 'Unhappy man! Unhappy man! What hast thou done?' she exclaimed in a low voice, and immediately disappeared in the crowd.

The aged bishop passed by. He cast a severe and scrutinising look upon me. My face presented the wildest aspect imaginable: I blushed and turned pale alternately; dazzling lights flashed before my eyes. A companion took pity on me. He seized my arm and led me out. I could not possibly have found my way back to the seminary unassisted. At the corner of a street, while the young priest's attention was momentarily turned in another direction, a negro page, fantastically garbed, approached me, and without pausing on his way slipped into my hand a little pocket-book with gold-embroidered corners, at the same time giving me a sign to hide it. I concealed it in my sleeve, and there kept it until I found myself alone in my cell. Then I opened the clasp. There were only two leaves within, bearing the words, 'Clarimonde. At the Concini Palace.' So little acquainted was I at that time with the things of this world that I had never heard of Clarimonde, celebrated as she was, and I had no idea as to where the Concini Palace was situated. I hazarded a thousand conjectures, each more extravagant than the last; but, in truth, I cared little whether she were a great lady or a courtesan, so that I could but see her once more.

My love, although the growth of a single hour, had taken imperishable root. I did not even dream of attempting to tear it up, so fully was I convinced such a thing would be impossible. That woman had completely taken possession of me. One look from her had sufficed to change my very nature. She had breathed her will into my life, and I no longer lived in myself, but in her and for her. I gave myself up to a thousand extravagancies. I kissed the place upon my hand which she had touched, and I repeated her name over and over again for hours in succession. I only needed to close my eyes in order to see her distinctly as though she were actually present; and I reiterated to myself the words she had uttered in my ear at the church porch: 'Unhappy man! Unhappy man! What hast thou done?' I comprehended at last the full horror of my situation, and the funereal and awful restraints of the state into which I had just entered became clearly revealed to me. To be a priest!—that is, to be chaste, to never love, to observe no distinction of sex or age, to turn from the sight of all beauty, to put out one's own eyes, to hide for ever crouching in the chill shadows of some church or cloister, to visit none but the dying, to watch by unknown corpses, and ever bear about with one the black soutane as a garb of mourning for oneself, so that your very dress might serve as a pall for your coffin.

And I felt life rising within me like a subterranean lake, expanding and overflowing; my blood leaped fiercely through my arteries; my long-restrained youth suddenly burst into active being, like the aloe which blooms but once in a hundred years, and then bursts into blossom with a clap of thunder.

What could I do in order to see Clarimonde once more? I had no pretext to offer for desiring to leave the seminary, not knowing any person in the city. I would not even be able to remain there but a short time, and was only waiting my assignment to the curacy which I must thereafter occupy. I tried to remove the bars of the window; but it was at a fearful height from the ground, and I found that as I had no ladder it would be useless to think of escaping thus. And, furthermore, I could descend thence only by night in any event, and afterward how should I be able to find my way through the inextricable labyrinth of streets? All these difficulties, which to many would have appeared altogether insignificant, were gigantic to me, a poor seminarist who had fallen in love only the day before for the first time, without experience, without money, without attire.

'Ah!' cried I to myself in my blindness, 'were I not a priest I could have seen her every day; I might have been her lover, her spouse. Instead of being wrapped in this dismal shroud of mine I would have had garments of silk and velvet, golden chains, a sword, and fair plumes like other handsome young cavaliers. My hair, instead of being dishonoured by the tonsure, would flow down upon my neck in waving curls; I would have a fine waxed moustache; I would be a gallant.' But one hour passed before an altar, a few hastily articulated words, had for ever cut me off from the number of the living, and I had myself sealed down the stone of my own tomb; I had with my own hand bolted the gate of my prison! I went to the window. The sky was beautifully blue; the trees had donned their spring robes; nature seemed to be making parade of an ironical joy. The Place was filled with people, some going, others coming; young beaux and young beauties were sauntering in couples toward the groves and gardens; merry youths passed by, cheerily trolling refrains of drinking-songs—it was all a picture of vivacity, life, animation, gaiety, which formed a bitter contrast with my mourning and my solitude. On the steps of the gate sat a young mother playing with her child. She kissed its little rosy mouth still impearled with drops of milk, and performed, in order to amuse it, a thousand divine little puerilities such as only mothers know how to invent. The father standing at a little distance smiled gently upon the charming group, and with folded arms seemed to hug his joy to his heart. I could not endure that spectacle. I closed the window with violence, and flung myself on my bed, my heart filled with frightful hate and jealousy, and gnawed my fingers and my bedcovers like a tiger that has passed ten days without food.

I know not how long I remained in this condition, but at last, while writhing on the bed in a fit of spasmodic fury, I suddenly perceived the Abbé Sérapion, who was standing erect in the centre of the room, watching me attentively. Filled with shame of myself, I let my head fall upon my breast and covered my face with my hands.

'Romuald, my friend, something very extraordinary is transpiring within you,' observed Sérapion, after a few moments' silence; 'your conduct is altogether inexplicable. You—always so quiet, so pious, so gentle—you to rage in your cell like a wild beast! Take heed, brother—do not listen to the suggestions of the devil The Evil Spirit, furious that you have consecrated yourself for ever to the Lord, is prowling around you like a ravening wolf and making a last effort to obtain possession of you. Instead of allowing yourself to be conquered, my dear Romuald, make to yourself a cuirass of prayers, a buckler of mortifications, and combat the enemy like a valiant man; you will then assuredly overcome him. Virtue must be proved by temptation, and gold comes forth purer from the hands of the assayer. Fear not. Never allow yourself to become discouraged. The most watchful and steadfast souls are at moments liable to such temptation. Pray, fast, meditate, and the Evil Spirit will depart from you.'

The words of the Abbé Sérapion restored me to myself, and I became a little more calm. 'I came,' he continued, 'to tell you that you have been appointed to the curacy of C———. The priest who had charge of it has just died, and Monseigneur the Bishop has ordered me to have you installed there at once. Be ready, therefore, to start to-morrow.' I responded with an inclination of the head, and the Abbé retired. I opened my missal and commenced reading some prayers, but the letters became confused and blurred under my eyes, the thread of the ideas entangled itself hopelessly in my brain, and the volume at last fell from my hands without my being aware of it.

To leave to-morrow without having been able to see her again, to add yet another barrier to the many already interposed between us, to lose for ever all hope of being able to meet her, except, indeed, through a miracle! Even to write to her, alas! would be impossible, for by whom could I dispatch my letter? With my sacred character of priest, to whom could I dare unbosom myself, in whom could I confide? I became a prey to the bitterest anxiety.

Then suddenly recurred to me the words of the Abbé Sérapion regarding the artifices of the devil; and the strange character of the adventure, the supernatural beauty of Clarimonde, the phosphoric light of her eyes, the burning imprint of her hand, the agony into which she had thrown me, the sudden change wrought within me when all my piety vanished in a single instant—these and other things clearly testified to the work of the Evil One, and perhaps that satiny hand was but the glove which concealed his claws. Filled with terror at these fancies, I again picked up the missal which had slipped from my knees and fallen upon the floor, and once more gave myself up to prayer.

Next morning Sérapion came to take me away. Two mules freighted with our miserable valises awaited us at the gate. He mounted one, and I the other as well as I knew how.

As we passed along the streets of the city, I gazed attentively at all the windows and balconies in the hope of seeing Clarimonde, but it was yet early in the morning, and the city had hardly opened its eyes. Mine sought to penetrate the blinds and window-curtains of all the palaces before which we were passing. Sérapion doubtless attributed this curiosity to my admiration of the architecture, for he slackened the pace of his animal in order to give me time to look around me. At last we passed the city gates and commenced to mount the hill beyond. When we arrived at its summit I turned to take a last look at the place where Clarimonde dwelt. The shadow of a great cloud hung over all the city; the contrasting colours of its blue and red roofs were lost in the uniform half-tint, through which here and there floated upward, like white flakes of foam, the smoke of freshly kindled fires. By a singular optical effect one edifice, which surpassed in height all the neighbouring buildings that were still dimly veiled by the vapours, towered up, fair and lustrous with the gilding of a solitary beam of sunlight—although actually more than a league away it seemed quite near. The smallest details of its architecture were plainly distinguishable—the turrets, the platforms, the window-casements, and even the swallow-tailed weather-vanes.

'What is that palace I see over there, all lighted up by the sun?' I asked Sérapion. He shaded his eyes with his hand, and having looked in the direction indicated, replied: 'It is the ancient palace which the Prince Concini has given to the courtesan Clarimonde. Awful things are done there!'

At that instant, I know not yet whether it was a reality or an illusion, I fancied I saw gliding along the terrace a shapely white figure, which gleamed for a moment in passing and as quickly vanished. It was Clarimonde.

Oh, did she know that at that very hour, all feverish and restless—from the height of the rugged road which separated me from her, and which, alas! I could never more descend—I was directing my eyes upon the palace where she dwelt, and which a mocking beam of sunlight seemed to bring nigh to me, as though inviting me to enter therein as its lord? Undoubtedly she must have known it, for her soul was too sympathetically united with mine not to have felt its least emotional thrill, and that subtle sympathy it must have been which prompted her to climb—although clad only in her nightdress—to the summit of the terrace, amid the icy dews of the morning.

The shadow gained the palace, and the scene became to the eye only a motionless ocean of roofs and gables, amid which one mountainous undulation was distinctly visible. Sérapion urged his mule forward, my own at once followed at the same gait, and a sharp angle in the road at last hid the city of S——— for ever from my eyes, as I was destined never to return thither. At the close of a weary three-days' journey through dismal country fields, we caught sight of the cock upon the steeple of the church which I was to take charge of, peeping above the trees, and after having followed some winding roads fringed with thatched cottages and little gardens, we found ourselves in front of the façade, which certainly possessed few features of magnificence. A porch ornamented with some mouldings, and two or three pillars rudely hewn from sandstone; a tiled roof with counterforts of the same sandstone as the pillars—that was all. To the left lay the cemetery, overgrown with high weeds, and having a great iron cross rising up in its centre; to the right stood the presbytery under the shadow of the church. It was a house of the most extreme simplicity and frigid cleanliness. We entered the enclosure. A few chickens were picking up some oats scattered upon the ground; accustomed, seemingly, to the black habit of ecclesiastics, they showed no fear of our presence and scarcely troubled themselves to get out of our way. A hoarse, wheezy barking fell upon our ears, and we saw an aged dog running toward us.

It was my predecessor's dog. He had dull bleared eyes, grizzled hair, and every mark of the greatest age to which a dog can possibly attain. I patted him gently, and he proceeded at once to march along beside me with an air of satisfaction unspeakable. A very old woman, who had been the housekeeper of the former curé, also came to meet us, and after having invited me into a little back parlour, asked whether I intended to retain her. I replied that I would take care of her, and the dog, and the chickens, and all the furniture her master had bequeathed her at his death. At this she became fairly transported with joy, and the Abbé Sérapion at once paid her the price which she asked for her little property.

As soon as my installation was over, the Abbé Sérapion returned to the seminary. I was, therefore, left alone, with no one but myself to look to for aid or counsel. The thought of Clarimonde again began to haunt me, and in spite of all my endeavours to banish it, I always found it present in my meditations. One evening, while promenading in my little garden along the walks bordered with box-plants, I fancied that I saw through the elm-trees the figure of a woman, who followed my every movement, and that I beheld two sea-green eyes gleaming through the foliage; but it was only an illusion, and on going round to the other side of the garden, I could find nothing except a footprint on the sanded walk—a footprint so small that it seemed to have been made by the foot of a child. The garden was enclosed by very high walls. I searched every nook and corner of it, but could discover no one there. I have never succeeded in fully accounting for this circumstance, which, after all, was nothing compared with the strange things which happened to me afterward.

For a whole year I lived thus, filling all the duties of my calling with the most scrupulous exactitude, praying and fasting, exhorting and lending ghostly aid to the sick, and bestowing alms even to the extent of frequently depriving myself of the very necessaries of life. But I felt a great aridness within me, and the sources of grace seemed closed against me. I never found that happiness which should spring from the fulfilment of a holy mission; my thoughts were far away, and the words of Clarimonde were ever upon my lips like an involuntary refrain. Oh, brother, meditate well on this! Through having but once lifted my eyes to look upon a woman, through one fault apparently so venial, I have for years remained a victim to the most miserable agonies, and the happiness of my life has been destroyed for ever.

I will not longer dwell upon those defeats, or on those inward victories invariably followed by yet more terrible falls, but will at once proceed to the facts of my story. One night my door-bell was long and violently rung. The aged housekeeper arose and opened to the stranger, and the figure of a man, whose complexion was deeply bronzed, and who was richly clad in a foreign costume, with a poniard at his girdle, appeared under the rays of Barbara's lantern. Her first impulse was one of terror, but the stranger reassured her, and stated that he desired to see me at once on matters relating to my holy calling. Barbara invited him upstairs, where I was on the point of retiring. The stranger told me that his mistress, a very noble lady, was lying at the point of death, and desired to see a priest. I replied that I was prepared to follow him, took with me the sacred articles necessary for extreme unction, and descended in all haste. Two horses black as the night itself stood without the gate, pawing the ground with impatience, and veiling their chests with long streams of smoky vapour exhaled from their nostrils. He held the stirrup and aided me to mount upon one; then, merely laying his hand upon the pommel of the saddle, he vaulted on the other, pressed the animal's sides with his knees, and loosened rein. The horse bounded forward with the velocity of an arrow. Mine, of which the stranger held the bridle, also started off at a swift gallop, keeping up with his companion. We devoured the road. The ground flowed backward beneath us in a long streaked line of pale gray, and the black silhouettes of the trees seemed fleeing by us on either side like an army in rout. We passed through a forest so profoundly gloomy that I felt my flesh creep in the chill darkness with superstitious fear. The showers of bright sparks which flew from the stony road under the ironshod feet of our horses remained glowing in our wake like a fiery trail; and had any one at that hour of the night beheld us both—my guide and myself—he must have taken us for two spectres riding upon nightmares. Witch-fires ever and anon flitted across the road before us, and the night-birds shrieked fearsomely in the depth of the woods beyond, where we beheld at intervals glow the phosphorescent eyes of wild cats. The manes of the horses became more and more dishevelled, the sweat streamed over their flanks, and their breath came through their nostrils hard and fast. But when he found them slacking pace, the guide reanimated them by uttering a strange, gutteral, unearthly cry, and the gallop recommenced with fury. At last the whirlwind race ceased; a huge black mass pierced through with many bright points of light suddenly rose before us, the hoofs of our horses echoed louder upon a strong wooden drawbridge, and we rode under a great vaulted archway which darkly yawned between two enormous towers. Some great excitement evidently reigned in the castle. Servants with torches were crossing the courtyard in every direction, and above lights were ascending and descending from landing to landing. I obtained a confused glimpse of vast masses of architecture—columns, arcades, flights of steps, stairways—a royal voluptuousness and elfin magnificence of construction worthy of fairyland. A negro page—the same who had before brought me the tablet from Clarimonde, and whom I instantly recognised—approached to aid me in dismounting, and the major-domo, attired in black velvet with a gold chain about his neck, advanced to meet me, supporting himself upon an ivory cane. Large tears were falling from his eyes and streaming over his cheeks and white beard. 'Too late!' he cried, sorrowfully shaking his venerable head. 'Too late, sir priest! But if you have not been able to save the soul, come at least to watch by the poor body.'

He took my arm and conducted me to the death-chamber. I wept not less bitterly than he, for I had learned that the dead one was none other than that Clarimonde whom I had so deeply and so wildly loved. A prie-dieu stood at the foot of the bed; a bluish flame flickering in a bronze patern filled all the room with a wan, deceptive light, here and there bringing out in the darkness at intervals some projection of furniture or cornice. In a chiselled urn upon the table there was a faded white rose, whose leaves—excepting one that still held—had all fallen, like odorous tears, to the foot of the vase. A broken black mask, a fan, and disguises of every variety, which were lying on the armchairs, bore witness that death had entered suddenly and unannounced into that sumptuous dwelling. Without daring to cast my eyes upon the bed, I knelt down and commenced to repeat the Psalms for the Dead, with exceeding fervour, thanking God that He had placed the tomb between me and the memory of this woman, so that I might thereafter be able to utter her name in my prayers as a name for ever sanctified by death. But my fervour gradually weakened, and I fell insensibly into a reverie. That chamber bore no semblance to a chamber of death. In lieu of the fetid and cadaverous odours which I had been accustomed to breathe during such funereal vigils, a languorous vapour of Oriental perfume—I know not what amorous odour of woman—softly floated through the tepid air. That pale light seemed rather a twilight gloom contrived for voluptuous pleasure, than a substitute for the yellow-flickering watch-tapers which shine by the side of corpses. I thought upon the strange destiny which enabled me to meet Clarimonde again at the very moment when she was lost to me for ever, and a sigh of regretful anguish escaped from my breast. Then it seemed to me that some one behind me had also sighed, and I turned round to look. It was only an echo. But in that moment my eyes fell upon the bed of death which they had till then avoided. The red damask curtains, decorated with large flowers worked in embroidery and looped up with gold bullion, permitted me to behold the fair dead, lying at full length, with hands joined upon her bosom. She was covered with a linen wrapping of dazzling whiteness, which formed a strong contrast with the gloomy purple of the hangings, and was of so fine a texture that it concealed nothing of her body's charming form, and allowed the eye to follow those beautiful outlines—undulating like the neck of a swan—which even death had not robbed of their supple grace. She seemed an alabaster statue executed by some skilful sculptor to place upon the tomb of a queen, or rather, perhaps, like a slumbering maiden over whom the silent snow had woven a spotless veil.

I could no longer maintain my constrained attitude of prayer. The air of the alcove intoxicated me, that febrile perfume of half-faded roses penetrated my very brain, and I commenced to pace restlessly up and down the chamber, pausing at each turn before the bier to contemplate the graceful corpse lying beneath the transparency of its shroud. Wild fancies came thronging to my brain. I thought to myself that she might not, perhaps, be really dead; that she might only have feigned death for the purpose of bringing me to her castle, and then declaring her love. At one time I even thought I saw her foot move under the whiteness of the coverings, and slightly disarrange the long straight folds of the winding-sheet.

And then I asked myself: 'Is this indeed Clarimonde? What proof have I that it is she? Might not that black page have passed into the service of some other lady? Surely, I must be going mad to torture and afflict myself thus!' But my heart answered with a fierce throbbing: 'It is she; it is she indeed!' I approached the bed again, and fixed my eyes with redoubled attention upon the object of my incertitude. Ah, must I confess it? That exquisite perfection of bodily form, although purified and made sacred by the shadow of death, affected me more voluptuously than it should have done; and that repose so closely resembled slumber that one might well have mistaken it for such. I forgot that I had come there to perform a funeral ceremony; I fancied myself a young bridegroom entering the chamber of the bride, who all modestly hides her fair face, and through coyness seeks to keep herself wholly veiled. Heartbroken with grief, yet wild with hope, shuddering at once with fear and pleasure, I bent over her and grasped the corner of the sheet. I lifted it back, holding my breath all the while through fear of waking her. My arteries throbbed with such violence that I felt them hiss through my temples, and the sweat poured from my forehead in streams, as though I had lifted a mighty slab of marble. There, indeed, lay Clarimonde, even as I had seen her at the church on the day of my ordination. She was not less charming than then. With her, death seemed but a last coquetry. The pallor of her cheeks, the less brilliant carnation of her lips, her long eyelashes lowered and relieving their dark fringe against that white skin, lent her an unspeakably seductive aspect of melancholy chastity and mental suffering; her long loose hair, still intertwined with some little blue flowers, made a shining pillow for her head, and veiled the nudity of her shoulders with its thick ringlets; her beautiful hands, purer, more diaphanous, than the Host, were crossed on her bosom in an attitude of pious rest and silent prayer, which served to counteract all that might have proven otherwise too alluring—even after death—in the exquisite roundness and ivory polish of her bare arms from which the pearl bracelets had not yet been removed. I remained long in mute contemplation, and the more I gazed, the less could I persuade myself that life had really abandoned that beautiful body for ever. I do not know whether it was an illusion or a reflection of the lamplight, but it seemed to me that the blood was again commencing to circulate under that lifeless pallor, although she remained all motionless. I laid my hand lightly on her arm; it was cold, but not colder than her hand on the day when it touched mine at the portals of the church. I resumed my position, bending my face above her, and bathing her cheek with the warm dew of my tears. Ah, what bitter feelings of despair and helplessness, what agonies unutterable did I endure in that long watch! Vainly did I wish that I could have gathered all my life into one mass that I might give it all to her, and breathe into her chill remains the flame which devoured me. The night advanced, and feeling the moment of eternal separation approach, I could not deny myself the last sad sweet pleasure of imprinting a kiss upon the dead lips of her who had been my only love.... Oh, miracle! A faint breath mingled itself with my breath, and the mouth of Clarimonde responded to the passionate pressure of mine. Her eyes unclosed, and lighted up with something of their former brilliancy; she uttered a long sigh, and uncrossing her arms, passed them around my neck with a look of ineffable delight. 'Ah, it is thou, Romuald!' she murmured in a voice languishingly sweet as the last vibrations of a harp. 'What ailed thee, dearest? I waited so long for thee that I am dead; but we are now betrothed: I can see thee and visit thee. Adieu, Romuald, adieu! I love thee. That is all I wished to tell thee, and I give thee back the life which thy kiss for a moment recalled. We shall soon meet again.'

Her head fell back, but her arms yet encircled me, as though to retain me still. A furious whirlwind suddenly burst in the window, and entered the chamber. The last remaining leaf of the white rose for a moment palpitated at the extremity of the stalk like a butterfly's wing, then it detached itself and flew forth through the open casement, bearing with it the soul of Clarimonde. The lamp was extinguished, and I fell insensible upon the bosom of the beautiful dead.

When I came to myself again I was lying on the bed in my little room at the presbytery, and the old dog of the former curé was licking my hand, which had been hanging down outside of the covers. Barbara, all trembling with age and anxiety, was busying herself about the room, opening and shutting drawers, and emptying powders into glasses. On seeing me open my eyes, the old woman uttered a cry of joy, the dog yelped and wagged his tail, but I was still so weak that I could not speak a single word or make the slightest motion. Afterward I learned that I had lain thus for three days, giving no evidence of life beyond the faintest respiration. Those three days do not reckon in my life, nor could I ever imagine whither my spirit had departed during those three days; I have no recollection of aught relating to them. Barbara told me that the same coppery-complexioned man who came to seek me on the night of my departure from the presbytery had brought me back the next morning in a close litter, and departed immediately afterward. When I became able to collect my scattered thoughts, I reviewed within my mind all the circumstances of that fateful night. At first I thought I had been the victim of some magical illusion, but ere long the recollection of other circumstances, real and palpable in themselves, came to forbid that supposition. I could not believe that I had been dreaming, since Barbara as well as myself had seen the strange man with his two black horses, and described with exactness every detail of his figure and apparel. Nevertheless it appeared that none knew of any castle in the neighbourhood answering to the description of that in which I had again found Clarimonde.

One morning I found the Abbé Sérapion in my room. Barbara had advised him that I was ill, and he had come with all speed to see me. Although this haste on his part testified to an affectionate interest in me, yet his visit did not cause me the pleasure which it should have done. The Abbé Sérapion had something penetrating and inquisitorial in his gaze which made me feel very ill at ease. His presence filled me with embarrassment and a sense of guilt. At the first glance he divined my interior trouble, and I hated him for his clairvoyance.

While he inquired after my health in hypocritically honeyed accents, he constantly kept his two great yellow lion-eyes fixed upon me, and plunged his look into my soul like a sounding-lead. Then he asked me how I directed my parish, if I was happy in it, how I passed the leisure hours allowed me in the intervals of pastoral duty, whether I had become acquainted with many of the inhabitants of the place, what was my favourite reading, and a thousand other such questions. I answered these inquiries as briefly as possible, and he, without ever waiting for my answers, passed rapidly from one subject of query to another. That conversation had evidently no connection with what he actually wished to say. At last, without any premonition, but as though repeating a piece of news which he had recalled on the instant, and feared might otherwise be forgotten subsequently, he suddenly said, in a clear vibrant voice, which rang in my ears like the trumpets of the Last Judgment:

'The great courtesan Clarimonde died a few days ago, at the close of an orgie which lasted eight days and eight nights. It was something infernally splendid. The abominations of the banquets of Belshazzar and Cleopatra were re-enacted there. Good God, what age are we living in? The guests were served by swarthy slaves who spoke an unknown tongue, and who seemed to me to be veritable demons. The livery of the very least among them would have served for the gala-dress of an emperor. There have always been very strange stories told of this Clarimonde, and all her lovers came to a violent or miserable end. They used to say that she was a ghoul, a female vampire; but I believe she was none other than Beelzebub himself.'

He ceased to speak, and commenced to regard me more attentively than ever, as though to observe the effect of his words on me. I could not refrain from starting when I heard him utter the name of Clarimonde, and this news of her death, in addition to the pain it caused me by reason of its coincidence with the nocturnal scenes I had witnessed, filled me with an agony and terror which my face betrayed, despite my utmost endeavours to appear composed. Sérapion fixed an anxious and severe look upon me, and then observed: 'My son, I must warn you that you are standing with foot raised upon the brink of an abyss; take heed lest you fall therein. Satan's claws are long, and tombs are not always true to their trust. The tombstone of Clarimonde should be sealed down with a triple seal, for, if report be true, it is not the first time she has died. May God watch over you, Romuald!'

And with these words the Abbé walked slowly to the door. I did not see him again at that time, for he left for S——— almost immediately.

I became completely restored to health and resumed my accustomed duties. The memory of Clarimonde and the words of the old Abbé were constantly in my mind; nevertheless no extraordinary event had occurred to verify the funereal predictions of Sérapion, and I had commenced to believe that his fears and my own terrors were over-exaggerated, when one night I had a strange dream. I had hardly fallen asleep when I heard my bed-curtains drawn apart, as their rings slided back upon the curtain rod with a sharp sound. I rose up quickly upon my elbow, and beheld the shadow of a woman standing erect before me. I recognised Clarimonde immediately. She bore in her hand a little lamp, shaped like those which are placed in tombs, and its light lent her fingers a rosy transparency, which extended itself by lessening degrees even to the opaque and milky whiteness of her bare arm. Her only garment was the linen winding-sheet which had shrouded her when lying upon the bed of death. She sought to gather its folds over her bosom as though ashamed of being so scantily clad, but her little hand was not equal to the task. She was so white that the colour of the drapery blended with that of her flesh under the pallid rays of the lamp. Enveloped with this subtle tissue which betrayed all the contour of her body, she seemed rather the marble statue of some fair antique bather than a woman endowed with life. But dead or living, statue or woman, shadow or body, her beauty was still the same, only that the green light of her eyes was less brilliant, and her mouth, once so warmly crimson, was only tinted with a faint tender rosiness, like that of her cheeks. The little blue flowers which I had noticed entwined in her hair were withered and dry, and had lost nearly all their leaves, but this did not prevent her from being charming—so charming that, notwithstanding the strange character of the adventure, and the unexplainable manner in which she had entered my room, I felt not even for a moment the least fear.

She placed the lamp on the table and seated herself at the foot of my bed; then bending toward me, she said, in that voice at once silvery clear and yet velvety in its sweet softness, such as I never heard from any lips save hers:

'I have kept thee long in waiting, dear Romuald, and it must have seemed to thee that I had forgotten thee. But I come from afar off, very far off, and from a land whence no other has ever yet returned. There is neither sun nor moon in that land whence I come: all is but space and shadow; there is neither road nor pathway: no earth for the foot, no air for the wing; and nevertheless behold me here, for Love is stronger than Death and must conquer him in the end. Oh what sad faces and fearful things I have seen on my way hither! What difficulty my soul, returned to earth through the power of will alone, has had in finding its body and reinstating itself therein! What terrible efforts I had to make ere I could lift the ponderous slab with which they had covered me! See, the palms of my poor hands are all bruised! Kiss them, sweet love, that they may be healed!' She laid the cold palms of her hands upon ray mouth, one after the other. I kissed them, indeed, many times, and she the while watched me with a smile of ineffable affection.

I confess to my shame that I had entirely forgotten the advice of the Abbé Sérapion and the sacred office wherewith I had been invested. I had fallen without resistance, and at the first assault. I had not even made the least effort to repel the tempter. The fresh coolness of Clarimonde's skin penetrated my own, and I felt voluptuous tremors pass over my whole body. Poor child! in spite of all I saw afterward, I can hardly yet believe she was a demon; at least she had no appearance of being such, and never did Satan so skilfully conceal his claws and horns. She had drawn her feet up beneath her, and squatted down on the edge of the couch in an attitude full of negligent coquetry. From time to time she passed her little hand through my hair and twisted it into curls, as though trying how a new style of wearing it would become my face. I abandoned myself to her hands with the most guilty pleasure, while she accompanied her gentle play with the prettiest prattle. The most remarkable fact was that I felt no astonishment whatever at so extraordinary ah adventure, and as in dreams one finds no difficulty in accepting the most fantastic events as simple facts, so all these circumstances seemed to me perfectly natural in themselves.

'I loved thee long ere I saw thee, dear Romuald, and sought thee everywhere. Thou wast my dream, and I first saw thee in the church at the fatal moment. I said at once, "It is he!" I gave thee a look into which I threw all the love I ever had, all the love I now have, all the love I shall ever have for thee—a look that would have damned a cardinal or brought a king to his knees at my feet in view of all his court. Thou remainedst unmoved, preferring thy God to me!

'Ah, how jealous I am of that God whom thou didst love and still lovest more than me!

'Woe is me, unhappy one that I am! I can never have thy heart all to myself, I whom thou didst recall to life with a kiss—dead Clarimonde, who for thy sake bursts asunder the gates of the tomb, and comes to consecrate to thee a life which she has resumed only to make thee happy!'

All her words were accompanied with the most impassioned caresses, which bewildered my sense and my reason to such an extent, that I did not fear to utter a frightful blasphemy for the sake of consoling her, and to declare that I loved her as much as God.

Her eyes rekindled and shone like chrysoprases. 'In truth?—in very truth?—as much as God!' she cried, flinging her beautiful arms around me. 'Since it is so, thou wilt come with me; thou wilt follow me whithersoever I desire. Thou wilt cast away thy ugly black habit. Thou shalt be the proudest and most envied of cavaliers; thou shalt be my lover! To be the acknowledged lover of Clarimonde, who has refused even a Pope! That will be something to feel proud of. Ah, the fair, unspeakably happy existence, the beautiful golden life we shall live together! And when shall we depart, my fair sir?'

'To-morrow! To-morrow!' I cried in my delirium.

'To-morrow, then, so let it be!' she answered. 'In the meanwhile I shall have opportunity to change my toilet, for this is a little too light and in nowise suited for a voyage. I must also forthwith notify all my friends who believe me dead, and mourn for me as deeply as they are capable of doing. The money, the dresses, the carriages—all will be ready. I shall call for thee at this same hour.

Adieu, dear heart!' And she lightly touched my forehead with her lips. The lamp went out, the curtains closed again, and all became dark; a leaden, dreamless sleep fell on me and held me unconscious until the morning following.

I awoke later than usual, and the recollection of this singular adventure troubled me during the whole day. I finally persuaded myself that it was a mere vapour of my heated imagination. Nevertheless its sensations had been so vivid that it was difficult to persuade myself that they were not real, and it was not without some presentiment of what was going to happen that I got into bed at last, after having prayed God to drive far from me all thoughts of evil, and to protect the chastity of my slumber.

I soon fell into a deep sleep, and my dream was continued. The curtains again parted, and I beheld Clarimonde, not as on the former occasion, pale in her pale winding-sheet, with the violets of death upon her cheeks, but gay, sprightly, jaunty, in a superb travelling-dress of green velvet, trimmed with gold lace, and looped up on either side to allow a glimpse of satin petticoat. Her blond hair escaped in thick ringlets from beneath a broad black felt hat, decorated with white feathers whimsically twisted into various shapes. In one hand she held a little riding-whip terminated by a golden whistle. She tapped me lightly with it, and exclaimed: 'Well, my fine sleeper, is this the way you make your preparations? I thought I would find you up and dressed. Arise quickly, we have no time to lose.'

I leaped out of bed at once.

'Come, dress yourself, and let us go,' she continued, pointing to a little package she had brought with her. 'The horses are becoming impatient of delay and champing their bits at the door. We ought to have been by this time at least ten leagues distant from here.'

I dressed myself hurriedly, and she handed me the articles of apparel herself one by one, bursting into laughter from time to time at my awkwardness, as she explained to me the use of a garment when I had made a mistake. She hurriedly arranged my hair, and this done, held up before me a little pocket-mirror of Venetian crystal, rimmed with silver filigree-work, and playfully asked: 'How dost find thyself now? Wilt engage me for thy valet de chambre?'

I was no longer the same person, and I could not even recognise myself. I resembled my former self no more than a finished statue resembles a block of stone. My old face seemed but a coarse daub of the one reflected in the mirror. I was handsome, and my vanity was sensibly tickled by the metamorphosis.

That elegant apparel, that richly embroidered vest had made of me a totally different personage, and I marvelled at the power of transformation owned by a few yards of cloth cut after a certain pattern. The spirit of my costume penetrated my very skin and within ten minutes more I had become something of a coxcomb.

In order to feel more at ease in my new attire, I took several turns up and down the room. Clari-monde watched me with an air of maternal pleasure, and appeared well satisfied with her work. 'Come, enough of this child's play! Let us start, Romuald, dear. We have far to go, and we may not get there in time.' She took my hand and led me forth. All the doors opened before her at a touch, and we passed by the dog without awaking him.

At the gate we found Margheritone waiting, the same swarthy groom who had once before been my-escort. He held the bridles of three horses, all black like those which bore us to the castle—one for me, one for him, one for Clarimonde. Those horses must have been Spanish genets born of mares fecundated by a zephyr, for they were fleet as the wind itself, and the moon, which had just risen at our departure to light us on the way, rolled over the sky like a wheel detached from her own chariot. We beheld her on the right leaping from tree to tree, and putting herself out of breath in the effort to keep up with us. Soon we came upon a level plain where, hard by a clump of trees, a carriage with four vigorous horses awaited us. We entered it, and the postillions urged their animals into a mad gallop. I had one arm around Clarimonde's waist, and one of her hands clasped in mine; her head leaned upon my shoulder, and I felt her bosom, half bare, lightly pressing against my arm. I had never known such intense happiness. In that hour I had forgotten everything, and I no more remembered having ever been a priest than I remembered what I had been doing in my mother's womb, so great was the fascination which the evil spirit exerted upon me. From that night my nature seemed in some sort to have become halved, and there were two men within me, neither of whom knew the other. At one moment I believed myself a priest who dreamed nightly that he was a gentleman, at another that I was a gentleman who dreamed he was a priest. I could no longer distinguish the dream from the reality, nor could I discover where the reality began or where ended the dream. The exquisite young lord and libertine railed at the priest, the priest loathed the dissolute habits of the young lord. Two spirals entangled and confounded the one with the other, yet never touching, would afford a fair representation of this bicephalic life which I lived. Despite the strange character of my condition, I do not believe that I ever inclined, even for a moment, to madness. I always retained with extreme vividness all the perceptions of my two lives. Only there was one absurd fact which I could not explain to myself—namely, that the consciousness of the same individuality existed in two men so opposite in character. It was an anomaly for which I could not account—whether I believed myself to be the curé of the little village of C———, or Il Signor Romualdo, the titled lover of Clarimonde.

Be that as it may, I lived, at least I believed that I lived, in Venice. I have never been able to discover rightly how much of illusion and how much of reality there was in this fantastic adventure. We dwelt in a great palace on the Canaleio, filled with frescoes and statues, and containing two Titians in the noblest style of the great master, which were hung in Clarimonde's chamber. It was a palace well worthy of a king. We had each our gondola, our barcarolli in family livery, our music hall, and our special poet. Clarimonde always lived upon a magnificent scale; there was something of Cleopatra in her nature. As for me, I had the retinue of a prince's son, and I was regarded with as much reverential respect as though I had been of the family of one of the twelve Apostles or the four Evangelists of the Most Serene Republic. I would not have turned aside to allow even the Doge to pass, and I do not believe that since Satan fell from heaven, any creature was ever prouder or more insolent than I. I went to the Ridotto, and played with a luck which seemed absolutely infernal. I received the best of all society—the sons of ruined families, women of the theatre, shrewd knaves, parasites, hectoring swashbucklers. But notwithstanding the dissipation of such a life, I always remained faithful to Clarimonde. I loved her wildly. She would have excited satiety itself, and chained inconstancy. To have Clarimonde was to have twenty mistresses; ay, to possess all women: so mobile, so varied of aspect, so fresh in new charms was she all in herself—a very chameleon of a woman, in sooth. She made you commit with her the infidelity you would have committed with another, by donning to perfection the character, the attraction, the style of beauty of the woman who appeared to please you. She returned my love a hundred-fold, and it was in vain that the young patricians and even the Ancients of the Council of Ten made her the most magnificent proposals. A Foscari even went so far as to offer to espouse her. She rejected all his overtures. Of gold she had enough. She wished no longer for anything but love—a love youthful, pure, evoked by herself, and which should be a first and last passion. I would have been perfectly happy but for a cursed nightmare which recurred every night, and in which I believed myself to be a poor village curé, practising mortification and penance for my excesses during the day. Reassured by my constant association with her,

I never thought further of the strange manner in which I had become acquainted with Clarimonde. But the words of the Abbé Sérapion concerning her recurred often to my memory, and never ceased to cause me uneasiness.

For some time the health of Clarimonde had not been so good as usual; her complexion grew paler day by day. The physicians who were summoned could not comprehend the nature of her malady and knew not how to treat it. They all prescribed some insignificant remedies, and never called a second time. Her paleness, nevertheless, visibly increased, and she became colder and colder, until she seemed almost as white and dead as upon that memorable night in the unknown castle. I grieved with anguish unspeakable to behold her thus slowly perishing; and she, touched by my agony, smiled upon me sweetly and sadly with the fateful smile of those who feel that they must die.

One morning I was seated at her bedside, and breakfasting from a little table placed close at hand, so that I might not be obliged to leave her for a single instant. In the act of cutting some fruit I accidentally inflicted rather a deep gash on my finger. The blood immediately gushed forth in a little purple jet, and a few drops spurted upon Clarimonde. Her eyes flashed, her face suddenly assumed an expression of savage and ferocious joy such as I had never before observed in her. She leaped out of her bed with animal agility—the agility, as it were, of an ape or a cat—and sprang upon my wound, which she commenced to suck with an air of unutterable pleasure. She swallowed the blood in little mouthfuls, slowly and carefully, like a connoisseur tasting a wine from Xeres or Syracuse. Gradually her eyelids half closed, and the pupils of her green eyes became oblong instead of round. From time to time she paused in order to kiss my hand, then she would recommence to press her lips to the lips of the wound in order to coax forth a few more ruddy drops. When she found that the blood would no longer come, she arose with eyes liquid and brilliant, rosier than a May dawn; her face full and fresh, her hand warm and moist—in fine, more beautiful than ever, and in the most perfect health.

'I shall not die! I shall not die!' she cried, clinging to my neck, half mad with joy. 'I can love thee yet for a long time. My life is thine, and all that is of me comes from thee. A few drops of thy rich and noble blood, more precious and more potent than all the elixirs of the earth, have given me back life.'

This scene long haunted my memory, and inspired me with strange doubts in regard to Clarimonde; and the same evening, when slumber had transported me to my presbytery, I beheld the Abbé Sérapion, graver and more anxious of aspect than ever. He gazed attentively at me, and sorrowfully exclaimed: 'Not content with losing your soul, you now desire also to lose your body. Wretched young man, into how terrible a plight have you fallen!' The tone in which he uttered these words powerfully affected me, but in spite of its vividness even that impression was soon dissipated, and a thousand other cares erased it from my mind. At last one evening, while looking into a mirror whose traitorous position she had not taken into account, I saw Clarimonde in the act of emptying a powder into the cup of spiced wine which she had long been in the habit of preparing after our repasts. I took the cup, feigned to carry it to my lips, and then placed it on the nearest article of furniture as though intending to finish it at my leisure. Taking advantage of a moment when the fair one's back was turned, I threw the contents under the table, after which I retired to my chamber and went to bed, fully resolved not to sleep, but to watch and discover what should come of all this mystery. I did not have to wait long, Clarimonde entered in her nightdress, and having removed her apparel, crept into bed and lay down beside me. When she felt assured that I was asleep, she bared my arm, and drawing a gold pin from her hair, commenced to murmur in a low voice:

'One drop, only one drop! One ruby at the end of my needle.... Since thou lovest me yet, I must not die!... Ah, poor love! His beautiful blood, so brightly purple, I must drink it. Sleep, my only treasure! Sleep, my god, my child! I will do thee no harm; I will only take of thy life what I must to keep my own from being for ever extinguished. But that I love thee so much, I could well resolve to have other lovers whose veins I could drain; but since I have known thee all other men have become hateful to me.... Ah, the beautiful arm! How round it is! How white it is! How shall I ever dare to prick this pretty blue vein!' And while thus murmuring to herself she wept, and I felt her tears raining on my arm as she clasped it with her hands. At last she took the resolve, slightly punctured me with her pin, and commenced to suck up the blood which oozed from the place. Although she swallowed only a few drops, the fear of weakening me soon seized her, and she carefully tied a little band around my arm, afterward rubbing the wound with an unguent which immediately cicatrised it. Further doubts were impossible. The Abbé Sérapion was right. Notwithstanding this positive knowledge, however, I could not cease to love Clarimonde, and I would gladly of my own accord have given her all the blood she required to sustain her factitious life. Moreover, I felt but little fear of her. The woman seemed to plead with me for the vampire, and what I had already heard and seen sufficed to reassure me completely. In those days I had plenteous veins, which would not have been so easily exhausted as at present; and I would not have thought of bargaining for my blood, drop by drop. I would rather have opened myself the veins of my arm and said to her: 'Drink, and may my love infiltrate itself throughout thy body together with my blood!' I carefully avoided ever making the least reference to the narcotic drink she had prepared for me, or to the incident of the pin, and we lived in the most perfect harmony.

Yet my priestly scruples commenced to torment me more than ever, and I was at a loss to imagine what new penance I could invent in order to mortify and subdue my flesh. Although these visions were involuntary, and though I did not actually participate in anything relating to them, I could not dare to touch the body of Christ with hands so impure and a mind defiled by such debauches whether real or imaginary. In the effort to avoid falling under the influence of these wearisome hallucinations, I strove to prevent myself from being overcome by sleep. I held my eyelids open with my fingers, and stood for hours together leaning upright against the wall, fighting sleep with all my might; but the dust of drowsiness invariably gathered upon my eyes at last, and finding all resistance useless, I would have to let my arms fall in the extremity of despairing weariness, and the current of slumber would again bear me away to the perfidious shores. Sérapion addressed me with the most vehement exhortations, severely reproaching me for my softness and want of fervour. Finally, one day when I was more wretched than usual, he said to me: 'There is but one way by which you can obtain relief from this continual torment, and though it is an extreme measure it must be made use of; violent diseases require violent remedies. I know where Clarimonde is buried. It is necessary that we shall disinter her remains, and that you shall behold in how pitiable a state the object of your love is. Then you will no longer be tempted to lose your soul for the sake of an unclean corpse devoured by worms, and ready to crumble into dust. That will assuredly restore you to yourself.' For my part, I was so tired of this double life that I at once consented, desiring to ascertain beyond a doubt whether a priest or a gentleman had been the victim of delusion. I had become fully resolved either to kill one of the two men within me for the benefit of the other, or else to kill both, for so terrible an existence could not last long and be endured. The Abbé Sérapion provided himself with a mattock, a lever, and a lantern, and at midnight we wended our way to the cemetery of———, the location and place of which were perfectly familiar to him. After having directed the rays of the dark lantern upon the inscriptions of several tombs, we came at last upon a great slab, half concealed by huge weeds and devoured by mosses and parasitic plants, whereupon we deciphered the opening lines of the epitaph:

Here lies Clarimonde
Who was famed in her life-time
As the fairest of women.*

* Ici gît Clarimonde
Qui fut de son vivant
La plus belle du monde.

The broken beauty of the lines is unavoidably lost in the translation.

'It is here without a doubt,' muttered Sérapion, and placing his lantern on the ground, he forced the point of the lever under the edge of the stone and commenced to raise it. The stone yielded, and he proceeded to work with the mattock. Darker and more silent than the night itself, I stood by and watched him do it, while he, bending over his dismal toil, streamed with sweat, panted, and his hard-coming breath seemed to have the harsh tone of a death rattle. It was a weird scene, and had any persons from without beheld us, they would assuredly have taken us rather for profane wretches and shroud-stealers than for priests of God. There was something grim and fierce in Sérapion's zeal which lent him the air of a demon rather than of an apostle or an angel, and his great aquiline face, with all its stern features, brought out in strong relief by the lantern-light, had something fearsome in it which enhanced the unpleasant fancy. I felt an icy sweat come out upon my forehead in huge beads, and my hair stood up with a hideous fear. Within the depths of my own heart I felt that the act of the austere Sérapion was an abominable sacrilege; and I could have prayed that a triangle of fire would issue from the entrails of the dark clouds, heavily rolling above us, to reduce him to cinders. The owls which had been nestling in the cypress-trees, startled by the gleam of the lantern, flew against it from time to time, striking their dusty wings against its panes, and uttering plaintive cries of lamentation; wild foxes yelped in the far darkness, and a thousand sinister noises detached themselves from the silence. At last Séra-pion's mattock struck the coffin itself, making its planks re-echo with a deep sonorous sound, with that terrible sound nothingness utters when stricken. He wrenched apart and tore up the lid, and I beheld Clarimonde, pallid as a figure of marble, with hands joined; her white winding-sheet made but one fold from her head to her feet. A little crimson drop sparkled like a speck of dew at one corner of her colourless mouth. Sérapion, at this spectacle, burst into fury: 'Ah, thou art here, demon! Impure courtesan! Drinker of blood and gold! 'And he flung holy water upon the corpse and the coffin, over which he traced the sign of the cross with his sprinkler. Poor Clarimonde had no sooner been touched by the blessed spray than her beautiful body crumbled into dust, and became only a shapeless and frightful mass of cinders and half-calcined bones.

'Behold your mistress, my Lord Romuald!' cried the inexorable priest, as he pointed to these sad remains. 'Will you be easily tempted after this to promenade on the Lido or at Fusina with your beauty?' I covered my face with my hands, a vast ruin had taken place within me. I returned to my presbytery, and the noble Lord Romuald, the lover of Clarimonde, separated himself from the poor priest with whom he had kept such strange company so long. But once only, the following night, I saw Clarimonde. She said to me, as she had said the first time at the portals of the church: 'Unhappy man! Unhappy man! What hast thou done? Wherefore have hearkened to that imbecile priest? Wert thou not happy? And what harm had I ever done thee that thou shouldst violate my poor tomb, and lay bare the miseries of my nothingness? All communication between our souls and our bodies is henceforth for ever broken. Adieu! Thou wilt yet regret me!' She vanished in air as smoke, and I never saw her more.

Alas! she spoke truly indeed. I have regretted her more than once, and I regret her still. My soul's peace has been very dearly bought. The love of God was not too much to replace such a love as hers. And this, brother, is the story of my youth. Never gaze upon a woman, and walk abroad only with eyes ever fixed upon the ground; for however chaste and watchful one may be, the error of a single moment is enough to make one lose eternity. lose eternity.

The True Story of A Vampire and More

by Eric Stenbock

The True Story of a Vampire

Vampire stories are generally located in Styria; mine is also. Styria is by no means the romantic kind of place described by those who have certainly never been there. It is a flat, uninteresting country, only celebrated for its turkeys, its capons, and the stupidity of its inhabitants. Vampires generally arrive at night, in carriages drawn by two black horses.

Our Vampire arrived by the commonplace means of the railway train, and in the afternoon.

You must think I am joking, or perhaps that by the word "Vampire" I mean a financial vampire.

No, I am quite serious. The Vampire of whom I am speaking, who laid waste our hearth and home, was a real vampire.

Vampires are generally described as dark, sinister-looking, and singularly handsome. Our Vampire was, on the contrary, rather fair, and certainly was not at first sight sinister-looking, and though decidedly attractive in appearance, not what one would call singularly handsome.

Yes, he desolated our home, killed my brother—the one object of my adoration—also my dear father. Yet, at the same time, I must say that I myself came under the spell of his fascination, and, in spite of all, have no ill-will towards him now.

Doubtless you have read in the papers passim of "the Baroness and her beasts." It is to tell how I came to spend most of my useless wealth on an asylum for stray animals that I am writing this.

I am old now; what happened then was when I was a little girl of about thirteen. I will begin by describing our household. We were Poles: our name was Wronski: we lived in Styria, where we had a castle. Our household was very limited. It consisted, with the exclusion of domestics, of only my father, our governess—a worthy Belgian named Mademoiselle Vonnaert—my brother, and myself. Let me begin with my father: he was old and both my brother and I were children of his old age. Of my mother I remember nothing: she died in giving birth to my brother, who was only one year, or not as much, younger than in self. Our father was studious, continually occupied in reading books, chiefly on recondite subjects and in all kinds of unknown languages.

He had a long white beard, and wore habitually a black velvet skull- cap.

How kind he was to us! It was more than I could tell. Still it was not I who was the favourite.

His whole heart went out to Gabriel—Gabryel as we spelt it in Polish. He was always called by the Russian abbreviation Gavril—I mean, of course, my brother, who had a resemblance to the only portrait of my mother, a slight chalk sketch which hung in my father's study. But I was by no means jealous: my brother was and has been the only love of my life. It is for his sake that I am now keeping in Westbourne Park a home for stray cats and dogs.

I was at that time, as I said before, a little girl; my name was Carmela. My long tangled hair was always all over the place, and never would combed straight. I was not pretty—at least, looking at a photograph of me at that time. I do not think I could describe myself as such. Yet at the same time, when I look at the photograph, I think my expression may have been pleasing to some people: irregular features, large mouth, and large wild eyes.

I was by way of being naughty—not so naughty Gabriel in the opinion of Mlle Vonnaert. Mlle Vonnaert. I may intercalate, was a wholly excellent person, middle-aged, who really did speak good French, although she was a Belgian, and could also make herself understood in German, which, as you may or may not know, is the current language of Styria.

I find it difficult to describe my brother Gabriel; there was something about him strange and superhuman, or perhaps I should rather say praeterhuman, something between the animal and the divine. Perhaps the Greek idea of the Faun might illustrate what I mean: but that will not do either. He had large, wild, gazelle-like eyes: his hair, like mine, was in a perpetual tangle—that point he had in common with me, and indeed, as I afterwards heard, our mother having been of gipsy race, it will account for much of the innate wildness there was in our natures. I was wild enough, but Gabriel was much wilder. Nothing would induce him to put on shoes and stockings, except on Sundays—when he also allowed his hair to be combed, but only by me. How shall I describe the grace of that lovely mouth, shaped verily "en arc d'amour." I always think of the text in the Psalm, "Grace is shed forth on thy lips, therefore has God blessed thee eternally"—lips that seemed to exhale the very breath of life. Then that beautiful, lithe, living, elastic form!

He could run faster than any deer: spring like a squirrel to the topmost branch of a tree: he might have stood for the sign and symbol of vitality itself.

But seldom could he be induced by Mlle Vonnaert to learn lessons; but when he did so, he learnt with extraordinary quickness. He would play upon every conceivable instrument, holding a violin here, there, and everywhere except the right place: manufacturing instruments for himself out of reeds—even sticks. Mlle Vonnaert made futile efforts to induce him to learn to play the piano. I suppose he was what was called spoilt, though merely in the superficial sense of the word. Our father allowed him to indulge in every caprice.

One of his peculiarities, when quite a little child, was horror at the sight of meat. Nothing on earth would induce him to taste it. Another thing which was particularly remarkable about him was his extraordinary power over animals. Everything seemed to come tame to his hand. Birds would sit on his shoulder. Then sometimes Mlle Vonnaert and I would lose him in the woods—he would suddenly dart away. Then we would find him singing softly or whistling to himself, with all manner of woodland creatures around him—hedgehogs, little foxes, wild rabbits, marmots, squirrels, and such like. He would frequently bring these things home with him and insist on keeping them. This strange menagerie was the terror of poor Mlle Vonnaert's heart. He chose to live in a little room at the top of a turret; but which, instead of going upstairs, he chose to reach by means of a very tall chestnut-tree, through the window. But in contradiction of all his, it was his custom to serve every Sunday Mass in the parish church, with hair nicely combed and with white surplice and red cassock. He looked as demure and tamed as possible. Then came the element of the divine. What an expression of ecstasy there was in those glorious eyes!

Thus far I have not been speaking about the Vampire. However, let me begin with my narrative at last. One day my father had to go to the neighbouring town—as he frequently had. This time he returned accompanied by a guest. The gentleman, he said, had missed his train, through the late arrival of another at our station, which was a junction, and he would therefore, as trains were not frequent in our parts, have had to wait there all night. He had joined in conversation with my father in the too-late-arriving train from the town: and had consequently accepted my father's invitation to stay the night at our house. But of course, you know, in those out-of-the-way parts we are almost patriarchal in our hospitality.

He was announced under the name of Count Vardalek—the name being Hungarian. But he spoke German well enough: not with the monotonous accentuation of Hungarians, but rather, if anything, with a slight Slavonic intonation. His voice was peculiarly soft and insinuating. We soon afterwards found that he could talk Polish, and Mlle Vonnaert vouched for his good French.

Indeed he seemed to know all languages. But let me give my first impressions. He was rather tall with fair wavy hair, rather long, which accentuated a certain effeminacy about his smooth face.

His figure had something—I cannot say what—serpentine about it. The features were refined; and he had long, slender, subtle, magnetic- looking hands, a somewhat long sinuous nose, a graceful mouth, and an attractive smile, which belied the intense sadness of the expression of the eyes. When he arrived his eyes were half closed—indeed they were habitually so—so that I could not decide their colour. He looked worn and wearied. I could not possibly guess his age.

Suddenly Gabriel burst into the room: a yellow butterfly was clinging to his hair. He was carrying in his arms a little squirrel. Of course he was barelegged as usual. The stranger looked up at his approach; then I noticed his eves. They were green: they seemed to dilate and grow larger. Gabriel stood stock-still, with a startled look, like that of a bird fascinated by a serpent.

But nevertheless he held out his hand to the newcomer Vardalek, taking his hand—I don't know why I noticed this trivial thing—pressed the pulse with his forefinger. Suddenly Gabriel darted from the room and rushed upstairs, going to his turret-room this time by the staircase instead of the tree. I was in terror what the Count might think of him. Great was my relief when he came down in his velvet Sunday suit, and shoes and stockings. I combed his hair, and set him generally right.

When the stranger came down to dinner his appearance had somewhat altered; he looked much younger. There was an elasticity of the skin, combined with a delicate complexion, rarely to be found in a man. Before, he had struck me as being very pale.

Well, at dinner we were all charmed with him, especially my father. He seemed to be thoroughly acquainted with all my father's particular hobbies. Once, when my father was relating some of his military experiences, he said something about a drummer-boy who was wounded in battle. His eyes opened completely again and dilated: this time with a particularly disagreeable expression, dull and dead, yet at the same time animated by some horrible excitement. But this was only momentary.

The chief subject of his conversation with my father was about certain curious mystical books which my father had just lately picked up, and which he could not make out, but Vardalek seemed completely to understand. At dessert-time my father asked him if he were in a great hurry to reach his destination: if not, would he not stay with us a little while: though our place was out of the way, he would find much that would interest him in his library.

He answered, "I am in no hurry. I have no particular reason for going to that place at all, and if I can be of service to you in deciphering these books, I shall be only too glad." He added with a smile which was bitter, very very bitter: "You see I am a cosmopolitan, a wanderer on the face of the earth."

After dinner my father asked him if he played the piano. He said, "Yes, I can a little," and he sat down at the piano. Then he played a Hungarian csardas—wild, rhapsodic, wonderful.

That is the music which makes men mad. He went on in the same strain.

Gabriel stood stock-still by the piano, his eyes dilated and fixed, his form quivering. At last he said very slowly, at one particular motive—for want of a better word you may call it the relâche of a csardas, by which I mean that point where the original quasi-slow movement begins again—"Yes, I think I could play that."

Then he quickly fetched his fiddle and self-made xylophone, and did, actually alternating the instruments, render the same very well indeed.

Vardalek looked at him, and said in a very sad voice, "Poor child! you have the soul of music within you."

I could not understand why he should seem to commiserate instead of congratulate Gabriel on what certainly showed an extraordinary talent.

Gabriel was shy even as the wild animals who were tame to him. Never before had he taken to a stranger. Indeed, as a rule, if any stranger came to the house by any chance, he would hide himself, and I had to bring him up his food to the turret chamber. You may imagine what was my surprise when I saw him walking about hand in hand with Vardalek the next morning, in the garden, talking lively with him, and showing his collection of pet animals, which he had gathered from the woods, and for which we had had to fit up a regular zoological gardens. He seemed utterly under the domination of Vardalek. What surprised us was (for otherwise we liked the stranger, especially for being kind to him) that he seemed, though not noticeably at first—except perhaps to me, who noticed everything with regard to him—to be gradually losing his general health and vitality. He did not become pale as yet; but there was a certain languor about his movements which certainly there was by no means before.

My father got more and more devoted to Count Vardalek. He helped him in his studies: and my father would hardly allow him to go away, which he did sometimes—to Trieste, he said: he always came back, bringing us presents of strange Oriental jewellery or textures.

I knew all kinds of people came to Trieste, Orientals included. Still, there was a strangeness and magnificence about these things which I was sure even then could not possibly have come from such a place as Trieste, memorable to me chiefly for its necktie shops.

When Vardalek was away, Gabriel was continually asking for him and talking about him. Then at the same time he seemed to regain his old vitality and spirits. Vardalek always returned looking much older, wan, and weary. Gabriel would rush to meet him, and kiss him on the mouth. Then he gave a slight shiver: and after a little while began to look quite young again.

Things continued like this for some time. My father would not hear of Vardalek's going away permanently. He came to be an inmate of our house. I indeed, and Mlle Vonnaert also, could not help noticing what a difference there was altogether about Gabriel. But my father seemed totally blind to it.

One night I had gone downstairs to fetch something which I had left in the drawing-room. As I was going up again I passed Vardalek's room. He was playing on a piano, which had been specially put there for him, one of Chopin's nocturnes, very beautifully: I stopped, leaning on the banisters to listen.

Something white appeared on the dark staircase. We believed in ghosts in our part. I was transfixed with terror, and clung to the ballisters. What was my astonishment to see Gabriel walking slowly down the staircase, his eyes fixed as though in a trance! This terrified me even more than a ghost would. Could I believe my senses? Could that be Gabriel?

I simply could not move. Gabriel, clad in his long white night-shirt, came downstairs and opened the door. He left it open. Vardalek still continued playing, but talked as he played.

He said—this time speaking in Polish—Nie umiem wyrazic jak ciechi kocham—"My darling, I fain would spare thee: but thy life is my life, and I must live, I who would rather die. Will God not have any mercy on me? Oh! Oh! life; oh, the torture of life!" Here he struck one agonized and strange chord, then continued playing softly, "O, Gabriel, my beloved! my life, yes life—oh, why life? I am sure this is but a little that I demand of thee. Sorely thy superabundance of life can spare little to one who is already dead. No, stay," he said now almost harshly, "what must be, must be!"

Gabriel stood there quite still, with the same fixed vacant expression, in the room. He was evidently walking in his sleep. Vardalek played on: then said, "Ah!" with a sign of terrible agony. Then very gently, "Go now, Gabriel; it is enough." And Gabriel went out of the room and ascended the staircase at the same slow pace, with the same unconscious stare. Vardalek struck the piano, and although he did not play loudly, it seemed as though the strings would break. You never heard music so strange and so heart-rending!

I only know I was found by Mlle Vonnaert in the morning, in an unconscious state, at the foot of the stairs. Was it a dream after all? I am sure now that it was not. I thought then it might be, and said nothing to anyone about it. Indeed, what could I say?

Well, to let me cut a long story short, Gabriel, who had never known a moment's sickness in his life, grew ill: and we had to send to Gratz for a doctor, who could give no explanation of Gabriel's strange illness. Gradual wasting away, he said: absolutely no organic complaint. What could this mean?

My father at last became conscious of the fact that Gabriel was ill. His anxiety was fearful. The last trace of grey faded from his hair, and it became quite white. We sent to Vienna for doctors.

But all with the same result.

Gabriel was generally unconscious, and when conscious, only seemed to recognize Vardalek, who sat continually by his bedside, nursing him with the utmost tenderness.

One day I was alone in the room: and Vardalek cried suddenly, almost fiercely, "Send for a priest at once, at once," he repeated. "It is now almost too late!"

Gabriel stretched out his arms spasmodically, and put them round Vardalek's neck. This was the only movement he had made, for some time. Vardalek bent down and kissed him on the lips.

I rushed downstairs: and the priest was sent for. When I came back Vardalek was not there. The priest administered extreme unction. I think Gabriel was already dead, although we did not think so at the time.

Vardalek had utterly disappeared; and when we looked for him he was nowhere to be found; nor have I seen or heard of him since.

My father died very soon afterwards: suddenly aged, and bent down with grief. And so the whole of the Wronski property came into my sole possession. And here I am, an old woman, generally laughed at for keeping, in memory of Gabriel, an asylum for stray animals—and— people do not, as a rule, believe in Vampires!

The Other Side: a Breton Legend

À la joyouse Messe noire.

NOT that I like it, but one does feel so much better after it—"oh, thank you, Mère Yvonne, yes just a little drop more." So the old crones fell to drinking their hot brandy and water (although of course they only took it medicinally, as a remedy for their rheumatics), all seated round the big fire and Mère Pinquèle continued her story.

"Oh, yes, then when they get to the top of the hill, there is an altar with six candles quite black and a sort of something in between, that nobody sees quite clearly, and the old black ram with the man's face and long horns begins to say Mass in a sort of gibberish nobody understands, and two black strange things like monkeys glide about with the book and the cruets—and there's music too, such music. There are things the top half like black cats, and the bottom part like men only their legs are all covered with close black hair, and they play on the bag-pipes, and when they come to the elevation, then—" Amid the old crones there was lying on the hearth-rug, before the fire, a boy whose large lovely eyes dilated and whose limbs quivered in the very ecstacy of terror.

"Is that all true, Mère Pinquèle?" he said.

"Oh, quite true, and not only that, the best part is yet to come; for they take a child and—." Here Mère Pinquèle showed her fang-like teeth.

"Oh! Mère Pinquèle, are you a witch too?"

"Silence, Gabriel," said Mère Yvonne, "how can you say anything so wicked? Why, bless me, the boy ought to have been in bed ages ago."

Just then all shuddered, and all made the sign of the cross except Mère Pinquèle, for they heard that most dreadful of dreadful sounds— the howl of a wolf, which begins with three sharp barks and then lifts itself up in a long protracted wail of commingled cruelty and despair, and at last subsides into a whispered growl fraught with eternal malice.

There was a forest and a village and a brook, the village was on one side of the brook, none had dared to cross to the other side. Where the village was, all was green and glad and fertile and fruitful; on the other side the trees never put forth green leaves, and a dark shadow hung over it even at noon-day, and in the night-time one could hear the wolves howling—the were-wolves and the wolf-men and the men- wolves, and those very wicked men who for nine days in every year are turned into wolves; but on the green side no wolf was ever seen, and only one little running brook like a silver streak flowed between.

It was spring now and the old crones sat no longer by the fire but before their cottages sunning themselves, and everyone felt so happy that they ceased to tell stories of the "other side." But Gabriel wandered by the brook as he was wont to wander, drawn thither by some strange attraction mingled with intense horror.

His schoolfellows did not like Gabriel; all laughed and jeered at him, because he was less cruel and more gentle of nature than the rest, and even as a rare and beautiful bird escaped from a cage is hacked to death by the common sparrows, so was Gabriel among his fellows. Everyone wondered how Mère Yvonne, that buxom and worthy matron, could have produced a son like this, with strange dreamy eyes, who was as they said "pas comme les autres gamins." His only friends were the Abbé Félicien whose Mass he served each morning, and one little girl called Carmeille, who loved him, no one could make out why.

The sun had already set, Gabriel still wandered by the brook, filled with vague terror and irresistible fascination. The sun set and the moon rose, the full moon, very large and very clear, and the moonlight flooded the forest both this side and "the other side," and just on the "other side" of the brook, hanging over, Gabriel saw a large deep blue flower, whose strange intoxicating perfume reached him and fascinated him even where he stood.

"If I could only make one step across," he thought, "nothing could harm me if I only plucked that one flower, and nobody would know I had been over at all," for the villagers looked with hatred and suspicion on anyone who was said to have crossed to the "other side," so summing up courage he leapt lightly to the other side of the brook. Then the moon breaking from a cloud shone with unusual brilliance, and he saw, stretching before him, long reaches of the same strange blue flowers each one lovelier than the last, till, not being able to make up his mind which one flower to take or whether to take several, he went on and on, and the moon shone very brightly and a strange unseen bird, somewhat like a nightingale, but louder and lovelier, sang, and his heart was filled with longing for he knew not what, and the moon shone and the nightingale sang. But on a sudden a black cloud covered the moon entirely, and all was black, utter darkness, and through the darkness he heard wolves howling and shrieking in the hideous ardour of the chase, and there passed before him a horrible procession of wolves (black wolves with red fiery eyes), and with them men that had the heads of wolves and wolves that had the heads of men, and above them flew owls (black owls with red fiery eyes), and bats and long serpentine black things, and last of all seated on an enormous black ram with hideous human face the wolf-keeper on whose face was eternal shadow; but they continued their horrid chase and passed him by, and when they had passed the moon shone out more beautiful than ever, and the strange nightingale sang again, and the strange intense blue flowers were in long reaches in front to the right and to the left. But one thing was there which had not been before, among the deep blue flowers walked one with long gleaming golden hair, and she turned once round and her eyes were of the same colour as the strange blue flowers, and she walked on and Gabriel could not choose but follow. But when a cloud passed over the moon he saw no beautiful woman but a wolf, so in utter terror he turned and fled, plucking one of the strange blue flowers on the way, and leapt again over the brook and ran home.

When he got home Gabriel could not resist showing his treasure to his mother, though he knew she would not appreciate it; but when she saw the strange blue flower, Mère Yvonne turned pale and said, "Why child, where hast thou been? sure it is the witch flower"; and so saying she snatched it from him and cast it into the corner, and immediately all its beauty and strange fragrance faded from it and it looked charred as though it had been burnt. So Gabriel sat down silently and rather sulkily, and having eaten no supper went up to bed, but he did got sleep but waited and waited till all was quiet within the house. Then he crept downstairs in his long white night-shirt and bare feet on the square cold stones and picked hurriedly up the charred and faded flower and put it in his warm bosom next his heart, and immediately the flower bloomed again lovelier than ever, and he fell into a deep sleep, but through his sleep he seemed to hear a soft low voice singing underneath his window in a strange language (in which the subtle sounds melted into one another), but he could distinguish no word except his own name.

When he went forth in the morning to serve Mass, he still kept the flower with him next his heart. Now when the priest began Mass and said "Intriobo ad altare Dei," then said Gabriel "Qui nequiquam laetificavit juventutem meam." And the Abbé Félicienturned round on hearing this strange response, and he saw the boy's face deadly pale, his eyes fixed and his limbs rigid, and as the priest looked on him Gabriel fell fainting to the floor, so the sacristan had to carry him home and seek another acolyte for the Abbé Félicien.

Now when the Abbé Félicien came to see after him, Gabriel felt strangely reluctant to say anything about the blue flower and for the first time he deceived the priest.

In the afternoon as sunset drew nigh he felt better and Carmeille came to see him and begged him to go out with her into the fresh air. So they went out hand in hand, the dark haired, gazelle-eyed boy, and the fair wavy haired girl, and something, he knew not what, led his steps (half knowingly and yet not so, for he could not but walk thither) to the brook, and they sat down together on the bank.

Gabriel thought at least he might tell his secret to Carmeille, so he took out the flower from his bosom and said, "Look here, Carmeille, hast thou seen ever so lovely a flower as this?" but Carmeille turned pale and faint and said, "Oh, Gabriel what is this flower? I but touched it and I felt something strange come over me. No, no, I don't like its perfume, no there's something not quite right about it, oh, dear Gabriel, do let me throw it away," and before he had time to answer, she cast it from her, and again all its beauty and fragrance went from it and it looked charred as though it had been burnt. But suddenly where the flower had been thrown on this side of the brook, there appeared a wolf, which stood and looked at the children.

Carmeille said, "What shall we do," and clung to Gabriel, but the wolf looked at them very steadfastly and Gabriel recognized in the eyes of the wolf the strange deep intense blue eyes of the wolf-woman he had seen on the "other side," so he said, "Stay here, dear Carmeille, see she is looking gently at us and will not hurt us."

"But it is a wolf," said Carmeille, and quivered all over with fear, but again Gabriel said languidly, "She will not hurt us." Then Carmeille seized Gabriel's hand in an agony of terror and dragged him along with her till they reached the village, where she gave the alarm and all the lads of the village gathered together. They had never seen a wolf on this side of the brook, so they excited themselves greatly and arranged a grand wolf hunt for the morrow, but Gabriel sat silently apart and said no word.

That night Gabriel could not sleep at all nor could he bring himself to say his prayers; but he sat in his little room by the window with his shirt open at the throat and the strange blue flower at his heart and again this night he heard a voice singing beneath his window in the same soft, subtle, liquid language as before—

Ma zála liral va jé Cwamûlo zhajéla je Cárma urádi el javé Járma, symai,—carmé—Zhála javály thra je al vú al vlaûle va azré Safralje vairálje va já? Cárma serâja Lâja lâja Luzhà!

And as he looked he could see the silvern shadows slide on the limmering light of golden hair, and the strange eyes gleaming dark blue through the night and it seemed to him that he could not but follow; so he walked half clad and bare foot as he was with eyes fixed as in a dream silently down the stairs and out into the night.

And ever and again she turned to look on him with her strange blue eyes full of tenderness and passion and sadness beyond the sadness of things human—and as he foreknew his steps led him to the brink of the brook. Then she, taking his hand, familiarly said, "Won't you help me over Gabriel?"

Then it seemed to him as though he had known her all his life—so he went with her to the "other side" but he saw no one by him; and looking again beside him there were two wolves. In a frenzy of terror, he (who had never thought to kill any living thing before) seized a log of wood lying by and smote one of the wolves on the head.

Immediately he saw the wolf-woman again at his side with blood streaming from her forehead, staining her wonderful golden hair, and with eyes looking at him with infinite reproach, she said—"Who did this?"

Then she whispered a few words to the other wolf, which leapt over the brook and made its way towards the village, and turning again towards him she said, "Oh Gabriel, how could you strike me, who would have loved you so long and so well." Then it seemed to him again as though he had known her all his life but he felt dazed and said nothing—but she gathered a dark green strangely shaped leaf and holding it to her forehead, she said—"Gabriel, kiss the place all will be well again." So he kissed as she had bidden him and he felt the salt taste of blood in his mouth and then he knew no more.

Again he saw the wolf-keeper with his horrible troupe around him, but this time not engaged in the chase but sitting in strange conclave in a circle and the black owls sat in the trees and the black bats hung downwards from the branches. Gabriel stood alone in the middle with a hundred wicked eyes fixed on him. They seemed to deliberate about what should be done with him, speaking in that same strange tongue which he had heard in the songs beneath his window. Suddenly he felt a hand pressing in his and saw the mysterious wolf-woman by his side. Then began what seemed a kind of incantation where human or half human creatures seemed to howl, and beasts to speak with human speech but in the unknown tongue. Then the wolf-keeper whose face was ever veiled in shadow spake some words in a voice that seemed to come from afar off, but all he could distinguish was his own name Gabriel and her name Lilith. Then he felt arms enlacing him.

Gabriel awoke—in his own room—so it was a dream after all—but what a dreadful dream. Yes, but was it his own room? Of course there was his coat hanging over the chair—yes but—the Crucifix—where was the Crucifix and the benetier and the consecrated palm branch and the antique image of Our Lady perpetuae salutis, with the little ever- burning lamp before it, before which he placed every day the flowers he had gathered, yet had not dared to place the blue flower.

Every morning he lifted his still dream-laden eyes to it and said Ave Maria and made the sign of the cross, which bringeth peace to the soul—but how horrible, how maddening, it was not there, not at all. No surely he could not be awake, at least not quite awake, he would make the benedictive sign and he would be freed from this fearful illusion—yes but the sign, he would make the sign—oh, but what was the sign? Had he forgotten? or was his arm paralyzed? No he could not move. Then he had forgotten—and the prayer—he must remember that. A—vae—nunc—mortis—fructus. No surely it did not run thus—but something like it surely—yes, he was awake he could move at any rate—he would reassure himself—he would get up-he would see the grey old church with the exquisitely pointed gables bathed in the light of dawn, and presently the deep solemn bell would toll and he would run down and don his red cassock and lace-worked cotta and light the tall candles on the altar and wait reverently to vest the good and gracious Abbé Félicien, kissing each vestment as he lifted it with reverent hands.

But surely this was not the light of dawn; it was like sunset! He leapt from his small white bed, and a vague terror came over him, he trembled and had to hold on to the chair before he reached the window. No, the solemn spires of the grey church were not to be seen—he was in the depths of the forest; but in a part he had never seen before— but surely he had explored every part, it must be the "other side." To terror succeeded a languor and lassitude not without charm—passivity, acquiescence, indulgence—he felt, as it were, the strong caress of another will flowing over him like water and clothing him with invisible hands in an impalpable garment; so he dressed himself almost mechanically and walked downstairs, the same stairs it seemed to him down which it was his wont to run and spring. The broad square stones seemed singularly beautiful and irridescent with many strange colours—how was it he had never noticed this before—but he was gradually losing the power of wondering—he entered the room below— the wonted coffee and bread-rolls were on the table.

"Why Gabriel, how late you are to-day" The voice was very sweet but the intonation strange—and there sat Lilith, the mysterious wolf- woman, her glittering gold hair tied in a loose knot and an embroidery whereon she was tracing strange serpentine patterns, lay over the lap of her maize coloured garment—and she looked at Gabriel steadfastly with her wonderful dark blue eyes and said, "Why, Gabriel, you are late to-day" and Gabriel answered, "I was tired yesterday, give me some coffee."

A dream within a dream—yes, he had known her all his life, and they dwelt together; had they not always done so? And she would take him through the glades of the forest and gather for him flowers, such as he had never seen before, and tell him stories in her strange, low deep voice, which seemed ever to be accompanied by the faint vibration of strings, looking at him fixedly the while with her marvellous blue eyes.

Little by little the flame of vitality which burned within him seemed to grow fainter and fainter, and his lithe lissom limbs waxed languorous and luxurious—yet was he ever filled with a languid content and a will not his own perpetually overshadowed him.

One day in their wanderings he saw a strange dark blue flower like unto the eyes of Lilith, and a sudden half remembrance flashed through his mind.

"What is this blue flower?" he said, and Lilith shuddered and said nothing; but as they went a little further there was a brook—the brook he thought, and felt his fetters falling off him, and he prepared to spring over the brook; but Lilith seized him by the arm and held him back with all her strength, and trembling all over she said, "Promise me Gabriel that you will not cross over." But he said, "Tell me what is this blue flower, and why you will not tell me?" And she said, "Look Gabriel at the brook." And he looked and saw that though it was just like the brook of separation it was not the same, the waters did not flow.

As Gabriel looked steadfastly into the still waters it seemed to him as though he saw voices—some impression of the Vespers for the Dead. "Hei mihi quia incolatus sum," and again "De profundis clamavi ad te"—oh, that veil, that overshadowing veil! Why could he not hear properly and see, and why did he only remember as one looking through a threefold semi-transparent curtain. Yes they were praying for him— but who were they? He heard again the voice of Lilith in whispered anguish, "Come away!"

Then he said, this time in monotone, "What is this blue flower, and what is its use?"

And the low thrilling voice answered, "it is called 'lûli uzhûri,' two drops pressed upon the face of the sleeper and he will sleep."

He was as a child in her hand and suffered himself to be led from thence, nevertheless he plucked listlessly one of the blue flowers, holding it downwards in his hand. What did she mean? Would the sleeper wake? Would the blue flower leave any stain? Could that stain be wiped off?

But as he lay asleep at early dawn he heard voices from afar off praying for him—the Abbé Félicien, Carmeille, his mother too, then some familiar words struck his ear: "Libera mea porta inferi." Mass was being said for the repose of his soul, he knew this. No, he could not stay, he would leap over the brook, he knew the way—he had forgotten that the brook did not flow. Ah, but Lilith would know—what should he do? The blue flower—there it lay close by his bedside—he understood now; so he crept very silently to where Lilith lay asleep, her long hair glistening gold, shining like a glory round about her. He pressed two drops on her forehead, she sighed once, and a shade of præternatural anguish passed over her beautiful face. He fled—terror, remorse, and hope tearing his soul and making fleet his feet. He came to the brook—he did not see that the water did not flow—of course it was the brook for separation; one bound, he should be with things human again. He leapt over and—

A change had come over him—what was it? He could not tell—did he walk on all fours? Yes surely. He looked into the brook, whose still waters were fixed as a mirror, and there, horror, he beheld himself; or was it himself? His head and face, yes; but his body transformed to that of a wolf. Even as he looked he heard a sound of hideous mocking laughter behind him. He turned round—there, in a gleam of red lurid light, he saw one whose body was human, but whose head was that of a wolf, with eyes of infinite malice; and, while this hideous being laughed with a loud human laugh, he, essaying to speak, could only utter the prolonged howl of a wolf.

But we will transfer our thoughts from the alien things on the "other side" to the simple human village where Gabriel used to dwell. Mère Yvonne was not much surprised when Gabriel did not turn up to breakfast—he often did not, so absent-minded was he; this time she said, "I suppose he has gone with the others to the wolf hunt." Not that Gabriel was given to hunting, but, as she sagely said, "there was no knowing what he might do next." The boys said, "Of course that muff Gabriel is skulking and hiding himself, he's afraid to join the wolf hunt; why, he wouldn't even kill a cat," for their one notion of excellence was slaughter—so the greater the game the greater the glory. They were chiefly now confined to cats and sparrows, but they all hoped in after time to become generals of armies.

Yet these children had been taught all their life through with the gentle words of Christ—but alas, nearly all the seed falls by the wayside, where it could not bear flower or fruit; how little these know the suffering and bitter anguish or realize the full meaning of the words to those, of whom it is written "Some fell among thorns."

The wolf hunt was so far a success that they did actually see a wolf, but not a success, as they did not kill it before it leapt over the brook to the "other side," where, of course, they were afraid to pursue it. No emotion is more inrooted and intense in the minds of common people than hatred and fear of anything "strange."

Days passed by but Gabriel was nowhere seen—and Mère Yvonne began to see clearly at last how deeply she loved her only son, who was so unlike her that she had thought herself an object of pity to other mothers the goose and the swan's egg. People searched and pretended to search, they even went to the length of dragging the ponds, which the boys thought very amusing, as it enabled them to kill a great number of water rats, and Carmeille sat in a corner and cried all day long. Mère Pinquèle also sat in a corner and chuckled and said that she had always said Gabriel would come to no good. The Abbé Félicien looked pale and anxious, but said very little, save to God and those that dwelt with God.

At last, as Gabriel was not there, they supposed he must be nowhere— that is dead. (Their knowledge of other localities being so limited, that it did not even occur to them to suppose he might be living elsewhere than in the village.) So it was agreed that an empty catafalque should be put up in the church with tall candles round it, and Mère Yvonne said all the prayers that were in her prayer book, beginning at the beginning and ending at the end, regardless of their appropriateness—not even omitting the instructions of the rubrics. And Carmeille sat in the corner of the little side chapel and cried, and cried. And the Abbé Félicien caused the boys to sing the Vespers for the Dead (this did not amuse them so much as dragging the pond), and on the following morning, in the silence of early dawn, said the Dirge and the Requiem—and this Gabriel heard.

Then the Abbé Félicien received a message to bring the Holy Viaticum to one sick. So they set forth in solemn procession with great torches, and their way lay along the brook of separation.

Essaying to speak he could only utter the prolonged howl of a wolf— the most fearful of all bestial sounds. He howled and howled again— perhaps Lilith would hear him! Perhaps she could rescue him? Then he remembered the blue flower—the beginning and end of all his woe. His cries aroused all the denizens of the forest—the wolves, the wolf- men, and the men-wolves. He fled before them in an agony of terror— behind him, seated on the black ram with human face, was the wolf- keeper, whose face was veiled in eternal shadow. Only once he turned to look behind—for among the shrieks and howls of bestial chase he heard one thrilling voice moan with pain. And there among them he beheld Lilith, her body too was that of a wolf, almost hidden in the masses of her glittering golden hair, on her forehead was a stain of blue, like in colour to her mysterious eyes, now veiled with tears she could not shed.

The way of the Most Holy Viaticum lay along the brook of separation. They heard the fearful howlings afar off, the torch bearers turned pale and trembled—but the Abbé Félicien, holding aloft the Ciborium, said "They cannot harm us."

Suddenly the whole horrid chase came in sight. Gabriel sprang over the brook, the Abbé Félicien held the most Blessed Sacrament before him, and his shape was restored to him and he fell down prostrate in adoration. But the Abbé Félicien still held aloft the Sacred Ciborium, and the people fell on their knees in the agony of fear, but the face of the priest seemed to shine with divine effulgence. Then the wolf- keeper held up in his hands the shape of something horrible and inconceivable—a monstrance to the Sacrament of Hell, and three times he raised it, in mockery of the blessed rite of Benediction. And on the third time streams of fire went forth from his fingers, and all the "other side" of the forest took fire, and great darkness was over all.

All who were there and saw and heard it have kept the impress thereof for the rest of their lives—nor till in their death hour was the remembrance thereof absent from their minds. Shrieks, horrible beyond conception, were heard till nightfall—then the rain rained.

The "other side" is harmless now—charred ashes only; but none dares to cross but Gabriel alone—for once a year for nine days a strange madness comes over him.

Mona Lisa

by Warren Lapine

Terrence Gregor lifted the 9-millimeter from his desk. It was a cold, stark thing of unearthly, wicked beauty. He put the pistol to his head and smiled. He wasn't going to shoot himself, not yet. There was one more night of work to be done on his final painting. Then, perhaps, he would pull the trigger.

He had a vision of them finding his body slumped over his easel; just a bit of blood on what would be his greatest triumph. "And this small brown spot is actually the artist's blood," he could hear a museum guide say. "Upon completing this painting, Terrence Gregor despaired; he realized that he would never again be able to achieve such a mastery of vision and form. Rather than go on, he killed himself." It wasn't all that far from the truth.

He put the pistol back on the desk. It was a nice fantasy, but if the wrong person found him, the painting might never be seen. The idea of dying frightened Terrence, but not nearly as much as the idea of living. It wasn't fair, it just wasn't fair. He had struggled all of his life to master his art; and now that his skills were such that his art could match his ambition, he was through. What a cruel joke. He wanted to scream at the universe—curse the day that he had been born. No one should be born with such a desire to create and then have the ability stripped from them. And in such a gradual manner.

Terrence stood and walked over to his painting. He let out a deep breath. Looking on what he had created, it was impossible to remain in despair. Surely this would earn him some degree of immortality. Could anyone look at this and be unmoved? For the hundredth time he wondered who the woman in the painting really was. He knew little about her. Every night she came shortly after dusk and left just before dawn. He'd tried to explain to her that if she'd just let him photograph her, he could complete the painting without her having to pose for such extended periods of time. She'd flat out refused. "I'd rather be here when you're painting. It lets me pretend that I'm part of the creative process." Strange woman.

Without her he would have given in to despair; some days she was all that stood between him and the dark abyss. His muse. Until he had met her, he'd never really believed in muses. One either had the fire or one didn't. Terrence Gregor had always had the fire.

In thirty five years nothing had slowed him down. Not until the morning that he had woken up with numb fingertips. It was then that he heard the words that ended his life.

Lou Gehrig's disease.

Three words.

The doctors had tried to comfort him, but what could they say? The disease was already fairly advanced. He'd lose fine motor control quickly. Eventually he'd be a prisoner trapped within his own body, depending on others for even the most basic bodily functions. He couldn't live with that. He'd been born for one reason, to create, and if he couldn't create it would be better that he not live.

He'd purchased a 9-millimeter pistol and a single bullet. After he used the first bullet, he wouldn't need another one, not ever. Terrence loaded the pistol and took it home only to find that he couldn't bring himself to use it. He stared at the gun in his hand for more than an hour, but he just couldn't pull the damn trigger. He put the gun down and cursed. "I've got to be able to do this. I can't let this thing run its course. I won't spend my last days in a nursing home."

"Oh look, the poor dear is drooling on himself," he could almost hear a nurse say as she wiped spittle from his face. "Do you think he really was a famous painter?"

"That's just talk. From the looks of him, I'm sure he never painted anything more ambitious than a paint by number clown set."

"You shouldn't talk like that in front of him. They can understand, you know."

"So what? He'll never complain. Once they get this bad off, there's no coming back.

Terrence pulled himself from the image. He couldn't let it happen. "I need to get drunk, that's all; then I'll be able to do it."

He grabbed a jacket and rushed out of his studio. Outside the early evening, spring air helped him collect his thoughts. There was still plenty of time to do what must be done. He pulled the keys to his Porsche 911 from his pocket then put them back. There was a bar just down the street, and the walk would do him good.

Terrence had never been to this bar before, it wasn't upscale enough for him. But tonight that would be just fine. He really didn't want to take the chance of running into someone that he might know. What would he say? "Oh, hi, good to see you, I'm planning to get drunk and blow my brains out." That would be a real conversation starter.

As it turned out the bar was a blue-collar pub. It was dimly lit and through the smoke-filled air, Terrence could see couples playing pool and even a group shooting darts. After finding that the bar didn't serve Bass ale, Terrence ordered a Rolling Rock; it was the closest thing to a passable beer in the place. Once the bartender gave him the bottle he took it and sat down at an empty table in the corner. The mood of the bar was perfect: no loud music or bright lights, and what little laughter that found its way to his table all sounded forced and subdued. It was just the right kind of place to sit, drink, and contemplate oblivion.

And that's exactly what he would have done if she hadn't walked into the bar. He noticed her immediately; she didn't belong in this bar. She was like a swath of bright red on a gray landscape, a spring flower in December. Long, jet black hair streamed over her shoulders and halfway down her back; her blue eyes, nestled within a delicate face, flashed with life and vitality. Terrence had never seen anyone so captivating. Strength, wisdom, and power all emanated from her. He had to paint her. If he could capture half of what he saw in this magnificent woman he would be remembered forever. She could be his Mona Lisa. Surely he had enough time to complete one last painting before the disease disabled him.

He picked up his drink and walked over to where she sat alone. "May I join you?" he asked.

"Certainly," she said motioning to a chair across from her.

Terrence caught a slight accent, but couldn't quite place it. "Your accent, it's European isn't it?"

"You have a good ear, it's Romanian. I've been in this country since I was a little girl; very few people notice it."

"I've spent some time in Europe. I'm Terrence Gregor."

"The painter?"

"You're familiar with my work?" Terrence was surprised; despite being very successful, he didn't run into a lot of people outside of the art community who knew who he was.

"Oh yes, your work is marvelous. I love your use of color, and your lighting techniques are second to none. I've often wished I could afford one of your paintings."

"How would you like to model for one?"

"Me?"

"Yes, I'd love to use you in a painting. That's why I came over here. You have a great deal of character. I think you could be my Mona Lisa."

"Oh come now, your Mona Lisa?"

"I mean it. There's something about you that I've got to capture on canvas."

She smiled. "I'd like to be your Mona Lisa. Yes, I'd like that very much."

Terrence pulled out one of his cards and handed it to her. "Could you start tomorrow?"

"I work during the day, but I'd be happy to stop by during the evening."

"I do most of my painting at night, so that would be fine. What I really need to do is photograph you and then I can work from the photos. You don't have to pose the entire time."

"I don't like photographs. If you want me to be your Mona Lisa, I'll have to sit for you."

"It's really not necessary."

"I insist."

There was something about the way that she said it that brooked no argument. "If you insist."

She nodded. "Is this one of your regular haunts? Uncle Gus' bar doesn't seem to suit you."

"No, this is my first time here, one of your regular haunts?"

"I like a change of scenery," she smiled, showing white teeth. "What brings you here?"

"I needed to get drunk, it's been a rough day, and this bar is close to my studio."

"I'm sorry about your day. Would you like to talk about it?"

Terrence started to say no but found that he couldn't. He told her the entire story almost as if he had been compelled to. When he'd finished she nodded and said, "It must be frightening knowing that you're going to die."

"It's not frightening, it's just hard to overcome my instinct to live. I love life, I love being able to create. I don't want to let go of the passion, but I know that I don't have a choice. I think I was twelve when I realized that I was going to die just like everyone else. It didn't frighten me, it made me angry. I mean, how dare the universe do this to me. Give me such ambition and then only seventy years or so in which to realize my dreams."

"It doesn't seem fair, does it?"

"No, no it doesn't. I have so much I want to share with the world, so many great paintings left within me. And now, now I'll only have time to paint one more of them. And then my life might just as well be over."

"It must take a lot of courage to decide to end it."

Terrence laughed. "To make the decision, no, I've done that. I just haven't been able to follow through on it yet. It's just as well, if I'd been able to pull the trigger I wouldn't have met you."

She smiled again. "You flatter me."

Suddenly Terrence realized that he didn't know this woman's name. "By the way, what's your name?"

"Mona."

"As in Mona Lisa?"

"Perhaps."

"Well, Mona, if we are to start tomorrow, I have some preparations to make."

"Until tomorrow, then."

Thinking back on it, Terrence had to admit that it seemed a bit strange. It was almost as if she'd been looking for him. But that didn't make any sense. She couldn't have known what his reaction to her would be, and she definitely wasn't a groupie.

The bell rang and Terrence went to the door and let Mona in. She smiled. "Ah, Terrence, it's good to see you."

Terrence breathed the smell of her in. "It's always good to see you. I can't believe that I'll be finished tonight."

"Do you really think so?"

He nodded. "I'm afraid so. I'm usually really excited when I finish a painting, but knowing that this is my last, well, I don't want it to end. I want to go on painting it for eternity, of course, I can't."

Mona walked over to the painting and gazed at it. "Do I really look that majestic?"

"More so, my dear."

She smiled up at Terrence, "Thank you."

"For what."

"For capturing me this way. You're the greatest artist of your age, and to think, I'm your Mona Lisa."

"Only history will be able to decide where I'll stand. We don't have the perspective. Maybe I'll be remembered, I certainly hope so, but one can only hope."

"Trust me, you'll be remembered," Mona said, taking her place on the couch.

Terrence went to work. His fingers were a bit more numb than he would have liked, but if he concentrated, he could still get the sharpness of line that he demanded. It was a frightening thing to realize that this would indeed be his last painting. His fingers were much more stiff now than they had been three weeks ago when he'd begun the painting. He continued through sheer force of will, losing himself in the radiance and magnificence of creating.

Finally he realized that the painting was complete. He'd captured the essence of Mona. She was like some pale immortal goddess, an ageless enchantress defying the universe. Strength and wisdom fairly leapt off the canvas. It was so magnificent that he started to cry.

Mona moved off the couch and over to Terrence. She put her arms around him, comforting him. "It'll be all right, Terrence. The painting is brilliant. You have nothing to worry about. This will make you immortal."

"But I'll never paint again."

"Terrence, look at what you've created. Most mortals never leave behind this kind of legacy."

Terrence looked up at his masterpiece. Mona was right, with this painting he'd accomplished greatness. What more could he want? Eternity, that was what he really wanted. "Mona, he whispered, "I'm not sure if I can pull the trigger, will you stay with me until I do?"

Terrence had expected her to be shocked, but if she was, she showed no sign of it. "I'll do better than that, Terrence."

"Better?"

She pulled him close and began kissing his neck. Terrence felt the thrill of desire course through his body. He wanted Mona more than he had ever wanted anyone. "Mona, I think I'm in love with you." Suddenly, Mona bit into his neck. Blood burst forth, splashing them and the painting. Part of Terrence was horrified, but that part was small and far away. Ecstasy like nothing that he had ever experience before exploded through his senses. He became one with Mona. He could feel her desire for him, her thirst, it ached to be quenched. "I'm yours, Mona."

The ecstasy went on and on. Finally she pulled her mouth away from Terrence' throat. He was weak and dazed and would have fallen had Mona not supported him.

"Terrence, listen to me," Mona said, blood dripping down her chin. "I'm a vampire, a creature of the night. I live forever, nothing is held back from me, nothing but the sun, that is all I am denied. I prey on mortals, I drain them of their life force, but I live forever. No disease can touch me. Think of what you could do with your art if you had immortality. You can have it, but you have to really want it. You have to have the fire—without it immortality is more a curse than a gift. If you would live forever, drink my blood. Do you have the fire, Terrence?"

He smiled, brought his lips to Mona's throat, and began to feed. Terrence Gregor had always had the fire.

www.ingramcontent.com/pod-product-compliance
Lightning Source LLC
Chambersburg PA
CBHW030352310726
48979CB00001B/278

* 9 7 9 8 8 8 0 9 2 5 0 3 2 *